Yvonne Roberts is an award-winning journalist who has worked in television and on many newspapers including *The Sunday Times*, the *Observer* and the *Guardian*. She grew up in Pakistan in the 1950s and is the author of two non-fiction titles and two highly acclaimed novels, *Every Woman Deserves an Adventure* and *The Trouble with Single Women*.

'A thoughtful and witty novel'   *Daily Telegraph*

'A witty and pacy novel'   *The Times*

'Yvonne Roberts is a natural. She's wonderful; the wittiest, most inventive novelette writer in ages'   *Image* magazine

'Both an entertaining satire on contemporary sexual mores . . . and a touching portrait of a woman's search for self-respect'
                                                                                    Vogue

Also by Yvonne Roberts

Every Women Deserves an Adventure
The Trouble with Single Women

A History of
Insects

Yvonne Roberts

review

First published in Great Britain in 2000
by HEADLINE BOOK PUBLISHING

First published in paperback in 2001
by HEADLINE BOOK PUBLISHING

A REVIEW paperback

10 9 8 7 6 5 4 3 2 1

ISBN 0 7472 6126 1

Typeset by Letterpart Ltd
Reigate, Surrey

Printed and bound in Great Britain by
Clays Ltd, St Ives plc.

HEADLINE BOOK PUBLISHING
A division of Hodder Headline
338 Euston Road
London NW1 3BH
www.headline.co.uk
www.hodderheadline.com

For my parents,
John and Nancy Roberts

Chapter One

Eye to the crack in the door, she could see most of the brightly lit room. A grown-up, blindfolded and wearing a party dress, was crawling around on her hands and knees, one arm outstretched, squeaking, 'Are you there, Moriarty? Moriarty, are you there?' Two ladies were standing on chairs, skirts held high, shoes in hand, shrieking with laughter. A man in a white jacket and black trousers was half lying on the sofa, his legs held stiffly off the floor, like a tumbling tin soldier. One of the women on a chair threw her sandal and screamed, 'Over here, over here. Cooee.' The blindfolded one sat back on her heels and pretended to pout. 'I'm not playing if you do that,' she complained. A second man, riding the arm of the sofa as if it were a horse, bellowed, 'She's cheating, she can see where we are, she can see where we are. She's cheating. Cheater, cheater.' The other grown-ups joined in, chanting, 'Cheater, cheater.'

And then everything went black.

The clunk, clunk, clunk of the sitting room's ceiling-fan was hushed and the crickets and the bull frogs went quiet. Only the sounds of the muezzins in the city's mosques, calling the faithful to evening prayer, continued. Alice Jackson, dressed in a turquoise cocktail dress, her short black hair carrying the singed smell which came from sitting under the ancient pre-war hairdryer in Belle's Beauty Parlour, made her way across the room, fumbling in the

1

semi-darkness, and almost fell over her nine-year-old daughter. As they collided, the lights flickered back to life, the fan staggered and revived. On the tape recorder, a female voice slurred drunkenly back into performance: 'Once, I had a secret luuurve . . .' Power was restored.

'Ella,' said Alice, gazing at her pyjama-clad daughter, 'whatever are you doing out of bed?' Behind her, Alice heard the laughter, muted at first, but growing in volume.

'Oh, what an absolute hoot!' said the woman sitting back on her heels, the blindfold pushed back.

Ella Jackson blushed, aware that, for some reason unknown to her, she was the source of the grown-ups' amusement.

'How dare you, Ella!' Alice was leaning forward, hissing in her only child's face.

Ella attempted a defence. 'I was going to get a drink of water, and saw you all . . .' She was about to say 'playing', but some instinct told her the word would not be welcome.

'Dear heaven . . .' said the tin soldier on the sofa.

Alice was now pulling at her daughter's arm agitatedly. 'You're a very bad girl, do you hear me? A very bad girl. Give me that, at once!' she demanded.

Ella caught the evening smell of her mother – a mix of perfume and cigarette smoke and Pond's cold cream, and the biscuity odour that came from the bright-red lipstick that she always wore. A little of the lipstick had smudged onto her teeth, like flecks of blood.

'Give me that, now. Do you hear me, Ella? Bill!' Alice added, summoning her husband.

Over her mother's shoulder, Ella could see more guests drifting in from the garden, drawn by the laughter. It was then that she remembered what she was holding in her hand. She had taken it the day before from the large cabin trunk, where it had lain in the corner, coiled like a fat pink rubber snake. One end was round, as if it had swallowed a golf ball, and when Ella squeezed, it made a satisfactory whooshing noise. She carried it now, because in the strange land of grown-ups she'd needed a weapon.

The woman who had been crawling on the floor got to her feet. Ella recognised her as the new wife of the Deputy High Commissioner, Noel Hargreave-Smith, her father's boss. She had arrived in Peshawar a few months before Ella and her mother. Sylvia Hargreave-Smith was several years younger than anyone else in the room, apart from Ella. The girl couldn't help but stare, because quite apart from her height – she was much the tallest in the room – it was the first time she had noticed how strangely the woman was put together.

Mrs Hargreave-Smith had a long, oval face, large, slightly bulging pale-blue eyes, and a very small chin that fitted uncomfortably, as if that particular feature had originally been intended for somebody else. Her neck was long, her hands enormous, like the paws of a puppy destined to become a very large dog. The bones in her wrists and elbows looked like nuts and bolts, they stuck out so. Her thin, dark-brown hair hung to her shoulders, crimped like corrugated iron, held back by two combs. She was wearing an ankle-length peach-coloured dress with short puffed sleeves, a frilled collar and diamanté buttons down the front. Prickly heat had spread itself across the part of her chest that was exposed. Her enthusiastic party game had added to the flush. Now, she was blinking hard, her eyes slightly red-rimmed, as if she couldn't believe what she was seeing. Ella realised that Mrs Hargreave-Smith was pointing in her direction. 'Can you beat it?' she was saying, as she giggled. 'The little shrimp has actually got her hands on her mother's douche. How frightfully amusing.'

It was then that Ella fled.

Sitting cross-legged on her bed, Ella occasionally glanced at herself in the dressing-table mirror as she wept tears of humiliation. She had dark-brown hair, woven into plaits, a round face and freckles. Sadly, she was not at all like Doris Day. Music seeped from the sitting room. 'Oh, Mein Papa, to me you are so wonderful . . . Oh, Mein Papa . . .' She heard the slap slap of sandals and the clink of ice against glass as Ijaz, the bearer, bore a fresh tray of drinks to the grown-ups. Ella liked having people in the house, because it made her parents act as if they were in love, just like in the films.

'She wears red feathers and a hula-hula skirt, she wears red . . .' The voice was suddenly muted as the sitting-room door shut. Ella dried her eyes, the drama of the situation exhausted. Her father had been ordered to deliver a punishment. He would eventually come into her room, sit on her bed, say, 'You know what your mother's like . . .' shrug, and leave.

Ella lay back on her bed and stared at the ceiling. If she stared hard enough, the cracks in the plaster would begin to jump and dance and turn into tiny lizards, chee-chees, darting backwards and forwards. Ijaz had told her once about a girl who slept with her mouth open. One night, a chee-chee had fallen from above, she'd swallowed it and choked. So Ella always slept with the sheet over her head, like a corpse, almost suffocating herself in the process. Suffocation was definitely better than choking.

Her bedroom was the smallest room in the bungalow. Each bed leg stood in a saucer of water to deter insects. The rest of the furniture was a peculiar mix. A large walnut dressing-table, a pine chest of drawers, a long, low bamboo bookcase, which held dozens of paperback thrillers, a garish army guarding one wall: John Dickson Carr, Ngaio Marsh, Agatha Christie, the property of the previous residents. In the ten weeks since Ella and her mother had joined Bill Jackson, already in post for six months, she had read most of the paperbacks in the hours when she was supposed to be asleep. Tales of murder and derring-do didn't stir Ella much, unless she woke up in the middle of the night. Then, victims with their necks gaping wide from stab wounds, heads smashed by axes, jostled each other in the shadows. 'I don't know what goes on in that child's mind,' Alice would say to her husband, 'but it comes from your side of the family. And it's bound to end in tears.'

Ella's room had a window and two doors, one leading to the bungalow's central hall, the second to a bathroom. Ministry of Works rules, on which Ella had been raised, dictated no posters or pictures hung on the walls and, no matter how many cigarette burns already decorated the wobbly furniture, all care should be taken not to add to the scarring. As a result, the only decorative touch was a framed poster showing a young woman on tiptoes, wearing an apple-green swimsuit and a captain's hat. On it were written the words, 'Welcome to Sunny Scarborough!'

In the corner of her bedroom, two packing cases held an assortment of books and dolls. Each packing case carried several labels, all of which read, 'Mr and Mrs W Jackson, Compound of the Deputy High Commissioner, Radcliffe Road, British Cantonment, Peshawar, North-West Frontier, Pakistan.'

Ella Jackson had spent most of her nine years camping out in other people's houses, occupying strangers' bedrooms. Home was always referred to as 'The Temporary Accommodation'. Her parents rarely gave her notice of any impending move. 'Why upset her unnecessarily?' Alice would reason. So, while Ella had often been uprooted, she'd rarely had the opportunity to make her goodbyes. As a consequence, she was wary of all adults. For some mysterious reason, when they were around, whatever happened today, wouldn't necessarily happen again tomorrow.

'Damn Bastard,' said a voice loudly in the hall outside. It belonged to the Jacksons' cook, P H Surindabash. P H as in Poor Honest. 'Damn Bastard' was his preferred name for

Ijaz, whom he treated with contempt. Ijaz, according to Surindabash, wasn't just a whisky drinker – bad enough to any Muslim – he was a drinker of the sahib's whisky, and that was not acceptable either to Allah or Surindabash's sense of propriety. It was Surindabash's mission in life to catch Ijaz at the bottle.

Ella heard a knock on her door. She expected it to be Surindabash, smuggling in a slice of his chocolate cake, icing made from semi-frozen condensed milk and cocoa powder, 'Favourite of Win-stone Church-Hill', according to Surindabash, who claimed he had once been his employee. But before Ella could speak, the door opened, and a woman slipped in.

She wore a full-skirted, belted shirtwaister dress, the collar up, in a shiny dark-green material. She had sparkling earrings and high-heeled, open-toed dark-green shoes which matched the colour of her dress. 'Hi, honey,' the woman said in a soft, slow voice. Her accent was American.

Ella's eighteen-year-old cousin, Vivien, read *Photoplay* and *Silver Screen* from cover to cover. She'd once told Ella that, in order to become a Screen Goddess, Rita Hayworth had had her hairline lifted and learnt to do as she was told.

Ella had no idea what had happened to the hairline of the woman now standing in her bedroom – or whether she did as she was told – but she was certain that she looked exactly like a Screen Goddess. As if on cue, as Ella watched, smoke from her visitor's cigarette lazily curled above her head, just as it did in photographs of Barbara Stanwyck and Lana Turner. 'May I?' the woman asked politely, indicating Ella's bed. Ella nodded, surprised that an adult would seek permission. The woman sat next to her, leaning against the iron bedstead, her feet up on the bed, apparently happy just to smoke her cigarette. Alice had always instructed her daughter that, in the company of adults, children must wait until spoken to, so Ella occupied herself drawing patterns with her finger on the white cotton sheet.

Eventually, the woman said, 'You know something? I was always in trouble when I was little.' Ella didn't appreciate the reference to 'little'. She didn't see herself as little, not any more. The woman went on: 'What I hated most was the way grown-ups would tell me to act my age and then they'd behave like great big babies themselves. You know what I mean?'

Ella nodded.

Her visitor stood up, put her cigarette in her mouth, and smoothed down her dress with the palms of her hands. Then she walked to the door, turned, and gave Ella a small wave. 'By the way, my name's Betty. See you around, honey.'

The following morning, Ella wasn't at all sure whether she had met the American woman in real life – or whether she'd come to her in her dreams.

'Gums, that's what gives the game away. One of these days, I'm going to get a damn good look at her gums.' Marjorie Rockingham sat in a cotton dressing-gown in front of the dressing-table of the master bedroom, removing her lipstick. She was thirty-two, married for eleven years, and the mother of eight-year-old twin boys, despatched at seven to boarding school, to her unspoken relief.

Marjorie came from a long line of women accustomed to attracting attention. Petite, fine features, snub nose, full lips, naturally blonde hair. The kind of female who, in looks and demeanour, encouraged a certain type of man to feel protective, assertive, dominant. In the case of Marjorie's husband, Piers, this had mutated a stage further. He found his wife's winsomeness and pliability increasingly grating. His reaction over the years had become more and more overbearing and critical. The more she conceded, the stronger became his urge to destroy. Occasionally, he found himself physically as well as mentally lashing out. A situation for which Marjorie blamed herself entirely.

So, she attempted to be even more conciliatory, soothing, subordinate. And, above all, grateful. Piers had, after all, saved Marjorie, who was not quite as perfect as she appeared. 'You're one of life's seconds,' her sister had once said to her cruelly. 'Nobody worth their salt will ever want you.' But Piers had.

At nineteen, Marjorie, drifting in and out of secretarial jobs, met Piers Rockingham, then twenty-two, and at Oxford. On the surface, they made a fine couple – and, for that reason, he had wanted her. She was adoring of him and this meant she was unlikely to cause him embarrassment, an important consideration for a career diplomat. Marjorie, the third of four daughters, also had the advantage of background, which Piers lacked. She came from minor landed-gentry; connections, but no cash. Piers' father, in contrast, had been the owner of a tool-making factory in Birmingham and had prospered on the black market during the war. Recently, he had diversified into the Fifties' appetite for cars.

Piers had been at Oxford when the war began. He served as an officer in the army, then resumed his degree, achieving a first in Oriental Languages – Persian and Arabic. The diplomatic service had so far failed to utilise his skill in either language. Instead, it had paid for him to learn Russian, sent him on classified courses, and then placed him in several sensitive posts as a Cold War expert. Piers' facility for languages was not remotely matched by his intuition, sensitivity or understanding of human nature, so in reality his diplomatic triumphs had been few. However, since at the outset he had been marked out to rise high, his career continued to blossom. None of which had come as a surprise to Piers.

Marjorie had learnt at an early stage in her marriage that she was not expected to do much in the way of thinking. Apart from taking care of her appearance, a dependable way of pleasing her husband was to devalue the character and performance of anyone with whom he came in contact. The more others were diminished, the greater his stature. Gradually, over the years, Marjorie also became addicted to the strong, if short-lived, charge that the denigration of others brought. Now, it was almost as if the only setting in which the Rockinghams could converse was the rubble of other people's attributes and reputations.

'I swear if you looked at her gums in daylight, they'd be blue.' Marjorie grimaced at herself in the mirror. 'She's got to be an Anglo-Indian or at least a gypsy. Did you hear her tonight? She puts on that frightfully posh voice and talks about, "Choosing serviettes . . ." Serviettes! Does she think she's running a Lyons Corner House? How vulgar can you get?'

Marjorie continued, interpreting her husband's silence on the subject of Alice Jackson as approval of her views. 'And flirt! God, how she can flirt. She even does it with those Pakistanis. I don't know how Bill puts up with it. I mean, she's doing it right under his nose. I'm sorry, but it has to be said, it's just so common. I could see Sylvia wasn't at all impressed.' Marjorie gave a small shudder and glanced at her husband.

He lay on the large double bed, semi-naked. On her first introduction to Piers, Marjorie had thought they'd met before. Then she realised that it was because he looked exactly like the young man seen on the cover of knitting patterns, photographed in Fair Isle jumpers, holding a pipe, leaning against a country stile, his lips as thin as a staple.

Now, Piers lazily flicked through a copy of the *Illustrated London News*. He wasn't much interested in the magazine, but he enjoyed the recognition that came with its temporary possession. Each month, a bundle of periodicals and newspapers would arrive from the UK in the diplomatic bag. These included an airmail compendium of *The Times* and the *Daily Sketch*, the *Illustrated London News*, *John Bull*, *Punch*,

Country Life, and *Horse and Hound*, among others. First, they spent time with Noel Hargreave-Smith. Then they were passed on to Rockingham, as number two, then to the number three, the commercial attaché, David Carnow, and finally they would be deposited, usually several weeks out of date, with Bill Jackson. Jackson was the only member of the small UK based staff who did not have diplomatic status, although he was senior to the half-a-dozen clerical and administrative people employed on local wages.

A small sticker on the cover of each periodical listed the names in order of rank. Rockingham never failed to receive a small thrill of pleasure that Jackson's name came last. Piers saw himself as brighter, more talented, more socially adept; an altogether different class of man from many of his peers, never mind someone of the dubious calibre of Bill Jackson. So it annoyed him intensely that Jackson had the knack of occasionally making him feel like a stupid little boy.

'Isn't he a brigadier or something?' Piers suddenly asked his wife, without raising his eyes from the magazine.

'Who?' Marjorie replied.

Piers put the magazine by the bed and pulled up the sheet. 'The Pakistani army chappy that you said was flirting with Alice.'

Then, without waiting for an answer, he snapped out the light, leaving his wife, still seated at her dressing-table, stranded in the dark.

An hour later, Marjorie left her bed and her sleeping husband and groped her way to the window. She drew back the dark-blue velvet curtains and looked out. In the distance, she could see the light of the two chowkidars on sentry duty at the gate. It did not reassure her. The perimeter of the compound had been allowed to return to the wild. She had convinced herself that it was only a matter of time before a couple of thugs slipped over the ten-foot wall and cut their way through the bougainvillea whose thorns were supposed to act as nature's barbed wire. Then they would move through the compound, slitting throats. What else would you expect from this barbaric, blood-soaked, Godforsaken country?

Her eyes adjusted to the dark. The compound of Her Majesty's British High Commission sprawled across a couple of acres, and, from the second floor, she had a view of much of it. Accommodation and offices were laid out in a rough semi-circle, linked by rose beds, a gravel drive, and open lawns. Housing expanded according to the rank of the inhabitant. The servants' quarters and a double garage for the official cars, a Hillman Minx and a Humber Super Snipe, were screened behind willow and palm trees, to the right of the double gates at the entrance. Next, came the Jacksons' three-bedroom bungalow. Adjoining it was a two-storey block of offices. David Carnow, living alone, a shy, shadowy figure, had been allocated a four-bedroom bungalow. Then, almost at the centre of the semi-circle, but set further back, was a mock-Victorian country mansion, encircled by veran- dahs on two floors. This was the home of the Hargreave- Smiths, referred to as The Residence. The semi-circle was completed by the Rockinghams' large six-bedroom house, complete with two minarets.

Ironically, only the Jacksons, in the least lavish accom- modation, enjoyed a modicum of privacy. They had a small garden surrounded by makeshift bamboo fencing, over- grown with ivy. As a result, while everyone knew who the Rockinghams or the Hargreave-Smiths entertained, the Jacksons' guest list was more difficult to ascertain. From what Marjorie had been able to observe, the Jacksons mixed with Pakistani army and air force officers, a few Americans, mostly in the business of aid, and even the occasional Anglo-Indian. Piers had predicted that this would speed Bill Jackson's demise, since fraternising with the locals was not considered on. Particularly given the delicate nature of Jackson's job.

Marjorie didn't say as much to her husband, but she enjoyed Bill's company. He made her laugh. Occasionally, in his company, she almost believed she might be interesting. She looked again. A small figure, dressed in pyjamas, was sitting on the steps of the bungalow's verandah. It was the girl. She looked up, as if aware that she was being watched. Instinctively, Marjorie Rockingham stepped back, surprised to find herself unnerved.

It was almost as if the child was waiting for something to happen.

'I swear I could have killed her with my bare hands when I saw her standing there with my douche,' Alice Jackson told her husband as she undressed, her words haphazardly sliding into one another. She clumsily removed one of her earrings.

'Are you all right?' Bill asked from the bed. He put down the book that he was reading.

'Are you saying I've had too much to drink?' his wife answered aggressively. Bill sighed. The role of the party jester had left him too weary for a battle with Alice. She was speaking again. 'Sylvia told me she thinks you're a hoot. Mind you, she seems to regard everything and everyone as a bit of a hoot. I swear she's a four-year-old in a grown woman's body. All those bloody party games. What on earth was Noel thinking of when he married her? She must be at least half his age. And she's not exactly a pretty picture, is she? You know what, Bill?' Alice addressed her husband's back as he retreated into the bathroom. 'Nobody can say that we don't give a damn good party. We're a team, you and I. That's what we are, a team. Nobody can beat us in the entertainment stakes.'

Alice suddenly sat down hard on her side of the bed. The crack was so loud, Bill heard the noise even above the sound of water running from both taps. 'Jesus bloody Christ,' he said out loud. Now, there would be no peace.

The Jacksons' double bed looked as if it had served the best of its time in a Blackpool bordello. The headboard was painted black with a pair of unnaturally pink naked cupids. Half the slats were missing or splintered. One of the legs was shorter than the others, so stability was maintained by a 1932 copy of *The Oxford English Dictionary*. But it was more than the state of the bed that irritated Alice. Each and every night, it reminded her of the poverty of her husband's career prospects. Why? Because he refused to practise the skill which mattered most to his employers in the Foreign and Commonwealth Office: the art of ingratiation.

It was Piers Rockingham who had the power to deliver a new bed. As the person in charge of Her Majesty's fixtures and fittings, he also had the authority to refurbish, withdraw or replace every curtain, bedspread, rug and stick of furniture in the compound. Hence, the interior of the Deputy High Commissioner's home was as chintzy as a Kent country house, while the Jacksons' bungalow resembled a second-hand furniture salesroom.

Alice Jackson had refused to be daunted. The family's heavy baggage had disgorged knick-knacks from three previous postings – Kuala Lumpur, Copenhagen and, very recently, Cairo. To these, Alice had added local Pakistani purchases: copper trays, cushions patterned with tiny mirrors, basket chairs.

Marjorie had, of course, expressed her admiration for Alice's ingenuity and her flair with colour. 'An almost Romany love of the flamboyant. Quite, quite different to what I'm used to – but awfully effective in this little bungalow,' she'd said. Alice had bitten her lip; she had long ago accepted that being patronised was the occupational hazard that went with her husband's job.

'Ask him, ask Piers nicely,' Alice now drunkenly demanded of her sober husband, as she swayed in the bathroom doorway. 'It says in the inventory we're entitled to a new bed. Just smile and say please. Everyone else does it, what's so special about you, that you can't?'

'Bollocks,' her husband replied.

Alice poked his chest aggressively as he manoeuvred past her. 'One of these days, you'll wake up and I'll be gone,' she slurred. 'Then you'll be sorry. And when I go, I'll take Ella with me.' It was a threat she had made many times before, not least because she liked to see the flash of fear in her husband's eyes. It allowed her to pretend that he really did care.

Early the following morning, Bill tiptoed into his daughter's bedroom. Short wisps had escaped from Ella's plaits, framing her face. Gently, he kissed her on the forehead, then left the room as quietly as he had entered it. Ella opened her eyes. She didn't know why her father found it hard to kiss and cuddle her when she was awake. She'd simply made it easier for both of them by learning how to feign sleep.

Chapter Two

'Alka-Seltzer, memsahib?' Surindabash asked, as Alice Jackson came into the dining room. He had been serving fried eggs, yolks the size of marbles, to Ella and Bill. Now, he enthusiastically polished the seat of Alice's chair with the teacloth he'd just used to tidy up the food on the plates. Outside, the early April sun was already so hot, every breath taken scalded the lungs.

Surindabash hummed to the music playing on his wireless in the kitchen, tuned to a Punjabi station. On her arrival in Peshawar, Alice had enquired about the going rate for the sweeper, the dhobiwallah who did the laundry, the bearer, the chowkidar and Surindabash. Then she'd paid each of them over the odds, much to Marjorie Rockingham's disapproval. As a result, while domestic staff elsewhere in the compound came and went, sometimes within the space of a few days, the Jackson team had remained intact. 'She thinks she's being so clever, but sooner or later they'll take advantage of her. They always do,' Marjorie had remarked cattily to Sylvia Hargreave-Smith.

Surindabash's wages were 140 rupees a month, plus a weekly ration of sugar, tea and flour (removing the need to help himself). Alice also sent exercise books and pencils to the two of his five children remaining at home. She turned a blind eye to Surindabash's lucrative sideline. Every so often, depending upon popular demand, he would bring an audience of two or three into his kitchen and unveil his modern miracle – a GEC electric cooker. Bill Jackson had bought it second-hand in the UK and had had it shipped out in the heavy baggage. Made in 1951, it had four rings, Queen Anne legs, and it came in speckled grey.

Surindabash refused emphatically to cook on the contraption, preferring an open charcoal fire, but he was happy to operate the cooker's switches. He would charge a few annas per person, then heat up all the rings, operate the grill and – praise Allah! – watch his audience's amazement as the cooker glowed consistently without any obvious source of fuel. Surindabash had assured his boss that when the time came for the family to leave, so widespread was the cooker's fame, he was sure he could obtain 'a very good price' on its sale. Plus, of course, a decent percentage for himself.

Surindabash claimed to be forty years of age. Heat and hard work had prematurely aged him. He was short, made even shorter by acutely bandy legs. His fortune lay in his mouth, furnished as it was with a significant number of gold teeth. He always wore a woollen hat on his head, no matter how high the temperature, and in his pocket, he carried the references which spanned a lifetime of cooking for the Raj.

During slack times, he would ask Ella to read out extracts from the bundle of yellowing, fragile letters. 'This man is very brave man in the cooking of mutton in Winzor style as served to His Majesty,' Ella would dutifully recite, while Surindabash smiled happily, mouthing the familiar words as she spoke.

'His egg-and-mango sandwiches are supper.' Once, she had tried to substitute the word 'super' for 'supper', but Surindabash had been most indignant. On other occasions, he would ask Ella to add or subtract a sentence here or there, replicating the handwriting as closely as possible, which is how she came to know that at least some of his commendations were self-crafted.

Surindabash's culinary repertoire was small. All soup was called mulligatawny, 'cutlet' covered a high proportion of meat dishes, and most desserts could be described as variations on cold rice pudding, fruit fool or coconut blancmange. Curry, he refused point blank to produce. 'Not good for Western bellies,' he would say, firmly if inelegantly. Such cooking was deemed, 'Bazaar chappy business,' and beneath his dignity.

Alice and Surindabash had so far clashed in only one area. At the Jacksons' first buffet dinner party, the table had resembled an accumulation of entrants for the best sandcastle competition. Surindabash had sculpted the Russian salad into a swan, the mashed potato into a Red Indian dug-out canoe, with tomatoes and cucumbers and peas providing intricate decoration, while the meat loaf had been reborn as a hedgehog, with cocktail onions on toothpicks representing its spines. Only the tinned ham, imported from the UK, had escaped untouched – literally – because Surindabash, as a Muslim, had refused to handle it at all.

It was established that he would, in future, produce only one work of art per occasion. He now regularly swore that he was so content (apart from the continuing irritation of Ijaz's presence) that he would lay down his life for the sahib and memsahib. 'No bloody lie,' he would add dramatically.

'Alka-Seltzer, sweet tea, fried eggs, plenty grease?' Surindabash suggested cheerily to Alice now. It was the formula for combating hangovers which he had offered to employers for years.

'Just tea, please,' she replied.

'May we go swimming today?' Ella asked. 'Tommy said he was going to the club and we haven't been for ages and . . .'

'The least heard from you, the better, young lady,' Alice

replied curtly, pouring milk into her cup. 'You're still in disgrace from last night.'

Bill interjected, 'She didn't understand about the bloody douche. She meant no harm.'

His wife gave him a scathing look. Her head throbbed.

Ella considered making herself invisible, then decided instead to take her cue from her father. 'May I go to the Old City with Surindabash, then?' she asked.

Alice stirred sugar into her tea and kept her eyes fixed on the cup. 'Don't be silly,' she answered.

'I'd really love to go for a swim, please, Daddy.' Ella turned to her father. 'I haven't seen Tommy for ages.' She knew this persistence was risky, but sometimes recklessness paid off.

'Of course you don't want to go swimming,' Alice announced firmly. She took a sip of her tea and, without looking up from her cup, added, 'Ask your father if he's working today.'

Bill, sitting on the opposite side of the table to his wife, winked at his daughter, whose face had tightened with anxiety. 'No, I'm not working today,' he replied evenly, pushing his chair back and beginning to get up from the table.

What Ella hated most was when she had to act as the messenger boy for days. 'Ask your father if he'd like ice in his water . . .' 'Tell your mother I'm out late tonight . . .'

She realised her mother was talking to her again. 'Tell your father I'm putting the bed out on the drive unless he does something about it today.'

'Whose bed?' Ella asked, anxious in case it might be hers.

'Never you mind,' Alice replied sharply. Then she added, 'I'm putting that bed out, do you hear me, Bill? Do you hear me?'

Her husband suddenly slammed his chair against the table. Surindabash, hovering by the kitchen door, instantly melted away. 'Do I hear you? Do I hear you?' he shouted. 'Of course I bloody hear you. I hear you last thing at night and first thing in the morning! I always bloody hear you.'

Alice rearranged her knife and fork, her face stony. Ella shut her eyes and took a deep breath and began counting. If she could reach twenty without taking in any more air, the row would end and everybody would be happy again. 'One . . . two . . . three,' she recited silently.

'Anyone home?' came a well-spoken voice from the verandah. 'Come on, Bill, you old bastard. You don't get out of a game that easily.'

Ella opened her eyes and let out her breath. Her mother and father were smiling. The magic had worked.

Colonel Ashraf Khan Afridi, 'Ash' to his friends, walked into the dining room from the verandah, wearing white tennis shorts and shirt and carrying a small parcel. Aged thirty-eight, he had steel-grey hair and a moustache to which he devoted much care, dark-brown eyes and a slightly hooked nose. Like many Pathans, he was tall and muscular. He came from four generations of zamindars, landowners and military men. His father, grandfather and great-grandfather had served in the Indian army. He was the first to serve in both the Indian and Pakistani military, transferring on Partition nine years before.

Ash symbolised much of what Bill Jackson resented most – authority, privilege, inherited money. But Bill still found himself strongly drawn to the man. In the first few months of his posting, in the autumn of 1955, before Ella and Alice's arrival, he and Ash had spent a good deal of time together. They had met at a cocktail party and Ash had offered to take him riding. That had led to flying lessons, organised by a fellow officer.

Ash slipped easily into the role of the convivial dandy but, from time to time, Bill – who had spent a lifetime disguising his own anger with anecdotes and humour – saw something darker beneath the Pakistani's surface amiability. Neither man drank: the lapsed non-conformist because he couldn't trust himself; the sceptical Muslim because he couldn't bring himself to trust others. But what especially endeared Bill to Ash was his refusal to give background and breeding the inflated value bestowed upon it by the British class system. Colonel Khan judged Bill Jackson as he found him – and chose to be his friend.

The colonel was from the Afridi tribe. Pukhtunwali was his code: honour, revenge, hospitality and friendship were what mattered most, along with land, gold and women. On a few occasions, Bill had visited Ash's substantial home, built next to the house of his father, uncle and two cousins. Fleetingly, he had been introduced to Ash's second wife, a woman in her early thirties. She had said little and was dressed in a burquah.

Once, Ash had delicately offered Bill female company. 'White, of course.' Bill had declined and nothing more was said. Ash had a number of women friends, almost all European or American, but he never discussed his private life, and Bill had no desire to ask.

Now, Ash bowed theatrically and kissed Alice's hand. 'See sense,' he smiled. 'Leave this chap for me.'

Bill looked on, amused. Alice might flirt with every man she met, but he could almost guarantee that she'd slept with none. Sex, for her, was a useless, grubby activity in which, if it weren't for procreation, she'd have no interest at all.

'Coffee, Ash?' Alice smiled. 'Ella, go and tell Surindabash to make fresh coffee, please.'

Ash took hold of Ella's hand as she passed, kissing her fingertips. The scratchiness of his moustache made her giggle. 'Wait a minute, Ella,' he instructed. 'Stand in front of me, and close your eyes. No looking.'

She did as she was told. She heard the rustle of paper. Her

mother's voice said, 'Oh, you shouldn't have. You spoil her to death already.'

Ash took hold of the girl's hands and guided her to the package, now unwrapped, on the seat. 'Miss Cinderella Jackson, you *shall* go to the ball! Open your eyes . . . now!' he instructed, and he chuckled at the speed with which the child obeyed his command. He liked Ella, he liked her air of self-sufficiency and her contrariness.

The child squealed with pleasure. It was what she had most wanted since first arriving in Pakistan. 'Can I wear it now, please? Can I? Can I?' she demanded, one leg already out of her shorts.

It took only minutes to put on the white baggy shalwar trousers and the pale pink qamiz tunic decorated with tiny rainbow-coloured rosebuds. She wound a deeper-pink dupatta scarf around her head and whirled round in excitement.

'Doesn't she look gorgeous, Mummy?' Ash asked Alice. He produced a small paper bag from his pocket. 'Now, you need to jingle,' he smiled.

Ella took the bag, and tipped its contents out on to the dining-room table. A dozen glass bangles in every shade of pink and blue and purple cascaded out. 'Are they all for me?' she asked, breathless.

Ash nipped her cheek with his fingers. 'Of course. Nobody in the whole of Peshawar is as beautiful as you,' he answered playfully. 'Only you have my heart, Miss Jackson. Remember that always. Only you have my heart, so take great care of it.'

Ella turned to her mother, her face alight, seeking approval. Alice looked away, as she so often did, then hated herself for her meanness.

Ash began to issue orders. 'Right, no time to waste,' he commanded. He pointed at Bill. 'You have a game of tennis to play with me. And you two, where are your swimming things? We're off to Sunday curry at the club and a lazy day with your Uncle Ash.'

Ella glanced uncertainly at her mother. 'Go on, do as Uncle Ash says,' Alice ordered. 'But take off your new things and change into something cooler.'

Her daughter began to shake her head furiously, but Ash was already intervening. 'Come, Alice, my dear,' he coaxed. 'The child's having fun. These clothes are designed for our heat, remember? We Pakistanis know about these things.' He smiled, but his voice held no laughter.

Bill took the initiative, aware that his wife would make him pay later. 'Ella, you're fine as you are. Some of us don't care as much as your mother about what the neighbours might say. Ash, have you come in your car?'

He nodded.

Cars were for the minority in Peshawar. The Jacksons normally hired tongas, gaudily painted carriages, pulled by horses so emaciated they resembled trotting X-rays. Ella hated travelling in a tonga, because she loathed the whippings to which the animals were constantly subjected. '*Bus, bus, bus*,' she would plead in Urdu to a bemused driver. 'Stop, stop, stop.'

Occasionally, she would see a horse that had collapsed in the street. Its equally emaciated owner would kick mercilessly at the ulcerated sores on the horse's body until it struggled upright again or died in harness, foaming at the nostrils, bright-red blood dribbling from its mouth. 'We can't do a thing about it,' Alice would say. 'They're just a naturally cruel people.'

But Ella didn't believe her mother. If Pakistanis were naturally cruel, why were Ash's polo ponies, which she'd visited several times, as sleek and as smooth and as well fed as the officers who rode them?

'Race you to the motor!' Ash shouted, as Ella emerged from her bedroom, swinging her bathing costume. She did as she was told, laughing delightedly.

Across the drive, on the opposite side of the compound,

Marjorie Rockingham stood on her verandah, close to tears. Sitting cross-legged at her feet, on a rush mat, was the tailorwallah. She had given him three lengths of material, sent out from the UK. He had now returned with the first of the dresses he had been requested to make.

'Memsahib, not happy?' he asked, ageless and anxious. A double row of needles was stuck into the breast of his long shirt, like a veteran's medals. A tape measure hung around his neck, a pin cushion was strapped to his wrist. One hand was poised like a crab's claw, as if to begin stitching at a moment's notice. Unhappy clients not only meant less cash, they also took up equally valuable time. The tailor needed to sew, not negotiate, for twelve hours a day, seven days a week, to make a living.

'Memsahib, no like?' he asked again, aware of the answer. This memsahib never liked anything. He already charged her twice as much, otherwise known as 'a very special price', to cover her bouts of disapproval, but even this premium was unlikely to yield a profit if she didn't speed up her discontent.

'I just don't understand how you people think,' Marjorie Rockingham said, shaking the dress in his face. 'Are you so stupid that you can't even follow an ordinary picture, for God's sake? Don't you possess any brains?'

The tailor smiled back. Even if he understood her, word for insulting word, it was better that he pretended otherwise. Marjorie suddenly sat down in a garden chair, as if defeated. 'Do again?' he suggested helpfully.

Marjorie had very carefully drawn a halter-neck day dress, with a straight skirt and a kick pleat in the back. Initially, she had drawn a pocket on the left-hand side, then she had changed her mind and crossed it out. The tailor had replicated the design literally. On the left hip of the otherwise perfectly executed dress was what looked like a very large rosette, the material folded in circles of frills, resembling a

23

hideous cotton anemone – the closest the tailor could come to copying a pencilled scribble. He failed to understand the problem. The memsahib had said, 'Follow exactly what I've drawn.' And that's precisely what he had done.

'Go, go, go,' Marjorie suddenly commanded, thrusting rupees in the man's hands.

'I come back?' he asked, self-respect always second to survival.

'No, yes, oh, I don't care. Tomorrow. *Imshe*, go, go.'

Marjorie sat and pulled at the dress that now lay in a crumpled pile in her lap. She was sick of it all. She wanted to leave Pakistan now and never see it again. She was tired of the rains, the heat, the beggars, the poor, the haggling in the bazaar, the putrid smells, the squalor, the ogling of the men, the bitchiness of the foreign women, the ineptitude of her servants, the idiocies of entertaining – rose-shaped pats of butter, bread rolls twisted into reef knots, napkins tortured into geisha-girl fans. Who cared? Who cared apart from Alice Jackson, that common little tart with her cheap cocktail dresses and Woolworths lipstick?

The Rockinghams had eight more months of their tour to complete, but Marjorie had hated this posting from the outset. Just as she'd hated every posting in Piers' career. She'd hated them for the simple reason that none of them were home – The Larches, 21 Bismarck Drive, Princes Risborough, Bucks.

Peshawar offered a unique set of miseries as far as Marjorie Rockingham was concerned. She loathed the humidity that destroyed her hair, the ants that ate the carpet, the mosquitoes that bored holes in her clothes, the silver fish that devoured the lacquer on her paintings, the lizards that snacked on the curtains and the locally bought food which periodically detonated her guts. In the fasting days of Ramadan, she couldn't stand the indolence and the irritability of the steady stream of men who came to sell her goods or services – the fruitwallah, the paniwallah offering bread, the dudhwallah selling milk. Always on the fiddle, trying to make more than their due. God, what she would give for one decent deferential British tradesman.

Marjorie had kept herself going so far because of the promise that, one day, Piers' career might take them to Paris and Rome and Washington. Then it would all be worthwhile.

One day.

'Morning, Marjorie,' Alice called out with a hint of defiance, as she climbed into Ash's black Wolsey, the door held open by an immaculately uniformed soldier. In Peshawar, the public and private lives of senior army officers tended to melt into one. Ella followed her mother into the rear of the car, proudly readjusting her dupatta, as she'd seen the older girls in school do, wrapping it round her head and throwing the end over her shoulder.

Ashraf Khan, seeing Marjorie, raised his hand in an informal salute. 'Would you care to join us? We're off for a swim and a bite to eat,' he called out. 'Plenty of room in the old banger if you care to come along.'

'She doesn't,' Alice whispered. 'No one's ever seen her in a swimming costume, never mind near water. Probably terrified of the effect on her immaculately waved hair.'

Marjorie gave a small wave. 'Another time, perhaps . . .' she said.

'Morning, Marjorie,' Bill Jackson smiled. Much to her surprise, she realised she was blushing.

The car nosed into The Mall, the driver hooting the horn furiously, ignoring the dilapidated road sign which read, 'Silence is Golden.' Ella adored life outside the compound. She liked the heat and the clatter and the colours and the dust and the smells and the frenzy of it all. Ancient lorries and buses, cannibalised and reconstructed from spare parts, observed no rules, veered from one side of the road to the other. Painted in shades of lime green and candy pink, they had pictures of fighter planes, Pakistani film stars, lions, moons and stars decorating their sides. Immediately ahead, a donkey laden down with bags of cereal had been brought to a dead halt, as the two small boys driving it stopped to watch the big black car, engulfed by a swarm of bicycles, ox carts and tongas. The boys waved and smiled.

Ella waved back. '*Asalam aleikum!*' she shouted, opening the window wider.

'Don't encourage them,' her mother chastised her nervously.

Encourage them to do what? Ella thought. Smile more?

Ash wound his window down too and began to bang on the side of the car. His curses and invocations to Allah in Urdu, Punjabi, Pashtu and Baluchi, plus his clenched fist, gradually created the gap in the traffic that the horn had failed to achieve. The car inched forward. Several women, dressed in dark-blue burquahs, stacked like human shuttle-cocks in the back of a tonga, looked on. Suddenly, a small hand was pushed through Ella's window. A child of five or so, with blonde-brown hair, matted with dirt, wearing a torn cotton dress and holding a baby on her hip, its eyes congealed with pus, kept repeating the same words, trotting by the side of the car as she did so. '*Baksheesh*, memsahib, *baksheesh . . .*'

'*Imshe! Imshe! Imshe!*' the driver shouted at her.

Ash reached into his pocket, acknowledging the duty of a Muslim to give alms. Alice looked the other way. Of course she was moved by the poverty, but really it wasn't a problem that she could solve.

'Here! Have this!' Ella's voice interrupted Alice's thoughts. She turned to see her daughter thrusting her new dupatta into the small girl's arms.

'*Shukria, shukria!*' the child shouted after the car as it picked up speed.

Ella sat back, not a little regretful that she had acted so spontaneously. 'Well,' she said defiantly, 'I didn't have anything else to give her, did I?'

'Whatever will Uncle Ash think of you now?' Alice demanded.

Ash put up his hands, as if refereeing this battle of wills. 'Look, it's no problem,' he coaxed. 'What's done is done. I'll get the driver to bring you a new one tomorrow. They're ten a penny in the bazaar. Really.'

Alice was about to remonstrate further when, suddenly, something cracked against her closed window. 'Christ, what's that?' Bill asked, pulling Ella towards him and covering her head.

On the right-hand side of the road, a large crowd of men had gathered. Almost as if in slow motion, the group was circling slowly around some fracas that was taking place in their centre. The traffic had once again ground to a halt, as everyone strained to have a look.

Ash gave rapid instructions to the driver, who immediately began tooting the horn with fresh gusto, manoeuvring the car out of the throng. Ash turned and smiled at his three passengers in the rear of the car. He appeared unperturbed. 'It's probably a Muslim having a go at a Sikh, or a Christian being beaten to a pulp. The usual kind of thing. You should know by now, bloodletting is our national sport. All in the name of God. Violent religion, it's what we do best. Don't give it another thought.'

As the car moved free of the crowd, and the adults' conversation resumed, Ella, unnoticed, turned and knelt on the back seat to look out of the rear window. She watched as a youth emerged from the crowd to cheers and shouts. He was holding a pole on which a flag was burning. He waved it backwards and forwards, before dropping it to the ground where it was trodden underfoot by a dozen or so men. Ella recognised the flag. It was the Union Jack.

27

Chapter Three

The British High Commission and the Peshawar Tennis Club both lay in a part of the city known as the British Cantonment. Created in the 1850s, when the Raj finally came to the North-West Frontier, the cantonment was orderly and manicured, a tribute to English suburbia. The car carrying Ash's party drove down boulevards shaded by palms and pipals, banyans and pines, willows and mulberry trees. It passed what the British regarded as some of the essential tools for a civilised life – Anglican and Catholic churches, a Masonic hall, a couple of bookshops, a handful of hotels, two schools, military barracks, riding stables. Behind high walls, guarded by dozing chowkidars, lay palatial houses and bungalows, built with high ceilings for coolness, and occupied by diplomats, aid workers, former members of the British Raj who had chosen to remain in the new country, and affluent Pakistanis and Anglo-Indians.

Peshawar, set at the foot of the Khyber Pass, a gateway to Afghanistan, China and Central Asia, had been invaded, sacked and rebuilt by one wave of marauders after another for two thousand years. Persians, Greeks, Huns, Tartars, Scythians, Mughals and Sikhs had left their legacy in the features of the city's inhabitants: carrot colouring, blond, black and brown hair with Western, Oriental and Asian faces. However, no trace of this diversity was to be found at the Peshawar Tennis Club. From its grand opening in 1873, until four years after Partition, in 1951, its selection committee had enthusiastically adopted an unspoken policy: whites only. Occasionally, an exception was made for an Anglo-Indian wife, but only if her mixed blood was so well disguised by a cream skin that she could 'pass' without too much dissent.

Eventually, economics dictated a change of policy. As many of the British returned to the UK, a fresh source of membership fees was required. It was decided that selection would no longer depend upon colour of skin, but clubbability. The fresh Pakistani intake generated desperately needed revenue. Club facilities were refurbished. This work was carried out at a highly inflated price by the brother of the North-West Frontier Province minister for home affairs. One favour deserved another, so the minister, in turn, for a generous bribe, issued a communal addicts' licence to the club. In the past, observing Islamic regulations, each member, if they wished to drink alcohol, had to acquire a signed certificate from their doctor, stating they were incurably addicted. That inconvenience was removed.

Now, the PTC was the centre of much of Peshawar's social life. Membership cost sixty rupees for a male, one rupee for a lady, and there was no charge at all for nurses. Among the entertainments offered were a Sunday buffet curry lunch, open-air cinema every third Saturday in the month, tombola night on a Thursday and a regular dinner-dance.

The club covered several landscaped acres. At the rear of the club house were ten chalet-style rooms and bathrooms for residential guests. Situated next to an open-air pool was the main club building, constructed in the form of a three-sided rectangle, facing a central garden, bordered with roses in every shade of pink and red. On this lawn, mid-morning and evening, cane chairs and tables were arranged in groups for the use of the members.

The club house offered a dance hall, walled with art nouveau mirrors, a library (with an extensive section in praise of Hitler and Nazi ideology), a dining room, a tea room, a cards room and snooker hall, and a small hairdressing and beauty parlour, named after its proprietor and sole beautician, Belle.

The tea room held a large Roberts' wireless which was perpetually tuned to the BBC World Service and God help the member who attempted to seek out a different radio station. The tea room also doubled as a venue for various events organised by the ladies to keep their mornings busy – flower arranging, toy making, lectures on the Tudors and Stuarts or Shakespeare's comedies, often given by visiting academics at the university or, more commonly, somebody's wife. Most important of all, of course, were the bars – four in total, one of which – the Campbell Room – had a men-only rule.

Predictably, the ceiling and walls of the Campbell Room were covered in tartan. The floor had originally been carpeted in tartan too, but such was the frequency with which socialising males vomited, tiling had been installed.

Rules may have been liberalised, but not attitudes. Occasional flare-ups at the bar, the way in which conversation suddenly stopped when a different face entered the Ladies, the manner in which the Pakistani maître d'hôtel, trained during the Raj, insisted on seating non-whites in the hottest part of the dining room, next to the kitchens, ensured that a sense of superiority could still find ways of nurturing itself.

As Ash's car pulled into the club now, Haji, the chief gateman, was on duty. He looked majestic. A Pathan, like Ash, he was dressed in a royal-blue jacket, white trousers and a spectacular blue pugree, the starched cotton cloth splayed out into a fan at the front of the turban. Ash ordered the driver to slow the car down. Haji, an ex-army man, saluted smartly. Ash slipped a rupee, a handsome tip, into his hand. The transaction was fluid, like a conjurer's trick.

'*Asalam aleikum*, sahib.' Haji waited until Ash had returned the greeting, then he added in English, grinning, 'Memsahib played tennis early and just gone, sahib. Coast is becoming clear, *inshallah*.'

Bill chuckled. 'I don't want to know which one of many memsahibs she might be, Ash, or why you're trying to avoid her,' he joshed, 'but, one day, you're going to come terribly unstuck. And who'll be around to pick up the pieces then?'

Ella threw her arms around Ash Khan's neck. 'I will,' she announced enthusiastically. 'I'll pick up the pieces, Uncle Ash, I promise. So don't you worry about a thing.'

The child couldn't fathom why the adults found her words so funny.

Tommy Larkhall sat under the shade of a parasol by the diving board at the corner of the adult swimming pool. He wore a tee-shirt and swimming trunks. He was eleven, but he had the body of a much younger boy. Everything about him was light, like a feather in a breeze. His skin was unnaturally white, almost translucent, with pale-purple shadows under his eyes. His limbs were not much fatter than the arms of the deckchair in which he sat. Every so often, his pattern of breathing would be interrupted by a slight shudder, like a second-hand car engine, turning over against the odds. Tommy was clapping his hands with pleasure.

The children's pool opposite was crammed full, the pool for grown-ups was empty, except for a woman whom the boy hadn't seen before. But then, he didn't visit the club all that often. His parents had explained to him that, while they could afford the fees, it was the lavishness of the entertainment that they found crippling. Even the most affluent member sometimes discovered, at the end of the month, that signing chits was a regrettably easy currency in which to deal.

The woman had been swimming lengths when Tommy first arrived. When she'd finished, she'd come over to talk to

31

him. She had an American accent, so Tommy guessed she might be a tourist, perhaps on her way to the Khyber Pass. Not many Americans stayed in Peshawar, unless they had no choice.

Now, he was throwing a stone into the pool for her and she was diving to retrieve it. A couple of older children had joined the game, and the woman was still finding the stone first, much to Tommy's pleasure. Most of the children at the club grew frustrated in his company, since he lacked the energy that they took for granted. Now, these two were tasting what it was like to be outstripped by somebody else. The woman seemed to understand why Tommy's enjoyment was so keen.

'Tommeeee, Tommy.' The voice came from the other end of the pool. Tommy turned and smiled broadly. It was Ella in her red swimming costume. She was dancing with excitement.

'Is she your friend?' the woman asked, as she hauled herself out of the pool, and dried herself with a towel.

Tommy nodded. 'She doesn't mind sitting down a lot,' he said, as if that was sufficient explanation. 'Ella's used to being on her own, like me.'

The girl came racing barefoot around the side of the pool, past the sign which warned, 'All Childs No Running,' her towel flapping like a cape. Breathless, she said, 'Tommy, do you know, we've got hours together? Come on, let's go. Hurry up, they're laying it out now. Put your hat on,' she suddenly added, remembering the state of her friend's health. Then she stopped, aware of the woman's presence.

'Hi, Ella,' the woman said, smiling.

'Hello, Aunty Betty,' Ella replied dutifully. Her mother had taught her to call all adults Mr or Mrs or Aunty or Uncle. Ella couldn't call Betty Mrs, since she didn't know her surname, so Aunty Betty it would have to be.

'Betty,' the woman corrected. 'Everybody calls me Betty.

Even my own children, sometimes.'

'That's nice,' Ella replied politely, impatient not to waste the time she had with Tommy.

The two children had met because Tommy's father, Albie, worked at the Deputy High Commission as a clerk. He was British, but employed on a local rate, which meant he earned very little. Ella knew this, because her dad talked about it quite a lot. He said it wasn't right. Tommy also had one older sister, Bertha, aged nineteen, who was married. His mother, Blossom, worked part-time as a nurse in the Quaker Hospital. She only worked part-time, because of her son's condition.

Tommy was spoilt. Adults gave in to him, but Ella was not inclined to be so indulgent. 'How can we have any fun if I just do what you tell me to do all the time?' she had demanded soon after they first met. Tommy was bright, so he'd seen the sense in this, although he still occasionally threw a tantrum. At those times, Ella worried that she might kill him – but she still refused to give in.

At first, Ella thought Tommy had been born in Wales, because he spoke with a Welsh accent. Then, when she'd met his sister and granny and mother, she realised it was probably more complicated than that. The boy was white – well, pale blue, really – while his mother was very dark brown and his granny and sister were the colour of milky coffee. Ella thought Bertha the most beautiful girl she had ever seen. She always smelt of flowers. When Ella told her mother, she said it was California Poppy, as if that wasn't very nice.

Tommy had a smell of his own, too, a sweet, strange, musty smell. Sometimes, when Ella was at his house and he was only able to lie quietly while she read out loud, the smell was almost overpowering. Ella had asked her mother what was wrong with Tommy and she'd said that it was best not to mention it. 'Is he going to die?' Ella had pressed.

'We're all going to die,' Alice had replied.

33

Tommy eventually broached the subject himself. He had a hole in his heart, he explained, so he wouldn't live long.

'Do you mind?' Ella had asked.

'Not really,' Tommy answered. 'Mama says that if you die young, that's because Jesus loves you so much, he wants you near to him.'

Personally, Ella hadn't found that at all reassuring.

Now, the two sat under a palm tree, watching the staff decorate the lunch tables with sugar-cane sticks and flower petals and green foliage. While they worked, other bearers brought out vast copper pans filled with rice and chicken curry and dishes of *karahi*, made of chillies and tomatoes and beef, all kept warm over large hissing gas-rings.

'How do you know her?' Tommy asked, referring to the American woman.

'She came to a party at our house last night. She's Mummy's friend,' Ella replied, then, conscious this wasn't terribly exciting, she added, 'Perhaps she was a famous film star once. You should've asked for her autograph.' Tommy was about to answer when there came the sound of smashing glass and swearing.

One of the bearers was attempting to wrap the cloth he normally carried over his arm around the hand of a man standing next to Tommy's father, at the outdoor bar. The man was trim and very tanned. He was wearing a brightly coloured sport-shirt and shorts and a heavy gold ring on his finger. He was waving his hand around and swearing. Blood, bright-red blood, was being flicked by the man, over himself, Albie and the servant. A streak landed on Albie's spectacles and he jerked his head back suddenly, as if struck.

'Daddy!' Tommy shouted. Instinct made Ella put her hand out to stop him, in case he tried to join the fray.

The man with the cut hand kept repeating himself, as if in a daze. 'Glass, for Chrissake, glass. Who would bloody believe it? Who the fuck uses glass? Give me plastic, nice, shiny plastic. You heard of plastic, buster? Plastic from the US of A?' he challenged the bearer belligerently. 'Cocktail glasses in plastic, that's what we use back home when we drink outside. Nice, pretty plastic in colours, lots of colours. None of this glass shit. See this?' The man picked up a second glass. It was as if this was the signal for action. Tommy's father and a couple of other members pushed the man down on to a chair.

The man was shouting again. 'I want a real doctor, you hear me? An American doctor. And whisky,' he demanded, and added with a roar, 'IN A FUCKING PLASTIC GLASS.'

Once the excitement had died down, Ella and Tommy sat in the shadier section of the pool, and kicked at the frogs' spawn which laced the water like tapioca.

'Why do you think that man was so angry?' Ella asked. Tommy had spent more time with grown-ups than she had, because of his illness, so she assumed that he understood their behaviour better.

'Oh, I expect he's just a bad person,' he answered casually.

'Do you think I'm a bad person, Tommy?'

The boy chuckled breathily. 'Of course not, you idiot,' he replied. 'Who said you were?'

'Mummy did, last night,' Ella said, kicking the water again with her feet.

Tommy waved his hand dismissively. 'Oh, I never believe what grown-ups say,' he answered breezily. 'They told Mama I'd be dead before I was ten, and I'm still here. What do they know about anything? My advice is, not to listen to what they say, and don't tell them anything either. They never listen properly, anyway. Not unless it suits them,' he added, shrugging his chicken-bone shoulders.

'Tommy,' Ella asked, her thoughts already moving on, 'what's a douche?'

The slice of purple aubergine sank and then resurfaced in the dung-coloured sauce, like a tyre bobbing in an oil slick. 'More, memsahib?' the chef asked, never surprised by how much club members could consume.

Alice nodded. First aid was required: a large gin and tonic and a plateful of chilli. If she set fire to her throat, at least that might distract her from the clanging in her head. As she took her plate and turned, she almost collided with Betty Brooking. The woman held a cigarette in one hand, a whisky in the other. 'I didn't know you were a member,' Alice said, as they made their way to the farthest side of the lawn, where Ash had secured a table and chairs.

'I'm not,' Betty answered. 'I'm not the joining kind. I prefer the joys of secret drinking. My husband's a member, he comes to play tennis.'

Alice had begun to believe that Mr Brooking was a ghost of a spouse. She and the American woman had been introduced a few weeks earlier, at an official reception to celebrate the establishment of Pakistan as an Islamic republic. Betty had been alone then and at every social occasion since.

'Aren't you eating?' Alice asked, discreetly inspecting the older woman's face and her immaculate white linen skirt and shirt. She had drunk steadily all through the previous evening too, so why didn't her skin resemble baking paper?

'The secret is not to stop.' Betty smiled, as if reading Alice's mind. 'When anyone asks, I say I drink a little – which is true.' She saluted with her glass. 'I drink a little, all the time.'

Alice laughed and, reaching the table, began to introduce the American to the other guests, already seated. 'Betty Brooking, please meet Claire and Chubby Whitstead. Chubby is going to be the new manager of Darnley's Bank. Ashraf Khan Afridi – what's your rank, Ash? I always forget,' she lied. 'Well, anyway, Ash is something very important in the army and his family has lots of money. He is also –' Alice looked at him with mock sternness – 'he is also married, but keeps his wife locked away in the house in a burquah.'

Ash smiled and, having risen from his seat when the two women approached, sat down again. 'Alice is inclined to exaggerate,' he said amiably. 'My wife lives the life she chooses. Islam is important to her.'

'And not to you?' Betty asked.

'I have little faith in anything,' he answered lightly.

'Oh, come on, you're an army man,' Chubby Whitstead commented jocularly. 'What are you? Nationalist, socialist, revolutionary, fundamentalist, what? What banner do you follow, Colonel Khan?'

Claire Whitstead's face was registering a look that Alice knew well from diplomatic circles – controlled panic that a scene might be about to ensue.

Ash relaxed back into his chair, as if to ease the woman's concern. 'Since you ask, Mr Whitstead, what I am is a realist,' he replied equably. 'In my humble view, unless this country changes drastically – and soon – fifty years from now, it will be what Americans call a busted flush, a broken wheel, a country crippled by corruption and lack of investment, used and abused by the big boys – the Soviet Union and the States.

'As for the poverty, that will be many times worse. And families like mine will be even richer. But as to what form change should take and who would be capable of bringing it about . . .' Ash shrugged his shoulders non-committally. 'I am merely a soldier trained to fight – not a politician.'

Whitstead was not in the mood to set his prey free. 'And no doubt you're one of those soldiers who put all the blame on the Brits?' he challenged aggressively.

His wife's hand moved to her husband's knee, as if to steady him on the tiller. 'It's the heat,' she interjected apologetically. 'He's not at all his usual self.'

Ella's voice interrupted, calling from the other side of the lawn, trying to attract her mother's attention. 'Mummy, Mummy, Aunty Blossom's leaving now. We're over here.'

Alice turned to see her daughter and the Larkhalls coming towards her table. Albie Larkhall, a muscular man with an open face and a military bearing, was gently carrying his son, Tommy, in his arms. His wife, Blossom, stood by his side, but came only to his shoulder. She was slim, in her early forties, with long black hair, knotted in a bun. She wore no make-up and a simple floral short-sleeved dress with white collar and cuffs. Around her neck was a gold cross and chain.

'Please, don't get up,' Blossom instructed the men in the group. 'We're off now, Alice. Tommy needs a rest. He's had such fun today, haven't you, little man?' She smiled at her son. 'I'm thinking Ella might like to come and spend the night next weekend? Perhaps after school on Friday?'

'Please, Mummy, please, please,' Ella begged.

'Let's think about that,' Alice answered.

The American woman was surprised that her tone was so cold.

Blossom moved forward, as if to kiss Alice on the cheek, but saw the embarrassment in her face. Instead, she patted her husband's arm and pushed Tommy's fringe out of his eyes. 'Time for home, boys,' she urged.

Claire Whitstead was the first to speak after the Larkhalls' departure. 'So what exactly is wrong with the little boy?' she asked.

Ella answered. 'He's got a hole in his heart and they can't afford to send him away to get better.'

'Ella,' Alice warned. 'You know what Mummy says. Children should be seen and not heard.'

Betty took a sip of her drink. 'I've never thought that made much sense,' she remarked casually. 'I mean, how are kids to learn if they never open their mouths?'

Claire Whitstead, her mind still on Tommy, commented perfunctorily, 'Tragic.' Then she added, 'And who exactly does the little boy belong to? I mean, she can't be his mother, can she? Is she a friend of yours, Alice?'

Alice put down her plate. 'Friend?' She wiped her mouth with her napkin, leaving a lip print. 'Blossom Larkhall? Oh, goodness me, no. Her husband works under Bill. He's locally employed, in charge of the clerks. Tommy is Blossom's son. And Albie's, of course.'

Ella looked at her mother in disbelief. Of course Aunty Blossom was a friend. When Ella was dropped off at the Larkhalls', her mother always stopped and chatted for ages. It was Aunty Blossom who had taken them to the bazaar when they first arrived. It was she who'd sent Surindabash for the job as their cook. They saw her all the time, so how could she not be a friend? Why was her mother telling this horrible woman, who couldn't care less about Tommy, such an awful fib?

'So the poorly little boy is actually her son?' Claire Whitstead's eyebrows signalled her curiosity.

Alice nodded. 'Tommy's Eurasian . . . Anglo-Indian. Albert, his father, was born in Southend. He came out here before the war to work on the railways and met Blossom. Blossom's grandfather was British too – he worked on the railways as well.'

'But the boy's so very white. It's difficult to believe he's just a chee-chee.' Claire Whitstead wrinkled her nose, as if Tommy Larkhall had committed some kind of sartorial blunder. 'And she's, well . . . she isn't, is she? White, I mean.'

Ella could stand no more. 'Tommy isn't "just a chee-chee",' she burst out furiously, perfectly mimicking the wonan's artificially polished accent. 'He belongs here. He comes from Peshawar. He loves Peshawar. He doesn't want to be British. He thinks we're horrible. Most of us, anyway. And he's not "just" a chee-chee. He's very, very special, because he might die at any minute. And . . . and . . .'

Her indignation ran out of words. Her mother stepped in. 'Ella, say sorry at once. How dare you be so rude to Mrs Whitstead. You will go straight to your room when we get home. I will not have this behaviour. Do you hear me? Say sorry immediately.'

Ella stood up abruptly and glared at her mother, then at Claire Whitstead, who had composed herself in preparation for the child's apology.

'Well?' Alice demanded.

'I will not say sorry,' Ella blurted out. 'Mrs Whitstead was rude about Tommy. And Aunty Blossom is your friend, she is, she really is. You know she is.'

Then Ella was gone, aghast at her own boldness in virtually calling her mother a liar. She ran out into the drive, a pair of flashing legs, dancing between the tongas waiting for passengers.

Ash rose to follow, but before he could move, he found his way blocked by the stranger with a heavily bandaged hand.

'Let her go, Ash,' Alice instructed, fuming at the humiliation Ella had inflicted on her. 'Just wait till I get her home.'

Ash did as he was told, turning his attention to the newcomer. 'Ah, the gentleman who would like us all to buy American plastic,' he said, his tone gently mocking. 'I do hope the wound isn't serious, sir?'

Betty stood up, drained her drink, and put on her sunglasses. 'Alice, Colonel Khan, Mr and Mrs Whitstead –' she gestured with her head – 'May I introduce you to my husband, Charles Jermaine Brooking Junior?'

'Hi, folks.' The man twitched his cheeks in a semblance of a smile. 'Call me CJ. All my friends call me CJ.' Then, without missing a beat or turning to look at his wife, he added abruptly. 'Siddown, Betty. Did I say we were leaving?'

'Crap?' repeated Bill Jackson a little later. He had joined the group in the hope of coaxing Alice to leave.

'Yeh, crap. That's my business.' CJ Brooking pointed a finger at Ash Khan. 'I teach you people how to deal with your shit. And, forgive me for saying so, that isn't a pleasant task.'

Betty Brooking, her eyes hidden behind her sunglasses, watched the Pakistani's reactions. A muscle in one cheek was jumping, but his manner remained relaxed. He spoke softly. 'So, you're working on the new sewage plant on the Jamrud Road. Is that it?' he asked.

CJ pretended to look crestfallen. 'Shiiitt! You guessed already,' he said, then, chuckling again, added, 'Shit. Get it?'

Alice was surprised. Betty appeared indifferent to her husband's behaviour. She would have been mortified.

'Ah, that sewage plant.' Bill Jackson nodded, as if everything had been made clear.

'What sewage plant?' Alice asked. 'For goodness sake, will somebody please speak plain English?'

'Allow me?' Ash sought permission from CJ, who nodded, still highly amused. 'Mr Brooking is working for Friends of America. FOA,' he explained. 'It's an aid organisation helping to improve the infrastructure of underdeveloped countries. Right so far?' he asked.

CJ nodded happily.

'The FOA is building us a sewage plant. We have a very, very large budget being poured into providing us with ways of dealing with our excreta, at a time when three-fifths of the population barely eats enough to produce any waste at all. A superb example of synchronisation between supply and demand, don't you think, Mr Brooking? Sorry, CJ?' Ash's charm couldn't hide the sarcasm.

The women exchanged glances, perplexed by the mysterious male game that was clearly underway.

CJ slapped his thigh. 'Do you know what, Mr Khan?' he chuckled. 'I guess I must have been a shit stirrer in my previous life.' He laughed uproariously and alone at his private joke. 'Isn't that what you believe in? Reincarnation? Being born again as an iddy biddy flea if you put a foot wrong?'

Betty placed a cigarette in her mouth and Ash immediately produced a lighter. The woman cupped her hands around his,

41

to protect the flame from a non-existent breeze. Alice noticed that she held his hands just a fraction longer than necessary. 'Thank you, Colonel Khan,' Betty smiled. Coolly, she turned to her husband and talked to him as you might a child. 'CJ, reincarnation is a Hindu belief. Colonel Khan is a Muslim. Pakistan is a Muslim country.'

'Whatever you say, honey,' CJ answered docilely, as if this was a matter for a domestic court, and therefore beyond his jurisdiction.

Betty stood up and addressed Ash. 'Colonel, I'd be grateful if you would introduce me to the doctor who tended to my husband's hand. I believe you know him? I just want to give him my thanks. Excuse us for a minute, won't you?'

Ash guided her across the crowded lawn, his hand on her elbow. They reached the interior of the club, a retreat from the heat, a cool, dark cave. In the gloom of the corridor, he stopped and leaned against a wall. The couple studied each other without speaking, testing who would be the first to break the silence. Ash smiled and slowly ran a finger down Betty's arm.

'Perspiration,' she said. 'What did you expect, Colonel? Neat Johnnie Walker? I brought you away from the table to apologise,' she added. 'My husband is not a pleasant man now, although, once, he carried all my dreams with him no matter where he went.' She spoke as if the information she was relaying had no effect on her personally.

'So why do you put up with it?' Ash asked.

She gave him an enigmatic smile, before answering almost lazily, 'Take your pick. Perhaps it's because I believe I deserve no better? Or, perhaps it's because I have no choice? A divorcee is not the most welcome human being in Cheyenne, Wyoming. Or, maybe I stay because this kind of relationship suits me?

'CJ leaves me to live the life I please because he can't imagine that I'm being anything other than his faithful wife.'

She shrugged. 'Or, then again, maybe the real reason I stay is because I made a promise when I married him and that remains strong even if the man has changed. Like you, Colonel Khan, I don't have much left in the way of faith but I hang on to a sense of duty. Hell, a girl's got to hold on to something to keep her out of trouble, don't you think? Do I look the dutiful type, Colonel?' she added almost mockingly. Then, before he had time to reply, she began to walk back down the corridor, heading for the sunlight.

Almost at the door, she stopped to slowly stub out her cigarette on the stone floor. Ash's eyes were drawn to the movement of her leg under her skirt.

'Do you know something, Colonel Khan?' she said casually over her shoulder. 'The older I get, the more I'm aware that nothing and nobody is quite what they seem.'

An hour later, the Jacksons were in a tonga on their way home. The day's socialising had succeeded in distracting Alice both from her aching head and this morning's altercation with her husband, but the dirt and the dust were beginning to reverse her mood. Ella, dozing, sat propped up between her parents. Earlier, Alice had chastised her. The words had sounded tired from repetition even to her: Ella had behaved very badly, she was a wicked girl, she must go to bed early without supper. The new shalwar and qamiz were in the swimming bag and Ella was now reluctantly dressed in a cotton frock. Still, Alice was only partially satisfied. She glanced at Bill, who had his arm protectively around his daughter. Rarely, nowadays, did he extend the same affection to her.

'I've been thinking that we should send Ella as a boarder to St Winifred's in Chowdiagalli,' she said. 'The Larkhall girl went and loved it. Ella would have plenty of friends to play with, lots of things to do. It's cooler in the hills. Anyway, she's bored to death most of the time in the compound. She hardly knows anyone her own age. She's with adults far too much for her own good.

'Besides,' Alice added, 'it's not you who has to put up with her all day, Bill. When you're not around she can be an absolute madam. She disappears for hours on end and I haven't got a clue where she is. Or she's under Surindabash's feet. The man's got work to do.'

Bill Jackson sat back on the tonga's shiny red plastic seat and took one of his sleeping daughter's hands in his, as if to anchor himself to her more firmly. 'Are you saying you want to send Ella away?' he asked.

Alice shook her head irritably. 'Not away – to school. For her own good,' she answered.

Bill closed his eyes. 'She's only nine, Alice,' he said evenly. 'She's only a little girl and you want to send her away? I thought we'd decided, if she has to go, it'll be when she's thirteen.'

Alice's voice was defensive. 'Lots of children her age are in boarding school in the UK by now,' she argued. 'Marjorie's boys have been away from home since they were seven and it's done them no harm.'

Bill Jackson smiled wryly. 'Well, in their case, given the father they've got, on the contrary, it's probably been the saving of them,' he said. 'But as for Ella, she stays with us.'

'You'd think you'd want something better for your daughter,' Alice muttered crossly.

'That's precisely the point,' Bill Jackson replied flatly. 'I do.'

Chapter Four

Later that same Sunday evening, Sylvia Hargreave-Smith smiled at her husband and gave him a peck on the cheek. 'See you in the morning, darling,' she said cheerily. Noel Hargreave-Smith watched as she walked up the stairs to her bedroom. As soon as she'd joined him in Peshawar, he had advised separate sleeping arrangements. Among the reasons he had given were his late nights and early risings and her need for more rest as she acclimatised to the heat. Sylvia had been generous in her response. 'How marvellously considerate you are.'

Early in their brief courtship, Noel realised that Sylvia reacted to most events in this sometimes maddeningly cheerful fashion. Everything and everyone was either 'marvellous' or 'nice' or 'super'. He wasn't sure whether this was the result of inexperience, since Sylvia had yet to meet with serious disappointment, or, much more troubling, a straightforward lack of imagination. Sylvia was twenty-nine to his fifty-two. She was the daughter of old friends and they had met and married during Noel's brief sojourn in the UK between postings. She had joined him four months after his arrival in Peshawar, a postponement caused by her sister's marriage.

He was fully aware that, when the party games of which Sylvia was so fond began to pall, he would have to seek out some other suitable endeavour to keep his new wife occupied. Noel knew from experience that a bored spouse could cause enormous mischief.

Now, he crossed the polished floor of the hall, walked into his study, and felt at peace. The room had a high ceiling and a polished wooden floor, partially covered in Afghan rugs. It was furnished with a brown leather three-piece suite and a mahogany desk, bought in Rangoon twenty years before. French windows looked out over a folly constructed by one of his predecessors: a walled and locked garden. Inside, a now bedraggled maze concealed a gazebo – or, more accurately, a dilapidated hut. With the exception of Shafi Akhtar, the gardener and occasional chowkidar and driver, only Noel had access to the garden.

By instinct and training, Hargreave-Smith was a man who not only lived by the rules, but believed that they were essential if man's natural tendency to anarchy and evil were to be contained. He had gradually come to realise that almost every senior diplomat he'd known, who'd displayed an unquestioning devotion to Queen and country, also had an area of his life reserved for a private act of rebellion. Some acts were more dangerous than others – small boys, mistresses, poker, even, of course, communism. It was as if a discreet cul-de-sac of risk enabled a man to adhere more easily to a lifetime of duty.

Noel smiled wryly. His personal indulgence was, ironically, perhaps the most difficult of all to satisfy: a desire for solitude. That's why he loved his garden. Of course, he had warned Sylvia, but it wasn't in her nature to understand. 'Look,' she'd said, without irony, 'it's just marvellous that you even want to marry me. If you need time on your own, I'm sure we'll work something out. Together.'

Inevitably, even before he'd left for Pakistan, it had been developing into a problem. He sighed. Why on earth did Rosemary have to go and let herself die? He picked up one of the silver-framed family photographs on his desk. It showed a woman in her late thirties, in a summer frock, standing with three teenage boys. His Rosemary. He smiled. She had always called him 'my perfect gentleman'. She had been able to cope so well with his – he searched for a word – his . . . distance.

Rosemary used to tease him, quoting Kipling, 'If neither foes nor loving friends can hurt you, if all men count with you, but none too much . . .' She had hurt him considerably by dying at the age of thirty-eight. Thirteen years later, when his sons had grown, Noel had met and married Sylvia. It had been suggested to him delicately that marriage might be appropriate, especially if promotion to the rank of High Commissioner and a knighthood was to be forthcoming. The Foreign and Commonwealth Office did so hate loose ends.

Noel didn't love Sylvia, but, then, he hadn't loved Rosemary either when they'd first married. Gradually, she had become what he called – somewhat unromantically, he admitted – his 'Life Enhancer'. Rosemary used to laugh and say it made her sound like a surgical truss. She had made few demands and shared his attitude to sex and, of course, she had left him alone for hours, even weeks, returning to the UK to be with the boys at Easter and, occasionally, in the summer.

Noel took out a small green book from his desk drawer and walked out through the study's French windows to the verandah. He settled into one of the recently arrived cane armchairs. Its crude equivalent could be bought in the furniture bazaar in the Old City, but Rockingham had insisted that a set of six, covered in hideous yellow cabbage-roses, should be purchased in the Army and Navy Store in Victoria and sent out by sea. The wait had been interminable.

Ten minutes later, Noel's reading was interrupted by the sound of the telephone. The telephone was rarely heard in the compound, because the Peshawar exchange was ancient and erratic. In most cases, within the city, it was quicker to send a boy with a written note than to wait for the operator to make a connection. For longer distances, the compound's residents booked a call. They then settled down to wait, sometimes for minutes, often for days.

He picked up the phone. 'Deputy High Commissioner here,' he said.

A smoker's voice replied, 'Hope I didn't wake you, Noel, old boy?'

Hargreave-Smith said nothing, for fear that his irritation might be obvious. Harry Webster was based near to the hill station of Abbotabad, founded as a British garrison town a hundred years earlier. Four hours' driving time to the east of Peshawar, the area was close to the border of Punjab and the disputed territory of Kashmir.

In Abbotabad, on Sundays, church bells pealed and brass bands played and the club served roast beef. Noel relished the place's resistance to change and would have visited more often, but for the presence of Harry and his boys from the Met, the weather men.

The Meteorological Office normally consisted of a staff of five, headed by Webster. It was now a man short, and awaiting a replacement from London. The Met men were ostensibly studying weather patterns. Their covert role was to monitor communications and atomic tests across the border in the USSR. Their findings were then sent to Peshawar by diplomatic bag, for encoding and communication to London. The man responsible for sorting what he referred to as 'the mildly interesting from the utterly useless' was David Carnow, Hargreave-Smith's number three, another MI6 employee, a cuckoo in the nest, seconded to the compound.

'You could call us the barometer of the Cold War,' Harry Webster had once said to Noel in his slightly pompous fashion. 'We're always the first to know if the temperature's changed.' The DHC suspected that the truth was much more prosaic. He was sure the Russians found it useful sometimes to feed the Met boys information. Certainly, each time he ran into Kolensky, the military attaché at the Russian consulate, the man would say, 'And how's the weather in the hills these days, old chap?' then grin broadly. It was the kind of levity in international relations that Noel could do without.

Most of all, though, he disliked the Met boys' arrogance and sense of superiority, especially since some were so young. They acted as if they knew best and he was far too well mannered to tell them otherwise.

'You there, Noel? It's a bloody awful line.' Harry Webster's voice faded and returned to full power. He was chuckling and sounded drunk. 'Guess what? You'll hate this. The bastards have sunk a boat, right bang in the middle of the Canal. How about that then? The Russians are bloody cock-a-hoop. Wait until London finds out.' The man was gleeful.

Webster was an Arabist. In private conversations with Noel in recent weeks, he'd voiced his view that Egypt's young leader, Gamel Abdul Nasser, was a star of Islamic imperialism in the making – and a trouble-maker.

Noel had remained unimpressed. Nasser, in his view, was a jumped-up son of a post-office clerk who lacked pedigree. Given time, in his opinion, Nasser would sink into the same swamp of greed and corruption and incompetence as all his predecessors. He was just another Egyptian Johnny who should be bought off or brought down.

'Is that what you phoned to tell me?' Hargreave-Smith replied. 'A boat sunk at Suez is hardly going to make much difference here, is it?'

''Course not, old man,' Webster said. 'I phoned because it's my birthday. Thought you might want to give me your good wishes. And to tell you that I've taken a bit of a liberty.'

Noel automatically viewed change as synonymous with loss of quality. Webster and his gang proved his point. He'd bet his money on Webster being a grammar-school boy. 'What sort of liberty?' he asked cautiously.

'Our new boy, a lad called Dan Cockcroft, he's arriving in

Peshawar the day before the Queen's birthday. I told him you'd invite him to the usual bash. Hope you don't mind, but it's the quickest way for him to meet all the local bods, get a lie of the land. Know what I mean? He's young, but not your usual sort. Bloody brilliant, apparently.' Webster laughed, as if enjoying a private joke. 'You still there, old boy?' His voice began to fade again. 'Listen to Uncle Harry. Go and get yourself some rest. According to our readings, we're all in for a bloody busy few months. Sleep while you can, that's my advice. Regards to Sylvia. Settling in, is she? Night, old fellow.'

Noel replaced the receiver. He could smell trouble in the air. And it was only partly to do with gaining a wife.

Chapter Five

C J Brooking sat in his den, under one of his favourite posters, an ad for General Electric. Three American fighter planes winged their way across the sky. The poster read, 'Dedicated to America's Defence.' That's why he instructed Betty to buy General Electric – refrigerator, toaster, blender. In his view, it was a clear duty of freedom lovers everywhere to spend, spend, spend and keep the American dream strong. Outside, the evening temperature hovered around eighty degrees, but in the den it was chilly, courtesy of General Electric's air-conditioning.

Nursing a Budweiser, CJ flicked through a three-year-old copy of *Playboy*; Marilyn Monroe across the centre spread, only to be viewed in private. He had always been a man's man, his family's rock, a disciplinarian, the breadwinner who laid down the rules and expected them to be obeyed. No soft-bellied tears for him when his only son had died. CJ saw public expressions of grief as a woman's indulgence, except that his wife hadn't wept much either.

Betty always wore the same necklace: four pearls for each daughter she had borne CJ and one diamond for their son, Gregory John Brooking. Greg had died four years earlier. The four girls were now in their twenties, married, and Marsha, Greg's twin, had two boys of her own. Betty had been a perfect mother and wife. How did CJ know? Because the gold cup on his very large desk told him so. In

1947, Elizabeth Caroline Hamilton Brooking had been voted Wyoming's Mother of the Year, in a statewide contest run by the radio station WBGT and screened on national television.

Betty had been nominated by the staff in the school where she taught part-time. They had listed her efforts as the mother of five, the time she devoted to looking after her ninety-year-old father, her reading classes for illiterate poor black children, and, of course, her prize-winning turkey meat loaf. Betty was always a doer, always busy, always well organised, always involved. She hadn't even known she'd been nominated. Her prize had included a new set of kitchen pans, a year's supply of Rice-a-Roni, a television set for the family home, a *Reader's Digest Cookery Compendium*, a weekend for two in New York to accept the accolade, and a set of golf clubs for the husband of the champ.

Afterwards, she was asked to sponsor all manner of consumer goods in exchange for handsome fees. 'Mother of the Year says you can't beat ZitAttack for tackling teenage acne.' 'Mother of the Year knows the way to make hubby tubby is with delicious Seltzer's Sausage Meat.' 'Wrap it up – with Holmer's Baking Foil, says Mom of the Year.' Betty refused it all. CJ even had to retrieve the gold cup and the publicity photographs from the refuse.

He had taken this particularly badly, since, not unnaturally, he saw his wife's success as his own. He had given her the opportunity and the income and, even more crucially, the children. Betty hadn't wanted quite so many, but if CJ was going to have a family, it was going to be a big family.

They had met and married within a year. Betty was nineteen, CJ twenty-three and going through law school. It was 1929, money was tight so, eighteen months through college, Betty dropped out and took a job as a waitress, because the tips were good and they helped meet the cost of her husband's college fees. Years later, she became a teacher, but CJ had never wanted her to work full-time. He knew he had done good by Betty. He had qualified as a lawyer, specialising in corporate affairs, mainly in construction. Then he made a mistake.

He had always been a man who needed a mission. Initially, the mission had been his own advancement – qualifications, career, wife. Then it had been to secure – heck – immortality. Or, rather, the establishment of a vast shopping mall, known as Brookings Bay, filled to overflowing with items that the average human being must acquire if he wanted to become a truly happy American.

CJ was good with the law, with construction, with money. What he knew nothing about was civic corruption. So Brookings Bay met hurdle after hurdle, until by the time he belatedly agreed to pay good money to bad people, it was all too late. CJ lost almost every penny he'd made. He blamed his misfortune on the commies and faggots who had capitalism by the balls. Senator Joseph McCarthy was right; J Edgar Hoover, head of the FBI, knew exactly what he was talking about; CJ even had time for Phyllis Schlafly, McCarthy's researcher, despite the fact she was a woman.

Normally, he preferred females to keep to their own area of the flight deck – schools, family, hospitals, that kind of thing. But Phyllis was smart. She'd contacted him over a couple of matters and, through her, CJ eventually discovered a fresh mission: working on the frontline in the fight for liberty. In 1950, he became a senior executive with Friends of America, 'building bridges to the American dream'. He worked abroad – Honduras, Vietnam, Korea – Betty remaining at home to see the kids through school.

CJ's (usually covert) task was to get a project built in far-flung corners, fast and efficiently, as an important defence against the Red encroachment. The foreign people on whom he had to rely were more often than not, in his experience, lazy, slow, unskilled, ill-disciplined and unappreciative of the

American investment intended to secure their futures. They most often also happened to be black or brown, certainly not white. White was best – CJ didn't regard this view as racist, he saw it as common sense. What's more, nothing could beat the US of A. He'd lived and flourished in the States, and he'd worked elsewhere. And, on the whole, elsewhere stank.

Three years into joining FOA, CJ's family fortunes had been considerably restored. He had been promoted twice. In addition, he had a handsome wife who had everything a woman could want, his girls had married well, his son had died a hero, he owned two Cadillacs, television sets, a ranch-style home on an exclusive estate, a log cabin in the mountains and, installed in a corner of his study in Peshawar, a state-of-the-art Grundig Majestic tape recorder with a two-speed multispeaker, a record player with a flip lid, and a radio, all encased in a sideboard with a walnut veneer and a cream leather finish.

Yet, somehow, however much there was, it was never quite enough. It was while waiting for a connection in Denver airport, Colorado, that CJ had picked up a paperback. It was called *The Power of Positive Thinking* by the Reverend Norman Vincent Peale. The date was 12 January 1954. And, suddenly, it had clicked. It wasn't life that was the problem, it was CJ's attitude towards it. He had found a new mission, one which almost rivalled stemming the tide of communism. It was – to think positive.

The book promised ten rules for developing confidence, three secrets for keeping your vigour, five ways to overcome defeat, and a ten-point guide to popularity. CJ had been a little unsure of the Biblical references, and the need to call constantly on Christ, but Mr Peale's belief in 'a higher power' tallied with CJ's Masonic commitment, so that was OK.

He had tried to convert Betty, too. He couldn't remember what she'd said or, indeed, whether she'd said anything at all, but, from that moment, he had discovered a whole new set of tools with which to play. Now, he was unbeatable.

'Big Boy!' CJ shouted. The door opened and the bearer entered, bowing. On a tray, he carried a can of beer, a slab of cheese and a cheese peeler; the Sahib's evening ritual. The bearer placed the food and drink on the desk and left. CJ carefully shaved a slim slice of Monterey Jack from the block. He poured his beer, sat back in his chair, and surveyed his den.

It was a man's room. The furniture was teak, the lighting was subdued, the décor plum-coloured, the Venetian blinds black. But ask him to describe any of this detail or recall the colour scheme and he would have been stumped. The look of it didn't concern him, it was the feel of it that mattered. It was the biggest room in the house – and it felt his. On the wall facing his desk, he had framed a few of the most telling thoughts of Norman Peale.

'Think defeat and you are bound to be defeated.' 'They conquer who believe they can'; 'Stop fuming and fretting'; 'Expect the best and get it'; 'Practise liking people' (CJ had difficulty with that one); 'Do the thing you fear and the death of fear is certain'.

CJ took pride in fearing nothing, but he did have a small but growing sense of unease. Throughout his twenty-seven-year marriage to Betty, it had been CJ who had had the status, the money, the career, the kudos (he didn't count domestic trophies) and, years ago, the occasional fling, conducted mainly to prove that he could. He had always viewed his wife as an indivisible part of himself. So much so, that when people commented on how attractive she was, CJ would be taken aback – as if they were faggots coming on strong to him. When he and Betty talked, it was about his life, not hers. That's what she was happy to do. Recently, however, CJ had begun to wonder if Betty was really quite as uncomplicated as he'd always assumed. And he found the thought unsettling.

Chapter Six

The scorpion was black with a purple shine and the size of Ella's smallest finger. 'Lookee, lookee,' the small boy excitedly instructed her. He tipped the jar up, cruelly causing the scorpion to tumble down its walls. She took the jar cautiously and peered at the insect. It had four pairs of legs and two claws. A tail almost its body length was curled up and over its back. Ella watched as, slowly, gracefully, its claws reached out, as if it was inviting her to dance.

'*Shukria*,' she said, handing the jar back. She had been playing, as she often did, with the group of half-a-dozen or so children who permanently hovered around the compound gate. Ella would bring sweets and they, in turn, would share what little they had, sticks of sugar cane or cakes.

'Lookee, lookee,' the boy said again. He set the jar down, freeing the scorpion. Another boy had released a small spider. The two insects faced each other, immobile. Then, the scorpion attacked. It flicked its tail forward. As Ella watched, its claws began to mash and crunch the smaller insect, rapidly reducing it to a pulp. Within seconds, the pulp was transformed into liquid. Then, as the scorpion feasted, the boy brought the glass down hard. '*Bus!*' he shouted, triumphant, waving the scorpion's splattered remains on the end of the jar. 'Finished!'

'It was sort of sucking up the spider, just as if it was orange squash,' Ella recounted excitedly to her mother, an hour later.

Alice was in the sitting room, reading a newly arrived copy of *Picture Post*, a magazine her sister regularly sent her from home. It was overflowing with photographs of the American film star Grace Kelly and Prince Rainier of Monaco, whose marriage was taking place in a few weeks. 'A Fairy Tale Come True,' the headline proclaimed. In one picture, Grace Kelly was wearing a dress with cap sleeves, a mandarin collar and a flared skirt. Easy enough to copy, Alice thought to herself. Part of the past that she preferred to conceal was her apprenticeship to a furrier at the age of fourteen. She had become an excellent seamstress.

Ella pulled at her mother's arm, to attract her attention. Without raising her eyes from the magazine, Alice murmured, 'Is that right?'

Encouraged, her daughter babbled out more details. 'You'd never believe how fast the scorpion ran. It ran really, really fast.' Ella tried again. 'And the poor spider, who should've tried to get away, just stood there and did nothing, as if he didn't have any choice. He just sort of gave up. I'd've run or something, wouldn't you, Mummy?'

'Mmm,' Alice answered.

Ella grew all the more determined. 'You wouldn't believe how big the scorpion was – really, really big. The biggest I've seen. It was about as big as my whole hand. When the boy killed it, there was blood everywhere and . . .'

'E-ll-a.' Alice elongated the word, as if issuing a warning. 'Don't be silly. It couldn't possibly have been as big as your hand. Besides, you might have got yourself badly stung and then who'd have had to take you to hospital? Me, that's who. Look,' she added, finally putting down her magazine, 'I don't really want to know about your scorpion or about any other creepy-crawly. It's bad enough dealing with them all day in the house, without having to know about their disgusting habits and their entire history. Anyway, there's something else we need to talk about. Come with me, young lady.' Alice beckoned as she walked out of the sitting room.

Ella's face reddened as she did as she was told, following her mother into the hall and stopping at the door of the store room, adjacent to the dining room. The store room was a walk-in pantry. Tins of ham and bacon and sausages were stacked in boxes of twelve. Alongside, there were also supplies of corned beef, pilchards, evaporated milk, fruit cocktail, sliced peaches, jelly cubes, jam, treacle, marmalade, porridge oats, tomato sauce, bottles of spirits and stacks of lavatory paper, plus an assortment of sweets in catering-size jars.

These rations had been shipped from Braham Masters, a London company which specialised in supplying ex-pats around the globe. Much of it had arrived at the beginning of the Jacksons' tour. Christmas was catered for separately, when festive food was ordered from catalogues which arrived in September.

Every Thursday morning, before her 9.00 am hair appointment at the club, Alice would check the stock and issue fresh weekly rations to Surindabash, recording the transaction in a small accounts book. Occasionally, she made a spot check. To her great satisfaction, this morning's spot check had revealed a discrepancy.

Alice threw open the store-room door and turned to face her daughter. 'So,' she said, folding her arms across her chest, 'what have you got to say?'

The girl looked down at her feet. Her white sandals were covered in dust from the street. Something vaguely resembling a spider's leg appeared to have got caught in the open toe of her left shoe. She hurriedly gave her foot a shake.

'Ella, this is not a joke,' her mother said. 'What have you got to say about the toffees?' She looked at the set of her daughter's mouth. Defiant, that's what she was. Defiant, difficult, unaffectionate and stubborn, just like her father.

'Ella, I'm talking to you,' she began again. 'A whole tin of toffees has disappeared. Surindabash says he wouldn't dream of taking sweets. Ijaz is only interested in whisky, so that leaves you. You know it's very naughty to steal, don't you?'

'Yes,' Ella answered.

'Don't be cheeky,' Alice snapped.

Ella fell silent again. Grown-ups were so confusing. 'I haven't taken it, Mummy,' she answered.

'Oh, yes, you have,' Alice answered. 'I can tell. One thing I will not have in this house is lies, Ella Jackson. You should know that by now. I'll give you until suppertime to tell the truth. If you haven't by then, we'll see what your father has to say when he gets home. Now, you're a thoroughly bad girl, so get out of my sight.'

Surindabash squatted in the kitchen yard, a chicken lying lifeless in his lap, while he plucked furiously at its feathers, rapidly revealing a breast of sagging saffron-yellow flesh. Ella sat on the step next to him, stick in hand, drawing aimlessly in the dirt. They were comfortable with the silence.

'Do you ever tell lies, Surindabash?' she eventually asked.

'No,' the cook said. 'Not unless very, very important,' he chuckled and stopped plucking. 'Allah understand if you lie to be safe. Lookee after number one.'

'God understands if you lie?' the child repeated, puzzled.

Surindabash nodded his head enthusiastically. 'He say it's OK. God is great,' he added, as if to give extra legitimacy to this dispensation.

'Does God think it's all right if you lie to protect somebody else?' Ella asked.

Surindabash paused to consider this dilemma. 'Maybe,' he eventually answered cautiously.

She persisted. 'What if other people find out that you've been lying to protect somebody else? Is that not so bad as lying to look after number one?' she asked.

Surindabash shrugged his shoulders. 'All the same,' he replied glumly, 'if found out, it means trouble. Big trouble.'

Half an hour later, Ella interrupted the pre-lunchtime gin and tonic Alice was enjoying in the garden. 'Mummy,' she said, 'I'm sorry. I did take the toffees. I promise I won't do it again.'

Alice looked at her daughter and decided she appeared suitably contrite. 'There,' she said, 'it's not so difficult to tell the truth, is it? Mummy doesn't like to get cross with you, but it's for your own good. You only had to ask and I would have let you have some toffees. It was a very silly thing to do, wasn't it?'

'Yes, Mummy,' Ella replied. She tried to raise a few tears, but they refused to come.

Alice gave her daughter a rare hug. 'Let's not say any more about this,' she said. 'But if you lie about anything at all in the future, I shall be very, very cross. Do you understand?'

Ella nodded. Of course, she felt bad – but no more than usual.

Later, she was playing a solitary game of hopscotch, when Surindabash emerged from the kitchen. He carried a parcel wrapped in a couple of tea cloths, which he strapped to the rear of his bicycle. '*Asalam aleikum*,' he called cheerily as he pedalled past. Ella stopped to watch his progress as he cycled down the drive, endeavouring to avoid the potholes and piles of horse manure left by the tongas. His efforts made him wobble furiously, causing one of the tea cloths to slip back far enough for her to read the writing on the tin it covered. 'Callard and Bowser,' she read. 'Assorted Toffees of Distinction.'

Ella was not in the least bit surprised. It wasn't the sweets that had attracted the cook, it was the tin. The container would have a very long life, put to a multitude of uses in Surindabash's house. And it hadn't hurt her all that much to take the blame.

Besides, her mother expected her to do wrong.

Sylvia Hargreave-Smith was bored. Her household was superbly run by the chief bearer, the cook told her what was planned for lunch and dinner, and her husband was hardly proving time-consuming. Just before the wedding, Noel had raised the issue of children. Gently, he had explained that he really didn't want to start another family and might this prove an impediment? Sylvia had heard herself saying no, of course not, when, actually, she'd meant to say yes. What else was a woman expected to do, if she didn't become a mother?

She walked out on to the verandah of The Residence and saw the Jackson girl opposite, playing hopscotch. On a whim, she called out, 'Ella!' and beckoned her over.

'Do you like dressing up?' Sylvia asked. The girl was watching her warily. 'Would you like a beautiful dress to play with?' Sylvia asked again.

'To keep?' Ella asked cautiously. The woman nodded. Mrs Hargreave-Smith was a mystery to Ella. For some reason, her mother treated her as if she was special, better than anybody else in the compound, better than anyone else in Peshawar, probably the whole world. Alice even tried to talk like Sylvia, making her voice sound very peculiar.

'Come with me,' Sylvia coaxed the girl. The two went up the stairs of The Residence and into Noel Hargreave-Smith's bedroom. He had an adjoining dressing-room, where his wife had stored some of her clothes.

'Who's that?' Ella asked. Her mother had told her it was rude to point, so she indicated with her head a framed photograph on the bedside table.

'That,' said Sylvia, grimacing, 'is Starburst.' Starburst was a two-year-old chestnut, with a distinctive white mark on his nose. He not only had pride of place by Noel's bed, but also in his heart. Sylvia and the horse had met only once and the dislike had been mutual. All the more woeful then that, on

61

his retirement, Noel intended to temporarily abandon her for Starburst. He planned to meander around the south-east of England, recreating some of the rural rides of the eighteenth- and nineteenth-century writer, William Cobbett.

'William who?' Sylvia would have said a year before. Now, she had an intimate knowledge of the man – or, at least, of his early life. Noel had explained that he had no interest in Cobbett once he became a republican and a radical. But, in his early years, Cobbett and Noel could have been as one. Both believed in everyone accepting their place in society with good cheer and mutual respect, poor man at his gate, rich man in his castle. Both had an enthusiasm for farm labourers which Sylvia couldn't understand at all – uncouth, illiterate, sexually deviant bunch that they were, always being caught with a sheep here and a hen there.

Both men had lived briefly in America, and both were inclined to become very sentimental about crown and country and the wonders of the British aristocracy. Naturally, Sylvia agreed one hundred percent on the question of the aristocracy, since it was her own heritage – but for the rest, privately she found Mr Cobbett an all-round bore.

'Is it your horse?' Ella was asking politely.

Sylvia picked up the photograph and laid it face down on the table. The gesture made her feel a lot better. 'He belongs to Mr Hargreave-Smith, who loves him rather a lot, I'm afraid to say.'

Later, as she dressed the child in cream satin, a tear unexpectedly ran down Sylvia's cheek and plopped on to her hand. Mentally, she gave herself a pep talk. 'You're a wifey now. Too grown-up to have regrets. Or miss Mummy and Pops. It's up to you to make things work.'

She knew exactly what had to be achieved: a knighthood for her husband, a child for herself and Starburst for the knacker's yard.

'Don't cry,' Ella comforted the young woman awkwardly,

unused to seeing an adult outside the family weep. 'Everything's going to be all right.'

Half an hour later, Ella ran into the Jacksons' bungalow. 'I've been playing with Sylvia,' she told her mother. 'She's asked if I'll go with her to the hospital to see Aunty Blossom. Can I go, please? Please?'

Alice put down her sewing. 'Ella, it's Mrs Hargreave-Smith to you – and I'm sure she hasn't suggested anything of the kind.' Then she realised that Sylvia was standing at the French windows.

Ella watched while her mother's mood and voice were magically transformed – another example of Sylvia's strange powers.

Alice gave her daughter a small push in the direction of the bedroom. 'Gosh, how lovely. What a splendid idea. How kind of you, Sylvia. Ella, run and change. Put on that nice blue frock and socks and . . .'

But her daughter had already gone.

At five, dressed in an apple-green sundress and white hat and gloves, Sylvia stood on the steps of The Residence, as the driver pulled up in the Humber Super Snipe. She had arranged an appointment with Blossom Larkhall at the Quaker Hospital. Mrs Larkhall was going to show her some of the wards, to see if acting as a volunteer for a few hours a week held any appeal. Sylvia had told Blossom that she thought it would be quite jolly, sailing around, dispensing biscuits, tea and medicine and a little bit of cheer.

Piers Rockingham emerged from the offices. 'Afternoon, Sylvia. Off somewhere interesting?' he asked.

Sylvia found Piers unsettling. She gave him a quick smile, busying herself by walking down the steps to the drive. 'Mrs Larkhall is going to show me the ropes at the hospital. See if I can give a hand.'

'Oh, you might bump into Marjorie,' Rockingham said. 'She's rolling bandages too, or whatever you girls do. She's going a couple of times a week. Doesn't talk about it much, but I expect it's jolly useful.'

He had come to a halt in front of Sylvia. Instinctively, she took a step back and almost tripped, dropping a glove. She fumbled to retrieve it.

'Sylvia, could I ask you something?' Rockingham asked, in a confiding tone.

She pretended to be absorbed by her driver, who, immaculate in a khaki uniform and white puggaree, had leapt out of his seat, run round the front of the car, polishing the bonnet with his cuff as he did so, and with a great flourish, was now holding the car door open for her.

The interval of a few seconds had given Sylvia a chance to compose herself. She turned to Rockingham. 'Of course, Piers,' she answered.

He rubbed the back of his head, in what he hoped was an appealingly boyish fashion, and looked puzzled. 'The truth is, I need a bit of help,' he said. 'I know it's Noel's birthday in a couple of weeks so I thought I'd get him a little something. I overheard him and Jackson having a bit of a chinwag about some writer chappy. Jackson's old man was a farm labourer and he was talking about what's changed . . . or, rather, what hasn't changed. But I didn't quite catch the writer's name . . . I'm not that much up on agricultural matters . . .' Rockingham was aware that he sounded peeved. Bloody Jackson, of all people, discussing bloody books with the bloody DHC. If that was anybody's job, it was his.

He smiled winningly. God, the woman was unattractive. He averted his gaze from the mosquito bite livid on her neck. 'Anyway,' he continued, 'Noel looked pretty animated, so I thought a book by this chap might be a good idea. Any clues?' he ended brightly.

Sylvia seized her chance. Rockingham, with his tin-plated

charm, was typical of the kind of man who, until she became Noel's wife, would never have spared her a second glance. 'Oh,' she replied sweetly, 'you mean William Cobbett. Noel just adores him. Try and find *The English Gardener*. Noel would be so pleased,' she added, fully aware that her husband loathed anything to do with shrubberies, flowers and pruning.

Rockingham clicked his fingers, as if to signal that his memory had suddenly been restored to working order, and said, 'Of course, Cobbett. Silly of me to forget. Published recently, was he?'

Ella skipped out of the bungalow and followed Sylvia into the back of the official car. The woman poked her head out of the window and gave Rockingham one of her warmest smiles. 'Published in eighteen twenty-nine, actually. Good afternoon, Piers. Good hunting.'

The Quaker Hospital was down a narrow alley off Dabgari Gate Road, on the other side of the railway lines from the British Cantonment. Built around a large, arched, open courtyard, where the families of patients set up temporary camp, it consisted of two storeys, constructed from wood and traditional burnt brick. At the entrance was a brass plaque. It read, '*Lumen ad Revolutionem Gentium*.' It continued, 'The hospital had been lighted by electricity in memory of Dr S Hansford, who for twelve years gave himself for the sick and poor and whose life was taken, like that of his master, by those he came to serve. b. 21 May 1894 d. 17 March 1931.'

The wards were basic: concrete floors, charpoi beds. In the very coldest months, elderly paraffin stoves would lose the fight to take the chill off the rooms. In the heat of the summer, patients would be moved on to the verandahs, protected from the sun and the mosquitoes by blinds and netting.

On the left of the main building were three operating theatres, a Quaker meeting house and an out-patients department. On the right was the small bungalow where the hospital's directors, George and Trixie Danvers, lived. George had trained as a surgeon, Trixie as a general practitioner. They had arrived in Peshawar twenty-seven years before, intending to stay for a few months. They had never been able to bring themselves to leave. A son and daughter, born at the hospital, were now medical students in London. The son's intention was to take his parents' place when they retired.

Danish and Swedish aid money had allowed the Danverses to expand the facilities and add a rudimentary leprosy and eye unit, but it did not provide resources to buy enough of even the most basic drugs. The hospital charged a pittance so, since the vast majority of the city dwellers (and those from the villages outside, too) were desperately poor, demand was unrelenting and overwhelming. Local people trusted the Danverses. At least, in their hands, death and deformity were more often delayed than accelerated, unlike in some of the costlier medical establishments.

A mile from the Quaker Hospital, a site had been excavated and a vast building half completed. Called the Roosevelt Hospital, it had been financed by the US Government and was intended to meet the needs of the ordinary people of Peshawar. Corruption ensured that it would never be completed. While children in the Danverses' care died for lack of penicillin, the annual running costs of this ghost establishment were liberally spread between a handful of politicians who, of course, travelled abroad for their own medical needs.

The Danverses relied on a medical staff of six local doctors and a small band of nurses and auxiliaries. From time to time, the team would be augmented by diplomats' wives with specific skills. The hospital had recently lost its only physiotherapist when the wife of the university's vice-chancellor returned to Britain. Local custom, as well as lack of resources, dictated that each patient had to be cared for by a family member, who lived with him or her until health was restored, cooking, washing and giving a hand to the nurses. Nonetheless, volunteers were vital, if scarce.

The car carrying Sylvia Hargreave-Smith and Ella stopped at the entrance to the street, since the road itself was too full of ruts and potholes to risk the car. Sylvia refused the driver's offer to accompany them to the hospital, but ordered him to wait. They began to pick their way through the horse manure, debris, chickens and goats. A dozen or more 'specialists' had set up business in the shadow of the hospital, attracting those who believed that the more costly the 'cure', the higher the chance of a return to good health. 'Kidney Specials,' read one sign. 'Tooth Surgeon The Best,' read another.

As the two Europeans walked on, the band of children following them grew louder and more boisterous. 'Baksheesh, memsahib, baksheesh,' they shouted, giggling with delight at their own cheek, jostling each other to push their hands in Sylvia's face, tugging at her skirt, pulling at her bare arm. Women walking in burquahs, babies on their hips, stopped dead to stare at this red-faced, harassed white woman and her child. A young man brushed up close to Sylvia, whispering something as he passed. She jumped back, panicking. 'Rukiya! Rukiya!' somebody shouted. 'Stop! Stop!' Out of the corner of her eye, Sylvia could see two bullocks, flicking their tails to ward off the flies, staring at her morosely.

Their wizened owner, sitting on a cart loaded down with rubber tyres, was so small, he looked as if he'd shrunk in the wash. He grinned, revealing a mouth empty of teeth. 'Rukiya, memsahib, *asalam aleikum*, memsahib,' he cackled, as Sylvia did as she was told and he and his load lumbered past.

Bullock dung splattered at Sylvia's feet, staining her skirt. She gripped Ella's hand so tightly the girl had to fight hard not to cry out. Why was Sylvia so frightened? Nobody meant any harm.

'Come,' a soft sing-song voice suddenly called out. 'Come, Mrs Hargreave-Smith, we've been expecting you. And, how nice, I am seeing you have brought Ella.' Sylvia turned to see Blossom Larkhall, beckoning from the hospital gate, just like a guardian angel.

'Be prepared,' Blossom warned. They had walked through the central courtyard. Everywhere there were queues and crowds, but there was no noise, hardly any movement, even. Sylvia thought it was as if everyone had settled down to sleep for a hundred years. The smells were different from those of the street. Here, they were a mixture of disinfectant and sewage and sickness and ghee cooking and vomit. Blossom suggested that Ella wait in her office, with paper and pencils to keep her amused. Then, she turned to her guest. 'Are you ready?' she asked. Sylvia nodded. But when the door opened, she wasn't at all ready.

The boy was sitting on the bed, a woman, who might have been his mother, was cross-legged on the floor by his side, massaging his feet. He was perhaps four or five. His head was several times its normal size, a distortion which reduced his crossed eyes to the size of rabbits' droppings and his mouth to a tadpole, lost in a sea of skin. He waved at Blossom and his head wobbled so much, Sylvia feared it might snap at his neck.

'Hydrocephalus,' Blossom explained, as she kissed the boy on the vast expanse of his cheek, and greeted the woman. 'Water on the brain,' she added. Sylvia tried to return the child's smile, but her face remained frozen in horror. 'He's dying.' The nurse smiled at the child, as if to counter-balance the visitor's reaction.

Sylvia's voice came out as a squeak. 'God, what rotten luck

to have a little one who's dying,' she said, then, realising the mother might understand English, she put her hand to her mouth. 'Oh, I'm so sorry. Gosh, I'm sometimes so stupid . . . I . . .'

Blossom had long ago wearied of trying to teach others the etiquette of dealing with those facing death. So, now, she simply nodded, as if in acceptance of the apology, and propelled her charge into a second room. Here, a woman of indeterminate age was lying fully dressed and unveiled on a charpoi. Her eyes were closed, while a girl of seven or eight stood by her head, patiently waving a paper fan to keep at bay the flies who persistently tried to settle on the woman's eyes and mouth. A small army of insects had already settled on a bandaged and bloody wound on her arm. Sylvia could smell what she now supposed must be rotting flesh.

Blossom stroked the little girl's head. 'The woman told us that her husband's mother burnt her with boiling water, because she said she was lazy. The woman went to a pir, who peeled away the skin and placed a small piece of the Koran, the holy book, in the wound. After a few days, it began to fester. She's come to us too late. Dr Danvers says he will have to amputate the arm below the elbow. She has six children. She says her husband will throw her out, because she will be of no use in the house. We don't have enough staff to change the dressings often enough. This child is too young to do it alone.'

'That's terrible,' Sylvia said, her tone perfunctory. The young girl was gazing at her impassively, while her arm moved back and forth, like an oiled machine. 'What's a pir, Mrs Larkhall?' Sylvia asked.

'Pirs are healers, mystics, medicine men, witch doctors, call them what you like.' Blossom shrugged. 'Many women here believe in them, believe in their magic. They go to them for spells and potions. They believe they can cure anything – impotence, infertility, lethargy, marital discord. A couple of pirs do business in this street. Their queues are almost as long as our own.' She laughed. 'Now, what else would you like to see?'

Sylvia said she'd really rather sit down for a few minutes, if Mrs Larkhall didn't mind. Blossom had given enough foreign women similar tours to know the signs. 'Is it perhaps a bit too much for you to take?' she asked, more gently than she thought the young woman deserved.

Sylvia nodded her head, relieved that she didn't have to deal in white lies, then said, 'Well, it's not very nice, is it? What I mean is, you must be used to it. I think it's awfully brave that you do what you do. But one does need an awfully strong stomach to tackle it, doesn't one? And, I mean, life can be pretty grim as it is, without seeing all this sadness every day. I think it might get me down just a teeny bit.'

Blossom hoped this rather silly young woman didn't have a gift for reading minds. 'It's all right, really it is,' she said, thinking precisely the opposite.

Sylvia went pink. 'Perhaps I could do a bit of fund-raising instead,' she suggested. 'A coffee morning, that sort of thing?'

Blossom nodded her head.

Reassured, Sylvia had already moved on to matters closer to her heart. 'These pirs,' she said brightly, 'I know it's probably mumbo-jumbo, but do you know if they know anything about . . . um . . . aan . . .' She struggled to find the appropriate word.

'Infertility?' Blossom suggested.

The young woman giggled. 'Well, not exactly infertility . . .' she replied.

Twenty minutes later, as she and Ella were saying their goodbyes, Sylvia remembered what Piers had told her earlier. 'How's Marjorie doing as a volunteer?' she asked. 'I bet she's made of much sterner stuff than me.'

Blossom looked puzzled. 'Mrs Rockingham?' she said. 'A

volunteer? No, you must have made a mistake. I don't think she's ever set foot in the hospital. You and Alice are the only ones to come here from the High Commission for a very long time.'

'Is that right? My goodness me, what a hoot,' Sylvia added, as the possible implications of what she'd just been told began to sink in. Who would have thought that 'Have-You-Met-My-Wonderful-Husband' Marjorie would be up to her own fun and games?

'Did you find out what you wanted to know?' Ella asked politely on the journey back to the compound, unsure – since the signals were so contradictory – whether to treat her fellow traveller as a playmate or a grown-up.

Sylvia smiled mischievously. 'Yes, Ella, I really think I did,' she answered.

Chapter Seven

Bill Jackson had shared his office with the same couple for several years – and he begrudged them the space. Their portraits varied in quality, but the effect was the same. The Duke of Edinburgh, dressed in naval uniform, posed, squinting irritably at his sombre-looking wife, Elizabeth II. She was always presented wearing evening dress, white elbow-length gloves and diamonds, as if she had no daylight existence. What made the Pakistani version different from the Malayan and the Egyptian pictures was the sugar-almond tinting added by a local artist – baby-pink cheeks, watery-blue eyes.

Now, Bill, feet on his desk, headphones around his neck, occupied himself by making paper darts out of classified material, due for the shredder. His aim was to see how many of the numerous medals pinned to the breast of the Queen's consort he could hit consecutively. Seven was his record. Three . . . Four . . . Not bad. Perhaps, tonight was going to be the night. Five . . .

Bill believed in neither God nor Queen nor the automatic privilege of class. He didn't believe in himself much either – which made him an angry man, a quietly angry man, except when he drank. Then, he could become very cantankerous indeed. Twice in the navy he had been demoted, once from chief petty officer. So, now, he struggled to remain teetotal. He reasoned that if he could keep his silence for another twenty-five years, his self-respect might be gone – but at least he'd have a pension.

He had been fifteen when war broke out. He'd added a year to his age and joined the navy. The extra year had never been shed. So, Bill had celebrated his thirty-third birthday on 2 January 1956, aged thirty-two. A sense of the absurd had always appealed to him. When he was eight, and his sisters five and three, his father had run away with the local greengrocer's wife. Before he did so, he'd left a box of fruit and vegetables on the back door step, as if in compensation. Bill's mother had subsequently tried often to secure love and money, but failed abysmally at both.

She swapped jobs as frequently as she changed boyfriends and addresses. Cleaning, barmaiding, picking potatoes came and went, as did Harry, Charlie, Les; Stockport, Leeds and Preston. Bill regarded one temporary dad very much like the next, give or take a clout. What they all had in common was the fact that, sooner, rather than later, they left. He did not intend to abandon Ella – not even if it meant a lifetime with Alice.

Ironically, or perhaps inevitably, Bill had found himself in a job in which he was expected to uproot every couple of years just as he had throughout his childhood. The staff list described William Jackson as the Deputy High Commissioner's technical advisor. On his first trip to the bazaar a couple of days after arriving in Peshawar, Bill had been amused to be greeted universally by stall holders as 'The Secret Wireless Operator Sahib'.

Jackson was the compound's Morse-code man, a member of the Diplomatic Wireless Service, a branch of the Foreign and Commonwealth Office. He was considered the lowest of the low in the compound's social hierarchy, but, without him, there could be no communication with the outside world. He was good at his job. Karachi, a two-day train journey away, was considered a soft three-man posting. In

Peshawar, a traditional centre for covert activity, the wireless operator worked alone; a shift in the morning, one at night. Much of what Bill sent was encoded, but more than he could sometimes stomach was written in turgid prose; windy ways of avoiding anything that could be construed as an unequivocal opinion. Bill often used to joke with Ash that London would have learnt a helluva lot more from a couple of conversations with his cook each week.

Among the material that Bill didn't categorise as bullshit, were the progress reports on the Friends of America scheme to the west of the city, supervised by CJ Brooking, an agent of the CIA. His sewage plant was a cover for the construction of a runway, the longest ever built in the world. It was intended for the U2, a plane with enormous range, now undergoing test trials in the USA. Eventually, it could be capable of flying high over Soviet territory and sending back satellite reports. Thus curtailing the much less spectacular tracking skills of the Met boys in Abbotobad. Progress was always somebody's short cut to the labour exchange.

Now, Bill picked up his sixth paper dart and aimed carefully. It missed the medals completely and bounced against the Duke's lapel. Shit!

'Not interrupting anything, am I?' Bill was about to throw his crucial seventh dart when he heard the voice of his boss at the door. 'All right if I come in?'

Bill gestured a welcome with his hand. Noel Hargreave-Smith, when pinned into a corner at official receptions, conveyed dignity and gravitas. He was tall and had a slight stoop, as if weighed down by wisdom. On the move, however, he appeared hesitant, as if undecided whether it was best that one foot should follow the other. Now, he shambled in and collapsed into a chair, his puppet's strings severed. Since the arrival of his wife, he had visited Bill fairly regularly on his two-hour evening shift. If work was slack, he'd stay for a chat.

Initially, Bill had viewed this development with alarm. Might he weaken and become as big an arse licker as Rockingham? Would Noel expect a comedy routine on a nightly basis? In the event, the Deputy High Commissioner had made it plain what he sought from the outset. He was after dirt – as in good agricultural soil.

The interest had been triggered when Noel overheard Bill at a reception, discussing his father's skill in building dry-stone walls. Since then, the two had debated the pleasures and pains of rural life and the iniquities of the Industrial Revolution. Noel had also discovered, to his surprise, that his wireless operator read books and had more than a passing knowledge of politics. So, gradually, William Cobbett had become the unlikely conduit for their respective diametrically opposed political positions. Hargreave-Smith openly admiring Cobbett's early enthusiasms; Jackson offering carefully muted praise for the man's later radical allegiances.

Now, Bill gathered some papers on his desk into a pile. 'Busy?' his boss asked, as he always did.

'Only the usual.'

Noel appeared distracted. He lived life irritatingly by the book, he could be condescending, his unswerving belief in the supremacy of Great Britain grated, but, much to his surprise, Bill sometimes felt sorry for the man. Or, perhaps it would be more accurate to describe his reaction as one of empathy. They were both trapped by the expectations of class and the disappointment of marriage.

The DHC stood in front of a page ripped out from the airmail edition of the *Daily Telegraph*, which Bill had pinned to the wall. It depicted a village pub buried in several feet of January snow. 'Lucky so and sos,' Noel commented wistfully, then added, 'Starburst would cut through that in no time.'

Bill made no comment. He was already familiar with the horse's every last detail. 'Surindabash tells me that the Brotherhood are active, recruiting in the bazaars,' he

eventually commented. The Brotherhood was a fundamentalist association, strongly nationalistic, and had been among
those groups who had successfully lobbied to have Pakistan
recognised as an Islamic republic. Bill continued, 'My guess is
that we might be in for an upset or two.'

'What do you mean?' Hargreave-Smith asked. 'Distur-
bances? He shook his head. 'You're wrong, old chap. We're
yesterday's enemy. It's a new order now. Or so they keep
telling me.'

Bill kept his silence. The Deputy High Commissioner
began to lever himself out of his chair disjointedly, as if each
limb required a separate set of instructions. 'By the way,' he
added, avoiding Bill's eye, 'Rockingham suggests that we
should take care with Colonel Khan. You see quite a bit of
him, don't you? Rockingham says he has his suspicions . . .'

'Is that right? Suspicions about what, precisely?' Bill asked
curtly.

Noel waved a hand in the air, as if orchestrating rumours.
'Never does to get too friendly, does it, old chap?'

Only after he'd heard the office's main door swing shut,
did Bill give his response. 'Fuck off,' he shouted. 'Just fuck
off, the lot of you.'

Chapter Eight

B etty Brooking lay back in the cold bath and squeezed the mango in her hands until the juice ran down her arms, tinting the water apricot. She licked her fingers and sucked at the fruit's hard stone, soaking up its perfume. Peshawar had once been called the City of a Thousand Vices – most of them dark, hidden, private, shrouded in shame. Betty knew about shame – shame about her body, about her appreciation of sex, about her compulsion to take risks, about her boredom with the perpetual, unchanging, unrelenting sameness of her life. Then, Greg had been killed, aged nineteen, a hero in Korea, a defender of freedom. And she'd ceased to care about anything very much, let alone shame.

Something very terrible happens to a parent when he or she has to bury their child. Now, Betty turned on the tap and watched as several dead insects shot out in a stream of dirty brown water. She waited until the water ran clear, then splashed her face, massaging the muscles at the base of her neck. She had just ridden hard for over an hour, across barren countryside, a few miles outside the city's perimeter. She had not ridden alone.

A little later, Betty gathered a pile of movie magazines together. They had been sent by Charlie, her oldest daughter, as postcards of the American dream; Charlie was definitely her father's child. Now, the mother had a use for them. She would drop them in to Ella.

CJ emerged from the bedroom, dressed only in shorts, rubbing his eyes. 'Any coffee?' he said, by way of a greeting. 'Where's the big boy?'

'It's too early for the servants yet,' Betty replied, giving her husband a kiss on the cheek, before lighting him a cigarette and placing it in his mouth. 'Don't fret. I'll make coffee and eggs and how about some pancakes and syrup, just the way you like them, hon?'

CJ snorted. 'You trying to kill me?' he joked.

'Think positive, sweetheart,' Betty replied. 'Think positive.'

At 6.30 am, Surindabash wheeled his bicycle – purchased by Sahib Jackson – into the kitchen forecourt and gave it a wipe down. He took pride in its immaculate condition. He whistled as he opened up the padlock on the wire-mesh door to the kitchen, then the main door. His humour had returned. The thirteen-year-old girl employed as a maid in his own household had failed to wake him on time. After shouting for several minutes, his ill temper had dissipated.

In the event, he had arrived at the compound early. Shafi Akhtar, on the gate, had made him tea – buffalo milk and sugar and tea leaves stewed together on his small primus stove. Shafi lived in one room in the servants' quarters. Surindabash had never asked him directly about his background. Partition was so recent, he had no wish to prompt painful memories. Instead, he'd pieced together a picture gleaned from the man's conversations. He judged that Shafi was a *mohajir*, a refugee. He had cousins in Peshawar, but no wife or children. Possibly, they had been killed. Unlike most gardeners whom Surindabash had known, Shafi actually took an interest in the soil. Thanks to his efforts, the compound was a mass of colour – roses, pansies, bougainvillea. Shafi never stopped working. Perhaps, Surindabash guessed, it was one way of avoiding time to think.

'Is that you, Surindabash?'

The cook heard the memsahib's voice. He put on the white Nehru jacket which he hated, because it made him look like a Hindu, and opened the connecting door into the dining room. On the table were four large tins of powdered baby milk. Alice was dressed in red shorts and a red-and-white check blouse. Even after years of service, Surindabash still found the Western women's lack of modesty highly disconcerting, but he had trained himself not to react.

'They finally came in the bag last night,' Alice said, genuinely pleased, tapping one of the lids. 'Carnow Sahib brought them with him from Karachi. He told me he was very pleased I was having another baby. I told him not quite yet,' she smiled. 'Take them home tonight and tell your wife I'll order some more. OK?'

'*Shukria*, memsahib, *shukria*.' Surindabash bowed by way of showing his gratitude. Powdered milk was available in the bazaar, but at a hugely extortionate price, and his wife considered herself much too well-off to breast feed.

'Have you seen Ella?' Alice added casually. 'She's not in her room and I don't want her wandering off with those boys at the gate.'

'I fetch her,' Surindabash promised. He knew exactly where she would be.

Ella peered through the archway of trees and stared at the sun, dappling the leaves. The trick was to see how long she could hold her gaze without blinking. Every day, sometimes twice a day, she came to the secret garden, in the hope that Shafi or Mr Hargreave-Smith had forgotten to lock the door. So far, she had been unlucky. The garden was surrounded by a high brick wall, overhung with ivy and topped with broken glass, as Ella had discovered the first and last time she had attempted to clamber over it. Entrance was by a single door, which faced the rear of The Residence. Along one wall of the garden was a copse of trees and a wooden bench, where Ella was now sitting. Hidden from view, she could see the verandah which ran along the back of the Rockinghams' house, where people were yet to come to life.

Most days, she and Shafi would sit on this bench and he would give her clues as to where the key to the garden door might be. She would spend ages on the hunt and then he would softly chuckle and say, much to her annoyance, 'I joke you, Missy Ella.' Ella watched as a troop of ants began to climb the mountain that was her hand, resting on the bench. She brushed them away and chewed on the sugar cane Shafi had given her five minutes earlier. He was constantly giving her local sweets and small presents – a few bangles, a mirror set in turquoise tin, flowers from the garden twisted into a garland.

Once, she'd asked him why he didn't have children and she'd felt very bad, because he didn't answer and his eyes had filled with tears. Ever since, Ella had tried to be kind. To be honest, she'd grown bored with the hunt to find the key, but Shafi seemed to like the game, so she continued for his sake. Now, he was sitting by her side, his hand on her thigh.

The sun suddenly broke through a gap in the trees and Ella, momentarily dazzled, squeezed her eyes shut until fireworks split the blackness inside her head. It was then, temporarily blinded, that Ella heard the crash of a door slamming and a scream. She quickly opened her eyes wide, but Shafi indicated to her to remain seated, putting a finger up to his lips for silence. Opposite, the Rockinghams' kitchen door had been pushed back so hard it had hit the brickwork. Aunty Marjorie, wrapped only in a towel, was now on the verandah, leaning against the wall. She was crying, quite red with crying, Ella thought. Except that, when the woman put her hand up to her forehead, the girl realised the redness was blood. Marjorie Rockingham had blood smeared down one side of her face.

'E-ll-a, *jaldi, jaldi*, Ella,' Surindabash's voice sang out across the lawn. Marjorie heard his call too. She turned, and half dropped the towel in her rush to retreat back into her house. 'Mummy say quick, quick,' Surindabash hollered from the other side of the lawn.

Shafi removed his hand from her leg. 'Speak nothing, Missy Ella. Speak nothing,' he whispered.

Ella looked at the gardener's face and she could see that he was frightened. But of what?

'Coming, Surindabash,' she shouted, jumping up from the bench, as Shafi melted away into the trees. 'Coming.'

'Pin the tail on the donkey?' Alice repeated the words slowly, as if to take them in fully. 'You want the entire staff to play pin the tail on the donkey?'

Petulance flashed across Sylvia's face. 'Don't tell me, a donkey is another of their blessed sacred animals?' she asked.

It irritated Alice that the woman kept playing with the strange medallion she was wearing around her neck. It looked like a small piece of stone rubble, crudely painted blue and yellow. A hole had been drilled through its centre and it was threaded with gold braid. In Alice's view, it did not go well with the brown-and-maroon printed frock that Sylvia was wearing. But, then, not much would.

Sylvia returned her coffee cup to its saucer. 'Don't you think it's a super idea? Everyone pays to have a go, the winner receives . . . oh, I don't know . . . something or other . . . we all have a bit of fun, and the money, lots of it, I hope, goes to the hospital for those poor little children. So, what do you think?'

Alice bit on a Peek Frean's pink wafer to give herself time to prepare a response. 'Pin the tail on the donkey,' she repeated, giving her best imitation of a smile, and removing a crumb from the corner of her mouth.

'Super,' Sylvia beamed back. 'I'm glad you're in favour. You won't believe what my next project is. It popped into my head on the way back from the hospital. I do so love being on the go, don't you?'

Walking out on to the verandah with Sylvia, Alice commented on her medallion. 'It's a taweez,' the woman explained.

'A lucky charm?' Alice asked.

Sylvia nodded. 'I only wear it because I like the colours,' she added hastily. 'I'm not one for dabbling in the black arts. Church of England, me. Don't believe a word of all that mumbo-jumbo, do you?'

'Can I help at all?' Betty Brooking asked half an hour later. She was standing in the doorway of the Jacksons' sitting room. In her arms, she carried a pile of magazines.

Alice was on her hands and knees, her mouth stuffed with pins, laying a paper dress-pattern out on what looked like a carpet of midnight-blue silk. She looked up, dropping pins as she returned Betty's smile.

Her expert eye took in the American woman's outfit: a sleeveless cream shirtwaister dress, brown sandals, belt and bag. Her hair was swept up in a French pleat.

'Come in, Betty, do. Would you like coffee?' she offered.

Her guest gave her a mock-quizzical look. 'Honey,' Betty replied, 'it's way past ten in the morning. I'll have bourbon, please, with soda, two cubes of ice, in a tall glass.'

The instructions were repeated to a plainly envious Ijaz and Ella was called in from her bedroom to accept the magazines. 'Say thank you, darling,' Alice instructed, as if her daughter was incapable of independent thought or deed. Ella disliked it when her mother called her darling. It usually meant she was about to be asked to perform in some way. 'Ella's going with Surindabash to the bazaar to buy vegetables,' Alice said. 'The cook is very good with her. You have fun with him, don't you, darling?'

Betty didn't wait to hear Ella's reply. Instead, she said, 'Well, why don't we all have some fun? I was wondering if you both might come with me to the Old City tonight? I hear there are some new comics in from England in the London Book Store. Perhaps Ella might like a couple?'

'I would, I really would.' The girl was bouncing up and down on the chair in excitement. 'Oh, please can we go, Mummy? Please. I love the Old City and we haven't been in ages. Please can we go? I could go with Betty by myself if you don't want to come. Please?'

Betty nodded confirmation, but Alice had already made up her mind. 'It's school tomorrow for you, Ella. Perhaps another time?' she added, smiling.

'I want to go to the bazaar, I really do,' the child insisted.

'That's enough,' Alice warned.

Ella stood in front of her mother, her face flushed with frustration. 'You never want to do anything I want to do. It's not fair, it really isn't. Why can't we go?'

'Because I say so,' she snapped. 'Do you know what I think? I think boarding school's the place for you, my girl. A few weeks away from home and then you'd appreciate how much Mummy does for you.' Alice was fond of referring to herself in the third person.

Ella burst into tears, as she always did when her mother threatened exile. 'I'm not going away to school. You promised that I wouldn't go until I was thirteen. I'll hate it. I'll really, really hate it. I'll run away and then you'll be sorry. You'll see.' She turned, dropping her magazines, and ran out of the room.

'Children can't always have what they want, and they certainly don't know what's best for them,' Alice snapped, as if her guest had challenged her.

Betty said nothing. Instead, she took a sip of her whisky and let the words hang in the air.

★　★　★

Ella sat on her bed and waited. Eventually, she knew from experience, she would empty out. She'd stop feeling sad or afraid; there would be nothing inside. She reached into the drawer of her bedside table and took out a cheap unused exercise book, bought in the market. On the cover, she carefully wrote, 'Ella Jackson.' Then she added the words, 'Private Property. Keep Out!' She turned to the first page, and inscribed the date, 9 April 1956.

Half an hour later, she was summoned back to the sitting room. Sylvia was sitting on the sofa. The girl could tell, from the look on her mother's face, that she was on her best behaviour and expected the same of her daughter. 'Here she is,' Alice said, as if Ella was a white rabbit, popping out of a magician's hat.

'Darling,' Alice continued, putting her arm awkwardly around her, 'Sylvia has invited us to go to the Old City this evening. She wants to buy a canvas to paint a picture of a donkey.' Ella's eyes widened, but she remained silent. Her mother continued, 'I said we'd love to go. We can buy another dupatta to replace the one you lost.'

Ella understood the bribe: say nothing about Betty's earlier invitation.

'Shall we say half-six?' Sylvia bounced out of her chair enthusiastically. 'You don't mind if Marjorie comes too, do you, Alice?'

'Of course I don't mind,' Alice replied. But Ella could tell that her mother did mind, very much.

Chapter Nine

Railway lines cut Peshawar in two. On one side, lay the British Cantonment. On the other, the Old City, sprawling and chaotic, veined with bazaars, plying legal and illegal trades. Smuggling, gun-running and drug-dealing flourished alongside the sale of trinkets, exhaust pipes and elaborately frilly baby clothes. The Old City was packed tight with dilapidated buildings, some with delicately carved overhanging balconies, which made the narrow shopping alleys below even darker. Dazzling and disturbing, sweet-smelling and stinking, it was the place Marjorie Rockingham hated most – and where Ella loved to be.

Chowk Yadgar was the centre of the Old City. Radiating out from it were a number of bazaars, each specialising in a single product – Ander Shahar for jewellery, Mochi Lara for leather, Pipal Mandi for nuts and grains. Ella would sometimes come to Sabzi Mandi, the vegetable market, with Surindabash. Stalls not much bigger than a walk-in wardrobe would offer pyramids of oranges, mounds of red tomatoes, sackfuls of emerald-green ladies' fingers, set against the piles of dark-brown nutmeg, deep-yellow saffron and orange turmeric. Stall owners never pitched against each other, since, as good Muslims, they believed that Allah would decide whom to send as a customer.

Now, the car stopped near the Kabuli Gate, one of sixteen set in the crumbling city walls, and the entrance to Qissa

Khawani, the Old Street of Story Tellers. Near were bazaars trading in brass and copper and shoes and carpets and woodwork and china and textiles, heavily embroidered by boys sitting cross-legged, working under naked lightbulbs in the heat of the day.

'*Bacha! Bacha!*' shouted a young boy. 'Mind out! Mind out!' He balanced on his head a tray of freshly cooked brilliant-orange *jalebi*, deep fried, sweet and shaped like pretzels as he carved a route through the women in burquahs, the beggars, customers and dealers.

Ella watched as a girl of five or six patiently collected discarded wrapping paper and cardboard for fuel; another sold coat hangers, carrying them on her arms like bracelets. In the street, vendors were busy setting up temporary shop, flogging eggs dyed bright-pink, pakoras, deep-fried vegetables and cheap plastic dolls from the gutter.

Deep into the bazaar, where the alley narrowed to allow only four or five abreast, Ella watched as a man wielded a machete to chop sugar cane. He ignored the hundreds of thousands of flies which enveloped him in a miniature black cloud. 'Pukka, pukka cane,' the man shouted at Ella, smiling to reveal black stumps. 'Number one.'

Ahead of her, the trio of Western women had attracted interest from a small squad of beggars demanding baksheesh. 'Oh, I say, that is gorgeous.' Sylvia had spotted a heavily embroidered swathe of material, and spun round, so fast, she almost floored a small boy, his face covered in dried snot. She recoiled, unconsciously wiping her hand on her skirt. A man close to her cleared his throat noisily and spat. A deep-crimson stain spread at her feet. Ella saw it too. 'It won't hurt,' she said. 'It's only betel juice, not blood.'

'Of course I know what it is,' Sylvia replied irritably.

Alice suddenly thought she was going to be sick. It had happened a couple of times recently. It was probably due to too much sun and Surindabash's cooking. Perhaps it was her imagination, but the atmosphere in the bazaar appeared less friendly than usual, almost hostile.

'In the shop,' she heard herself say curtly to Sylvia, in the tone a mother uses on a persistently disobedient child. She indicated a stall selling hardware, its entrance illuminated incongruously with the face of a smiling Father Christmas and fairy lights. 'Now.' She turned and tried to grab Marjorie who appeared to be bobbing away in a sea of faces. 'And you, Ella, quickly.'

The girl responded to the urgency in her mother's voice. Alice's eye caught a flash of silver. A small boy was hurrying towards Marjorie with a cargo of tiny cups of hot tea, held high above his head on a large tin tray. 'Watch out, Alice,' called Marjorie, who, distracted, was looking down as something brushed her legs. She saw a grown man propelling himself towards her on a makeshift wooden trolley. He was without legs. Each hand clutched a pad of filthy rags, which he used to paddle his truncated torso forward. 'Baksheesh, memsahib.' His face took on a theatrical expression of martyrdom, as if his physical deformity alone was insufficient to move the heart. He stroked Marjorie's leg again with one of his cloth pads. 'Baksheesh.'

Alice heard the sound of china smashing. Marjorie was screaming as if she might never stop. At her feet, the boy lay in a puddle of tea, amid broken cups. Impetuously, Ella rushed past her mother, to try to help. Marjorie's hysterical screams grew louder. Alice slapped her hard around the face. The crowd was growing, and so were their murmurings.

'Look,' Ella said. In her hand was a large rock, the size of a child's fist. 'Somebody must have thrown it at the boy. Why would they want to hurt him?'

'Oh God. Oh God. Oh God . . .' Marjorie kept repeating, a reaction which, without the benefit of interpretation, sounded to the crowd like an admission of guilt.

'Have you got a hankie, Mummy?' Ella asked, anxious to

help the soaked boy, who was crying, his flesh blistered by the hot tea.

Alice ignored her request. 'We've got to go, now. Quickly. Where's Sylvia?' she asked.

'Cooee, over here,' Sylvia replied, head and shoulders above the throng, clearly excited by the mêlée. 'I've found somebody who can help us out.'

She was standing outside a small bookshop. Next to her was Betty Brooking. Alice's embarrassment at being caught out in a lie was almost immediately overcome by relief. Betty, accompanied by a man, possibly in his sixties, spoke to the crowd in Urdu, reassuringly, apologetically. The crowd slowly, sullenly began to melt away.

'Who on earth would want to throw a stone and hurt the boy?' Marjorie asked Betty later, as she recovered her composure, sitting inside the bookshop.

'The boy, honey? Not him, you,' Betty replied. 'It was you they were trying to hurt.'

'What on earth do you mean? I haven't done anything. I really haven't.'

Betty gave a small smile. 'Not you personally. It could have been me, or Alice, or anyone – Western, that is.'

'Oh, of course,' Marjorie answered.

An hour later, the three British women and Ella were sitting in the kitchen of Betty Brooking's home. All four were impressed and made no attempt to disguise it. The room was vast and appeared to have been transported wholesale from the USA, a treasure trove of gadgets – blender, ice-cream maker, a refrigerator the size of a wardrobe, even Formica surfaces.

'Is it wipe-clean?' Marjorie asked breathlessly, running her hands along a breakfast counter coated in jazzy patterned plastic.

Betty was occupied mixing Tom Collinses in a large jug,

while sipping on a glass of Scotch. She paused to examine Marjorie's face and then, having decided she was serious, gave a slow smile. 'Sure,' she replied, deadpan, 'I don't know where my life would be without it.'

Ella was thrilled at how messy the kitchen was – a tip of opened cartons, jars, bottles and packets, as if everyone had the right to help themselves any time they liked. Half the products, she'd never seen before – maple syrup, waffles, cornflakes with marshmallow chips, blueberry pancake mix. It all seemed a lot more exciting than Surindabash's banana fritters and pounded-chicken and tomato sandwiches. What was even more surprising was that Betty didn't even seem to notice how lucky she was to have so very, very much.

Marjorie shivered. 'God, even your air-conditioning works.'

'Too cold?' Betty asked. 'CJ likes to pretend that he's living in Alaska. That's how he got pneumonia last fall. Can you imagine? The only pneumonia patient in Peshawar. Of course, if you know my husband, you'll guess he saw that as commie infiltration of the air-conditioning system. Come, let's go and sit in the garden and hope the mosquitoes are having a lazy day.'

The British contingent, reared on rationing, were reluctant to leave this domestic Aladdin's cave, but were too polite to say so. Betty led, carrying a tray of drinks; the women and Ella, now happy with a bottle of lemonade, followed.

'Did I hear you speaking Urdu in the bazaar?' Marjorie asked, once they were settled again.

'Sure,' Betty smiled. 'The man in the bookshop – Mr Murad Ali – he's teaching me. I speak it very badly, but I'm trying.'

'Why on earth would you want to learn Urdu?' Marjorie asked incredulously.

'I like the language. I like it here,' Betty replied.

'You like it here?' Marjorie pretended to choke on her

89

drink. 'You actually like it here? God forbid.'

Betty took another sip of her Scotch. Her eyes narrowed slightly, but otherwise there was no change in her delivery. 'Do you know much about Pakistan, Marjorie?' she asked evenly. 'Have you travelled anywhere outside Peshawar? Have you been to Swat or Chitral or to Sindh?'

Marjorie shook her head. 'Of course I don't know any-thing about this awful country, and I have no wish to know,' she answered, giving a little shudder. 'It's all right for you Americans, you act as if you're still in the States, with all the luxuries and whatnots. It's home from home for you. We have to live like the locals, put up with all the filth and heat and the bloody awful insects, and that's no joke. Is it, Sylvia?'

Betty gestured with her empty Scotch glass. 'Well,' she said, 'it looks to me as if Sylvia likes the place a little more than you do. Don't you have a taweez around your neck, Sylvia?'

Sylvia had weathered the early evening's experience less well than the others. Her hair was sticking to her forehead with perspiration. A half-moon sweat-stain marked her dress under each arm. The prickly heat on her chest and throat had turned crimson as a result of her distracted scratching. Now, her hands became entangled in the medallion around her neck, as if she was literally tying herself in knots.

'What's a taweez?' Marjorie asked.

'It's magic,' Ella replied. 'Has someone put a spell on you, Sylvia?'

'Ella,' Alice warned.

Betty helped herself to another drink from the bottle of whisky on the table, then sat back in her chair. 'Ella's right,' she replied. 'A pir gives you a taweez. Some of the pirs carry out amazing feats. One was supposed to have stood on one leg in a river for months and months, as the fish nibbled away at his flesh until he was standing on only a stump. When he came to the bank, he was whole again. This experience gave him the power to help others with problems. Especially love problems.'

'Have you got a love problem, Sylvia?' Ella asked eagerly.

'Ella, don't be rude,' Alice chastised her daughter, aghast. 'And it's Mrs Hargreave-Smith to you.'

Ella was baffled. If Sylvia didn't want to talk about it, why have that thing hanging around her neck?

Sylvia tugged at the necklace. She did so hope the spell would work on Noel. But she couldn't possibly broach the subject with wives of junior members of her husband's staff.

Betty offered a toast. 'To whisky and men,' she said.

Ella had read about men. In an old copy of her mother's *Woman's Weekly*, she had read that love in a cottage with Mr Right was better than all the riches in the world.

'Have you had a look at these beautiful Pathans?' Betty continued provocatively. 'Tall, strong, manly. Did you know they come from Aryan stock? Some call them the lost tribe of Israel.'

'But they're still, you know, Pakistanis,' Sylvia interjected. 'Surely, you wouldn't . . . with a person who was . . .' She searched for a word.

'Brown?' suggested Betty, one eyebrow raised quizzically. 'Sure, I would. If he was handsome and courteous and willing,' she added dryly. 'And if, of course, he was no trouble.'

'I say, Betty, does that mean you've got a Pakistani lover?' Sylvia asked gleefully.

Alice cleared her throat noisily, as if to remind the adults of Ella's silent presence. All eyes turned to the small girl, who took it as her cue to speak.

'Was it your lover who hurt you the other day, Aunty Marjorie?' she asked. 'When your head was bleeding?'

Chapter Ten

'She's on her own so much, she's living entirely in her imagination. It's got to the point where Ella doesn't know what's fantasy and what's fact. It's not good for the child.'

Alice was recounting the evening's events to her husband, who had just come home from an unusually long stint in the office. London was in a state of anxiety, because Egypt's Gamel Abdul Nasser had recognised Communist China. It had asked the Met boys in Abbotobad for as much feedback as possible. Now, Bill was drinking from a bottle of lemonade and leaning against the bedroom door, watching Alice as she undressed for bed. Normally, his wife disliked being watched. Her mother had always called sexual intercourse 'monthly rape', and Alice had taken heed.

She slipped her knickers off under her cotton nightgown. 'I nearly died,' she told her husband, mentally editing Betty's conversation to omit the references to lovers. 'Marjorie had been talking about – something . . . and, suddenly, out of the blue, Ella asked her if she'd been hit by Piers. Well, actually, hit by somebody nameless close to her. Of course, we were all flabbergasted. I didn't know where to put my face. You could've heard a pin drop. Naturally, the woman said she didn't have a clue what she was on about.'

Alice stopped to brush her hair, counting the strokes as she did so. Bill watched the motion of her nipples against the thin cotton. She resumed her monologue. 'Ella would not back down. She's adamant she saw Marjorie coming out of her kitchen with blood on her face. If you ask me, the sooner we give her a chance to mix with children of her own age, the better,' she added.

She lay on top of the bed, her tanned legs entwined in the sheet. Bill finished his drink and began to take off his shirt. He wondered what it would be like to sleep with a woman who gave herself freely, willingly. He smiled wryly. It would probably be bloody terrifying.

Alice propped herself up on the pillows and folded her arms over her chest. 'I don't care what you say. I've made up my mind. Ella's going to St Winifred's. All we've got to do is send the first term's fees. She will love it. I know she will.'

'Alice,' Bill answered quietly, 'the truth is that you want Ella away so you can add a few flourishes to your personal bloody family history now and then, without her buggering it up. Father a brickie? Absolutely not.' He mimicked his wife's voice. 'A rather important construction entrepreneur, don't you know. If anyone's bloody fantasising around here, it's you, not her. Perhaps Ella did see Marjorie? Perhaps the woman did get a belting from our Piers? It wouldn't be the first time such things have happened.'

Alice flushed. 'Do you know what your sweet little daughter said, when I told her I didn't believe her? She said that she hated me, and she wished I was dead.'

Piers Rockingham bent to avoid clobbering his head, as he walked into the London Book Store off Qissa Khawani. He had worked with Noel Hargreave-Smith for nine months and he was stumped. Usually, it took only weeks for him to forge a mutually satisfactory relationship with a superior, but Noel had proved surprisingly resistant. Now, Piers had renewed hope. He would find the old man a copy of this blasted Cobbett and present it to him as a thoughtful gift.

'May I be of help, sahib?' said a cultivated voice. Murad Ali, Betty Brooking's Urdu teacher, bowed a welcome, simultaneously switching on several neon strip lights as he did so, revealing a much larger interior than the cubby-hole entrance implied; a cavern of literacy. Four large, cumbersome brass fans whirred into action overhead, while two middle-aged men began to half-heartedly dust shelves of books – Islam, Shakespeare, Norman Mailer.

'*Asalam aleikum*,' Piers replied, trying to curtail the time-draining courtesies which initiated every conversation in Peshawar. He pulled one book off the nearest shelf, *Home Cooking from the Prairies*, published in 1949 on crude, pirated paper.

The bookshop owner stepped forward. '*Lucky Jim*,' he said, handing him a paperback. 'Kingsley Amis. Very high-spirited, although not to my taste. Give me Dickens any day.'

Piers took the book politely, then returned it. 'Actually,' he said, 'I'm looking for something by William Cobbett.' The man moved his head in a sympathetic fashion. A badge on his lapel said: 'Mr M Ali, Bookshop Owner in Charge.'

'Why not?' he answered.

Piers wished these people would learn to speak English properly. What did he mean, 'Why not?' It couldn't be every bloody person who walked in off the street and asked for a book written a hundred bloody years ago.

'Do you mean you've got a copy?' he asked cautiously.

'I shall try,' the man replied, beaming.

Piers' face fell. In Pakistan, 'I shall try' roughly translated into a flat no.

Mr Ali patted a chair next to his, indicating that Piers should take a seat. Then he clapped his hands, a signal which sent the tiny chai boy scurrying for fresh tea. In Mr Ali's view, books were timeless, so why should those interested in acquiring them exercise undue haste?

'Mr Rockingham . . .' Mr Ali began.

The Englishman wasn't surprised that the man knew him by name. He'd never been in the shop before, he could hardly describe himself as bookish, but, in this city, no one remained anonymous for long. He told himself that Mr Ali undoubtedly also knew what he'd had for breakfast.

The bookshop owner continued, 'I am thinking there are at least two Cobbetts. One is an American writer of particularly nasty thrillers, a lot of guns and blondes,' he chuckled. 'That, I am thinking, is not what you are after. The other is most interesting. A man who moved from right in his youth to left in his middle age. But, of course, you knew that, Mr Rockingham.'

Piers accepted the sweet, aromatic tea and gave his host a sharp look. The man couldn't be mocking him, could he?

'And, of course, you know that Mr Cobbett was also quite prolific?' Mr Ali added.

Piers finished his tea. 'Yes, yes, of course,' he answered, growing impatient. 'So, have you got any of his books?'

Mr Ali looked pained. Ignorance displayed by those who had the opportunity to acquire knowledge was particularly distressing.

'Well?' Piers demanded.

'Sadly, no,' the man smiled.

Piers Rockingham stood up abruptly, furious that he had wasted so much time.

Mr Ali put up his hands, as if to make an offering. 'I have an idea, if I may suggest it, sir?' he said.

'Well?' Piers answered rudely, all pretence of civility dropped.

'An old friend of mine, Lutyens Jamieson, he was a railway man here for many years, but his hobby was British history. Sadly, he died recently, but one of his daughters still has many of his books. She's called Belle. She runs the beauty salon at the club. Belle Masters. Perhaps you could ask her. Good luck, Mr Rockingham.'

Murad Ali watched, as Rockingham left his shop at too fast a pace for the heat of the sun. He behaved like a man accustomed to success. Such a pity, Mr Ali reflected, since so many more lessons are learnt in the wake of failure.

Belle's Beauty Parlour at the Peshawar Tennis Club consisted of one room and a store cupboard. Piers Rockingham arrived just before eleven. He gingerly pushed the door open and poked his head round.

'Come, come,' said a voice impatiently. A dark-brown hand flapped in his direction. It had long nails, painted pink. His eyes adjusted to the gloom. The room had a line of mirrors running along one wall, three ancient washbasins, and three seats covered in torn green plastic, plus a cumbersome hairdryer on wheels. Dark-brown, black and crimson stains streaked the basins, each of which appeared to be plugged with multi-coloured hair; dirty pink towels lay in a pile; jars of pastel-coloured goo, minus their tops, littered the shelves, as well as curlers, brushes, bottles of nail varnish, cotton wool and bowls of brightly jewelled combs and clips. Alongside magazine photographs of Pakistani and Hollywood movie idols, cardboard gold stars had been pinned to the walls, their points curled by the heat. The beauty parlour had one small window and a large black fan in the far corner, revolving ineffectually in a semi-circle.

The pinks and browns and maroons of the room, and its squalor, reminded Rockingham of the putrid flesh of a rotting guava – the mixture of smells emanating from the salon's cluttered mess simultaneously repelled and attracted him, just like the perfume of the decomposing fruit.

'Yes, honey?' said a voice.

Rockingham became aware that a woman was sitting in a chair, with her legs up on the counter and crossed. Her toenails, none too clean, were painted to match her finger-tips.

'Are you looking for someone?' the woman asked again, coyly. 'We're closed today – for stocktaking,' she added, as if an excuse was required. She appeared unembarrassed by the mess.

Rockingham knew instantly the kind of chee-chee she was: a bed 'n' breakfast Betty. She was pretty – oldish, but pretty, in an Alice Jackson sort of way.

The woman had short, curly hair, very full lips, and dark skin, almost black under her eyes and in the wonderful crease of her arms. She wore a blouse, off the shoulder with puffed sleeves, and a full red skirt, patterned with brown cowboys on black horses, wielding lassoes. Her feet were bare. Her jewellery was cheap gold from the bazaar, too thin and too yellow.

'Shampoo and set?' the woman asked, and laughed, still making no attempt to move.

Piers Rockingham reverted to habit. 'I was looking for Miss Belle Masters,' he explained. 'Nobody told me she was the highly attractive Miss Belle Masters.'

'Mrs,' the woman corrected. 'It's Mrs Masters.' She acted as if the compliment was only her due. Now, she got up and walked over to Rockingham, rolling her hips in an exaggerated fashion. She pretended to inspect his hair. He could smell sweat and coconut oil and a perfume that was too sweet, too intense. Up close, he could see she had black hair on her upper lip, and dark whiskers sprouting from a trio of small moles on her cheeks. She had garlic on her breath and a small trickle of perspiration sliding down between her breasts. She wore too much lipstick, too much rouge, too much blue eyeshadow. She was excessive and dirty in a particularly female way, and repellent. Rockingham was intoxicated.

His experience lay with females whose own carnal appetites were minimal, but who possessed, instead, a rapacious desire to please. He liked it that way. He preferred his women chained by inhibition. That was less threatening, tidier, cleaner – safer. Belle Masters would eat up a man; swallow him whole.

Ten minutes later, Piers Rockingham emerged from the club. He had been rapidly disabused of any possible involvement with t;he woman when she revealed that her brother-in-law, Albert Larkhall, was a lowly member of the DHC's staff. Her sister, Blossom, was also a nurse at the Quaker Hospital and might therefore know Marjorie. Belle had proposed that he come after lunch during the afternoon siesta to view her father's books for himself.

'Let's see if I've got what you want,' she had suggested. 'Then we can decide how best to proceed.'

In the compound of the High Commission, Ijaz the bearer brought a small blue exercise book to the memsahib, who was sewing in the sitting room. He explained that he had been changing the beds, so the dhobiwallah could wash the sheets, and he'd found an exercise book inside the bibi's pillowcase. Perhaps the memsahib should take care of it for Missy Ella?

'*Shukria*,' Alice said curtly. If Ijaz spied on her daughter, he would undoubtedly also spy on her. When the man had gone, she flicked through the exercise book. She experienced no guilt. It was for Ella's own good that she had no secrets from her mother. The pages were blank. Alice was about to place the book on the coffee table, when she changed her mind. Her child was methodical. She turned to the first page. She read the date first. It was followed by eight words: 'I hate Mummy. I wish she were dead.' The same eight words were repeated again and again, as if Ella had been writing out lines.

Chapter Eleven

The Convent of Jesus and Mary had a tradition of being long on piety and short on conversions. It had been opened in the 1890s by the Sisters of Clair de Lune, an order based initially in France, and then in Ireland. The nuns had grown weary from years of teaching the word of the Lord to every creed except Christian, with almost no genuine recruits to the faith. Out of a desire to please, girls would embrace the Lord on one day, then appear shocked that their newfound fidelity was expected to be permanently maintained. Before Partition, pupils included Hindu, Parsee and Sikh children, now they were mostly Muslim. The nuns had long accepted that they were training girls to be their mother-in-law's feudal servant and their husband's possession.

This had been Ella's school since her third day in Peshawar. She found the school work easy, since, apart from Robert Louis Stevenson's *The Black Arrow*, which she found as incomprehensible as her classmates, much of the curriculum she had already been taught in other schools, several times over. She had made one friend, Sherry Masters, age eight, daughter of Belle, niece of Blossom, and cousin to Tommy.

Mystery surrounded the identity and whereabouts of Sherry's father. She lived with her mother and a couple of great-aunts in a run-down bungalow off the Jamrud Road. Ella adored Belle. She was indulgent, affectionate, and disorganised. The bungalow looked like a rubbish dump, routine was non-existent, and whereas Alice's instinct was to say, 'We'll see,' meaning no, Belle Masters' response was usually an expansive yes. Two ice creams each after lunch? Why not? A water fight in the sitting room? How funny. At Sherry's house, Ella never felt in the wrong.

At 1.30 pm, when the school bell rang, Ella and Sherry scooted through the playground dominated by the life-size bleeding body of Christ, looking down from the crucifix, his skin as pink as a Western baby's bottom. They skipped into the street beyond. Safiyah, Sherry's ayah, bundled them into a tonga and, within minutes, they were at the Masters home.

'I'll race you to the kitchen for a lemonade,' Sherry squealed, dropping her school bag in the drive.

The spine of the house was a long corridor, off which were several rooms. Ella ran ahead, but something caught her attention on the right. The door to Belle's bedroom was ajar. Ella glimpsed random piles of books, clothes strewn on the floor, necklaces and scarves looped over the back of a chair. A man sat on the bed, in front of a long mirror, putting on his shirt. In a split second she caught his reflection as he looked up. It was Pier Rockingham.

Ella ran as fast as she could – out of the back door and into the garden. She remained there until she heard the sound of a car driving away. 'You look as if you've seen a ghost,' Belle teased later. 'Come here, honey, let me give you a hug.'

Bill sat on the edge of his daughter's bed and watched, helpless, as the tears spilled down his nine-year-old's face. Tears literally petrified him. He forced himself to take her hand.

'Please, Daddy, please, don't send me away. Promise I won't have to go to that school. I'll hate it, I know I will. I don't want to leave you. How will I know you'll be here when I come back?' Ella pleaded. 'Promise me I won't have to go, promise, please. I'll be good, I really will. I won't do anything or say anything. I won't cause trouble, please . . .'

Ella gulped for air in between sobs. Bill clumsily used a corner of the sheet to dry her tears. 'Mummy was cross because you'd written something horrible about her. I know you didn't mean it, but she was hurt,' he said softly.

'It was my notebook. Why did she have to read it? It was private. It said so on the cover.' The child's crying began to abate, as a sense of injustice took its place.

'She's your mother,' Bill replied, as if that was sufficient explanation. 'She only wants what's best.'

'No, she doesn't,' Ella was almost shouting, a small part of her beginning to enjoy the drama. 'She wants to send me away. But you won't let her do that, will you, Daddy? Promise? Please?'

'I promise,' Bill lied.

'Think the best and get it,' might have worked for the Reverend Norman V Peale, but it had failed to deliver the goods for CJ Brooking. The project was two months behind schedule, and looked nothing like an aeroplane runway – although, ironically, the small sewage plant was progressing well. Fasting during the Ramadan period had slowed construction down almost to a stop and no matter how CJ roared for more effort, no matter how hard he strove to think positive, the practical results recently had been negligible.

'*Jaldi, jaldi,*' he shouted now, banging a rhythm on the jeep's dashboard, urging his driver to go faster. 'Get the fuck out of the way,' he shouted in English at goats, children, women in purdah and indolent young men. Occasionally, a bus or a truck loomed out of the dark, minus headlights, honking its hooter, passengers clinging to its sides and sitting on its roof.

Humidity made CJ's shirt stick to his back. He was

mildly drunk. Ten minutes ago, at 8.40 pm, the telephone had rung. The message was brief. There were some difficulties at the project, major difficulties. He knew instantly in his gut it was a *subversive* Commie kind of a problem. Bellowing for Betty produced no results. He had always taken it for granted that, when he retired to his study for several hours most evenings, she was elsewhere in the house, doing whatever it was that women do. Tonight, she wasn't. So CJ had left her a curt note – 'Where the hell are you?' – and left.

It took thirty-five minutes to get out of the city. CJ could see the flames as soon as he arrived at the Jamrud Road. Christ. He regarded the average Pakistani as slow-witted, born clumsy, and inherently lazy – too lazy to sabotage his baby. If it wasn't the Pakistanis, CJ knew that must leave only one other possibility – the Russians had come.

The project site had been surrounded by an eight-foot fence and had only three entrances. CJ was waved through one. On the left, the nearly completed single-storey building which was to have provided the hub of the sewage plant had been almost completely destroyed. Four lines of men had formed a chain, using every available container to supply water to fight the flames still burning fiercely. As he came closer, CJ realised that the majority of the men were in the uniform of the Pakistani army. He knew the figure who appeared to be supervising operations from the tennis club. It was Colonel Ashraf Khan Afridi.

The colonel walked towards him and extended his hand in greeting. 'Mr Brooking,' he said, 'this is a sad night for you, but we have to be grateful for small mercies.'

'What d'ya mean?' CJ replied, ignoring Ash's gesture of friendship.

The Pakistani shrugged and said, 'The fatalities are small. Three security men are dead and five labourers have minor—'

'Any of our boys?' CJ interrupted. 'Any military police, aid workers?'

Ash shook his head and continued, 'The main target was the runway.' He gave the American a wry look. 'Or whatever it is that you call that area of land. They've done a minimal amount of damage. We've neutralised some devices.' He shrugged again. 'Shabby workmanship, so they failed to go off on time.'

'Reds?' CJ asked crisply.

The military man gave a bitter laugh.

'What's so funny?' CJ asked.

Ash surveyed the fire-fighting exercise now slowly bringing the flames under control. 'Mr Brooking, it's not the communists who are your main enemy in this country.'

CJ looked at him suspiciously. Maybe this guy wasn't what he pretended to be? Back home, a lot of them were in uniform, even decorated with medals.

According to *The Power of Positive Thinking*, it wasn't facts that mattered, but attitude. Now, the facts were that several months of work had been destroyed in a matter of minutes and CJ's attitude to this was just about as negative as anybody can damn well get. And that annoyed the hell out of him.

'You know what I'm thinking?' The American poked the army officer belligerently. 'I'm thinking, fuck 'em. I'm thinking, we'll build this again and twice as fast. And we'll have that plane flyin' down this frigging runway in less time than it takes to say their afternoon prayers. And forget the fucking shit-house. Everyone craps in the street anyway. I'll get this runway built if it fucking kills me. I'll . . .'

Much to CJ's annoyance, Ash Khan turned and walked away.

An hour later, a temporary generator was bringing light to the site again. CJ and the colonel had directed salvage operations from the bonnet of an army jeep. The American was in the process of sending a driver back to his house for coffee, water and fresh clothes. 'Give this to Memsahib Betty,' he instructed the man.

Ash rested his back on the jeep. 'I've just enjoyed the pleasure of your wife's company,' he commented mildly. 'I doubt she'll be home yet.'

'And what the hell does that mean?' CJ demanded.

The Pakistani decided the man had the control of a two-year-old. 'It means that I saw your wife at the Quaker Hospital. I went to question a boy who was involved in an incident in the bazaar. She'd arranged for him to have treatment. He's been scalded and the wound's gone septic. I didn't realise, but she's got quite a good grasp of Urdu.'

'She has?' CJ replied, then made a clumsy attempt to disguise his ignorance. 'She likes the place. She likes this shit hole. Can you beat that?' he added, oblivious to whom he was talking.

Betty was in the garden, writing letters, when her husband returned at eight o'clock the following morning. He pulled up a seat next to her and called for coffee. For several minutes, he studied her without speaking. After smiling a welcome, she had continued to write. Years of experience had taught her not to attempt to second-guess CJ. In the past, she had credited her husband with more imagination than he had, or at least, was willing to exercise. Asking him about the night's events would also be fruitless. He would speak when he was ready.

Coffee arrived and the silence continued. Betty shot a quick glance at CJ's face and realisation dawned: he was afraid.

'What's with the hospital, then?' CJ eventually asked casually. 'You a volunteer or what?'

Betty put down her pen and laughed. 'Me?' She smiled. 'Hell, no. You know I gave all that up years ago.'

CJ could tell by the look in his wife's eyes that this was as much information as he was likely to receive. Spontaneously, he reached out for her hand. Betty reacted as if she'd received a small electric shock. Since their sex life had died, CJ had avoided all physical contact. He had become impotent, and it was as if by non-contact he was attempting to train her needs to lie dormant too.

'I'm sorry,' he said.

Betty removed her hand from his and took a cigarette out of the packet on the table. She lit it before she spoke. 'You wouldn't be turning soft on me, now would you, honey?' she asked softly.

CJ couldn't be sure, but it almost sounded like a threat.

Chapter Twelve

It was the rattling that woke her. Ella lay in bed and held her breath, so that she could hear more clearly. Netting had been placed over the plug hole in the shower, to prevent snakes sliding up the drain and into the bathroom. Now and then, one would try and noisily break through the barrier. Ella stared into the darkness. A snake might, at this very minute, be slithering across the bedroom floor, coiling itself round the bed leg, its head raised, tongue flickering, sliding silently across her white sheets. The scream was long and piercing, but it was not her own voice Ella heard, it was her mother's.

She jumped out of bed, oblivious of cockroaches, scorpions or snakes, and ran barefoot out of her bedroom into the hall. Her parents' door opened and her father stepped out, carrying Alice in his arms. Ella had never seen him look like this before in her life. It was as if his face belonged to a stranger. She saw that her mother was wearing a pale-lemon nightdress. It was covered in patches of brightest red. Her tanned face was blotched and her eyes were closed. Instinctively, Ella reached out and touched the cotton garment. Her fingers came away damp. Blood was running down her mother's legs.

Bill registered his daughter's presence. 'It's all right, it's all right,' he kept repeating. 'It's nothing. It's really nothing. Go back to bed, sweetheart. Mummy's going to be fine. Go back to bed, there's a good girl.' He half ran past his daughter, towards the door leading to the verandah.

Ella heard the sound of a car screeching to a stop. Spots of blood tracked her parents' path, the brightest red she had ever seen. Dazed, she walked slowly to the door of her parents' bedroom. Sheets and towels littered the bed, all sodden with blood, her mother's blood. Ella turned on her heel and ran to her own room, slamming the door, her heart thudding, tears pouring down her face. She had said she wanted her mother to die, and now it had happened. Oh, what had she done? What had she done?

Ella told herself that it was all her fault. She had killed her mother. She should never have said it, written it, thought it. 'I love you, Mummy. I love you,' she cried out loud. 'I'm sorry. I'm sorry. I'm sorry, please don't die. I'll never be bad again. Please don't die. I didn't mean it. Please don't die.'

Half an hour later, Marjorie Rockingham arrived to persuade the child to sleep in her house.

'Is Mummy dead?' she asked. 'Will she be all right? Where has Daddy taken her? What will happen to me?' The questions spilled out as Marjorie hustled her on to the verandah.

She bent down to Ella's eye-level and spoke softly. 'Everything's going to be all right, it's nothing.'

Ella stared at the woman, bewildered. How could it possibly be nothing? And why should she believe anything that Aunty Marjorie said, when she already knew she told lies?

A clock in the Rockinghams' sitting room told Ella that it was 1.30 am. She sat on the edge of a hardback chair. The spiky rattan seat scratched her bottom through the thinness of her pyjamas. It hurt, so Ella knew this couldn't be a dream. 'Am I staying here for a long time?' she asked.

'Gosh, no,' Marjorie replied. 'Mummy will be as right as rain tomorrow. Really, she will.'

Just before two, Marjorie returned to her own bed. She

had been woken by the Jacksons' chowkidar banging on her front door. Only then did she realise that Piers had still not come home. He'd said that he was attending a Masons' dinner and he'd be back by midnight. He could, of course, be drinking at the tennis club. Marjorie touched the small scar under her fringe, and refused to allow herself to cry. Then, she reached for the telephone.

Alice was in the Quaker Hospital, in the section reserved for Europeans. She had miscarried nine weeks into her pregnancy. It was her second miscarriage in three years. Bill was desperate for another child. Alice had complied, but, secretly, at each miscarriage it had been relief, not grief, that had overwhelmed her.

Her room had two chairs and a bedside table, and looked out on to the lawns which led to the hospital's small Quaker meeting house. Alice rested. She rested from the turbulence of her relationship with Bill and she found peace from the nagging guilt that dogged her about Ella. The guilt that she found criticism so much easier to voice than praise. Introspection did not come easily to Alice Jackson; the façade she had created for herself was far too fragile. Instead, several years ago, she had decided that the cause of the difficulties between herself and her husband lay not with themselves, but with another. Alice had convinced herself that her marriage had really been quite good – until the arrival of Ella. Of course she loved the child, nevertheless; of course.

Blossom called in on Alice's second day. She described the recent visit of Sylvia, laughing at the rapidity of her exit.

'She came back again and bought a charm from one of those dreadful old pirs in the street outside,' Blossom smiled. 'She told him she wants her husband to sleep with her often to give her a child. Oh, I'm sorry,' she added quickly, not wishing to seem tactless.

Alice smiled reassurance. 'I'm all right, really I am.'

In the late afternoon, Bill and Marjorie appeared.

Marjorie gave an artificial laugh. 'Ella was telling me all about her great-grandfather. She kept saying he'd been a black man.'

Alice's face set in a mask. More giggles from Marjorie.

'Your daughter insisted he was a black man who had a horse and cart. Then, of course, I realised. She meant *coalman*!' More peals of laughter. 'You never told me your grandfather was a coalman, Alice. How perfectly quaint.'

A few minutes later Marjorie excused herself. Bill, too, was about to leave, when Trixie Danvers, the head of the hospital, poked her head round Alice's door. Embarrassed, she asked permission to seek a favour. 'We have a very simple operation we perform to remove cataracts,' she explained. 'Our cauterising gun requires a copper wire. A cheap copper wire.' She paused.

'Is it money you need?' Alice asked.

Trixie shook her head. 'Not exactly. We have these wires sent from Britain, but if they come through the post, we have to pay an import tax. The cost is enormous. Too much for us . . . Bill, we were wondering if you might bring some through your diplomatic bag. I know it's a cheek to ask, but we're desperately short . . .'

Alice rested her head on her pillows and closed her eyes. Bill hated asking favours from his superiors. She opened her eyes again to see Trixie Danvers beaming. 'Oh, thank you so much,' she was saying. 'You've no idea how many people you'll help.'

After Dr Danvers had gone, Alice asked Bill what he'd said.

'I told her I didn't have much clout, but I'd see what I could do,' he replied.

'Well, when you're crawling to Noel about the wires,

perhaps you might mention a new bed, too,' Alice commented sarcastically.

Bill and Ella leant side by side against the kitchen door and watched as Surindabash's thin fingers flew hither and thither, patting, piling, willing the construction to stay in shape. A small fan pitted itself against the late-morning heat and the open charcoal fire fiercely roasting the lunchtime lamb chops. A bead of perspiration plopped from Surindabash's forehead into the pile of vegetables he was using to build his creation. He selected a wafer-thin slice of carrot and, using a cocktail stick as a flagpole, he transformed it into a pennant. Chunks of potatoes, a few beginning to blacken, mixed with citrus-yellow homemade mayonnaise, were transformed into a miniature fortress. Cold peas did service as a moat; sliced runner-beans were being used to delineate windows and the portcullis; a cucumber cut vertically had been brought into service as a bridge.

'So, tell me, Surindabash,' Bill said, taking a swig from his bottle of lemonade, 'what's the word in the bazaars? Are there going to be riots?'

The cook stepped back from the kitchen table, frowning, adjusted the carrot, then smiled. 'OK?' he asked Ella.

She grinned and nodded. 'It's lovely.'

Alice had been in hospital for four days and was due to be discharged the following morning. Surindabash had suggested hiring a temporary ayah, but Bill had said they could manage. Ella had gone to bed late, showered infrequently, left her hair uncombed, eaten chocolate for breakfast, put her elbows on the dining-room table when eating, and left her books and comics scattered around the sitting room. She had also had her first riding lesson at the polo club, going with her father and Ash. They had bumped into Marjorie, who had joined them for a drink.

Ella had also given the cook – with her father's permission – the last jar of Callard & Bowser humbugs from the store cupboard. Betty had taken her to the open-air cinema in the Old City to see *Singin' in the Rain*. She had decided that, when she grew up, she was going to be a tap dancer. Surindabash had helped by tying metal shoe-polish lids to the soles of her sandals. Nobody had objected when she clicked round the bungalow for hours. Of course, Ella had missed her mother terribly.

Bill was happy. He could roam around his daughter's world – with no Alice as gatekeeper, deciding when, how often, and on what terms he should have access. He had met his wife when she was eighteen and they'd married two years later, having spent only a matter of weeks in each other's company. His tours of duty in the navy had kept him away. When Alice was twenty-four, Bill had joined the Foreign and Commonwealth Office, and she had begun a new apprenticeship, reinventing herself as a product of the middle classes. She'd changed the way she held a knife and fork, stopped referring to dinner at midday, and learnt how to organise coffee mornings, finger buffets and complex place settings. She was fun and attractive and the men indulged her, even if the women didn't.

No matter how cruelly some might snigger at her occasional faux pas, Alice – unlike her husband – preferred life among her 'betters'. Sometimes, Bill believed that incompatibility hadn't gradually emerged in their marriage, it had been there at the outset, disguised as love. On other occasions, he appreciated his wife's loyalty more than words could say.

Bill stole a slice of beetroot. 'So, Surindabash, when the Brotherhood tell you to leave your job and work for a good Muslim, what are you going to do?' he asked.

The Pakistani wiped his hands on a tea cloth. 'I say British do many good things here – roads, railways, schools. You're a

good sahib and Queen Victoria was a bloody fine bloke. Why
for should I leave job?' He cackled happily as he stabbed at a
lamb chop that resembled cooled molten lava. 'I'm a Pathan,
sahib,' he added, clicking his heels together. 'Nobody tells us
what to do. Nobody touches a Pathan.'

At lunch, Ella asked her father again what was the matter
with her mother. She had inquired several times before, and
he'd always avoided the question. Now, embarrassed, he said,
'You wouldn't understand, Ella. It's women's troubles.'

Later, in her bedroom, the girl flicked through the magazines that Betty had left. She had never previously paid
much heed to the advertisements. Now, they leapt out at her.
Women's troubles. They were all about women's troubles.

She was drawn to a photograph of a mother and daughter.
Ella read out loud, 'A mother must tell her grown-up
daughter how important it is to always put Zonite in her
fountain syringe.' What was a fountain syringe? And what, for
that matter, was Zonite? Why was it important? And why
only grown-up daughters? Why not young ones, too?

Intrigued, she read on with increasing alarm. 'A mother
will certainly warn her daughter about an odour she might
not detect herself, but is so apparent to others . . . One
greater even than body odour or bad breath!' Ella sniffed the
air around her cautiously. At what age did this odour take
hold? And why? The words themselves provided no further
clues.

On the following page, a different danger loomed. This
was called 'periodic function distress'. Whatever it was,
caused 'dim-out days' and inflicted cramps, headaches and
nervous irritability. Bad breath, nervous tension, underarm
irritation, lipstick smears, unwanted hair . . . Ella decided
that she would postpone becoming a woman for as long as
she possibly could.

Late in the afternoon, Bill and Ella visited the hospital
again. Alice told her husband that she'd arranged for her

daughter to spend the night with Tommy and the Larkhalls. She wanted them to coax Ella into going to St Winifred's.

'But I've organised a riding lesson,' Bill protested. The look on his wife's face spoke volumes. He shrugged, accepting defeat. Ella was once more Alice's business.

Chapter Thirteen

The Larkhalls' bungalow, a modest detached property, was shabby. The verandah at the front was treated as a second sitting room. It was jammed with several charpoi beds covered in rainbow-coloured cheap cotton mattresses bought in the bazaar. Here, the family would sit cross-legged and talk in the evenings.

The front door led straight into the sitting room, which contained an assortment of furniture, including a glass-topped fake-marble coffee table and a large Philips wireless, bought by Albie in 1934. On the walls were a number of family photos and a framed advertisement for Cussons Imperial Leather soap, 'The Exquisite Soap that Lasts Longer'. It showed a window box full of dwarf trees and alpines. Also on display were several images of Jesus and a film poster for an American film called *Three Came Home*, starring Claudette Colbert.

Ella loved spending the night, because the place overflowed with relatives, friends, animals – dogs, cats, birds, chickens, goats – and the smell of cooking, most often curries. Somebody was always staying, clothes and suitcases scattered higgledy-piggledy. Blossom's grandmother, Thomasina, aged ninety-six, had brown skin spread so taut over her bones, Ella feared that one day she would split open before her very eyes. Thomasina would sit in her rocking chair in a corner of the verandah, and spend a lot

114

of time singing – mostly hymns and music-hall songs. 'Two
Little Girls in Blue' was a favourite, sung many times each
day.

This evening, Shafi had driven Ella, since Bill was working.
She had sat in the front of the official car, while Shafi fed her
a supply of sweets made from coconut and milk and sugar,
dyed a luminous lime-green, and taught her new words in
Urdu. *Bohat ach-ha* – very good. *Ap kaha jateh he?* – Where
are you going?

Occasionally, he would pat the top of her leg, letting his
hand rest for a few seconds at a time. It didn't bother Ella.
Shafi was a friend.

Tommy was waiting with his sister, Bertha, at the gate. She
had shiny black hair, which she wore in a page-boy style. She
favoured elastic waspie belts, to show off her small waist, and
peep-toe sandals bought especially in Karachi. She also over-
laid a fake American accent on to her sing-song tones –
when, that is, she could remember.

'Hi, kid,' Bertha greeted Ella now. 'Long time no see.' As
they walked up the path at Tommy's slow pace, Bertha
shivered theatrically. 'What a creepy driver,' she said, to Ella's
surprise. 'He gives me the heebie-jeebies.'

Tommy had had a nap that afternoon, so his normal early
bedtime was postponed in Ella's honour. The family sat
talking on the verandah, the conversation periodically punc-
tuated by the splat of the shocking-pink fly swatter wielded
by the vigilant Thomasina.

'Ask Mum, she'll know,' Tommy instructed Ella.

The girl shook her head, embarrassed. Blossom smiled
encouragingly. She noticed how, in the company of grown-
ups, Ella was often so retiring it was as if she was willing
invisibility upon herself.

'Go on,' Tommy repeated, giving his friend a little push.
'Ask Mum.'

He addressed his mother himself. 'Ella wants to know

which women's troubles Aunty Alice has got. She thinks it's all her fault she's in hospital.'

'Come.' Blossom beckoned to Ella, who obediently settled on her knee. 'Your Mummy had a baby in her tummy. It wasn't healthy, so it went away. It was nothing to do with you, I promise. You must have been very worried if you thought it was your fault, poor darling.'

She rubbed the girl's rigid back.

Ella, unused to having her emotions confirmed rather than denied, at first said nothing, while she digested Blossom's information. Then she gave a small smile. 'So Mummy isn't going to die?'

The woman shook her head. 'Goodness me, no. One day, she may even have more babies.'

'Mummy doesn't want any more children,' Ella answered solemnly. 'She told me one like me is more than enough.'

Later, Blossom mentioned boarding school.

'I don't want to go,' Ella responded, her lip quivering. 'I won't love it,' she added defiantly, anticipating a possible line of argument.

'Perhaps you're right,' Blossom answered gently, and let the subject slide.

At bedtime, Ella told Tommy how her mother had discovered her exercise book. He was scathing. 'Don't you know anything?' he demanded. 'If you want to keep grown-ups away from what you're doing, the last thing you write is "Keep Out!" They immediately think it's their business and start nosing. If you want to get away with something, you have to think like they do.'

Ella was impressed, but pretended otherwise. Tommy might be dying, but she didn't want him dying with a big head. 'What would you do, then, if you're so clever?' she asked casually.

He propped himself up on his elbows. 'First, you have to know the risk. If you do things they don't like, grown-ups can make you disappear. Just like that.' Tommy enjoyed frightening Ella, she made it so easy.

'Just like that? Are you sure?'

He nodded. 'Very sure. One minute you're here, next minute you're gone. I've seen it happen.

'Second, you have to call your book, or diary, or whatever it is, something really boring, something grown-ups aren't interested in – like *The Anglo-Saxons*. I've just done those with Mum and I know she found them as dull as ditchwater. Or how about *Shells on the Seashore*? Then you disguise what you're writing about. Miss out every second word or something.'

Ella sighed. 'But if I do that, how will I know what it all means when I read it in years to come?'

Tommy tutted. 'If you can't work it out in years to come, you shouldn't have written it down in the first place. Only write what matters.'

The following morning, Ella took a long time to copy an illustration of a scorpion from Tommy's book, *A Child's World of Knowledge*. She painted it pale green, so it ended up looking more like a grasshopper. Directed by Tommy, she also drew ants and a caterpillar and then worried whether a caterpillar was technically an insect, but Tommy told her it was. Finally, she took pains with the title on the cover, carefully colouring in the block capitals in yellow: *A History of Insects* by Ella Jackson, aged nine and five months. She felt safer already.

She had a hiding place in mind. She turned to a blank page and picked up her pen. Then, suddenly fearful, she put it down again.

'Don't worry if you can't think what to write,' Tommy comforted her, misreading her actions. 'Something pretty awful will happen to you soon. It always does at your age.'

Chapter Fourteen

M arjorie Rockingham was aghast. 'You can't do that, Sylvia, you really can't.'

The woman opposite her waggled her glass of gin and tonic, so that the ice cubes tinkled against each other, the wind chimes of the diplomatic circuit. 'Oh, yes, I jolly well can,' she answered. 'It's time this stuffy old place was pepped up a bit.'

Sylvia had asked Marjorie to join her for an evening chota peg or two. The ritual required that the servants lay a carpet on the lawn and furnish the area with four armchairs, a coffee table and a standard lamp. Marjorie had dressed carefully for the occasion. A pale-green taffeta dress, made in Singapore. It was exquisite, but much too hot.

Her shock had been triggered by Sylvia's announcement that the Queen's Birthday Party on 21 April was to be a joint celebration. Noel's birthday fell a week later. Official guests and friends would toast not only the young Elizabeth, but the rather older Noel as well. In all her years as a diplomat's wife, Marjorie had never heard of such a breach of protocol. Her Majesty never shared her celebrations.

'The joint birthday party,' Marjorie ventured. 'It's just not done. Cheke doesn't even consider it.'

'Bother Cheke,' Sylvia announced airily.

Ten years earlier, Sir Marcus Cheke, vice-marshal of the diplomatic corps, had been considerate enough to write a

handbook on etiquette for the wives of British diplomats.
Thus, Marjorie had learnt to arrive ten minutes before the
start of an official function, never to light a cigarette in the
company of an ambassador, a high commissioner or his
deputy, and to introduce guests to each other, but only if they
were of equal rank.

'It's all planned,' Sylvia announced. 'Noel won't know a
thing about it, until the night. Bill is organising a military
band through his colonel friend. The club chefs are helping
my lot to do the food. Harry Webster from Abbotobad is
coming, because he has a new man arriving from London,
who's promised to bring some lovely records. Albie is sorting
out the extra guests. And we're all going to play pin the tail
on the donkey. It's going to be a hoot.'

Marjorie smiled wanly, then rallied. 'Who's making Noel's
birthday cake?' she asked.

Sylvia smiled mischievously. 'Alice has volunteered. She's
such a pet. But, of course, if you'd rather . . . Could you do
something very simple, nothing out of the ordinary?' she
instructed, then added, without any sense of irony, 'You
know how Noel hates to be surprised.'

The exercise book scratched against Ella's skin. She had
pushed it up her blouse, and it was resting against the
waistband of her shorts, hidden from view. It was the day
after she had stayed at the Larkhalls'. She and Shafi were
tiptoeing round the edge of the compound, making their way
to the walled garden. Every so often, Shafi would stop dead,
feigning fright, and Ella would give a small squeal of delight.
Security lamps, stationed at intervals on the compound
walls, provided flickering and unreliable light; shadows,
crackles, whispering leaves set Ella's nerves deliciously on
edge.

She and Shafi ran through the clearing which, with the
help of an old sheet doubling up as a tent, she had already

turned into a camp. Now, the sheet flapped menacingly, as if in warning. In the tangle of trees and bushes, the two passed a crumbling stone weather vane, standing tall like a sentry on guard. A creature scuttled near Ella's feet, making her jump.

'Sssh!' Shafi suddenly ordered, pinning her back against a bush with his hand. Something told her he was no longer play acting. In view was the walled garden. Across to their left, through the brambles, was the expanse of lawn and the normality of the compound's buildings – Ella's home, the offices, Mr Carnow's bungalow, The Residence and the Rockinghams' house. They were lit up, but there was no sign of life. It was the time for the evening rites to begin: showers, fresh clothes, drinks.

The walled garden, set in the furthest corner of The Residence's grounds, was a short distance away. Ella's heart was thudding. As she stood concealed in the shrubbery with Shafi, the door of the garden creaked open. Shafi suddenly stepped in front of Ella, blocking her view. '*Imshe*,' he said urgently, turning her by the shoulder, almost roughly, and shoving her back in the direction they had just come. '*Imshe, jaldi*.'

Ella did exactly as she was told.

Three hours later, at ten o'clock, she slid out of her bedroom, having dressed herself again in shorts and top, hidden her exercise book once more, and placed plimsolls on her feet. She let herself out of the dining-room verandah doors and ran round the edge of the lawn, accompanied by the barking of a few stray dogs, sniffing around the closed gates of the compound. The Jackson household was the only one still awake. The servants' quarters, from which Shafi now emerged, a white ghost, were also in darkness.

He beckoned for her to follow. This time, they skirted the edge of the lawns. When they reached the bench, Shafi sat down, and patted the spot next to him, smiling. Ella joined him. He offered her coconut ice and the two sat in companionable silence for several minutes, while she finished her sweet.

'So where is it, Shafi?' Ella eventually asked. Excitement had receded and now only the bites of the mosquitoes were keeping her awake. Smiling still, Shafi placed his hand at the top of her leg, under her shorts, his fingers working their way into her knickers. He let his fingers rest. This was hardly forbidden territory, so Ella wasn't unduly alarmed. Ayahs and amahs had fiddled with her when she was small, to make her laugh. Perhaps Shafi found this funny too.

He withdrew his hand, gave her another sweet, then beckoned to her to follow him. On the left-hand side of the door to the walled garden hung a small, weathered wooden box. On it was written the word 'Key'. Ella knew it was empty, because it was the first place she had looked. Shafi lifted the box and removed the loose brick behind it, pulling out a non-descript key.

Ella performed a little jig of triumph. Now, in the walled garden, she finally had somewhere safe in which to keep her secrets. Her efforts dislodged the exercise book. Shafi stopped to pick it up. 'It's called *A History of Insects*,' Ella said. To her satisfaction, he showed no interest.

'Only go inside garden when you are with me,' Shafi warned. 'Big trouble if you go alone.'

Ella laughed, not listening to a word he said.

Chapter Fifteen

'Bala Hissar Fort is built on a high plinth, ninety-two feet from the ground level, occupying a dominant position in the north-western corner of Peshawar – step back, memsahib, I am thinking, step back into the shade, if you please.'

Mr Ali Shah Shaukat, a very tall, very thin man, immaculately dressed in whites so sparkling he was almost phosphorescent in the sunshine, took off his cheap sunglasses and used hand signals to direct Betty Brooking back under the large umbrella being held with some difficulty by his assistant, a boy of about twelve.

Mr Shaukat, a retired teacher, was now chief guide at the Peshawar Museum. Betty had asked him to become her personal tutor, giving her weekly lessons in the architecture and history of the city and its surroundings – earning more in an hour than he did in a month at the museum.

For these tutorials, Mr Shaukat would accompany Betty to an historical building, ignore all traffic hazards, and station her with the umbrella boy in a spot with the best view, often in the middle of a road. Then, he would repeat parrot-fashion large chunks of the guide books he'd learnt off by heart, showing impatience if his pupil interrupted his flow with a question. Now, he resumed his thread, watched by a curious and giggling gang of children.

'The fort was originally constructed by the first Mughal emperor, Babur – that is spelt B-A-B-U-R. It was later destroyed by the Afghans and reconstructed in its present form by Sikhs who ruled over the Peshawar valley between seventeen ninety-one and eighteen forty-nine. The British – happy felicitates! – replaced the mud walls with brick masonry. It is now occupied by both the police and the army. A magnificent view of the countryside can be enjoyed from the fort's massive and frowning structure.'

Betty looked up the fort's sheer, dung-coloured walls. 'Can we go inside and see the view, Mr Shaukat?' she asked.

He smiled enigmatically, mopping the sweat from his forehead. 'Why not?' he answered brightly, his head waggling from side to side – a polite way of saying no.

'Why not, indeed,' interjected a half mocking voice. Betty turned to see Ash Khan, in uniform, sitting in an army jeep, accompanied by a driver. 'I have my office in the fort. Hop in,' he invited.

An hour later, the two were sitting under the trees in the gardens of Deane's Hotel, a sprawling, single-storey building, which comprised the best hotel in Peshawar.

'Tell me about yourself,' Ash coaxed.

Betty gave him a wry smile. 'You must remember that a woman has no past when she mates with a god,' she replied deadpan.

He burst out laughing. '*Quo Vadis*,' he guessed. 'Not the best movie in the world. Coffee?' he asked, as the waiter approached to take their order.

'Please.'

Ash raised an eyebrow in mock surprise. 'So you don't drink as much as you pretend?' he asked, smiling.

'More, actually,' Betty replied. 'But experience has taught me that I never learn much when I'm drunk. And I like Mr Shaukat's lectures very much.'

Ash leant forward, his arms on his knees, an enigmatic expression on his face. 'Yes, well, you would,' he said, gently enough to take the sting out of his words. 'No doubt he teaches the kind of history you like to hear. Your kind of history, Western history. I went to school here in Peshawar and boarding school in Abbotobad and I was barely taught a word about Indian history, my history before Partition. I was taught British history – Robert the Bruce, Elizabeth the First – the history of my betters. We were inferior, therefore our history didn't matter. But then I fought in the war – and discovered that I and my colleagues did matter, very much indeed.

'Did you know that three million Indian men, including me, fought for Britain in the war? Do you ever hear stories of the heroes who happened to be black or brown?' His tone was teasing, but Betty Brooking heard his anger.

'When you have your little lectures around Peshawar, does Mr Shaukat peddle tales about how much the Raj brought to India and Pakistan? As if we had no justice or culture to speak of before the British appeared on the scene? I bet he doesn't tell you how an Englishman, a complete stranger to this continent, sat in a room with a pile of maps, years out of date, and drew a line down the middle of the Punjab, chopping in half one village here, another village there? Deciding arbitrarily one side Pakistan, the other India?

'Does Mr Shaukat tell you about the throats cut and the brains of babies bashed out and the family farms destroyed? Does he tell you of the bankrupt country the British created? Pakistan – two broken wings on either side of the plump breast of India? Does he tell you how India refused to pay its debts to my new country, so we had an air force with no planes and ministers of state paying for official stamps and stationery? And nobody in the civil service drawing wages for months?'

Ash suddenly stopped, aware that his mask as the playboy, happiest splashing in the shallow end of conversation, had slipped badly.

'Go on,' Betty demanded, her voice low and husky.

Her response surprised him. He expected her to be offended or defensive or even bored. Instead, she seemed genuinely hungry for more information. Or perhaps, Ash told himself cynically, she was just hungry. He could smell mangos and jasmine and Chanel No 5.

He took a sip of coffee and sat back in his chair, watching her for a few seconds, as if to gauge how much more he could risk revealing.

'Let me tell you something, Mrs Brooking,' he eventually said. 'I was a pupil at Edwardes College, here in Peshawar. Beautiful building, education the epitome of the best of British. But it had an ugly side. A side the British preferred to ignore. I was one of a handful of Muslim boys amongst hundreds of Hindus. It wasn't a question of discrimination. Oh, goodness me, no. Muslims weren't considered clever enough. Pig fat would be smeared on our seats, bad names written across our exercise books.

'It suited the British. The Hindus were the middle class, the bureaucrats, the professionals. We Muslims were the donkeys, the providers of raw materials, the rats in the Hindu-owned wheels. So, what happens when Pakistan is created? Over-night, literally overnight, the Hindus and the Sikhs leave. For every one professional, educated, middle-class Hindu that departed, ten impoverished, illiterate Muslims arrived. We had no civil service to speak of, too little expertise to run our businesses and industry. And did the British government – the fair and just and decent British government – help? Of course not. Not as long as Pamela Mountbatten was dancing in the arms of Pandit Nehru in Delhi. It's always been India, the jewel in the crown – and Pakistan, the badly made paste bauble, the Empire's embarrassment.'

Betty, listening intently, moved to rest her head on her hand. Ash saw the curve of her breast, his eyes were drawn to a small smear of white cream on her brown flesh that had yet to sink into her skin.

'And where did you come from?' she asked lightly. 'Are you the poor, illiterate Muslim who arrived with nothing?'

Ash smoothed his moustache and rubbed his cheek, as if to check his own identity. 'My family own a great deal of land an hour's drive from Peshawar. Mr Shaukat may not have told you, but we landlords are feudal and corrupt and resistant to change. We are not the middle class. We are not politicians. We deal in giving and calling in favours, ideology is of no interest to us. I look after you, you look after me – that's the only -ism in which we believe.'

He shrugged. 'Your husband and his sort will work hard to keep us in power. Why? Because we want only more of the same. So, our army grows more bloated on bribes, the landowners take the cream of the foreign aid – and the poor die on the streets. And our fledgling middle-class? They struggle to pay the backhanders to ministers and officials before they can even begin to do business.'

Ash stopped and gave a bitter laugh. 'Your husband likes conspiracies, doesn't he, Mrs Brooking?' he asked. 'Pinkos and Faggots and Commies. Well, some of us believe there was a conspiracy at the birth of Pakistan. Nehru and the British believed that if they made us, the new baby, enough of a weakling, eventually we would beg to be allowed to return to Mother India, one whole country again. Well, we haven't begged – but neither has the weakling baby grown strong enough to cope.'

Betty put down her coffee cup. 'So are you the future saviour of Pakistan, Ash? The angry young army officer? Are you another Nasser, letting the communists in through the back door, while you dance and play with the British and the Americans out front?'

Ash narrowed his eyes, then laughed. 'You speak as a good wife, Betty Brooking,' he smiled. 'But don't believe everything your husband tells you. Nasser, like me, is a nationalist, not a communist. He wants a—'

'I've never shared CJ's beliefs. I'm interested in facts, not bigotry,' Betty interjected sharply. 'That's why I'm interested in history.'

Ash wagged his finger. 'Aaah,' he said, 'but whose history is it? Whose version of the truth do we decide to trust? Hindus are bad, Muslims are good. Americans are to be admired, because they believe in freedom; Americans are wicked, because they worship profit. Which of these truths do you prefer, Mrs Brooking?

'Look at Bill Jackson – a close friend of yours, I believe,' Ash continued, with a change of inflection that didn't escape Betty. 'He spends most of his day bashing out a record of "truth" on his Morse key. Most of which is hypothesis, guess work, plain hot air. As I'm sure he's probably told you.'

Betty spoke crisply. 'He hasn't,' she replied. 'But, then again, he is, as you know, a man of great discretion.'

Ash waved his hand airily. 'Whatever,' he smiled.

Betty bridled. 'Come on, Ash, what are you saying? Never trust anything you're told at all? Throw out all official records? What? Why, for that matter, should I trust your version of events any more than the next man's?'

Ash was pleased. He had finally drawn a reaction from this woman who affected to be the cool and uninvolved outsider. One way or another, he would eventually force her into the ring. 'Well, now, here we face a new dilemma,' he said. 'Sometimes, of course, the truth lies not in the information that you are given, but in seeking out what you have not been told, in discovering what is omitted from the official record, in unearthing the witnesses who would otherwise have no voice. In believing there is always another version.' He suddenly leant forward. 'Allow me,' he said.

He picked up a napkin from the table, dipped a corner of the cloth in a glass of iced water, and gently wiped away a non-existent smudge on the woman's cheek. At this point, in Ash's experience, a woman dropped her eyes, perhaps blushed, and normally expressed some confusion. Betty Brooking's gaze held his own, unwaveringly.

'That,' she said, deadpan, 'reminds me of a scene from *The Rains of Ranchipur*. Was it Tyrone Power who played your role? What was it you were saying about your version of the truth?'

Ash Khan sat back in his chair, roaring with laughter, attracting the attention of the other hotel guests. 'The truth, Mrs Brooking, is that I dislike your husband intensely. Do you know much about his sewage plant? Doesn't it strike you as odd that a country with so many who are so starved they hardly produce any waste has allegedly sanctioned a fortune invested on the recycling of excreta? Think about it, Mrs Brooking.'

He took a sip of his coffee, studying her face as he did so. He spoke again, this time so softly Betty could barely hear his words.

'Sometimes, when I loathe a man, I seduce his wife – a Western man, of course, since a Pathan would rightly shoot me dead.' Ash gave a dry smile. 'The ladies are almost always highly responsive.' He paused. 'Even grateful. I know that this is shocking bad manners on my part and very juvenile behaviour. Bill tells me that, one day, an irate husband is going to give me a poke on the chin. But most of the husbands imagine that no wife of theirs would dream of sleeping with a Pakistani. But dream – and more – they jolly well do.'

He sat forward and cupped one of the woman's hands in between his two. He expected her to tense a little, but she remained relaxed.

Betty was surprised that a man who appeared so muscular had skin so soft. His fingers were long and graceful, almost feminine, his nails grown almost to a woman's length. He wore one ring, a thin gold wedding band. He used his thumb to slowly draw circles on the palm of her hand, as if exploring its contours. Then, with his index finger, he traced her lifeline, like a fortune-teller tracking a future.

Ash put his head closer to hers and, as if they were already intimates, added softly, 'Revenge is usually my first excuse for taking a woman to bed, Mrs Brooking, but should you and I ever choose to become lovers – truthfully – my motivation would be based on nothing more than pleasure.'

Betty studied him coolly. 'Honey,' she answered, 'those are the only terms I accept.'

Chapter Sixteen

The woman had been annoyingly specific. 'It has to be a kiss-stick in a pink-and-gold cocktail case. I am thinking it said in the magazine it was six shillings and sixpence. It said, "Smooth as silk, it never smears, it never dries. Coty's kiss-stick is wonderfully creamy, giving you luscious, glossy, vital lips." You like my lips, don't you, Piers?' And she had touched him where he didn't like to be touched, not outside the act of copulation, not at all by her any more. He smelt the stale odour of perspiration, coconut cream and cheap powder. Her mascara had run, leaving black blobs in the corners of her eyes like the ticks bloated with blood on stray dogs.

As she spoke, she was sucking on an orange. Shreds of the fruit were stuck between her teeth. A towel, wrapped around her body, had loosened and fallen around her waist. She appeared not to care that her breasts were free, and hanging. It was almost as if she liked her own body, although God knows why, Piers thought. He realised how much he preferred Marjorie's secrecy, her obsession with remaining covered, concealed, sparing him a reminder of the ugliness of the female form, her female form.

In contrast, *in daylight*, Belle Masters had spread her legs, inviting him to look at what he had never seen before in his life, guiding his hand, licking his fingers. Then, he had run away. She had laughed, knowing he would be back. He had to come back, he told himself, because she had yet to give him the blessed book. So, in his own mind, Piers had transformed an act of adultery into a necessary career move – not that he'd ever felt any guilt. No, his strongest emotion was one of disgust. He wanted her to do things, but then he hated her for doing them. Worse, she made no attempt to hide her own enjoyment – a horrible, guttural sound, her eyes rolling, dribble on her chin. The silence of his own wife was so much more . . . dignified.

'So beautiful,' Belle would say, again and again. 'So beautiful,' as they slipped and slid. Naturally, at first, he'd assumed she meant him – she wouldn't be the first woman to pay him the compliment. But rapidly it dawned on Piers that Belle was actually referring to the act in which they were engaged. And he was deeply disgusted.

Almost immediately, she had begun to make demands, material demands. Over the past few days, Piers had found himself in the ridiculous position of stealing from his own pantry, providing excuses to Marjorie, who carefully annotated their stock. A tin of biscuits here, a jar of blackcurrant jam there.

Now, he looked at Belle, naked from the waist up, as she sat at the table in the bedroom, orange juice running down her arms in rivulets. Her nipples were deepest brown, huge and spreading, like creatures with a life of their own, sprouting several long, black hairs. She was talking again. 'A lipstick will be no problem for you, sweetie pie. They can send it in the diplomatic bag, isn't it? And I am so fed up with the shit they sell in the bazaar. Honest to God, it doesn't stay on for five minutes. Not five minutes, I'm telling you.'

Embarrassingly, the shade which Belle had demanded was called 'Tru-luv'. Piers would have to write to his sister, requesting that she buy the lipstick and send it to him. He would tell her it was a present for Marjorie. As if his wife would ever reduce herself to anything as common as Tru-luv.

'It's by the bed,' Belle instructed, pinning up her hair on the top of her head.

Piers reached out for the parcel. Relief and disappointment took hold. He had his prize, a copy of William Cobbett's *The English Gardener*, but his excuse for these visits, five so far, would now be gone.

'Guess what?' Belle said, slipping a cotton dress over her head. 'I've been invited into the hallowed grounds of your compound.'

Piers thought he was about to be sick.

She smiled at his obvious discomfort. 'Don't worry. I'm not coming as a guest. Albie is helping to organise the Queen's Birthday Party and he asked me if I'd give a hand with the floral displays. It's my skill. My other skill,' she added lasciviously. Piers was sure she exaggerated her vulgarity to annoy him. 'Still, who knows?' she teased. 'Once I'm there, I might hang around in the background, have a drink or two. See if I can be of service?'

She reached under the sheet for his naked body. In a flash of anger, he knocked her hand away. Her knuckles cracked as they hit the bedside table. Belle's face was expressionless. 'If naughty boys have a temper-tantrum,' she said evenly, 'they have to be punished.'

Alice had been home from hospital for several days. She had a fresh sense of achievement. A date for Ella's departure for boarding school had been decided – 24 April, three days after the Queen's Birthday Party. She was also making a cake for the Deputy High Commissioner. She had already spent an hour or so this morning making sure that the white icing on the large, square fruit cake was as smooth as alabaster.

The first few days after her discharge had been difficult. She had remonstrated with Bill that Ella had become totally out of control, refusing to go to bed, disappearing God knows where, spending more time riding with her father than doing her homework. Alice had been surprised, too, how much Ash had become part of the Jackson household. He claimed that the visits were part of an overhaul of the compound's security, since the army was responsible for the safety of foreign diplomats. When he came on official business, however, he would always find time to play Ludo or chess with Ella.

Alice went into her bedroom. Even here, there had been progress. Piers had given Bill a form, consisting of three pages, which had to be filled in, detailing the history of their existing bed, reasons for removal and details of the replacement preferred. This, he had said, would take a certain amount of time to process. Then, of course, the question of a new bed would produce a further reel of red tape. 'Sorry, old man,' Piers had smiled at Bill. 'You're looking at a good few months. You know how it is. Probably arrive just as you're on your way out. Bastard, isn't it?'

Alice had a surprise for her daughter. Laid out on the double bed were two navy-blue gymslips, both darned, but perfectly wearable, second-hand from the Larkhalls; three white blouses, almost new; two grey cardigans; and an assortment of grey and white knickers, plus a navy-blue beret – the uniform of St Winifred's. Alice had been puzzled, because Blossom's original enthusiasm for giving Ella her daughter's old school wardrobe had mysteriously cooled.

'I'll pay you, of course,' Alice had offered, misunderstanding Blossom's change of mood.

'Certainly not,' Blossom had said. Then she added, 'Are you sure that sending Ella away is a good idea? Bertha was much older when she became a boarder.'

Alice had been dismissive. 'I know Ella,' she'd said firmly. 'It will do her the world of good.'

Now, she picked up Ella's pyjamas, neatly folded for packing and buried her face in the cotton. They smelt of Johnson's baby powder and calamine lotion. To her surprise,

Alice realised she was crying. A sadness swept over her, sucking her down to depths she didn't want to reach. She knew that the tears weren't for Ella, but for herself, a very long time ago.

'You promised! You promised, Daddy. You really did promise. I heard you promise!' Ella's face was contorted with disbelief and shock and grief, as she looked from the school clothes on the bed to her father.

Bill, upset by the severity of his daughter's reaction, reached out his hands, as if for forgiveness.

Alice interrupted brusquely. 'Listen, my girl, you'll do as we say, and make no mistake. I wish I'd been as lucky as you when I was your age. Mummy would have loved to have had all these new clothes and . . .'

Ella seized the nearest gymslip and flung it on the floor. 'They're not new and, if you like them so much, you wear them. Daddy promised I wouldn't go away and now he's broken his promise. And you —' she turned her now tear-stained face to her mother — 'you, you, you fib all the time, I've heard you.'

Ella stopped abruptly. Now, there would be no forgiveness, she would never be loved again. She was horrible, wicked. She might as well be dead.

Alice took a step towards her, her hand lifted, as if to strike. 'How dare you speak to your mother like that,' she shouted. 'I wouldn't dream of telling a lie. You come back here, my girl!' she screamed at her daughter's retreating back.

Bill began to run after Ella, Alice following, into the hall, through the dining room. Their child was already jumping from the verandah, speeding down the drive to the compound gates. Alice turned and came back into the dining room. Only then did she realise that Sylvia was sitting at the dining-room table, the half-iced cake in front of her.

'Hope I haven't intruded?' she said brightly. 'Yummy cake. Only, there's a bit of a problem.'

Alice looked at Sylvia. The urge to speak her mind, to tell her what a ridiculous, infantile, spoilt, insensitive brat of a lazy cow she was, was so strong, for a brief moment, Alice almost imagined the words had popped out. Then she realised that Sylvia was speaking again.

'Gorgeous cake, but the thing is, we won't be needing it after all. Hope you don't mind? I hadn't realised, but Marjorie had already taken it upon herself to do the baking. You know how it is? It's a bit difficult for me to say no, what with Piers being number two and . . . well, I'm sure you understand. I bet Bill and Ella will gobble this one up in seconds. Super cake,' she continued enthusiastically. 'Quite marvellous. I'm surprised someone like you knows how to cook so well,' she added unthinkingly.

Alice smiled woodenly. 'Thank you,' she said.

Ella ran out of the compound, across the road, and into the park opposite. Already, she was dampening down her disappointment and fear by propelling herself into the more secure world of make-believe. She was a secret agent, dropped in France, fighting the Germans. She was Violet Szabo. She must cut off contact with her family. She must begin again. She would die for Britain.

'Ell-a, Ell-a.' At first, she thought it was her father calling. Then, she realised that one of the street boys with whom she occasionally played was beckoning to her from behind the dilapidated bandstand. As she ran towards him, she told herself to take care. He could be a German in disguise. She joined the boy and they both ducked down, as if he instinctively knew that she required cover. Peeping round the podium, hidden from view, the boy and girl watched as Bill Jackson stood at the gates, talking to the chowkidar.

Ella saw her father cross the road into the park. Standing

only a hundred yards from her hiding place, he was calling for her.

'Ella, please come home. You won't be in trouble. Nothing will happen, I promise.' Then, as if he recognised the diminished value of his word, Bill added, 'When I say I promise, I mean it this time. I really do.'

'Chewing gum?' said the small boy by Ella's side, offering her a sugared tablet.

'*Shukria*,' she whispered. She would never go home. Never.

An hour later, Ella slipped back into the compound. She followed the perimeter of the wall behind the willow trees. Everyone would be at lunch now, followed by a nap. The sun, past its fullest strength, had baked the day to a hazy, sleepy turn; all movements, whether by humans, insects or animals, were now rationed, energy sucked by the heat. Even the chee-chees, normally frantic as they scaled walls and explored cracks, were stilled.

Ella was hot, hungry, sweaty, frightened, poisoned by her badness. She reached the walled garden, found the key, but realised, as she placed it in the lock, that the door was already open; it just required a push. She walked through. A series of bushes gave the effect of a crude maze. Each turn she took, another hedge would obstruct the view. The hedges were as high as Ella's head, but she calculated that they would probably reach a grown-up's chest. At the heart of the maze was a simple wooden hut raised a foot above the ground on bricks. It was open on the side which faced a small, neatly gravelled clearing.

The hut was furnished with two straight-backed chairs, a table covered by a map and a large fan which took up the top of a tea trolley. The trolley also held a solitary bottle of whisky, four tumblers, and a small pile of books. Ella crept around to the other side of the hut. She knew only two people could be in the garden besides herself – Shafi, who would be saying his one-thirty prayers, and Mr Hargreave-Smith. She stopped. In the shade, a deckchair, a large parasol and a red ice bucket had been set out on a small carpet. To Ella's left was a rusted-iron bench. She stooped and moved one of the ornate stones, carved like a lion's paw, which anchored the seat to the ground. Here, she had hidden *A History of Insects*.

Her book clutched to her chest, she crept on. Now, concealed by a hedge, she had a full view of the occupant of the deckchair. Mr Hargreave-Smith lay asleep. He held something unfamiliar in one hand. She couldn't believe her eyes when she came closer. It was a child's tiny wooden horse.

Ella retreated carefully and sat behind a bougainvillea bush, oblivious to the scratches inflicted on her bare arms and legs. She wrote quickly. Tommy had said to use some kind of code, but that was too fussy. She read her first sentence back to herself and smiled. She had written, 'Mr Hargreave-Smith plays with toys.' If she'd told anyone what she'd just seen, nobody would have believed a word.

Chapter Seventeen

T he material was the colour of a peacock's breast. The
tailorwallah threw the bale with theatrical skill, letting the
cloth unravel in extravagant loops at Marjorie Rockingham's
feet.

'Do you think you can make it in time?' she asked
anxiously. 'And this one has to be right, do you understand
me?'

The tailorwallah bowed and smiled, unconsciously rubbing his hands. 'You draw, me sew,' he replied. 'Very, very
jaldi. Tonight, I come with dress for you to fit. Finish
tomorrow. OK? Very good price,' he added hastily.

Marjorie rose from her chair in the sitting room. As she
did so, she heard the hall door slam. That morning, Piers had
demanded that she stop her hospital voluntary work. He said
that she was never at home when he needed her. For the first
time in her life, she had refused point blank to do as he
instructed.

'Can you make this?' Marjorie asked. She gave the tailor a
page ripped out of a *Ladies' Home Journal*, borrowed from
Betty Brooking. The dress had an elaborate bolero and a drop
waist.

'You want jacket?' the tailor asked, incredulous that a
Western woman would *choose* to wrap up.

'I wouldn't ask you to make it, if I didn't want it, would I?'
Marjorie replied waspishly.

138

Hastily, the tailorwallah took the page and in return gave her the simple black taffeta cocktail dress with two thin sequinned straps she had ordered on his previous visit. This was the garment that Marjorie had intended to wear to the Queen's Birthday Party, if the consequences of her husband's temper hadn't upset her plans.

She took the dress, ordering the man to wait, and went upstairs to her bedroom. She undressed swiftly and pulled the tailor's latest effort over her head. It fitted beautifully, but exposed large purple and yellow bruises across both shoulders. She'd been lucky. She had crouched and protected herself with her arms, so Piers' kicks had missed her face and head.

In the past, he'd always avoided hitting her where it might show. Now, it was as if he no longer cared. As if he'd sensed that, somehow, a part of her had already broken free.

'What do you think?' Sylvia was almost levitating, she was so excited. It was late morning, on the compound's main lawn. Alice, Marjorie and Ella had all been summoned at short notice by Sylvia's bearer. Around the group, Albie was busily directing a gang of men, setting up tables, chairs and lights. Sylvia was on tiptoes in front of a crudely painted picture of a donkey, minus its tail.

The tail, plaited out of wool, was in Sylvia's hand. 'Isn't he frightfully handsome? Do you want to have a go, Ella?' she asked, pushing the tail into her hand.

The girl shook her head shyly. She decided that Sylvia was quite, quite potty. Nobody played Pin the Tail on the Donkey past the age of five.

Sylvia stuck the tail on the board at random. 'Now,' she announced, 'where's the driver? Come on you lot, I've something really important for us to do. I shan't tell you what it is until we get there, but I promise it's jolly useful. Have I got my little army with me? Chop, chop, ladies. We won't be long, back before lunchtime, absolutely ready for our G and Ts. Come along, Ella.'

The women found themselves marshalled into the official car.

The driver turned off The Mall, right on to Hospital Street and took the left fork into the Jamrud Road – a route that led to the university and, beyond that, to the Khyber Pass. After ten minutes or so, it pulled up outside the unmarked gates of a large walled enclosure. Marjorie and Alice exchanged glances. Sylvia beamed at them both. 'Here we are, ladies! The British Cemetery,' she announced. 'We've come to the relief of our fellow countrymen, our dead fellow country- men, but no matter. They need our help. Let's get to it.'

As she was speaking, the driver unloaded from the boot three pairs of garden gloves, shears, several armfuls of paper flowers, an eclectic mix of lurid orchids, poppies and sun- flowers, available cheaply in the Old City, a dozen or so brilliant-blue tin vases and a very large drum of whitewash, plus brushes.

'Follow me!' Sylvia commanded, producing a fountain pen and a leather notebook from her bag. Then, she marched through the gates, brusquely rousing the chowkidar, asleep on his charpoi.

Ella read the large notice at the entrance. 'Christian Cemetery Board,' it said. 'Burial rate: adult Rs 40; child Rs 20; Special Burials Rs 250.' The graveyard was parched brown, and it looked to her as if a giant had kicked and stamped his way carelessly through tombstones, cherubs and open Bibles. Slabs of marble and stone lay cracked and broken across grassed-over paths; weeds choked the life out of delicately carved angels. Only a few of the graves were still intact. In the corner, a mound of fresh earth covered in bunches of decaying flowers indicated that the cemetery was still in use.

Ella, Marjorie and Alice wandered between the graves, while Sylvia busied herself making notes on the improvements she intended to implement.

Marjorie spoke first. 'It must have been awful for the very first people in the cantonment,' she said. 'So many died so young. And so far away from home. Look how much they valued every minute of what little life they had. We should learn a lesson from that.' She read out loud from a tombstone close to the entrance. ' "Jane, beloved wife of Sergeant John Turner, ordinance depot, Cherat. Died the ninth of June eighteen seventy-five, aged thirty-two years, six months and ten days." Ten whole extra days.' Marjorie paused briefly, then continued:

'She is dead one so dearly loved
Freed from the world of pain
Gone to dwell in heaven above
Where we shall meet again . . .'

'Chin up!' barked Sylvia. 'We're here to do a bit of good, not feel sorry for ourselves.' She rapidly issued instructions. 'The workmen can do most of this stuff, but, while we're here, why don't we make a bit of a start tidying up? Put some flowers in vases on the graves? That sort of thing?'

Marjorie objected weakly, 'In this heat? But I don't even have my sun hat . . .'

Sylvia waved her hands impatiently. 'An hour or so won't hurt. Besides, it's shameful it's been allowed to get into this state. Whatever will the locals think? That we don't look after our own people? Ella, I want you to look after the children's graves – or at least, make a start. The driver is going to whitewash the walls outside. Come on, buck up, do, Marjorie.' Sylvia gave her shoulders a quick squeeze.

The woman let out a sharp yelp of pain. Then added

quickly, 'It's nothing, really. I'm just a bit tender; sunburn I expect.'

The chowkidar showed Ella the area reserved for the dead children of the Raj. The girl walked from one small grave to another. She stopped in front of a tombstone decorated with an angel. Neglect or vandals had clipped its wings. She read, ' "In loving memory of our little Mavis, born 6 September 1903 died 1 May 1904. The dearly loved child of Arthur and Maud Tyler. If thou shouldst call me to resign what most I prize, it ne'er were mine. I only yield thee what is thine. Thy will be done." '

Ella bent to replace a tile dislodged from the adjacent grave. On a small engraved stone, now in two, were the words 'Edward, dearly beloved son of Major and Mrs W R Diamond passed away 7 April 1928, aged seven.' Two years younger than her, Ella thought. What if Tommy was right? What if grown-ups did hold the power to make you disappear, pass away? *Thy will be done*? Ella knelt to read the tribute to a fourteen-month-old child who'd died on 12 April 1916. 'Just as our bud was opening in glory to the day, Down came the heavenly gardener and plucked our bud away . . .'

If Tommy was one day plucked, Ella mused, is this where he would come to rest? Would he lie here, uncared for, forgotten, a verse on a tombstone?

Her mother's voice suddenly broke into her thoughts.

'Sylvia,' Alice was saying determinedly, 'I've had enough. So has Marjorie. It's too hot and we're not achieving all that much. Don't you think we should call it a day?'

Sylvia's head bobbed up in the middle of a bush which had taken root in and around a large sarcophagus. She looked startled by this unexpected rebellion. 'Oh, quite, quite, of course . . .' she twittered. 'Still, we've made a super start, don't you think, girls?' She swung out her arms, as if to embrace the whole cemetery. 'I'm sure they'd be jolly grateful if . . . well, if, you know what I mean.'

Marjorie bent down to pick up the garden shears. As she did so, her dress slipped slightly off her shoulder. She hastily readjusted it, but not before Alice had seen that her flesh was so bruised it looked like the skin of a rotten banana. Before she could stop herself, she instinctively reached out her hand in comfort. 'Are you all right?' Alice whispered, so that Ella and Sylvia couldn't hear. 'Is there anything I can do?'

Marjorie shook her head, her face guarded. 'Do? Do about what? I really don't know what you mean,' she replied coldly. Then she walked brusquely away.

Back in the compound, Noel Hargreave-Smith looked at the young man sitting in his office in disbelief. Harry Webster had an amused smile on his face, enjoying the impact that had been made. Daniel Cockcroft was twenty-four or twenty-five, Noel guessed. His hair was in a sort of quiff at the front, heavily greased. Webster had told him he was a Cambridge University entrant, marked as a high flyer, and therefore his 'unconventionality' was deemed acceptable. He'd spent eighteen months in Athens and this was his second posting.

The DHC noted that young Mr Cockcroft was wearing whites, like every other member of staff, but in his hand he held a beige flat, peaked cap; not a panama or a basket-weave trilby, a flat, peaked cap, a working man's cap. He was reasonably well spoken, Noel decided, if a little sloppy, but he looked like a barrow boy. He sighed. One more working-class entrant, another grammar-school dilutee.

The three men had been joined by David Carnow. Webster was on his pet hobby-horse. 'The trouble with the bloody Americans is that they want to go around like the school bully, giving everybody a bloody nose. It's all black and white with Dulles. You're either for communism or against it, no shades of grey, no neutrality. What kind of madness is that? As if diplomacy was some kind of cowboy shoot-out. Personally,' Webster continued, 'I can't see the point in cutting off all economic aid to Nasser. That's what Dulles is pushing hard for us to do. If Nasser is forced into the arms of Kruschev, where does that leave our oil supplies and our policy in the Middle East?'

'What policy in the Middle East?' Carnow replied softly. 'We can't afford a policy in the Middle East, or anywhere else, for that matter. The Empire's shut up shop, Harry. The Americans ask our advice, then ignore it completely. They call on our experience, then explain how they'll do it differently. We pretend we're exercising power, when all we're really doing is spreading our troops too thin in four corners of the world and waiting for the next command to come from Washington. And I'll tell you this for nothing,' he added, 'if Eden continues to behave as if we're still a big hitter, he'll end up making one almighty cock-up. The trouble is, I think the man actually believes it. Somebody ought to tell him, the wardrobe's full of emperor's clothes.'

Hargreave-Smith turned to the newcomer. 'Anything to say, Cockcroft?'

'No, sir,' he replied.

Noel Hargreave-Smith decided the boy couldn't be all bad.

Custom dictated that when the Met chaps were in Peshawar, usually only for a couple of nights at a time, they stayed with the Deputy High Commissioner. It soon transpired that Cockcroft had other plans. 'If it's all right with you, sir,' he said, 'I'm going to stay with the Jacksons.'

'The Jacksons?' Noel repeated, taken aback.

'Yes, sir,' Cockcroft replied. 'Bill knows my father – and me, of course.'

Noel raised an eyebrow. 'Is your father in the DWS?' he asked.

'No, sir,' the young man replied. 'He's an ambassador. In Paris at present.'

Under Webster's amused gaze, Hargreave-Smith sat a little straighter in his chair. Paris, by God. 'I see, yes, of course,' he added, flushing with embarrassment, as if his earlier thoughts on Cockcroft had been exposed to the world.

The new arrival continued, 'We met Bill in Kuala Lumpur. I think it was his first post. I was a schoolboy at the time. He taught me how to sail a dinghy in the holidays.'

'Did he now?' Noel said. 'So, you've turned out to be a chip off the old block? Following in Father's footsteps, eh?'

Cockcroft smiled. 'You could say that, I suppose, but not quite the same style. I'm what my father would call "a bloody moderniser". Not his sort at all.'

'And precisely what "sort" are you?'

Cockcroft hesitated before replying, then said, 'I think we should open the service up, sir, make it more accountable, recruit outside the establishment, reflect society more, that sort of thing. Father doesn't agree, of course. He has a profound mistrust of the plebs. By the way,' he added, rummaging in the canvas hold-all at his feet, 'I had word that Mrs Hargreave-Smith wanted these . . . For the Queen's Birthday Party. They're the very latest.'

Cockcroft handed over half-a-dozen 45 rpm records. Bemused, Noel read the label on the first – then shuddered. 'Oh dear,' he said. 'Oh dear, oh dear . . .'

Alice spun Ella round faster and faster.

'Up, round, back and under,' instructed Dan Cockcroft, shouting to compete with Bill Haley and the Comets on the record player in the Jacksons' sitting room.

'We're going to rock around the clock tonight!' bellowed Bill Haley.

'Under and round and back again,' Dan bawled.

Eventually, mother and daughter collapsed in a heap on the floor. Dan, laughing, helped Ella up. 'Now you know how to rock 'n' roll,' he smiled.

Alice ordered another gin and tonic from Ijaz. 'I say, do you really think Noel is going to let Sylvia play that sort of stuff tomorrow night?' she asked Dan flirtatiously.

Bill answered for him. 'Of course. Up against Sylvia, Noel doesn't stand a chance. My view is, he's misread her completely – poor bastard.'

Chapter Eighteen

Saturday morning, 21 April, hours before the Queen's Birthday Party, and Sylvia stood stunned at the gate of the British cemetery. Shafi had arrived earlier with a couple of men, to continue the attempt to bring the graveyard to order. Instead, he'd discovered that vandals had been at work. Red paint dripped down the white walls of the cemetery from words daubed in Urdu. Inside, the flowers left on the graves had been scattered, and the empty vases crushed.

'What do the words mean?' she asked.

Shafi shook his head, reluctant to translate the anti-British insults.

'Where's the cemetery chowkidar?' the woman demanded angrily. 'Why didn't he stop them?'

Shafi shrugged his shoulders. 'He's gone.'

Sylvia was already stepping back into the official car. 'I shall demand that they put a policeman or a soldier on duty here, twenty-four hours a day.'

Shafi shook his head. 'Soldiers, policemen not a good idea,' he advised gently.

'Why on earth not?' she snapped.

Shafi briefly considered whether it was better to allow the woman to follow her own foolish course. 'Soldier here means you are afraid. You are weak. They come back for more. Give soldier baksheesh, he goes away. Then, people do bad things even more. Bad, bad things. Very angry at the British.'

'Why on earth would they be angry with us, when we've done so much?' Sylvia asked, genuinely incredulous.

Shafi, accustomed to disguising his emotions in the presence of his employers, avoided her eyes. To him, this woman was physically repellent, ignorant, as unappealing as a child whose selfishness is still monstrous, because she has yet to become aware of the needs of others. *We've done so much.* He had heard this so many times from the British. By which they meant railway lines and irrigation canals. But what about what they had taken away? What of the human cost?

What of his family – his mother, father, wife, two sons, a young brother, buried with far more indignity than was ever conveyed by a fallen tombstone? Buried under layers of the dead and dying, jammed into a railway carriage, which pulled into the station in Peshawar, as he stood there – arms wide in welcome. Welcome to the new homeland of Pakistan. Welcome to corpses with their throats cut, so they are no longer able to say thank you to the British. Thank you to Memsahib Hargreave-Smith. Thank you. Thank you so much.

Shafi picked up the paint brush, still wet with paint discarded by the culprits, and turned towards Sylvia Hargreave-Smith. He wanted to daub her face, watch her struggle with the paint's stickiness, confront her with the terrible redness that he could never forget; didn't wish to forget. Sikhs or Hindus may have slaughtered his family, but the fault lay with the British. How often had he wished since that they had instigated his death too.

'Do put that down, Shafi,' Sylvia admonished. 'We haven't got all day. Come now, *jaldi, jaldi.*'

The gardener carefully laid the brush on the ground and did as he was told.

Ella had spent most of Saturday left to her own devices. In the morning, she sat with Surindabash on the kitchen steps and watched as the trestle tables were set up, covered in white cloths, and elaborately decorated with palm leaves and gladioli and roses in preparation for the buffet. Twin portraits of HRH Queen Elizabeth II and the Duke of Edinburgh were set up at the entrance to the lawn and garlanded with jasmine. Fairy lights linked the bushes and trees and the small plinth from which Noel Hargreave-Smith would propose the royal toast. Albie Larkhall had borrowed speakers from the Army Officers' Club and these were connected to the interior of The Residence. Much of the lawn was covered with overlapping Afghan carpets. In the sunlight, they looked to Ella like vast trays of crimson and purple jewels. At night, of course, bumpy and uneven, they would trip up even the stone-cold sober.

Extra chowkidars had been brought in to help with parking; staff had been seconded from the tennis club to dispense drinks and food; Belle Masters, clattering around on impossibly high heels, had spent all morning working on one of The Residence's verandahs, making bouquets, one for each of the numerous small tables edging the temporary wooden dance-floor. Ella wove herself in and out of the arrangements, excited by the flurry, continually negotiating with her mother as to how late she could stay up.

'Please, can I go to bed at nine?'

'No, that's much too late.'

'Quarter to nine?'

'No. I don't want to hear another word. Eight o'clock and no later.'

'If I'm very, very quiet, can I go to bed at half past eight?'

'Only if you're in your nightdress early and before your supper and there are no arguments when it's time for bed,' Alice finally conceded.

Ella was thrilled. 'I promise, I promise,' she said, hoping that, when the time came, her mother would be too involved in the party to remember.

By seven, all was ready and the compound appeared

deserted as the staff – British and Pakistani – dressed for the evening. Ella, in her nightdress, wandered unobserved around the tables now glinting with silver and decorated with serviettes folded into fans. The carpets, deepest red and purple in the darkness, were rough and ticklish under her bare feet. On an impulse, Ella picked up the skirt of her nightdress and began to dance as if she was the queen of the ball, surrounded by admirers. She wove in and out of the tables, her dance turning into a wild, exuberant jig. As she spun, the fairy lights flickered on – pink, blue, green, yellow – and the entire lawn was suddenly illuminated in a rainbow of colour. Ella was caught at its centre, like a small white apparition.

Noel Hargreave-Smith glanced at his tuxedo, laid out on the bed, and then at his wife, who had come into his room to help him with his black bow-tie. He would have preferred a smaller function, inside The Residence, but if it kept Sylvia happy and occupied, then so be it. She had returned earlier in the day from the British Cemetery, demanding an armed guard, complaining about vandalism and very cross indeed. It had reminded Noel yet again of her youth and inexperience. What he did not want on the eve of the Queen's Birthday Party was some public fracas, however minor. Far too embarrassing, when he was hosting a reception with half the North-West Frontier Province administration bigwigs in attendance and all of the foreign diplomatic circuit.

Sylvia had sulked a bit, but had eventually seen sense. She agreed it would be best to ignore the state of the cemetery for a few days and then think again. 'Think again' was, of course, her husband's euphemistic way of saying, 'Do nothing.'

He was telling her about Dan Cockcroft. 'No one knows their place any more,' he sighed. 'No one, not even me.' He closed his eyes as if to shut out the horror of this new world.

'Noel,' Sylvia began hesitantly, 'I was going to let this be a surprise, but perhaps it's best that you're a bit forewarned. It's this party,' she continued.

He opened his eyes. 'What about it?'

'It's yours,' she blurted out.

Noel looked at his wife and gave an irritated snort. 'I know it's mine.' For the first time, he noticed what she was wearing. A long black dress, as if she was in mourning, and a ridiculous pendulum thingy round her neck, on a bit of old cord. 'What about the pearls?' he said gruffly. 'I mean, you look very nice and all that. But I'd've thought the pearls would look a lot better. The pearls I gave you for Christmas.'

Sylvia ignored his suggestion and pressed on with her confession. 'What I mean, darling, is that this is your birthday party as well as the Queen's. I've told everyone, you're fifty-three next week, so this is a joint party. Everyone's bringing presents and we're going to have games and . . .' She stopped. Her husband's face was aflame. His usually watery-blue eyes were the colour of steel plate. It was only a silly old party, what difference did it make?

'How dare you?' Noel roared. 'How dare you interfere? I wouldn't dream of insinuating myself on Her Majesty's festivities. I don't want virtual strangers bringing me birthday presents. I don't want party games and . . .'

'Not even a birthday cake?' his wife squeaked, in the little girl's voice she had always relied upon when facing her father's wrath. 'It's a beautiful cake. Marjorie made it and I've got tons of candles and . . .'

Noel was shaking. He was aware his anger was out of all proportion to Sylvia's offence, but rules and protocol existed for a reason; they protected people from themselves.

'Take that damn thing off,' he bellowed, pointing at his wife's neck. 'You look ridiculous.'

Sylvia's hand flew protectively to her charm. 'I couldn't, I can't,' she mumbled, her cheeks reddening.

He stepped forward, grabbing the cord. 'Of course you can,' he replied. He pulled hard and it fell to the floor, the cheap ceramic splintering in pieces. 'Good riddance,' he added defiantly. Embarrassment at his uncustomary display of emotion was beginning to edge out his anger.

Sylvia threw herself at her husband. 'Look what you've done, look what you've done. I hate you, I hate you,' she screamed, like a thwarted child in the nursery. 'You've broken the spell,' she added, then stopped abruptly, aware of what she'd let slip.

The Deputy High Commissioner's voice was icy. 'What spell?' he asked.

She told him. She told him she wanted him to share her bed more often, that she longed for a family and that she was frightened that, one day, he would abandon her and retreat back to a Britain that had never existed, galloping around on Starburst, in search of what had never been. 'Happy ever after for you,' she sniffed. 'But not for me.'

She expected a modicum of sympathy, perhaps an under-standing of the good will behind her birthday arrangements, possibly even an undertaking to consider the issue of a child. Starburst, she knew, would be sacrosanct. Noel rose, and for one brief, insane moment Sylvia, nourished by romantic fiction, believed that her husband was about to literally sweep her off her feet and ravish her passionately on the bed. Instead, he turned his back.

'Go to your room,' was all he said.

Chapter Nineteen

It looked a picture. Ella sat on the verandah stairs and watched, unnoticed, as the Queen's Birthday Party unfolded before her. The tongas and cars had come and gone all evening. Now, the main area was filled with guests, some eating, some drinking, some dancing. The military band that had played a welcome at the beginning of the reception had been replaced by a group of Anglo-Indian gentlemen and a lady singer. Ella knew the song, because her father played it on his tape recorder. 'I'm feeling so bad . . . I hope you make the music, dreamy and sad . . . I could tell you a lot . . . But you've got to be true to your code . . . So make it one for my baby and one more for the road . . .'

A number of Pakistani wives were without burquahs and dressed spectacularly – shalwar-qamiz and dupattas heavily sequinned, embroidered and hand-painted. Sylvia was wearing a black frock, which Ella decided made her look like a stick of liquorice. Presents for Mr Hargreave-Smith had piled up on a table near the plinth. He'd looked sad when the band played 'God Save the Queen' and even sadder when everyone sang, 'Happy Birthday to you . . . Happy Birthday dear Deputy High Commissioner . . .' followed by 'He's a Jolly Good Fellow'.

Belle had waved at Ella from the verandah of The Residence, where she sat with a record player and records, waiting for the lady to stop singing. She wasn't wearing an evening dress, just a black shirt and slacks, and she'd spent a long time talking first to Dan Cockcroft and then to Aunty Marjorie. Dan kept bringing them both drinks.

Twice during the evening, Alice had left the party to suggest to Ella that it was time for bed. Each time, truthfully, Ella had told her mother that she was easily the prettiest lady at the party. Bedtime had been postponed.

Later, as Belle was playing one of the records that Dan had brought – 'Sixteen tons and what do you get? Another day older and deeper in debt,' a big black car pulled up and the driver, in army uniform, opened the rear door. Ella beamed when she saw Colonel Ashraf Khan Afridi step out, splendid in a tuxedo.

He spotted the little girl instantly. 'My Cinderella,' he said, laughing and kissing her hand. 'And why aren't you at the ball?' For one giddy moment, Ella thought he was going to sweep her into the midst of the dancing couples, who would stand back, amazed, as they waltzed like no couple had ever danced before. Instead, he put one hand up the other sleeve of his jacket. 'Watch!' he ordered.

'Abracadabra!' Ash shouted above the music. 'Abracadabra!' And he pulled out a long sliver of pale green seethrough material heavily embroidered with silver threads and sequins. The dupatta shimmered in the fairy lights like an exotic snake. Throwing his head back and laughing, Ash hurled it in Ella's direction. She thought the dupatta would float in the air forever.

'Allow me,' she heard her Prince Charming say. But he was no longer paying her any attention. He was talking to an unescorted Betty Brooking, and offering her his arm.

Ella watched as Uncle Ash and Betty came into view of The Residence's verandah. She saw Marjorie Rockingham look up, just as Aunty Belle tried to dance with Mr Rockingham. Then, Aunty Marjorie burst into tears and ran off through the darkness on the edge of the lawn, towards her house. Someone turned up the volume on the player. 'How much is that doggie in the window? The one with the waggley tail? How much is that doggie in the window? I do hope that doggie's for sale . . .' So only Ella saw her flight.

Later, the girl curled herself up on one of the verandah chairs. She was almost asleep when Sylvia persuaded the remaining guests to play musical chairs. Ella remembered a lot of the grown-ups falling over, skirts flying, shirt tails hanging out, and Mr Hargreave-Smith and her father standing to one side, not taking part, like children whom nobody wants to pick for their team.

Piers Rockingham had carefully wrapped the battered leather-bound copy of *The English Gardener* in tasteful navy-blue paper. He had waited all evening for the appropriate moment. Now, he seized his chance. He saw Harry Webster join Noel and Bill Jackson, observing the party games, and he sauntered over. At a break in the conversation, Piers produced the book from behind his back with a flourish. Thrusting it into Noel's hands, he began to quote from Cobbett. 'It is far better to be in the greenhouse than to be blubbering over a stupid novel or, worse still – ' Piers raised his finger, as the three men gazed at him as if he'd gone completely mad – 'or, worse still, to be trapped in the injurious enjoyments of the card table.'

'What on earth are you going on about, man?' Hargreave-Smith asked, crossly. It had been a difficult and unsettling night for the Deputy High Commissioner. Too much that was different, including the tenor of his relationship with Sylvia.

Piers patted the parcel in his boss's hands. 'Open it, sir. I think you'll like it,' he added smugly.

Noel did as he was told. He read the title blankly and said, 'Most kind.' Privately, he wondered what on earth had possessed the man to buy a book on a subject in which he had about as much interest as a blacksmith had in a gearbox.

He put the book, somewhat carelessly, in Piers' opinion,

on the tray of the nearest waiter, who bore it away to the pile of presents on a distant table.

'Sylvia said you were rather keen on his stuff on gardening. It wasn't that easy to find, I can tell you,' Piers added petulantly.

Harry Webster seized the opportunity to goad. 'Gardening? Surely not, Piers. Didn't you know? Noel, here, is planning a trek around the south-east of England, on horseback, following in Cobbett's footsteps. Or perhaps that should be hoofprints. More countryside than gardening. You should write your own book, old man,' he added, addressing Hargreave-Smith directly. '*Rural Rides Revisited*. Bill's read the original, haven't you, old boy? Part of a good grammar-school education. Poor Piers. Shame the public-school curriculum is so blasted narrow, what?' Webster added, before walking away, chuckling with pleasure at the mischief he'd just made.

Noel, too, made his excuses and moved to a group of guests saying their farewells. After he'd gone, Piers kicked at the leg of the nearest table savagely.

Bill lit up a cigarette, drew on it deeply, then observed casually, 'Difficult, isn't it?'

Piers shook his head. 'I haven't a clue what you're on about,' he answered.

Bill ignored his response. 'Do you know why the DHC imagines he and I have a special bond? Do you know why he thinks I'm such an interesting chap? I don't think it can be because I lick his arse better than you do. I don't even think it's because I play Snap! with poor, misguided Sylvia. Shall I tell you the real reason why Hargreave-Smith has taken to me?' Bill continued. 'You'll be pleased to hear it's got nothing to do with me personally. It's because of the romanticised crap that he carries around in his head. He sees me as salt of the earth, whereas you, Piers, old man, are sadly regarded as the intruder. You are the son of a boxwallah, and therefore to be despised.' Bill was enjoying himself.

Piers spluttered, 'Boxwallah? What do you mean, boxwallah?'

His junior raised an eyebrow. 'It grieves me to say this, Piers, but, in the boss's eyes, you're the wrong sort. He's at the top, I'm at the bottom, and you are a boxwallah in the middle who has ideas beyond his station. He can't abide your lot – the upstarts, the exploiters, the dirty mill-owners who carved up his beautiful countryside in the Industrial Revolution and put my ancestors to the machines. You can buy all the bloody gardening books you like, Piers, old man, but, as far as Noel's concerned, you're just not his cup of tea. And never will be. You are the pool from which salesmen, poofs and traitors are drawn. He doesn't like you – and there's not a damn thing you can do about it. Tragic, isn't it?'

Bill walked away before Piers could think of a reply. He knew the man would make him pay dearly but it had been more than worth it.

Ella dreamt she was falling, and awoke with a start. Somebody had put her to bed and left her slippers on. Her bedroom door leading out to the hall was ajar. She walked on to the verandah. She waited until her eyes had adjusted to the near dark, then she realised that the trestle tables and chairs had already been stacked in neat piles, the carpets rolled. Large converted oil-drums had been filled, one with empty bottles, the second with piles of cut flowers. She could smell their perfume across the drive.

She walked across the gravel, and jumped as something ahead of her, startled by her steps, scattered stones – probably a lizard. Somewhere nearby, a cock crew, impatient for the dawn, but the dogs lay quiet. She ran straight across the lawn. Unusually, the door to the secret garden was ajar. On the other side, someone had stacked heavy stones. An adult determined to gain entrance would have sent them flying

157

noisily. Ella knew that Mr Hargreave-Smith wouldn't have any need to do that, and nor would Shafi. So who else had become an intruder like herself? Fear almost made her turn and run back to the safety of the bungalow, curiosity proved stronger.

The layout of the garden and the maze now offered no surprises. Over several visits, Ella had come to know the ground well. Now, as she zig-zagged in and around the half-dead bushes, she heard the rustle of leaves, a murmur of voices, a woman's stifled laugh, and breathing. Could Sylvia be out here too? Or Shafi and a friend? But Shafi didn't have any friends.

The blackness of the night was lifting. Shadows took on a familiar form. She saw the bench, the lion's foot. Ella lifted it, retrieved her exercise book, and rolled it up in her hand. Then, she turned the corner of a hedge, so that the front of the hut came into view. Uncle Ash, his back to Ella, was on top of a woman who was crying out, as if hurt. He was holding her arms out from her side, his hands in hers. She was spread-eagled and he was lying on top of her as if she was his cross.

Ella caught a flash of black. For a moment, she imagined that she'd glimpsed her mother's hair. Why would Uncle Ash be hurting her? What should she do? Then, she realised that it wasn't hair. It was a long, flimsy dupatta, covering the woman's head. Ella's eyes darted from the scarf to Ash Khan's trousers. They were round his ankles. 'Please, please . . .' the woman was saying over and over, and now her arms were round Uncle Ash's body, but, to Ella's surprise, she wasn't trying to shove him away, she was holding him tight.

The girl shut her eyes. Whatever was happening was too horrible, too awful, too strange. It was so ugly, she had to look again. In the few seconds since she had closed her eyes, everything had altered. The woman was sitting with her naked back to Ella, shaking as if she would never stop. The dupatta had slipped on to her shoulders and the girl could see from the yellow hair and the profile of her face that it was Marjorie Rockingham. Her husband had appeared from nowhere and was kneeling on the other side of Uncle Ash, who lay face forward.

Suddenly, as Ella watched, Mr Rockingham pulled his wife towards him, stuffing the scarf in her mouth as he did so. Aunty Marjorie punched silently at his white dinner-shirt, leaving a bright-crimson trail down his chest. It was then Ella realised that both the Rockinghams' hands were streaked with blood. Somebody was bleeding.

Instinctively, she began to get to her feet, to open her mouth to speak, to offer to run to get help, when she found herself pushed roughly back under cover. Shafi's face loomed above hers, ordering silence.

Mr Rockingham began to walk towards their hiding place, while, behind him, his wife cried quietly. Ella froze. He stopped and turned around. 'Don't move,' he snapped at his sobbing wife, and sprinted past her and Shafi towards the garden door.

Ella could see the gardener's face clearly now. His brown skin was dappled with blotches of white. His eyes were bloodshot, like her mother's when she had too much to drink, but there was no alcohol on Shafi's breath. He pushed his cap back on his head, and she noticed that his hands were trembling. Until that point, Ella had experienced fear, but it had see-sawed with excitement, a sense that she was taking part in a mysterious make-believe adventure; another party game for grown-ups. The sight of Shafi's face dispelled that instantly. Now, she knew terror.

'Come,' he whispered. And they both slipped away from their hiding place to the door. A few minutes later, Ella sat down on a fallen tree trunk, in the compound's undergrowth well away from the secret garden. She put her head in her hands and her exercise book on her lap and rocked backwards and forwards, trying to make sense of what she had seen. Had Uncle Ash been punishing Aunty Marjorie? Was he alive or dead?

Shafi put a hand on her shoulder, and crouched down in front of her. 'Say nothing,' he said, agitated and sweating. His years of longing for the liberation of death had now been replaced by a determination to survive the aftermath of whatever it was that he and the child had just seen. 'Say nothing about tonight, Missy Ella. Don't speak. Me and you big friends for a long time. You are very pukka girl. I like very much. I go now,' he added.

'Shafi,' Ella said. 'Is the Pakistani sahib hurt? What's happened? Why did we run?'

He shook his head. He had no answers for such questions. He touched Ella's cheek then pushed her in the direction of the lawn. He waited until he saw that she had returned safely to the bungalow, before retreating to the servants' quarters.

Ella, still holding fast to her exercise book, slid into her bed, pulling the sheet over her head, not this time to fend off falling lizards, but to shut out what she didn't understand.

Chapter Twenty

The scream cut through Alice Jackson's dream. Shaking Bill awake, she ran into her daughter's room. Ella was sitting up in bed, tears streaming down her face, pointing at the wardrobe. Its door had swung open. Alice couldn't make any sense of what she was saying. Her shoulders were hunched with grief, and she was hiccoughing and crying. Only fragments emerged.

'Mr Rockingham . . . he's come after me . . . Aunty Marjorie was crying . . . he put stuff in her mouth . . . and Uncle Ash was lying there asleep and it was all bloody . . . I want you, Mummy, I want you . . .'

Bill was the first to the bed, wrapping his arms around Ella, stroking her head. He whispered in his daughter's ear, 'It's only a dream, a nasty nightmare. Look, it's morning. Everything's all right. Nothing's happened. Mummy and Dad are here. We'll look after you.'

Her sobs began to grow calmer. 'Can I come in your bed?' she asked.

'I'm not—' Alice began.

Bill interrupted, signalling at her over Ella's head. 'Hop on, I'll give you a piggy back,' he suggested to his daughter.

Halfway across the room, Ella began to cry again, her tears trickling down the back of her father's neck.

'You're going to be cross with me,' she sobbed on his shoulder. 'You're going to be so cross. But it wasn't my fault. I promise it wasn't my fault. Shafi was there, he saw too, he knows,' she added, as if aware, in the midst of her terror, that she would never be believed without an adult's corroboration.

An awful fear took hold of Alice. 'Has anybody touched you? Has anyone hurt you?' she asked, lifting her daughter from her husband's shoulders and holding her close, stroking the hair from her eyes. 'Don't be afraid. We won't be cross.'

Ella slowly tried to describe scenes which had made no sense to her. She'd seen Aunty Marjorie and Uncle Ash on the floor, perhaps fighting, or perhaps not. Then Mr Rockingham had appeared and Aunty Marjorie was crying and there was a lot of blood and Shafi told her to run away.

'Do you think something horrible has happened to Uncle Ash? Will he be all right? Is he playing about again?' she added, brightening at the thought.

Her parents exchanged glances. 'Christ,' Bill Jackson muttered under his breath, dressing as he spoke. 'Jesus bloody Christ. I told Ash he'd go too far one day. But Marjorie Rockingham? I can't believe it . . .' He turned to his daughter, one leg in a pair of shorts. 'Are you sure you saw blood, Ella?' he asked gently. The girl nodded her head as her eyes filled with tears again.

Alice sat on the bed next to her daughter. 'You are telling us the truth, aren't you?' she asked. 'We won't be cross if you tell us, you know, if you've been telling—'

'Oh for God's sake, Alice,' Bill interrupted his wife. 'Can't you see the state she's in? Of course she's telling the bloody truth. I'll go over to the garden and then I'll see Shafi. He'll know what's gone on. You give Ash a ring at home. If he's not there, leave a message telling him to call as soon as he gets in. If he's hurt, he might have gone to the hospital.' Bill checked his watch. It was just before six. He and Ash had arranged to play tennis at 8.00 am. He never missed tennis.

Within minutes, Bill was sprinting through the maze,

shouting as he ran. 'Ash,' he called. 'Ash, where are you? Are you OK?' At the rear of the hut, he stopped and walked cautiously around it, unsure what he might find.

Noel Hargreave-Smith was standing with his back to him, hands in his pockets, staring into space. 'Morning, Bill,' he greeted him, without turning round. 'Just having a bit of a ponder. Lost something, have you?'

Ten minutes later, Bill was walking towards the servants' quarters, his temper beginning to rise. If Ella had sent him on a fool's errand, she would be very sorry indeed. Perhaps Alice was right, perhaps his daughter did suffer from too fertile an imagination. He was annoyed with himself, because he had told Hargreave-Smith a lie. Why, he didn't know. Perhaps because the child's story now appeared too fantastical. He had told him that he was looking for Ella and thought that she might be hiding somewhere nearby. 'I thought I heard you call a different name?' Hargreave-Smith had remarked. Bill had pretended not to hear. He could see no signs of a body, of blood, of anything other than what looked like an ordinary changing hut in the middle of a maze that had seen better days. 'Good party last night?' his boss had asked with a sigh, then added, before Bill could reply, 'No, I didn't think so either.'

Now, in the servants' quarters, patrolled by emaciated chickens, Bill knocked on the door of Shafi's room, one of several surrounding a communal courtyard. He knocked for a second time. 'Shafi,' he called through the door. 'It's me. Jackson sahib.' No answer.

'*Asalam aleikum*,' someone said behind him. Bill turned to see Shafi coming towards him from across the yard. He explained he had been to the mosque and then to the market for breakfast. No, he hadn't seen Missy Ella, not since yesterday. No, he hadn't been in the garden in the night. No, he hadn't seen the soldier sahib.

'Thank you,' Bill said.

'*Koi bat nai*,' Shafi answered politely. 'It's no problem.'

While Bill was away, Alice tried to reach Ashraf Khan's home by telephone several times. The operator provided first one excuse and then another for not making the connection. 'Engineers no damn good, memsahib,' he explained chattily at one point. She was in the dining room drinking coffee when Bill returned. He ignored her and went straight to Ella's room. She was dressed for school and sitting on her bed, scribbling in a battered exercise book.

'Ella,' Bill said, more irritated than annoyed. 'What the hell is going on? I've been to the garden and it looks perfectly normal, no blood, no bodies. And Shafi didn't have a clue what I was talking about. It's a good job I didn't go barging into the Rockinghams' and make a complete fool of myself.'

His daughter's response surprised him. She didn't defend herself, or apologise or admit to any fabrication. Instead, silently, she resumed writing as if her life depended upon it.

At the Peshawar Tennis Club, Bill waited for Ash for forty-five minutes. First on the tennis court, then drinking coffee on the lawn, then in the secretary's office, fruitlessly trying to call Ash's home and army head quarters. Of course, nothing had happened in the maze, he told himself, but if it did transpire that Ash had been hurt, he would personally take Piers Rockingham apart limb from bloody limb. And sod the bloody pension.

At 8.45 am, a jubilant switchboard operator finally succceded in putting him through to the Khan residence. A servant told him that the sahib was not at home. 'And the memsahib?' Bill asked. As he waited for the servant to bring Ash's wife to the telephone, it dawned on him that he hadn't a clue how to word his concern, without causing embarrassment.

He hadn't seen Ash leave the party but then he hadn't seen

anyone leave, as he'd taken to his bed soon after he'd had words with Rockingham. If Ash had been caught with Marjorie and there had been a fight, then it was perfectly feasible for him to lie low for a couple of days. Or, perhaps, Ash had left the party with a different woman and was still busy being wayward elsewhere?

A soft female voice came on the line. 'Good morning,' Ash's wife said. 'Is there some way I can help?'

Bill fumbled through an introduction, before blurting out, 'I wondered if you'd seen Ash . . . What I mean is . . . well, you see, we had a tennis game arranged this morning and he's not turned up, and . . .'

The tone of the woman's voice remained even. 'My husband told me he was staying at the club last night,' she said. 'He said he had to leave at dawn to go to the Jammu and Kashmir region on army business. He said he'd only been given his orders yesterday. It's always one sort of emergency or another, isn't it? You know how these things are, Mr Jackson. But I am sorry he didn't think to cancel your game . . .'

As Bill replaced the receiver, he should have felt a sense of relief, but he didn't. *You know how these things are, Mr Jackson.* Bill knew very little about Ash's private life. So, no, he didn't know how these things were.

In the afternoon, after lunch, goodbyes were said to Dan Cockcroft. He left for Abbotobad, hungover and oblivious to the Jacksons' early morning drama. Alice and Bill asked Ella to come into the sitting room. Bill was cross – less so now with the child and more so with Ash for his lack of thought and with Alice because of her smugness. Once again, she had been proved right. Ella must have thought it all up.

'Ash is away with the army,' he said curtly, as he gestured to Ella to sit on the sofa.

The child's face broke into a smile. 'So he's not hurt after all?' she asked delightedly. 'Have you seen him?'

Alice took two steps across the carpet and gripped the little girl by the shoulders, shaking her hard. 'Stop it, Ella. Just stop it!' she hissed. 'Just stop this nonsense instantly. I think you started all this because you're jealous if Ash pays attention to anyone else. Is that it, you silly little girl?'

'Alice!' Bill interrupted. 'Let me handle this.'

Ella's bottom lip had begun to quiver uncontrollably. She looked for sympathy in her father's face but saw only cold-ness. If it would make him happy, she would willingly say she had imagined every minute of her time in the garden; every single second. All he had to do was ask. But he didn't. Instead, Bill pulled up a chair and, facing his daughter, took both her hands in his, and looked into her eyes intently as if searching for the truth.

'What's this really about, pea hen?' he asked, more gently.

Anger flashed in Alice. 'Oh Christ, give her a medal, why don't you, Bill?' she snapped. 'Really, do you have to be so bloody pathetic?' She turned her attention to Ella and took up a position behind Bill's chair, as if to correct any notion in her daughter's head that her parents were adopting anything other than a united front.

'What Daddy's about to tell you is that we've decided that it would do you a lot of good to go to St Winifred's. In a couple of days, in fact. Isn't that right, Bill?' Her husband nodded his head in agreement, miserably.

A single tear slid slowly down Ella's face. Soon, she told herself, she would move into that place where she felt nothing. Then, it would be all right.

In the early evening, Alice packed Ella's trunk while her daughter watched silently, sitting on her bedside chair. Alice could tell from the set of her mouth that she was anything but contrite – on the contrary, she now appeared almost defiant, as if she didn't care at all where she went, or when.

'I hope you're taking in what I say,' Alice said, folding vests and shirts and pyjamas, neatly labelled with the words, Ella Jackson.

'I want only good behaviour at St Winifred's, do you hear me, young lady? No fibs, no stories, no creeping around in the middle of the night, no going where you shouldn't be.

'You know what happens to naughty girls who tell stories, don't you?' Alice asked. Ella decided it was best not to answer. She shrugged, since no response at all might antagonise her mother even further. It was a gesture Alice interpreted as a cockiness.

Her mother continued, 'Nobody loves them and they get left in boarding school for ever. For ever, mind.' Alice saw the flicker of fear in her daughter's eyes and knew she had gone too far. Instantly, she softened, her anger gone like a boil lanced. She knelt down and put her arms around the child's thin body. Ella tensed, wary of her mother's change of mood.

Alice whispered, 'Daddy and I love you, Ella, you know that, don't you? We only want what's best for you. Really, we do. One day, when you've grown up, you'll realise just how much we sacrificed especially for you.'

Later that evening, the Rockinghams did something they hadn't done for a very long time. They instructed the servants to lay a carpet on the lawn in front of their verandah, and to bring out table, chairs and standard lamp. Then, they sat together enjoying their drinks.

Alice pointed out the scene to her husband. 'I ask you,' she said. 'Do they look like a couple with blood on their hands?'

Chapter Twenty-One

An hour out of Peshawar, driving east, the road began to cut into the mountainside, bending and winding upwards. Gradually, the colours grew lusher, the valleys shrouded in purple and pale-blue clouds. Ella decided they were so high, the first floor of heaven must have already been passed. One by one, the hill stations came and went, each straddling the road untidily. During the Raj, they had been the refuge of the women and children who left the men to roast on the plains during the hot months. After independence, affluent families based in Lahore and Karachi and Peshawar often maintained a permanent second home in the hills, taking over bungalows and villas with names such as Bluebell Cottage and Dingley Dell House. Chowdiagalli, home of St Winifred's, was the last hill station in the chain.

It consisted of one main street, inevitably called The Mall, lined with souvenir shops, an Anglican church, a Catholic cathedral, a small mosque and several tea shops and guest houses. Most offered 'Traditional English Breakfast', except that the bacon was mutton and the toast a close cousin to cardboard.

The richer residents lived above The Mall, high on the ridge, in lavish houses, some modelled on Swiss chalets, others ugly marble monstrosities with views of the Pir Panjal range and beyond into Kashmir. Here, too, were the expensive hotels with tennis courts and croquet lawns and honeymoon suites and children's playgrounds with swings and see-saws made of wrought-iron – burning hot in the spring sun; freezing and sticking to the skin in the snowbound winter. All year round, in Chowdiagalli, the twin perfumes were those of pinewood being burnt for fuel and lamb and beef cooking on charcoal.

St Winifred's lay a mile out of town, built in a dip. It consisted of a small chapel and a line of wooden huts, employed as classrooms, linked by a corrugated iron walkway to an attractive Victorian four-storey grey-stone building, covered in ivy. The main house backed up against the mountain which cast a permanent shadow on its interior. The land at the front of the school dropped away gently, offering a natural play area. To the right, was a large wood, on a sharp incline, which offered a short cut to The Mall. To the left, was a dirt track, which linked the school to the single road in and out of Chowdiagalli.

St Winifred's, established in 1877, took female boarders from the age of three to eighteen. In practice, apart from the Anglo-Indian girls, the majority left between twelve and fifteen, many destined for arranged marriages. The pupils came from all over Pakistan, from the regions of Sindh, Baluchistan, the Punjab, and the North-West Frontier Province, as well as outside the country, from Kashmir and Afghanistan. All teaching was in English, the only religious instruction was that of the Church of England, supervised by the deaconesses, 'The Grey Ladies', who made up some of the senior staff, dressed in grey flannel cowls. While girls were expected to attend church and chapel, they were not required to eat pork.

St Winifred's main vacation was dictated by the weather – three months' break, from December to March, when the snow lay thick. Even in spring, when the stone-flagged school was heated in the evenings by stinking paraffin stoves, the temperature came close to that of an ice box.

The first term of the school year had been underway for five weeks when Ella Jackson was brought to St Winifred's on the afternoon of Tuesday 24 April. As with many parents before them, the Jacksons were neither offered nor requested a tour of the school, since the facilities (or lack of them) were not a deciding factor. St Winifred's was the only boarding school on offer in the North-West Frontier Province.

Still, Alice was hugely impressed by the little she did see, misguidedly assuming that the décor and ambience of the head's sitting room applied to the whole establishment. 'The deaconess was so pleased to see Ella,' she recounted to Betty later. 'She looked a bit strict at first, dressed all in grey, but she gave Ella a little hug and took us into her sitting room. It was so comfortable. There was a lovely Axminster carpet and cosy three-piece suite and a huge, roaring log fire.

'The head told us there are only three pure-British girls in the school, all the rest are Pakistani, with about three-dozen Anglo-Indians, so she expects Ella to set a high standard. Then she called for a very jolly Pakistani girl called Zuhra, to come and collect her. This girl couldn't do enough for Ella. So friendly and polite.'

Zuhra Iqbal, a girl with striking almond-shaped eyes, had the longest plaits that Ella had ever seen, made even longer by black woollen extensions with tassels on the ends. She wore a blue gymslip over baggy shalwar trousers. They were almost the same height, although Zuhra said that she was nearly twelve.

Her previous amiability in front of the adults was immediately replaced by a distinctly hostile air as she directed Ella through a door on the right of the main reception area. The contrast between what was on one side of the door and what was on the other reminded Ella of the little weather men on cuckoo clocks, smiling in the sunshine and crying in the rain.

She found herself in a long, wide corridor, so dark that it took time to adjust to the gloom. It was uncarpeted, the walls painted brown. Without speaking, Zuhra began to give her a speedy tour.

Ella had calculated during the journey from Peshawar that she had exactly nine weeks, five days and four hours at St Winifred's until the first holiday, a ten-day break at the end of June. Her mother had promised to come for a Sunday visit in a fortnight. She hung on to that promise for comfort now, but the tears were never far away.

The dining room had a stone floor and wooden tables and benches. 'It's always cold in here,' Zuhra announced with relish. 'But no one spends much time eating anyway, the food is so horrid.' She pinched Ella's spindly arm viciously. 'You're fat, but you won't be for long,' she said with satisfaction.

Through large, open swing doors, Ella could see village girls outside, some younger than her, gossiping hard, using tree trunks as makeshift tables, cutting lumps of yellow fatty meat and chopping vegetables, their glass bangles jangling as they did so. Alongside them, on open charcoal fires, huge blackened pots steamed. 'We're always finding bits of glass in our food. You do know that if you swallow glass you're dead, don't you?' Zuhra stated matter-of-factly. 'In true life,' she added menacingly.

The girl pushed Ella out of the room and pointed to the stairs. 'To the dormitories,' she instructed. Upstairs, on the threshold of each room, Ella's weepiness increased, an ache was spreading through her body. The dormitories were named after local flowers – Speedwell, Salvia, Violet, Periwinkle. They were long, narrow rooms, each holding twenty or thirty beds, with linoleum on the floor, and walls painted in a green that reminded Ella of the frogs that she and Tommy used to fish out of the club pool. Zuhra informed her that each girl was allowed a chair on which to fold her next day's clothes, and a doll or bear in the centre of the bed. The rest of her uniform would be kept in a wardrobe in the corridor. In each dorm-itory, one corner was curtained-off, to allow the monitor, a senior girl, some privacy.

'This is your dormitory,' Zuhra added curtly, stopping outside a room labelled 'Buttercup'. Here, as in the other dormitories, small windows were open, making the room even more chilly. But not cold enough to conquer the smell, the odour that comes from too many unwashed bodies and spices cooking and damp clothes and cheap talcum powder of the kind that Belle used in her bedroom. Ella ached even more. She wondered what Surindabash might be doing now, and Tommy. And if her friend, Sherry, had been told that she wouldn't be going back to the convent. Not ever. And whether Uncle Ash was dead. Or perhaps she really had imagined it all . . .

Then, Ella noticed that one of the beds in Buttercup was occupied. A small face, belonging to a girl of five or six, peered above the blankets. 'What's wrong with her?' she asked Zuhra.

'Sick,' she replied. 'Or pretending to be.'

Ella shivered. She might die in this place and nobody would ever know.

Zuhra pointed to a bed halfway down the room. On it was Ella's trunk. 'Unpack,' she commanded abruptly. Ella wished the other girl would go away, so she could climb under the covers and cry. To her horror, tears began to well up again now. Furiously, head down, she began to take out her clothes. Her nose dripped. First came the heart-shaped pyjama case made by her mother. 'Not allowed,' Zuhra said. Next came the framed photograph of her parents, taken at a cocktail party, arms around each other. 'Not allowed,' said Zuhra. Then she retrieved a small, yellow china duck, a lucky mascot. 'Not allowed,' Zuhra repeated impassively. Ella's fighting spirit rose. Two items she intended to keep close by her side, no matter what. She gave Zuhra a determined look.

One was her increasingly battered exercise book. The letter 's' had been smudged almost to invisibility. Ella almost smiled as she read, '*A Hi tory of Insects*.' The second was the dupatta Uncle Ash had given her on that night. It lay now at the bottom of her trunk, pale green, shaped like a puddle of blood. The cold had made Ella's nose run again. She wiped it on the back of her hand. She picked up the two items and held them to her chest, staring stony-faced at the Pakistani girl. Zuhra remained silent.

Finally, she shrugged and said, 'If you want to keep something that's not allowed, it's up to you. But don't put it under your mattress. That's where they look first. Here, I'll show you what to do.'

Zuhra took the book and the scarf and folded one around the other. Then, she slid the two between the second and third blankets on the bed, smoothing the covers flat.

'Thanks.' Ella smiled tentatively. Perhaps she had found a friend after all.

'If you get caught and say I told you what to do,' Zuhra answered, not returning her smile, 'I'll do something really, really, really horrible to you that you won't forget. If you think you're miserable now,' she added confidently, 'just wait until Miss Patterson gets hold of you. She really is bloody hell, I'm telling you.'

Mabel Patterson's room at St Winifred's was on the third floor, overlooking the playground. It could be noisy, but she had requested the room specifically, because evil requires vigilance. As the Bible says, 'The evil spirit worketh in the children of disbelief . . .' And she knew that St Winifred's had an abundance of disbelieving heathens camouflaged as church-going Christians. Miss Patterson's room was furnished in accordance with her view that indulgence weakened the spirit. Other members of staff, even the most devout, had customised their rooms – warm carpets, thick

173

curtains, perhaps a gramophone player, some cushions. Miss Patterson's private domain was only suited to a permanent state of mortification.

She had recently acquired a small cotton rug to put by the bed, because years of praying on the bare linoleum had aggravated the arthritis in her knees. In addition, she had her books, a wireless, an upright chair and she chose to hang her limited wardrobe behind a drab cotton curtain.

Winter and summer, Miss Patterson wore a grey cotton dress, long-sleeved and buttoned to the neck, and crocheted mittens. In winter, pullovers would be added in layers. Her skin was translucent milky white; bright-blue veins ran across her temples, like cracks in the ice. Her hair was long and silver-grey (nobody knew quite how long, but her younger pupils swore that, like Rapunzel, she could let her hair down out of her window and it would almost reach the ground) and she wore it with a centre parting, coiled on the nape of her neck.

Miss Patterson had taught at St Winifred's for fourteen years. Aged sixty-two, she had arrived in India as a lady's companion in the 1920s. Soon after, she realised that her true vocation lay in teaching. She studied for a diploma in Quetta and eventually became an employee of the Lahore Diocesan Board. For Miss Patterson, education was an act of worship. Her overriding aim was not to satisfy an appetite for learning, but to instil humility and obedience to the Creator's will. The more literate a child, the better she could understand the consequences of transgression. 'The fear of the Lord is the beginning of knowledge', Proverbs one, verse seven.

Miss Patterson had reduced life to the most simple of equations. Pleasure equals sin and therefore should be extracted from life. The Pakistani girls in her class ranged in age from ten to twelve, depending upon their ability with what Miss Patterson always referred to as the mother tongue. British girls were often younger. All were taught that singing and dancing were the devil's tools. ' "The whole world is lying in the power of the wicked one," John five, verse nineteen,' Miss Patterson would remind her children. Her God was the God of the Old Testament, vengeful and angry, rather like herself. She had no need to wield the cane – her ability to evoke fear was so much more lethal.

Now, she stood at the window, surveying the scene in the playground below, using an ancient pair of binoculars. Small dust-storms of rust-red clay were continually being kicked up by girls skipping and chasing and hopping. Girls at play before Monday tea and prep. Her attention was drawn to the corner of the playground nearest to her. Half a dozen of her girls were sitting on the bank. Standing in front of them was Zuhra Iqbal, waving a stick. Miss Patterson spanned the line, then reached for her heavy wool jacket. What she had just witnessed simply would not do.

Five minutes later, Zuhra continued chattering, pretending to be unaware of her teacher's presence. Miss Patterson took the opportunity to inspect the new girl. She had stick legs, the makings of a sty on one eye, a smattering of freckles, an open face, and a stubborn tilt to her chin. Her uniform was shabby; a hand-me-down. The girl's gymslip had been heavily darned and her cardigan ended in a shapeless frill from one too many washes. The child under inspection looked back at the teacher gravely.

'What are you playing, girls?' Miss Patterson asked.

Zuhra remained silent. Mubeena spoke up, as she always did, ferociously anxious to please. 'We're playing schools, Miss Patterson. Zuhra's the teacher.'

Miss Patterson took the stick away from Zuhra and thrust it into Ella's hands. 'I want you to be the teacher, Ella,' she instructed. 'Come now, come and stand in front of the others.'

'Why?'

The word snapped out of the air. 'Why her?' Zuhra

repeated, her tone unmistakably insolent. 'Why has she got to be the teacher? What's so special about her?' Everyone froze in the face of Zuhra's daring.

Miss Patterson looked Zuhra in the eye. 'I shall tell you why, Zuhra Iqbal. Ella is new. You have been asked to look after her. I want you to make sure you do that properly. That includes making her welcome in the games you play. No ifs and buts. Is that understood?' She turned on her heel and began to stride across the playground, making sure she was well out of earshot before the wretched child could react with her usual nonsense.

Zuhra waved her arms, as if gathering the gang to her. 'Come on,' she shouted, 'I'll race you to the wood.' The girls began to giggle and shove. Ella moved forward too. Zuhra turned to her. 'Not you,' she said. 'We don't want you. We don't like teacher's pets. Especially if they're British scum.'

Chapter Twenty-Two

Night-time. Ella both longed for and dreaded it. All that first day she had stored so many tears she felt like an overflowing bucket. Between the afternoon and bedtime, the routine of St Winifred's took over. Play, prep, then supper — black bread and soup, eight girls to a table, headed by a monitor. Each meal time, each pupil moved up a place. The two girls on the monitor's right fetched and carried and cleared for the rest of the table. Soup was followed by tuck. Again, Ella courted unwanted attention. Her mother had given her tins of Milo, a chocolate drink; Robertson's black-currant jam; Cadbury's wafer biscuits; and a large jar of pear drops. Everyone else had the gaudy orange and pink and yellow sweets from the bazaar. So they stared. Zuhra, a sulky escort, helped herself to some pear drops, until Ella hastily hid her tuck away in her locker. She wanted to be the same, not different.

Next, came a wash — St Winifred's had no running water, so each girl was given a bowl — then prayers and lights out. No talking allowed, no kiss goodnight, no attention paid to the small ones, some as young as four and five, holding tight to their pillows, as if, without them, they might sink in the night and be lost without trace.

Now, the lights were out. The moon was up at the curtainless window, just above Ella's head. It sent shadows in bars across her bed. She was too frightened to close her eyes, for fear of what she might see.

In spite of herself, Ella must have drifted into sleep. She woke with a start. A figure in white was gliding down between the beds. Ella's heart stopped. It started again as the figure went past and Ella could see in the dim light that it was an older girl, with a mass of black curly hair. She was wearing a frilly white nightgown and a cream woollen dressing-gown. Silently, she slipped into the monitor's cubicle. Ella heard whispers, giggles, the creaking of bed springs. She tucked her covers round her chin for warmth, and realised that Zuhra Iqbal, in the next bed, had her eyes wide open and was watching her. The girl turned over and said nothing.

The rising bell went at 6.00 am. 'Did you see the girl go into the monitor's cubicle last night?' Zuhra asked at bed-making, supposedly conducted in silence.

Ella, grateful for any communication, nodded enthusiastically. 'Yes,' she said, 'I did.'

Zuhra gave her a look of complete contempt. 'You must be seeing things, then,' she said.

At breakfast, a tall, striking, Anglo-Indian girl arrived. Aged sixteen or seventeen, she had coal-black straight hair cut to her chin, and full lips, permanently set in a sneer. She was unusually tall, with angular shoulders. She seemed vaguely familiar to Ella. Zuhra explained that this was their monitor, Caroline Chakrati, known as Caro. She was in charge of Buttercup, although she'd been absent before lights out on the previous night. As instructed on the previous evening, Ella moved up a place, to sit on Caro's right side. 'Hop it,' Caro instructed in a low drawl, without looking at Ella. Embarrassed, Ella sought her cue from Zuhra, who, again, was regarding her with contempt.

'Don't you know anything?' Zuhra said loudly, giving Caro an ingratiating smile. 'That's Milly's place. Nobody else sits there, do they, Caro?'

Two minutes later, almost as the head was saying grace,

Milly – Promilla Sebastian – flounced to their table. Ella recognised her instantly as the ghost she had seen floating through the dormitory. In daylight, Ella could see that she was dark-skinned and very, very pretty. She was probably Caro's age, but she was much shorter. 'Hi, honey,' Caro greeted her. Milly pulled the bench closer to her friend at the head of the table, making all the younger girls, still standing to hear grace, shuffle along to resecure their seats. Milly appeared to be in a sulk and Caro reached out to tickle her under her chin. Ella looked away, embarrassed, although why she should be embarrassed, she wasn't quite sure.

Sneaking a second look at Caro, Ella realised why she was familiar. Now, it was obvious. She was Elvis Presley's double. One of the magazines that Betty had given her had three black-and-white photographs of the singer with his quiff and his guitar, his shoulders hunched forward, and his lips in a sneer, just as Caro's were now. Momentarily, Ella forgot how unhappy she was. Poor Caro, looking like a man. Except that she didn't appear at all put out. On the contrary, Caro appeared to be loving it.

The girl kept trying to coax a smile out of Milly, calling her 'Baby' and 'Honey'. Ella left her grey porridge and black bread untouched. She wished Tommy was with her now. He would know exactly what was going on. The sudden reminder of home caught her unawares. A tear spilled before she could take control. She bit her lip hard. 'Cry baby,' Zuhra hissed.

Later that Tuesday morning, Miss Patterson had her class exactly as she wanted them – sitting in rows, backs straight, feet flat on the floor, hands on desks, looking neither to left nor right. 'What do you see in this picture, Ella?' she asked. She had pinned a large blown-up photograph on the black-board. The new girl was perplexed. It looked like a massive mushroom-shaped cloud, but, apart from that, she hadn't a clue. She flushed.

'Well, child?' Miss Patterson boomed. The other pupils began to giggle, and a forest of arms shot up. 'Tell her, class,' Miss Patterson instructed.

A triumphant chorus parroted, 'The H-bomb, Miss Patterson.'

'And what does the H-bomb do, Rukhsana?'

A thin, beaky girl with a reedy voice stood up and answered, 'It burns us alive horribly, Miss Patterson. Nobody can escape. And the strontium-ninety finds its way into our milk and our food and destroys us from the inside. Especially,' added Rukhsana dutifully, 'if we have been very, very bad.'

Ella looked from the photograph to Miss Patterson and back again. She had been very, very bad. Would she be destroyed from the inside? And what if this bomb exploded when she was here in Chowdiagalli and her parents were miles away in Peshawar? What should she do? Who could she turn too?

'The good Lord,' said Miss Patterson, as if reading her mind, fixing her eye on Ella again. 'The good Lord is our only refuge.'

She was pleased to see the impact that The Bomb had had on the new girl. The others, of course, knew her lecture off by heart. Miss Patterson tapped the monster cloud with her cane. 'Repeat after me, class,' she ordered. 'Even though the devil is on my shoulder, I shall not sin . . . Even though the devil is on my shoulder, I shall not sin . . .'

Mabel Patterson knew that Armageddon was imminent. This certainty had been born on 1 November 1952. On that day, three years and five months before Ella Jackson's arrival at St Winifred's, Eniwok Atoll in the Marshall Islands had been vapourised by a mushroom cloud twenty-five miles high and one hundred miles wide, statistics Miss Patterson repeated often to her girls. A few months later, the Russians exploded the first hydrogen bomb. The Americans, in turn, employed an even larger bomb to destroy Bikini Atoll and much else around it. Incineration in a nuclear holocaust in this world was inevitable, sooner, rather than later, Miss Patterson would say, as she passed around images of the survivors of Hiroshima. So was burning in hell for ever. 'Unless,' she would add, 'you are prepared to follow me in the ways of the Lord.'

Mystified Muslim pupils would soon surmise that the ways of the Lord primarily consisted of a series of 'Don'ts' – among them, don't dance, don't sing, don't cheek or challenge an adult. Childish exuberance, Miss Patterson regarded as the devil's calling card – ' "The whole world is lying in the power of the wicked one," John five, verse nineteen,' she would say. Passivity and piety, in her mind, were indivisible, one and the same. By this standard, it was inevitable that she would categorise Zuhra Iqbal as Lucifer's daughter. Now, however, Miss Patterson had high hopes that Ella Jackson, being British and Christian, and – so far – subdued and solemn, would show Zuhra how a well-brought-up young lady ought to behave.

'Come, come, Ella, we're waiting,' Miss Patterson said, tapping the desk with her cane. 'Are you prepared to follow the Lord?' She put a small, thin book on Ella's desk. 'Is God in your life?' she asked.

Ella looked at the book. It consisted of four double pages. Each double page was a different colour – red, white, black, yellow. There were no words. Miss Patterson picked up the book and turned each page as she explained. 'Red for the blood of Christ.' Flick. 'White for the purity that comes from good.' Flick. 'Black for the evilness of sin.' Flick. 'Yellow for the glory that is God's love. Red, white, black, yellow . . . Do you know God's love, Ella?'

The true answer to this question was that Ella wasn't entirely sure. Her religious education had been sporadic and mostly focused on Jesus, a man with long, wavy hair, riding around on a donkey, performing miracles. God had hardly figured.

Miss Patterson's irritation was increasing. She had expected an instant response, not this wavering in the presence of disbelievers. She rapped Ella's desk with her knuckles.

'What does the Good Book say? If ye have faith, nothing shall be impossible to you . . . Stand up, Ella. Stand up, girl. Tell us all how God is your protector. Speak child, speak!'

'Is he?' Ella asked, shyly getting to her feet. 'Does he? I mean, will he protect me?' Delighted by her response, the class began to giggle, wrongly assuming that the new girl had the nerve to tease Miss Patterson. But she was making a genuine enquiry. Alone, at St Winifred's, dogged by the malign Zuhra, what she needed most was somebody on her side. 'Does God protect you?' she asked. 'Even if you're bad?'

Chapter Twenty-Three

Zuhra Iqbal had declared war. For the remainder of Ella's first week, she made life impossible for her. She stole her arithmetic exercise book; sent her to the wrong classroom for geography; hid her outdoor shoes; and took every opportunity to remind the other girls that Ella was the teacher's pet. Ella's only defence was to remain silent. And she counted the days – thirteen, twelve, eleven, ten – until her mother's promised visit. Ella's isolation was made worse because it soon became apparent that she found the schoolwork easy.

On Friday morning, at the beginning of an English comprehension lesson, Zuhra feigned enthusiasm. 'I bet the new girl's come first again, hasn't she, Miss Patterson? She's so clever, isn't she, Miss Patterson?'

'Zuhra, that's quite enough. Do you hear me?' the teacher instructed, giving the girl an icy glare. 'If you tried just a little bit harder you could do just as well as Ella.'

Zuhra pretended to sulk. 'I was only being nice about the new girl and saying how clever she was. Much cleverer than the rest of us . . .'

Mubeena broke in. 'If you carry on being so wicked and answering back, Zuhra Iqbal,' she whimpered, genuinely distressed, 'that blasted bomb will drop on the lot of us, I'm telling you now. So do shut up. It will, won't it, Miss Patterson?'

183

The teacher whacked the desk with her ruler. 'You have a choice, Zuhra Iqbal,' she said. 'Decide to refrain from commenting and sit quietly, or go and stand in the corridor, where you'll be less of a distraction.'

Zuhra theatrically slammed her desk shut and stood up. The other girls in the class sucked in their breath. Such insolence. As she passed Ella's desk on her way out to the corridor, Zuhra bent down and, in a loud whisper, said, 'Now, look what you've done.'

Spontaneously, Ella did exactly what her enemy intended her to do. She turned to Miss Patterson and said pleadingly, 'I'm sure she didn't mean it, Miss. I'm sure she didn't mean any harm.'

'Harm?' The old woman rolled the word round her tongue, as if it had an alien taste. 'Harm? Of course she meant harm. She has the devil in her. She's a thoroughly bad lot. She's a Muslim and—'

Zuhra stopped dead, turned, and faced the teacher. 'I'm glad I'm a Muslim. I am not bad and I'd hate to be like you!' she shouted angrily. 'You British are liars and cheats and greedy little clerks. My father says so. I'm not frightened of you or your silly bomb or your devil. So there, Miss Patterson,' she added, before running out of the classroom and banging the door behind her.

Mabel Patterson looked at the stunned class, her face impassive. 'Get out your history books,' she instructed, 'and begin reading chapter five, "The Battle of Trafalgar". I shall go and deal with Zuhra.'

Later that morning, Ella made her way to the school chapel. It was a large room with whitewashed walls and a simple altar. As punishment, Zuhra had been instructed to clean the chapel floor. This involved carrying all the benches outside, with the help of the maintenancewallah, then rubbing the linoleum with a mixture of oil and hot water, and finally polishing it until all the oil was removed.

'I'd like to help,' Ella offered, standing behind Zuhra as she scrubbed on her hands and knees.

'Go away,' was her only response.

For one brief moment Ella contemplated kicking Zuhra Iqbal right up her backside. Then she reasoned with herself. Zuhra had something that she was desperate to acquire. She must persevere. 'Give me a cloth,' she tried again. 'Two can do it far more quickly than one.'

'Is that right?' Zuhra responded sarcastically. 'I'd rather die before having help from you. So go away.'

Ella refused to be deterred. 'How long will this take you?' she asked.

Zuhra stopped scrubbing. 'Normally, it takes two days,' she replied. 'But that's because the others come and help me. I'm their leader,' she added defiantly. 'Because I won't let Miss Patterson scare me. Not one bit.'

'Why don't you mind when Miss Patterson says you're bad?' Ella asked, pursuing the real reason for her visit. 'Don't you feel bad?'

Zuhra had turned to face Ella and was now sitting back on her heels, her face flushed from her physical efforts.

'Just because she says I'm bad, it doesn't mean it's true, stupid,' she replied. 'Besides,' she added, 'I don't want to go to your heaven, so I don't care what that silly old goat, Miss Patterson, thinks. You should be a Muslim. I've got an angel looking after me. It's here on my shoulder. So how can the devil be there too? But you've got nobody. You're all alone in this place and nobody cares for you at all. If I were you, I'd be really, really scared. Now, go away.'

That night, Ella woke from a nightmare to the now familiar whispers and groans emerging from Caro's cubicle. Ella couldn't stop herself. She got out of bed and quietly walked towards the sounds. Her hand at the curtain, she stopped and looked down. She expected to be standing in a puddle of blood. But there was only cold, brown lino.

★ ★ ★

On Saturdays, the girls rose later, at 7.00 am. They had white bread for breakfast and, soon after, the vendors from Chowdiagalli drifted up to the school, their goods in baskets on their heads. They would set up shop on the drive and fight furiously for the few annas each girl was allowed to spend as pocket money. They offered coconut ice; charcoal-grilled pieces of corn on the cob, rubbed with salt and lemon; deep-fried pakoras; sweets such as *halweh*, *barfi* and *jalebi*; and the juice of sugar cane to drink.

Mubeena, chubby and constantly eating, offered to supervise Ella's transactions. 'I'll get you plenty, plenty for your annas,' she announced. 'Then you give me some and we have a damn fine bargain. OK?'

Ella understood she wasn't in a position to argue. She didn't much care. What she was most looking forward to was letter-writing, later in the morning.

Miss Patterson, ever vigilant, and on patrol, circling the vendors and the girls, overheard Mubeena's offer. 'Tell me, Mubeena,' she asked, 'why is it our good Lord was able to fast for forty days and forty nights, and you can't bear to go five minutes without putting something in your mouth? I shall look after Ella's transactions.'

The new girl hid her resentment at the latest example of Miss Patterson sabotaging her efforts to become like the rest, and dutifully handed over her five annas. She watched silently while the teacher haggled furiously with a couple of vendors. Her reward was two mangos and five gaudily wrapped toffees. 'You might appreciate coconut ice and *puris* more, child,' Miss Patterson announced, 'but they aren't good for the developed Western digestion. Mubeena, you're dribbling,' she added, as she handed over her booty.

Letter-writing at St Winifred's was a structured activity. Ella duly handed in her three pages to Miss Patterson for inspection then returned to her desk. 'Child,' the teacher called from her desk. 'Come here, please.' Ella did as she was told, her hands behind her back to hide the darn in her gymslip which was beginning to fray. She knew enough about Miss Patterson's facial mannerisms to understand that something unpleasant had occurred – and she was probably the cause of it.

The other girls watched. Some had already encountered the initiation rite now facing Ella. They, too, had experienced elation in detailing all their miseries, fears and bouts of homesickness in their first letter home, ending in a plea for rescue – only to have their hopes dashed by the hand of the censor. Miss Patterson did not approve of pessimism.

'Think how concerned and worried your parents will be about your welfare,' she intoned. 'Think how upset they will be if they discover you are wasting their good money because you are behaving in such a selfish fashion. It's your responsibility to put your good parents' fears to rest. I thought you had far more backbone than this, Ella. If you can't convey any happy events to your mother and father,' Miss Patterson concluded, 'then I suggest you write nothing at all. I will pop a note in the post.'

Privately, Miss Patterson decided she would advise the Jacksons to postpone their first visit to their daughter until she had adjusted better.

'Now, let us move on. Zuhra, bring me your letter, please.'

Zuhra began to search her desk. 'It was here a minute ago, Miss Patterson,' she said. 'It really was. I'd written just the kind of letter you like, very jolly and all that. But where has the blasted thing gone now?'

The girls began to titter. Mabel Patterson told herself to take several deep breaths. What she really loathed about Zuhra Iqbal was her sense of herself. Such confidence, such precociousness was unnatural in a child.

'Zuhra, I don't want any of your games. Remove yourself from the classroom this instant, go to the hall, and write out, "Be sure your sin will find you out," one hundred times. Is that—'

She stopped, because the new girl had stood up from her seat. 'Please, Miss Patterson,' she began, her voice trembling slightly, 'it isn't Zuhra's fault. She has written her letter. I saw her.'

'Sit down, Ella.'

The child stood firm. 'Somebody else took her letter,' she persisted, unwilling to name Mubeena. 'I saw somebody else take her letter. It's not Zuhra's fault. You're always picking on her. You are, you really are,' she added, her face flushing. 'It's not fair.'

Watched by a monitor, Ella and Zuhra sat side by side in the hall, writing out their lines, not speaking. Once the task was completed, Zuhra turned to Ella and said, 'You're more stupid than I thought. You should have kept your mouth shut.'

Ella had ceased to care. She was satisfied. She had removed herself from the pedestal on which Miss Patterson had been so keen to install her. The rest of the class must see her now as one of them.

At rest, after lunch, Ella sat on her bed and scribbled away at length in her exercise book, before restoring it to its hiding place between the blankets.

'Is it a diary?' Zuhra asked, sitting cross-legged on her own bed.

Ella shook her head guardedly. 'No, it's not,' she replied. 'It's just that I don't know what I think until I write it down.' She blushed as she spoke, suddenly aware that this might sound silly.

'Think about what?' the other girl asked.

Ella shrugged, wary of Zuhra's interest. 'Just things,' she said.

★ ★ ★

On Sunday afternoon, after church, Mabel Patterson wrote
two letters. One was to the parents of Zuhra Iqbal, advising
them to speak to their daughter in the strongest terms about
her behaviour. They wouldn't listen, of course. They were
both lawyers, politically active nationalists, who came from
Bhakkar in the Punjab. They had sent Zuhra, the only
daughter among a family of six, to St Winifred's because they
believed in the education of girls. Miss Patterson had clashed
with the parents before during Zuhra's two-year stay at St
Winifred's.

The other letter was to the Jacksons. She told them that
Ella had settled in well, made friends and was coping
excellently with her academic work. However, it would be
advisable if the Jacksons postponed their first visit until a
later date.

Bill read Miss Patterson's letter and was not impressed.
'Why can't we bloody well see her when we like? How about
talking to Ella on the phone?'

Alice shook her head. 'It's impossible to get a connection
and, besides, it's not allowed. I told you she'd be fine. All that
nonsense about the Rockinghams is obviously forgotten. I'm
sure it was those damn murder stories in Ella's room. Why
don't we find somewhere else to put them while she's away?'

'It's her room,' Bill said. 'Leave it be. Have you told her
about Shafi yet?'

Alice shook her head. Four days after the Queen's Birthday
Party, the gardener had disappeared. Surindabash had said that
he was running from his gambling debts.

'No point in upsetting her,' Alice said.

Bill made no reply. Until Ella came home, this was dead
time; a marriage embalmed. And he knew he probably had
nobody to blame but himself.

Chapter Twenty-Four

Mrs Naseem Chaudhary had a moustache and eyebrows that met in the middle, and she dressed lavishly. Ella met her for the first time on Monday morning, third period. Mrs Chaudhary lived in nearby Murree and came to the school to teach needlework and biology. She was as excessive as Miss Patterson was spartan. Today, she was wearing an orange silk shalwar-qamiz and a matching dupatta, embroidered in gold sequins. She wore a miniature gold candelabra at each ear, a multitude of bangles and rings, and heavily jewelled sandals. Her fondness for lentils meant that she was inclined to let off wind, a weakness she preferred to blame on whatever group of pupils she happened to be teaching.

'Who has made that terrible smell?' she would cry out, bangles crashing, as she redirected the odour elsewhere. 'Who has expressed themselves flatulently?' No class was absolutely fart-free, so collective guilt would descend. Ridicule was Mrs Chaudhary's speciality.

At her first needlework lesson, Ella was issued with a piece of cotton cloth the size of a handkerchief, three skeins of thread, in green, yellow and orange, and a pencil.

Mrs Chaudhary had her feet up on the table, and was reading a magazine while the class sewed. She instructed Ella to draw a daisy in the corner of her cloth, then embroider it in chain stitch. Ella had watched her mother sew often enough, but she hadn't a clue what a chain stitch might be.

'Please, Mrs Chaudhary.' She raised her hand. She began to walk towards the teacher. 'Could you show me, please, how . . .' she began.

'Stop!' bellowed Mrs Chaudhary. 'Don't come any closer than that. White girls have a very strange smell about them that I really can't bear. Stay away, girl. That's right, stay away. Farting and all. I can't be doing with it.' She resumed reading her magazine about the love lives of Indian film stars.

Ella sat down again, humiliated and embarrassed. She attempted to draw a daisy, but the pencil was too faint. Harder and harder, more and more desperately, she attacked the cloth. 'Here, give it to me,' said a voice. Zuhra had come to sit next to her. Mrs Chaudhary looked up and returned to her magazine, picking her nose as she read. She was unconcerned what her girls did, so long as they remained quiet.

Zuhra took the cloth, deftly drew a daisy, threaded the needle, and slowly showed Ella a chain stitch. 'Try it,' she instructed. Ella tried. She pulled the thread too tight, the size of the stitches varied hugely and the cloth had turned grey and grubby because of the lead on her fingers, but at least her tears had stopped. 'You're hopeless,' Zuhra said. But for the first time in a week, she smiled.

Zuhra Iqbal, like most passionate individuals, was a person of extremes. Ella the enemy had become Ella the best friend. Zuhra had decided that the new girl was, in her own way, just as much of an outsider as she, Zuhra, was. Mrs Chaudhary had proved the catalyst. She picked on Ella, just as Miss Patterson picked on Zuhra. Besides, Zuhra was easily bored – and she'd grown tired of animosity. Ella, for her part, was relieved, but cautious.

'A best friend always stands by you. Always speaks up for you. Always fights for you. And you tell each other absolutely everything. Agreed?' Zuhra asked. They were sitting in the wood, in a secret den, a natural cave of fallen branches and thick ferns.

'I thought you were Rukhsana's best friend. And Mubeena's?' Ella replied warily.

The other girl shook her head impatiently. 'Cut yourself,' she ordered. She gave Ella a pair of nail scissors. 'And we'll mix our blood and make a pact.'

Ella paused. Might this be disloyal to Tommy? She had promised him that she was *his* best friend. How many best friends were you allowed to have? And what about Shafi? He'd told her he was her good friend. Did that count?

*A best friend always stands by you . . . always speaks up for you . . . always fights for you . . .*Shafi hadn't stood up for her.

'So, cut yourself, then,' Zuhra demanded impatiently. 'Like this.' She unceremoniously stuck the point of a scissor blade into her thumb. A small bright berry of blood appeared.

Ella looked at Zuhra. If she became her best friend, might something terrible happen to her? Might she disappear like Uncle Ash?

'Cowardy cowardy custard,' Zuhra was saying, dancing a jig, waving the scissors in the air.

'Horrible things happen to people who know me,' the British girl burst out, then she reddened, because the words sounded so silly.

Zuhra stopped dancing, intrigued. 'What sort of things?' she asked. 'Are they the things you write about?'

Suddenly furious, Ella threw herself at the older girl and they both tumbled to the floor. Sitting on Zuhra, she got hold of her hair and pulled hard. 'Have you read my book?' she yelled, ignoring her protesting screams. She wanted to hurt somebody, anybody, very, very badly. She wanted to kick and punch and bite and tear and watch the blood flow. Above all, she wanted to be released from the fear that it was all her fault, that she was to blame. 'Have you read my book?' Ella shouted. 'Have you? Have you?'

Zuhra gave her a sharp shove in the chest, and rolled away. 'Of course I have,' she hissed. Then added quietly, 'I looked at one page, but it didn't make much sense, so I stopped. Honestly.'

In reply, Ella took the scissors and jabbed them hard into the fleshy part of her thumb. She would mix her blood and swear to be best friends. 'If you've just lied and read my private stuff, Zuhra Iqbal,' she said fiercely, 'then, if bad things happen to you, it will only be what you deserve.'

On the following Saturday, in her letter home, Ella delivered the kind of bland propaganda that Miss Patterson preferred. On these terms, after half a page, she ran out of events to report.

The briefness of Ella's note encouraged Alice to believe that her daughter was happy enough for her to delay her Sunday visit, already postponed once by Miss Patterson, by a further two weeks. 'I know you won't mind, darling,' she wrote, 'but since Aunty Marjorie has been rather ill, I've been giving Sylvia much more of a hand with her fund-raising for the cemetery. We have a garden party planned on that Sunday and Sylvia has asked me especially to be there. Isn't that nice? Daddy said he would try to come to see you on his own, but not to bank on it, because he has a lot of work at present. Anyway, you'll be home for the holiday in a very short time.'

Of course, when she received the news a few days later, Ella did mind, very much. The post was issued before lunch in the dining room, while the girls were waiting to say grace. Her acute disappointment was slightly offset by the arrival of a large brown envelope. It came from Betty Brooking. She had sent several film magazines, some chocolate Hershey bars, and a card which read, 'I hope school is fun. Your mom says you are enjoying it and doing very well. I'm planning on coming with her to collect you for the mid-term break. Not long now! I'm thinking of you. Fond regards, Betty.'

Ella liked the idea that somebody in Peshawar was keeping her in mind. 'Fond regards' made her feel grown up.

Caro was whispering sweet nothings in Milly's ear as Ella, at the dining table, half pulled the first magazine from the envelope. 'Give it here,' the monitor ordered, winking at Milly. 'Magazines are forbidden in the dining room. You know that, Ella Jackson. I'm confiscating what you've got.'

'But it's my post,' the junior protested hotly, putting the magazines on her knee under the table. Zuhra, sitting next to her, slipped three on to her own lap and passed them down the line of girls, each manoeuvre hidden from Caro's view. 'Besides, I'm not reading it. I've only just got it. I haven't even opened it yet,' Ella argued.

'Give,' Caro snapped in her mock-American accent, pulling up her shirt collar. 'Right this minute.' Reluctantly, Ella handed over the envelope, now holding only a single magazine. Caro began to flick through it casually. It was *Photoplay*, 'the world's top film magazine'. It had Janet Leigh on the cover, dressed in an off-the-shoulder pale-blue negligee. '*Guys and Dolls* – first pictures. Wow,' Caro mocked. 'Look what you're missing, Ella Jackson. Goodness, Milly, did you know that Joan Crawford has allowed her eyebrows to grow back naturally?'

'Why should you read it if I'm not allowed?' Ella broke in crossly, taking the bait.

Caro sneered, 'Well, you know how it is, kiddo, life ain't fair, is it Milly, honey?'

Later, safe in the secret den, Ella and Zuhra devoured the magazines which Caro had failed to forfeit. 'Who do you want to be?' Ella asked.

'Jayne Mansfield,' Zuhra replied. 'How about you?'

'Doris Day,' Ella answered. 'Let's pretend we're best friends. And we live in Hollywood. We wear white polonecks and flared skirts. Mine will be in pink . . .'

'I'll be in blue,' Zuhra agreed, her long plaits flying. 'And we drive around in Cadillacs that match our skirts.'

Over the following days, Ella's imagination, previously overflowing with images of Marjorie and Piers Rockingham and Ash Khan, now found a happier diversion in Hollywood. She and Zuhra transformed St Winifred's. Each day, as Jayne and Doris, they would drive up and down the playground in their automobiles, convert the woods into their palatial second, third and fourth homes, pretend they were attending film galas at mealtimes, and stage entertainments during playtime. And they plotted against Caro.

'What we have to get is proof,' Zuhra announced one evening, as they were making their way to the dormitory.

'Proof of what?' Ella asked.

'Proof that Caro and Milly are doing something they shouldn't be doing, what do you think?' her friend replied scornfully. 'Then we can decide what to do about it.'

'What do you think they're doing?'

Zuhra clucked her tongue disapprovingly. 'How do I know?' she protested. 'That's why we're going to follow them, isn't it, silly?'

Ella fell silent, her thoughts elsewhere.

'What are you thinking?' Zuhra asked, as she doubled the top blanket on her bed for extra warmth.

'Nothing.' Ella blushed. She wanted to tell her friend about that night in the secret garden, but she didn't dare. Not for fear of facing more disbelief, but because of the possible consequences for Zuhra. What if the angel on her shoulder failed to offer her adequate protection, and she disappeared too?

Ella improvised. 'I was thinking that we ought to make a secret society and follow Caro and Milly around until we find out what they're up to.'

'OK, we'll start tonight,' the Pakistani girl agreed. 'We'll wait for Milly and then we'll creep up and peek at them through the curtains.'

The two girls went to bed determined to maintain their vigil. Both were sound asleep long before Milly made her moonlit walk. It was Ella's first full night's rest since the events of 21 April, almost three weeks earlier.

Chapter Twenty-Five

Each Sunday, a crocodile line emerged from St Winifred's, and took the Quaid-I-Azam Road (known before
Partition as Marlborough Street) down into Chowdiagalli,
and into St Michael's Church for the morning service. At
this time in the season, the congregation was small, easily
outnumbered by St Winifred's girls. By June, the church
would be packed, for social rather than spiritual reasons.
Tradition dictated that Miss Patterson led the procession, a
grey coat over her black Sunday dress, a beret on her head,
and her Bible under her arm. The juniors came behind her,
the seniors at the rear, and two more staff members would
prowl like sheepdogs, ready to herd the strays.

Ella had hated her first three Sundays. Partly, because it
was the day she associated with the best times at home – her
father and mother, most often in the company of others, so
at peace with each other; Surindabash's cooking; time with
Tommy; or uninterrupted play by herself. Sometimes, it was
the way the day dribbled away with little of anything
achieved that made it special for Ella – no one rushing to
work or school, just being together – so long as there were
no rows.

At St Winifred's, the regime was adjusted on the day of
rest, but it was no less taxing. Rising bell an hour later,
breakfast, dormitory cleaning, early morning prayers, Bible
reading for an hour, walk into Chowdiagalli, church, walk

back, lunch (always chicken curry and tubs of ice cream), rest, play, evening prayers, book reading, bed.

Partly, Ella hated Sundays at St Winifred's because her mother had failed to supply her with a white dress for church-going, so she had been issued one from the second-hand box. It was too long and too tight across the back and everybody knew it wasn't hers. Alice had promised to make a dress and despatch it quickly, but, so far, nothing had arrived. 'It will come,' Ella told Zuhra often. 'Mummy promised.'

'In God's house,' Miss Patterson said, reprimanding her for her concern, 'there is no place for vanity.'

Ridicule, however, was apparently perfectly acceptable, because none of the teachers intervened as Ella was constantly teased.

In addition to the uniform, Ella also disliked the service. It lacked the drama, the sense of imminent doom and disaster which made Miss Patterson's monologues terrifying, heart stopping and stomach turning, and therefore strangely enjoyable. In contrast, the only part of Ella's anatomy the church sermons reached was her bottom, numbed by the wooden pews.

The vicar, Mr Rodney John, round-faced and fair-haired, looked about twelve. He could barely see above the pulpit. Mindful of the sensibilities of an adult congregation who did not wish to be put off their more pleasurable pursuits by reminders of the seven deadly sins or the ten commandments, he stuck to preaching about Jesus, the Redeemer, gentle and forgiving. As he spoke, Miss Patterson, the Old Testament stalwart, would orchestrate her disapproval of his words, issuing a stream of *tuts* and *pshaws* interwoven with heavy sighs, sometimes shaking her head so hard, wisps of white hair would begin to come loose from her combs. As a result, she frequently looked much more attractive leaving church than arriving.

Ella shared Miss Patterson's concern about the vicar's

message. If God was going to come into her life, and she was seriously considering the proposition that he ought, she wanted him at his most vengeful and wrathful (at least to those who might wish her harm) – the Son seemed a soppy substitute.

This Sunday, however, she and Zuhra had a mission to perform. Each week, Caro and Milly would linger so they could enter the church last and sit in the back pew. Everyone but the teachers knew that, once the service was underway, they would then slip away. Miss Patterson, in the front pew, might be all-seeing, but, since she did not have eyes in the back of her head, she was unaware of their habit.

'We plough the fields and scatter, the good . . .' Miss Patterson sang in a tuneless voice. Three rows behind her, separated by four girls, sat Ella and Zuhra. Miss Patterson took every opportunity now to keep the two apart. Ella was concealed from the other two members of staff by a pillar. Zuhra was in full view, in the middle of the pew. Ella and Zuhra read this to mean that Fate had selected Ella as the chosen one. She duly slipped out during the third verse of the first hymn, keeping her eyes down, on the assumption that, if she didn't look, she wouldn't be seen.

Once out of the church, she ran down the path which led into The Mall, heady with the sense of freedom and not yet fearful of the consequences of her actions. At the corner, she saw the backs of Milly and Caro as they turned left down a sharp slope into a side street. Chowdiagalli was new to Ella. The Mall, the width of a country lane, was crowded with people, milling about, buying chewing gum from children and sweet, sickly drinks from the street vendors. Ella side-stepped the salesmen attached to each identical knick-knack shop. They were working the crowd, trying to woo customers into their respective stores. 'Very special price. For you, lady, very special price,' was the chant up and down the street.

Briefly, Ella stopped outside a makeshift café. It had battered iron tables and chairs and a large, cracked, orange-and-white plastic sign, which read, 'Freddy's Broast Chiken Palace.' In the gutter, a teenage boy was sitting on his haunches, washing tin plates in a bowl of grey water. Next to him, was a life-size cardboard cut-out of a cute all-American girl, dressed in bobby sox and shorts, with a blonde ponytail, smiling and holding a Kodak camera. Suddenly, a dwarf popped out from behind the cut-out's left leg. He was dressed in a miniature shalwar-qamiz and a grey waistcoat. 'Yum yum, nice eats,' he smiled at a startled Ella. 'Come inside,' he coaxed, assuming that, no matter how young, if she was white, she was bound to have money.

Ella shook her head, then remembered her manners. 'No, thank you,' she answered, trying to cover her confusion. 'I'm not hungry.' Her rumbling stomach contradicted her. She moved on, attracted by the sight of a butcher at work. She watched as he held a large lump of raw meat, checked with creamy fat, steady with one hand, and cut it with a knife held between the toes of his left foot. A younger man threw a bucket of water into the street, washing away the blood as it drained away.

Remembering the reason why she was in The Mall, Ella ran in the direction she'd seen the two older girls go, through the bazaar, and along a quieter road whose wrought-iron streetlamps leant one way and then the other. Turning a bend, Ella found herself surrounded by a herd of bellowing cows. A small dirty-faced boy, dressed in torn shorts, stick in hand, was riding on the back of one, digging his bare feet into its side. 'Hello.' He smiled and waved. Skipping and dodging to avoid the animals, she said hello back. Caro half turned, as if she'd recognised the voice. Her pursuer ducked behind the nearest cow's flank. On cue, it lifted its tail and released a stream of dung, splattering her dress. The small boy laughed so much at the expression on her face, he almost fell off his steed. 'Shit! Shit! Shit!' he kept shouting. Ella frowned, then grinned.

By the time she had emerged from the cattle scrum, the couple were out of sight. Ella ran hard, the road now steepening into a hill. Glancing down to her left, she glimpsed a rear view of Milly, following Caro down a flight of steps, towards a house screened by thick, tall bushes. Now, she could hear Milly's thin, baby voice, singing, 'Love and marriage, love and marriage, go togetherrrr like a horse and carriage . . .' She waited until they had disappeared into the house, then she followed the sound of Milly's humming.

The place was dilapidated and boarded up. Wooden shutters hung off hinges; the net screening on the front door was full of holes. Ella went round to the rear. The back door was missing, but a rusting water butt had been placed across the entrance. She squeezed past it, scraping her knee and marking her dress with mildew.

The kitchen had been stripped bare, apart from an old stone sink and single tap. A scratching noise in the far corner of the room made Ella jump. A chicken emerged from an empty cupboard, squawking indignantly. She left the kitchen and moved into a long, dark L-shaped corridor. Proof. She had to bring back proof. Her heart was beating fast. Milly's joyless voice acted as her compass. 'Hey, there, you with the stars in your eyes . . . Love never made a fool of you.'

As she tiptoed down the hall, moving in and out of shadows, Ella swore she was floating in blackness. She could feel the prickle of dry grass, the roughness of stone, the smoothness of paper, next to her skin. There were moans and sighs and a smell, a certain smell, the smell of the meat shop in Chowdiagalli, or somewhere else . . . She struggled to resuscitate a memory that perhaps she had never had.

Then, she was at the threshold of a large room, wood-panelled, and with every window open but shuttered, so it was darker even than the corridor. She waited until her eyes had adjusted, not moving. Gradually, she could see, in the far corner, a carpet, cushions, magazines, *her* magazine, empty bottles of lemonade, a packet of cigarettes and unlit candles. The darkness and the trees meant the room was cool. A shape, difficult to identify at first, began to move. Ella heard Caro's voice, muffled, but insistent. 'Come on, honey, come on, sugar pie.' Suddenly, Milly gave a small scream. Her leg and arm flopped out from under the other girl. Ella had seen this before. She half turned, looking, in panic, for Shafi.

'Stop it, stop it, stop it, you're hurting her!' she shouted. She took several steps into the middle of the room, her shoes crashing on the bare wooden floor – and then she turned and ran.

At the end of the service, Mabel Patterson smiled as she passed Caro and Milly in the last pew, still kneeling in prayer. Such a strong friendship, such commitment to the Church. Often, in the week, they requested permission to attend early communion in St Michael's, the only two seniors to do so. In a few months, each would go their own way, leaving school, living at opposite ends of the country – Caro in Karachi, Milly in Lahore. They would be dutiful wives and, eventually, attentive mothers – well, as attentive as any rich, spoilt girls could be, Miss Patterson told herself.

Zuhra was elated. She and a subdued Ella held hands as the crocodile line of which they were a part coiled its way back to St Winifred's. 'You saw them doing something they shouldn't, didn't you? Did you sneak up on them? What were they doing? Were they smoking? Drinking? What? Have you got the proof? Have you . . .?'

'Zuhra Iqbal, please try to walk like a lady,' chastised Miss Hope Fernandez in a chummy tone, prodding the girl's dancing legs with her walking stick. Miss Hopeless, as she was universally known, was the school matron, a young woman who had chosen to compensate for lifelong acne by adopting a permanently bubbly personality. Recently, she had become engaged. An event that had turned her permanent smile into the most extreme rictus. The girls liked her because, although she interfered, she did so only in the mildest fashion.

'Tell me what you saw,' Zuhra begged, skipping over the matron's stick. 'Please.'

Ella shook her head.

'Tell me, please, Ella,' she persisted.

Ella refused to look Zuhra in the eye. 'I didn't see anything,' she mumbled in reply.

Zuhra began to laugh. 'Don't be an idiot. Of course you did. I know you did. Was it really bad?' she asked eagerly. 'Were they meeting boys?'

Ella stopped and turned on her friend, causing a minor collision in the crocodile line. 'What's the point in telling you what I saw? What I really saw. You won't believe me,' she exploded, much to Zuhra's surprise. 'People always think I make things up. And do you know what grown-ups do, if you say things they don't want to hear? They make you disappear. Oh, yes, they do,' Ella insisted fiercely, as Zuhra began to shake her head, unsure how to react to her friend's outburst.

'My friend Tommy told me they do. And I've seen it happen. They can make people disappear.'

Zuhra gave her a little push, to make her begin walking again, then she linked arms with her friend. 'Don't be silly,' she chided gently. 'Nobody's going to make us disappear. Besides, I'm here to look after you. You're safe with me. Nobody will lay a finger on us. If they do, I'll write and tell my papa.'

Ella gave her a look. 'How can you? Miss Patterson reads everything.'

Zuhra chuckled mischievously. 'Not quite everything. One day, if you're really, really nice to me, I'll tell you my secret, OK? Now, what about Caro and Milly?'

Ella cupped her hand and whispered conspiratorially in the other girl's ear. 'Zuhra,' she breathed, 'they saw me.'

The Pakistani girl stopped dead, her eyes wide. 'Oh, my sweet Christ,' she said.

Monday night was bathtime at St Winifred's. Monitors worked on a rota, one monitor supervising four girls. The wash house was on the ground floor of the main building. It was a long, windowless room, with a concrete floor, a low ceiling and vents to ease the problem of condensation. Bowls and jugs were used for morning and evening ablutions. Each girl, except the youngest, would collect cold water from one of six taps, to pour into her bowl. After washing, the bowl was emptied into one of several drains. The stone floor was rutted with gutters, but, inevitably, a small sea of scum and hair and dirty, soapy water would eventually gather, swirling and slopping around dozens of pairs of bare feet. The luckier girls had wooden platforms to stand on; the majority paddled.

In addition, each Monday afternoon, giant-sized gas rings were lit and vast tubs of water heated. Monitors were responsible for conveying the hot water to sixteen cubicles, each furnished with a tin bath, and a peg for towel and clothes. A bath of water filled no more than six inches high would serve each child. A bath and hairwash had to be completed within ten minutes. Two monitors would then drain the water and repeat the ritual for the next child.

On Monday evening, the day after Ella's surveillance of Caro and Milly, she and Zuhra stood with the rest of Buttercup dormitory in a line in the corridor outside the wash house's double doors. They waited barefoot, naked under their dressing-gowns. The doors banged open and the girls from Gentian tumbled out, red-faced and noisy, pyjamas sticking to their still-wet skin. Immediately, Buttercup filed in and obediently waited to be allocated cubicles and monitors.

Ella looked around. She hadn't visited the bath house so late in the rota before. The gas rings roared and hissed, sending off a welcome heat. Boiling water bubbled and spat in giant urns. Monitors toing and froing with buckets of water were strange, disembodied shapes, their outlines erased by clouds of steam. Suddenly, Caro appeared from a cubicle at the opposite end of the room. Unsmiling, she beckoned Ella towards her.

Ella walked very slowly past one, two, three, four cubicles.

'In,' Caro said. The floor of her cubicle was a soapy mess. The tin bath was full to overflowing. No steam rose from the surface of the water. Ella didn't have to test it to know that it would be very, very cold. 'In,' Caro repeated, her top lip curled in best Presley tradition. She pulled her blouse collar up and pushed her hair back. She gave the younger girl a hard shove in the small of her back. Ella dropped her washbag and heard it splash like a stone in a lake. Dressing-gown flapping, she ran out of the cubicle, back towards the door, and the giggling, gaping mouth of the newly arrived Miss Hope.

Ella knew her feet had slid from under her – and then there was nothing.

Chapter Twenty-Six

Betty Brooking, in a stranger's house, refilled her glass from the bottle of Johnnie Walker on the silver tray by her side. The dhobiwallah had starched her linen skirt so sadistically that now, in spite of the softness of the over-stuffed yellow brocade sofa, it was as if she was sitting on shards of glass. She heard footsteps in the corridor. A servant opened the ornate door and a woman followed him in. She was veiled, but removed her burquah once the servant had gone.

'Good morning, Mrs Brooking,' the new arrival said evenly, in impeccable English. 'My name is Faryal. I'm Colonel Ash's wife. I've been expecting you.'

A few minutes later, after pleasantries had been exchanged, Betty lit a cigarette. 'Do you mind?' she asked.

Faryal Khan Afridi shook her head, then opened a cigarette case on the ornate ivory-inlaid coffee table, and lit up her own. 'Surprised?' she asked, amused.

Betty was aware she was undergoing appraisal.

'Did you imagine that I would be illiterate and barefoot, capable only of preparing hookah pipes for my husband?' the woman asked, her tone mocking, but not impolite.

Betty chose not to answer. Instead, she drew on her cigarette and took a sip from her glass. 'Thanks for the whisky,' she smiled. Faryal Khan Afridi was in her early thirties and strikingly pretty. Betty hadn't expected that. Why would a man have affairs when he had so much better at home? Ash's wife resembled a brown-skinned version of Audrey Hepburn – gamine face, high cheekbones, full lips, hazel eyes. Her black hair had been wrapped in a bun and she wore kohl around her eyes. A face without stress.

The woman shifted in her seat, as if squaring up for combat. She saw before her a well-preserved, composed, middle-aged woman, dressed in a pale-blue linen sheath dress, a colour which matched her eyes. Her brown hair was caught in a clasp at the back of her neck. She wore no jewellery or make-up, except for a pale lipstick. Her assets were such that she could afford understatement. She carried an air of cynicism – or was it sadness? She was, thought Faryal Khan Afridi, a dangerous woman; a woman without an anchor.

'So, your husband believes my husband to be a spy?' Faryal said. It sounded more like a statement than a question.

'Probably.' Betty gave a small smile.

'Does your husband also imagine you are having an affair with my husband?' The woman's gaze was unwavering, her tone light. Betty picked up on the word 'imagine'. It was as if Begum Khan was expertly playing a game of chess.

'Probably,' Betty answered. 'But it's quite likely the suspicion was only fleeting. CJ is too busy saving the world to worry about minor details such as how his wife spends her spare time.'

Faryal Khan Afridi smiled. It cheered Betty. She did not appear to be a wife in mourning.

The woman gave her a bemused look. 'Have you come to find out where Ash is?' she asked outright.

'Yes,' Betty answered simply. Why pretend otherwise?

'He's on secret manoeuvres in Kashmir,' Faryal answered, then gave a small shrug. 'On the other hand, he might be with one of his lovers in Nathiagalli or Pindi or Murree, justifying his lovemaking by pretending he's taking revenge for all the sins committed in the name of the British Empire. There are, of course, a multitude of sins,' she added, raising one eyebrow. 'So there's a great deal of lovemaking still to be done.'

Betty laughed, too much she knew. Begum Khan was clever. 'Don't you mind – about his girlfriends, I mean?' Betty asked.

'Why should I?' She shrugged. 'It makes him a better lover. The Koran tells us he has a duty to make me happy. Did you know that? I read in *Time* magazine that you American women are not at all happy in bed – or out of it. Such a pity,' she added, without sincerity.

'Presumably, you don't have much choice?' Betty regretted the words as soon as they were out of her mouth.

Faryal sat back in her chair. 'You mean, do I have to put up with what he does, no matter what? Choice, now there's an interesting word, Mrs Brooking. My husband may take Western women as lovers, but he chose me, in spite of my education, in spite of my barrenness.

'Many Pakistani men would be wary of a woman with my qualifications, without hope of sons. My marriage was arranged, but I could have chosen a different suitor. I chose Ashraf because he believed strongly that I had a right to do as I wished. Surely you agree that to do something, however small, is better than to do nothing?'

She paused, but not long enough for Betty to answer. 'I exercise a great deal of choice within my marriage, because I had a husband who knew that, in order to love me, in order for me to be the kind of woman in whom he could maintain an interest for many years, I had to be free. And with that sense of freedom comes responsibility to others and to myself.'

'But you couldn't leave him, you couldn't divorce, could you? Where's the choice in that?' Betty despised herself for sounding patronising, but, for the first time in a long time, she was unsettled.

'And why do you choose to stay with a husband who – so Ash tells me – gives you so little emotional nourishment? Your choice is, in different ways, as limited as mine, is it not?'

'You're right.' Betty gave a small smile. Somehow, the woman opposite made her feel pathetic, powerless, self-pitying. It is these small moments that change lives.

Faryal Khan Afridi rose from her chair. 'If you'll excuse me, Mrs Brooking, I have appointments to keep. Should Ashraf contact me, I will pass on your concern. Sometimes, it is several weeks. If you would like to stay, feel free. My garden is very beautiful, a peaceful place.'

Betty got to her feet. Her linen skirt had broken into an accordion of unwanted, untidy pleats – but it wasn't just her appearance that made her feel shabby in comparison with Ash's wife.

'Do you go out much?' Betty asked.

Begum Khan inclined her head quizzically. 'Is that code for, "Are you locked up all day and beaten at night?" I choose to wear the veil,' she added. 'Ash would prefer I didn't. He is suspicious of tradition and religion. But Islam matters a great deal to me. It gives me strength.'

She began to walk to the door and Betty followed, aware for the first time how noisily her heeled sandals clacked on the polished floor.

Faryal stopped and extended her hand in farewell. 'In answer to your question, Mrs Brooking, I go out six days a week. I have private patients and poor patients. I am a gynaecologist. My religion and my tribe mean that, when I discover an unmarried girl is pregnant, I tell the brother or the father or the uncle who has brought her, and she is never seen again. Barbaric, you would say.

'And when I see a sick woman, bearing her eighth or ninth child into poverty, I have no alternative but to help. To stand by and watch is a choice, but a disgraceful one, don't you think, Mrs Brooking?'

Only later, driving to the Peshawar Tennis Club, with the intention of swimming away her unease, did it dawn on Betty that Faryal Khan Afridi had referred to her husband mostly in the past tense.

'About Thursday,' Alice Jackson said. She tried not to flinch as, in the day clinic of the Quaker Hospital, she helped Blossom, who was tending to a woman with acute elephantiasis, folds of flesh hanging around her ankles. 'I'm really sorry, but I won't be able to make the clinic. Have you anyone else who can cover for me?'

Blossom said a few cheering words in Urdu to her patient and called for the next. She moved the hair out of her eyes with the back of her hand and bent to tickle a small child under the chin. The child's top lip was a bloodied mass.

In the few weeks since Ella's departure, Alice had been promoted as a volunteer, from general dogsbody to Blossom's assistant in this daily clinic.

'Do you see what they've done, Alice?' Blossom said. 'This child had a lump on her lip and the mother says the pir told her to cut it off with a razorblade and apply—' she turned to the increasingly anxious mother and asked a rapid series of questions – 'and apply the medicine he gave them – cow dung, probably. The lip's infected and the girl is probably scarred for life. Now they want doctor medicine to work the miracle that the pir failed to deliver. Ironic, isn't it? What were you saying about Thursday?'

'I said I couldn't do the clinic – nor Friday, I'm afraid. Can you manage?'

Blossom, never critical, smiled. 'All our volunteers are already beginning to flee to the hills, but of course we'll manage. Don't you worry. Are you going up to see Ella?' she added. 'She'll be so excited. How is she?'

Alice shook her head. 'No, Miss Patterson has suggested that it's best we don't see her until the first break. I'll go up then, with Betty, to bring her home. Very few of the other girls receive termtime visits, so Ella probably won't even notice we've not been up. It's only three weeks away and time will fly.' Alice felt uncomfortable bending the truth – she'd meant to see her daughter before now; it was just that life had become so busy.

'Does Ella know you're not planning a visit?' Blossom asked casually.

Alice gave a quick smile. 'Not exactly. She writes to ask when we're coming and I just say soon. No point in upsetting her unduly, is there?' she added.

Then, anxious to change the subject, she said, 'I'm going away this weekend with Sylvia. It's Harry Webster's birthday. He's having a bit of a party in Abbotabad and we're going up with some booze and bits that have come through in the diplomatic bag.' Alice stopped, embarrassed at her insensitivity. Instead of booze and bits, it should have been the copper wires that the hospital so desperately needed. Blossom turned away.

'Ah, yes,' Blossom murmured. 'I passed the British cemetery the other day. Very smart and tidy and manicured. And a permanent armed guard too. I'm sure the dead will be very appreciative. It's a great pity that we couldn't get Mrs Hargreave-Smith to exercise her enormous fund-raising talents in our direction. The living have needs too.' Her tone was soft, but her eyes blazed.

Alice took it as a personal criticism. 'I'd say something to Sylvia, but . . .' she began defensively.

'But?' Blossom pushed gently. Then she added, 'No matter. Tell me, does Ella know about Tommy?' She was putting a clean dressing on the child's lip. She took a sweet from her pocket and put it in the little girl's hand.

'*Shukria, shukria,*' the mother said, bowing as she backed out of the room.

Tommy Larkhall had collapsed the week before and had

been admitted to hospital. He had improved since, but slowly. The Larkhalls had been told that he probably had only weeks to live. His heart was literally worn out. To add to his difficulties, Tommy's antique wheelchair, patched and repatched, had finally given up the ghost. Once he was released from hospital, his mobility would be heavily restricted, since the Larkhalls lacked the resources to provide a replacement. Pride had prevented Albie or Blossom telling anyone else. Besides, they saw themselves as blessed. Charity should be reserved for those with nothing.

'I thought it best not to tell her. She'd worry and there's nothing she can do, is there?' Alice smiled brightly. 'It's not always a good thing to tell children everything, don't you agree? She told me she'd written to Tommy a couple of times. Did she tell him how much she's loving St Winifred's? She really seems to have settled in well. Perhaps Tommy can drop her a line once he's up and about again?'

Blossom busied herself washing her hands. She wondered, not for the first time, why Alice so often treated the truth like an ill-fitting jacket, taking in a seam here and letting out a seam there, when it would be more than adequate left well alone? Ella's letters to Tommy were formal, flat, bereft of any of the sense of mischief that Blossom associated with the child. Oddly, there was no mention of what she thought of the school. Instead, she wrote about how much she was looking forward to her mother's visit, almost as if it was a lifeline.

Blossom was sure that Ella's letters to Alice similarly smelt of sadness and longing, no matter what the words conveyed on the paper. She sighed. She'd met people like Alice before. They went through life ignoring the unpleasant and inconvenient, embroidering the ordinary – playing hopscotch with their conscience and blaming others when the gap between their fantasies and reality became a chasm that claimed casualties. That was the true danger of those reared in the belief they had no worth: they were better than anyone at destroying others.

Alice looked at her wristwatch. 'Do you mind if I slip away now, Blossom?' she asked. 'Bill's picking me up. He's playing tennis with CJ while Ash is away. I don't know why Bill bothers. CJ always gives him such a thrashing, he's depressed for days,' she laughed. 'I'm going to have a drink at the club while they play. We must fix a date for you and Albie to come over,' she added clumsily, aware that, in Ella's absence, she had made no attempt to meet the Larkhalls socially.

'Wouldn't that be lovely?' Blossom replied, giving a small, enigmatic smile.

Bill was waiting in the courtyard of the hospital on the Vespa scooter he used more now Ella was away. In the weeks since she had gone, the Jacksons had spent very little time alone together. Instead, they entertained or were entertained. At the end of every night, Bill would go to their bed thinking how empty the bungalow seemed, and how alone they were with each other. Alice, in contrast, told herself all was going well. She had a daughter in boarding school; she was the personal friend of the wife of the Deputy High Commissioner; she kept a very good table. She would fight very hard before she would allow anyone to spoil it.

'That's one helluva queue,' Bill commented, as Alice hopped on the back of the scooter. He indicated a silent, subdued mass of people spilling out of a building on his right.

'It's the eye clinic,' Alice replied. 'Dr Danvers says he can't keep up with the demand. An East German relief agency has promised an eye specialist on loan for three months, but the Government won't give him a visa. Frightened of upsetting the Americans, I suppose. They're mostly cataract cases.'

'How about the wires I made?' Bill asked casually. 'For the cauterising gun. Any use?'

'The copper wires?' Alice repeated. 'Well, of course, Dr

Danvers was appreciative, but they're still desperate for the real thing. And then I felt pretty awful because I let out to Blossom that Noel had bent the rules to bring half of Fortnum and Mason in through the bag for Harry's party.

'You're not thinking of asking Noel for the wires, are you?' she added anxiously.

Bill opened the throttle of the scooter, as Alice climbed on behind him. 'Oh no,' he replied sarcastically. 'I've got my priorities right. Much better that Harry's fat gut is filled to overflowing with tinned asparagus and fois gras. Who wants to save the eyes of a few piccaninnies? Oh dear bloody no. The white man's burden is acute fucking indigestion while the black man's curse is to stumble around in the dark. And we call ourselves decent?'

'You're not going to ask Noel, though, are you?' Alice repeated anxiously, yelling into the wind on the back of the scooter, as she clutched Bill round his waist.

Her husband's reply was lost in the bedlam of the Jamrud Road.

Piers Rockingham bounced up and down on the mattress. He stroked the dark mahogany wood. Marjorie, pale, her hair spiked with perspiration, stood at the foot of the bed, dressed in a baby-pink dressing-gown. Briefly, he wondered if the two of them – her and the Pakistani – had done it here, where he was sitting. All the more reason to replace it.

'They'll think it's a bribe,' she said, sounding as if she was close to tears. She put her hand to her back, as if supporting herself. Since last night, her back had hurt more and more. She almost welcomed the pain as a private punishment. Let Him wrap barbed wire around her soul and squeeze hard. No penance would be enough.

Her husband moved suddenly, bounding to his feet. She flinched and stepped back. Her reaction gave Rockingham pleasure.

'Let me explain something, Marjorie,' he addressed his wife. 'We have a new bed, due to arrive tomorrow. I cannot store our old bed, because we have no room in the compound warehouse. The only place to put this bed, therefore, is in the Jacksons' bungalow. They have been banging on about a bed for months. Let them enjoy our cast-offs. We know nothing, they know nothing, so how can it be a bribe? You must stop viewing life through the filter of a few unfortunate minutes. If it makes it any easier, why not tell yourself you imagined it all?'

Much of Piers' energy over the past few weeks had been invested in keeping Marjorie on an even keel. She had wanted to return to the UK immediately. He had refused point blank. Imagine how that would have looked, coming out of the blue? Piers told her an unstable wife on the old report card would write off any chance of further postings behind the Iron Curtain, the quickest route to promotion. So, he for one, wasn't about to allow a single, small mishap destroy his future. He told Marjorie that her infidelity would, of course, take a very long time to forgive. In the meantime, at least she could do as she was told.

Piers couldn't pretend that the disappearance of the gardener hadn't temporarily unnerved him. Occurring, as it did, so soon after the event. But, as the weeks passed, he had grown more relaxed. Now, he had almost begun to enjoy the subterfuge, the reconstruction of two lives – his and Marjorie's – on the foundation of the death of another. He saw the skill with which he conducted the cover-up as his private confirmation that he could master any situation – even murder – without fuss or fall-out. Now, if that didn't constitute ambassadorial material, what did?

Of course, Marjorie was beside herself with guilt. But then, he'd never known her when she wasn't beside herself about something. She'd been lucky that he'd married her, and now she was fortunate to have him on hand, to save her from herself. Even if he said so himself, Piers was good at tying up loose ends. On that night in the maze, his hands sticky with blood so thick it was almost black, he knew this was the greatest catastrophe of his life. Now, such was his arrogance, he almost saw it as child's play.

'I'll lay a bet that he'll be found out and exposed for the charlatan he is within weeks. You mark my words.'

Noel Hargreave-Smith, looking haunted, was speaking, sitting on the edge of Albie Larkhall's desk in the admin section in the foyer of the compound's offices. Albie was busy dealing with passport applications. Bill had emerged from his room to collect a lemonade from the office refrigerator. Hearing the sound of voices, Piers Rockingham emerged from his office to join in the discussion.

'Aaah, Piers.' Noel Hargreave-Smith had worked hard to mask his dislike of his number two, for the sake of morale – his own morale, mostly. He was, after all, a man of manners. So much so, that Piers' vanity was once again deluding him into believing that his superior held his talents in high regard. 'We were just chatting about this Egypt business. Bill, here, was saying that, now our troops are out, it might spark a bit of trouble. He seems to think the chap carries a lot of clout.'

Bill took a swig from his bottle of lemonade. 'We left Cairo a couple of months before the riots in January last year,' he explained. 'They hit anything to do with the British – the BOAC offices, Thomas Cook, Barclays Bank, the Turf Club – half a dozen or so were killed . . .'

Noel interrupted. 'Anything you want to know about the Suez Canal, Piers, old man, ask Bill. He's our resident expert. Two years in Cairo and he now has an encyclopaedic knowledge. Ask him anything, go on, do,' he urged enthusiastically, as if anxious that the performing monkey should deliver his best tricks.

Piers smiled sarcastically. 'I'll bear that in mind in the

unlikely event that the Canal becomes a central part of my life.'

Hargreave-Smith chuckled. 'Eden certainly wasn't over-keen when he met Nasser. Must've been during your posting, Bill? Saw him as a cheap, greasy matinée idol.'

'Eden's disapproval? All the better, as far as the Egyptian in the street was concerned,' Bill answered, warming to his theme. 'When we were there, Nasser had begun to make a big song and dance about the profits of the Canal. It's one of the best bargains Britain ever acquired, that's for sure – four million pounds sterling for a forty-four percent stake. Although, of course, it was only the common grocers who deigned to invest. What were the Canal's profits last year? Something like eleven million, with almost five of that going to the UK. Not bad at all.'

'You're surely not suggesting that the wogs get more, are you?' Piers asked. It was unclear whether the contempt in his voice was for Bill or the 'wogs'. 'Nasser's got absolutely nothing between his ears,' he went on. 'All that tripe about Arab socialism. He'll be as greedy as old Farouk, given a chance. Look at how badly he's played the Americans. First, he demands millions of dollars for his dam which will turn him into a local hero. Then, he goes and does his shopping for arms in Prague and recognises Red China. Not the cleverest of diplomatic moves, but, then again, the man has hardly had any education to speak of . . .'

As he spoke, Piers noticed with some satisfaction that a vein had begun to throb in Bill Jackson's temple.

Bill's smile was terse. 'He's read Voltaire, Rousseau, Dickens . . . depends what you call education, I suppose,' he replied. 'Not bad for the son of a peasant. And Nasser has done his sums. He argued that six percent of the Egyptian population owns sixty-five percent of the land, so something's got to change.

'Of course,' Bill added, belatedly trying to inject levity, 'it was so much easier when the third secretary in the British Embassy in Cairo was sent foxhunting every Friday with the Crown Prince, to find out what old Farouk was up to. You any good at hunting with the hounds, Piers?'

'Blooded as a baby,' he replied.

Three of the four men laughed, mostly out of relief that Bill had stepped away from his lectern.

Later, in the privacy of the Deputy High Commissioner's office, Piers Rockingham said, 'I've got some concerns about Bill, Noel. Never too sure where his political sympathies lie. And since all that business with . . .'

The Deputy High Commissioner frowned. 'You mean his interest in Egypt? Nonsense. That's not about ideology, that's about Bill's appetite for knowledge. He was posted there for a couple of years and made the most of it. Besides, he's much too working class for betrayal. Leave that to our Cambridge set. Those are the people we have to watch,' Noel added sourly.

'I'm just suggesting vigilance, sir, that's all,' Piers demurred. 'It's not just his politics, it's his personality too. In spite of all the charm, he gives me the impression he's on a very short fuse. Can we afford a bod like that in a one-man post?'

His superior's face showed his irritation. 'Actually, I find him very amiable and easy-going,' Noel insisted. 'Bill's no firebrand, he's got too strong a respect for the natural order of things. He long ago made peace with his lot in life. Wish that attitude was more widespread in the service. Ambition is all very well, but self-advancement in the wrong hands is so damn corrosive,' he added pointedly. 'A tide of talent carries you all the way up the shore, but the overly ambitious, instead of saying, "Look how far I've come," complain about how they've been beached. Bloody stupid, if you ask me. No, Bill's not the type who takes pleasure in rocking the boat. He has too much to lose.'

Piers was far from put out. As he left the room, he wore a

small smile of satisfaction. Doubt now hung in the air. Once Bill Jackson sensed it, it would speed him on his way to self-destruction. Of that, Piers Rockingham was certain.

Starburst was missing. The framed photograph of the horse on Noel Hargreave-Smith's bedside table had been removed. He had spotted the gap immediately. It happened a week after the Queen's Birthday Party.

On that evening, Sylvia had witnessed her husband at his most angry and it was as if, having experienced the worst, she was no longer fearful of courting his displeasure. On the contrary, she had begun to make demands of her own. Much of it was the result of a private conversation she'd had with the delightful lady who had woven together palm leaves and bougainvillea and lilies and peacock feathers to create the table decorations for the birthday party. At one stage in the evening, Sylvia, very tipsy, had had to be restrained from seizing a couple of these arrangements to use in an impromptu floral fan-dance.

On the following day, Belle Masters had appeared in the compound to collect her numerous vases and buckets. She was Eurasian, of course, and frightfully common, but very jolly, and Sylvia was desperate for some jollity. Marjorie moaned all the time, while Alice was perfectly pleasant, but certainly not the type of person with whom Sylvia would choose to spend her time in different circumstances. Mrs Masters, in contrast, was light, frothy, fun. Not a pal, but certainly a brief divertissement. So, the two women had gossiped.

In the course of which – much to her surprise – Sylvia had found herself disclosing far too much about the silly horse, and Noel's plans to trot round England, and her own desire for a child and – she blushed to recall it – her husband's reluctance to visit her bed. Sylvia knew it was all far too indiscreet for a diplomat's wife but, after all, she was only a beginner. And Belle *was* a hairdresser. Hearing Confessions was, after all, part of the job.

Belle had very casually made a couple of points. First, that Sylvia was in rather a strong matrimonial position, since it would not be in her husband's interests to sue for divorce or provoke behaviour on the part of his spouse which might prove embarrassing – not at this stage in his career.

'But I don't want to make him unhappy,' she had remarked plaintively. 'I want to be a good wife.'

Belle had wagged her finger reproachfully in Sylvia's face. 'A good wife knows what's best for her husband,' she had explained.

Sylvia decided that made an awful lot of sense.

The second point Belle had made was that her hair could do with a good cut, perhaps a short bob?

So, Sylvia now had a sort of Eton crop. The perm hadn't settled down yet, but Belle had assured her that it would. As it was, in the humidity and heat, Sylvia was the first to admit that it did rather look as if she'd put her fingers in a socket and suffered instant electrocution. Still, at least it wasn't lank and flapping around her ears any more. It made her feel rather seductive, actually, which was no bad thing.

'Bit sticky tonight, don't you think?' Noel had murmured one evening, after listening to the news on the World Service. Coded language meaning he wished his sleep uninterrupted by a visit from his wife.

Sylvia's heart had been thumping hard in time to the signature tune. Dum-de-dum-de-dum-de-dum. She was so nervous. But when the cue came, she was ready. She took a deep breath and said, more jauntily than she felt, 'Sticky? Yes, it is, darling. Very. Good job I asked the servant to switch on your air-conditioning after tea, so your room will be lovely and cool. I'm afraid I'll have to stay with you tonight, because my air-conditioning doesn't appear to be working at all and the other beds aren't properly aired. Don't mind, do you, darling? Follow me,' she'd added.

Noel, always the perfect English gentleman, had done exactly as he was told. He had also remembered to say thank you afterwards, although Sylvia could see from his expression that he hadn't felt in the least bit grateful.

Starburst had been the next target. Sylvia removed his portrait, but didn't quite have the nerve to dispose of it completely. That would come later. Instead, she'd put it at the bottom of the camphorwood chest in the guest room and covered it with the linen sheets they'd been given as a wedding present.

'Have you seen Starburst?' Noel had asked fretfully at breakfast the following day, as if he expected the horse to be wandering around the compound.

'Oh dear, darling,' Sylvia had replied. Noel had noticed strands of his wife's frizzed hair waving at him like a strange sea creature, as she shook her head sympathetically. 'The bearer knocked the table flying when he was dusting. Bit of a fall-out, I'm afraid. Starburst has a nasty crack in the glass, but it will soon be fixed and good as new. Then he'll be reinstated.' She took care not to say when.

Of course, Noel understood that the terms of his marriage had changed. There was little point in raising the issue, since he was enough of a diplomat to know that his wife would affect ignorance. So, he retreated. He spent more and more time in contemplation, sitting alone in the secret garden. Alone, except for his model horse and his map of the south-east of England, and his route notes and his copy of *Rural Rides*.

Surprisingly, Rockingham's gift of *The English Gardener* had proved extremely useful. The table at which Noel worked in the hut in the middle of the maze had developed a tilt. The book, propped under one leg, provided an instant cure.

Bill sat by Tommy's hospital bed. On the opposite side, Albie slept, slumped in a chair, exhausted by the vigil. Bill wondered what his daughter might be doing now. It was early evening. Would she be getting ready for bed? Or doing her homework? He had telephoned the school three times, with difficulty. On each occasion, he had spoken with Miss Patterson, who had assured him all was well. School policy was against parents calling their children. Still, Ella would be home in a couple of weeks, and then he would hear all the news. Life would come back into the house.

He smelt jasmine and knew without turning that Blossom had entered her son's room. 'Doesn't it ever make you angry?' Bill asked gently. 'Don't you ever say, "Why Tommy? Why my son?" '

The woman smiled and took the flannel out of the bowl of cold water by the side of the bed and wiped her son's forehead. She had long ago stopped asking why. She couldn't afford the energy that anger required.

'What the bloody hell is that?' Bill indicated a corner of the room, where a new electric wheelchair was parked.

Blossom gave a small sigh. 'Betty arranged for us to have it,' she explained.

He flicked a switch on the arm of the wheelchair and sprang back in pretend alarm.

Blossom obliged by chuckling. 'It doesn't work,' she said. 'Wrong voltage. And we can't charge the batteries.'

Bill gave the dormant machinery a small kick. 'You're not going to tell me it's the thought that counts, are you, Blossom?' he mocked gently. 'That the Lord is generous in his mercy? And the Americans aren't too bad either? Perhaps it's time we all stopped being so bloody obliging, so thoroughly bloody overjoyed to be given so bloody little.'

Wearily, she pulled up a chair and patted Bill's arm. 'Really, you know, it's better now for a lot of us than it was before.'

'That's what they keep telling me,' he answered sourly.

★ ★ ★

The legs had to come off; four stumpy carved pieces of mahogany. The bed had come through the French windows of the Jacksons' sitting room easily enough, but then the difficulties began. Surindabash added to the confusion by insisting on giving instructions like a demented traffic policeman. Three chowkidars and the Rockinghams' bearer sweated and strained. They chipped a chunk off the frame of the bedroom door – and then finally decided to remove the legs.

An hour later, an ox cart pulled into the compound, hired by Bill. Surindabash once again took charge of proceedings, his Pathan's woolly hat pushed back on his head, his chest almost visibly swelling with pride. The Jacksons' battered and repatched bed was placed on the cart, followed by the mattress, bound for Surindabash's house. 'Make sure he signs all the right chitties,' Bill heard Rockingham's bureaucratic voice shout from the steps of the office. He pretended not to hear.

Later, Bill sat alone in front of the dressing table in the bedroom he shared with Alice, and stared at himself in the mirror. Two sources of conflict had recently been removed from the life he shared with his wife – Ella, and now the bed. He could rub along with Alice, he could provide for his family, he was easily among the best of the Morse-code operators, he hadn't had a drink for months. In other words, he had done better than his father before him – he had stuck to the same job, refused to renege on his responsibilities. But, Christ, while he knew he had a duty to others, didn't he have a duty to himself too?

He got up and pulled the mattress more securely on to the bed. It was then that he noticed the stain. Not on the top, but on the right-hand side of the mattress, there was a rust-brown set of smudges, almost like a handprint. What do you expect from a second-hand mattress? he told himself. What the hell do you expect?

Chapter Twenty-Seven

'She said it was like liver, fresh liver, sliced clean off. First one, then the other. And hardly any blood at all. You wouldn't think that, would you?'

Ella Jackson woke to the sound of the deputy matron, Mrs Saleh's voice. Instinctively, she opened her eyes just a fraction. She was in the sick room. Much smaller than the dormitories, it housed four beds and had a worn carpet on the floor. A tin bucket was stationed by each bed, and a kidney-shaped bowl on each locker.

Mrs Saleh's voice, rattling along with excitement, intruded again. 'Her only daughter, aged thirteen, killed before her very eyes. Torture, isn't it, Miss Hope? Breasts cut off at thirteen and horribly dishonoured. I can't forget it. Years ago, but I can't forget it. I have to speak, it helps me to forget.' Mrs Saleh sighed deeply.

Ella tried not to think of the girl with her breasts cut off. And how had she been horribly dishonoured? Ella heard a rustle. She guessed from the whiff of Germolene and antiseptic, Mrs Saleh's unique aroma as she patrolled the corridors at night, that the deputy matron was adjusting her sheets. Eyes closed, she heard the click of a bedside light.

Mrs Saleh was resuming her story. 'Now, I know you are unmarried, Miss Hope . . .'

'Engaged,' Miss Hope interjected coyly.

Mrs Saleh continued, 'Well, these are delicate matters . . .'

Ella opened one eye. It was evening. In the corner, Mrs Saleh and Miss Hope sat with their backs to her bed, warming themselves around a small paraffin stove. Ella's head suddenly began to throb. She turned to ease the pain, shutting her eyes tight, as the women reacted to the movement from the bed. A tear trickled down Ella's nose. She wanted her mummy. She would make her promise never to leave her again. Really promise, a promise that you keep. Although, deep down, Ella had little belief that grown-ups knew much about those kinds of promises.

'. . . I am lying on my side.' Mrs Saleh's voice had risen two or three octaves. 'I am thinking, pretend dead, because if they discover I am Christian, the punishment might be far, far worse, isn't it?'

Miss Hope clicked her tongue sympathetically.

'I hid my face with my dupatta. Sheer silk it was, a beautiful orange colour, like the peaches on Wensleydale Road. My sister bought it for me long before the troubles began . . . I'm lying covered in blood – not my blood, of course, but looking, I hope, dead enough. A Hindu comes back into the carriage and drags out a girl, twelve, thirteen, from under my seat. She is crying and sobbing.' Mrs Saleh's voice began to tremble.

'He pulled down his trousers, hit her round the face so hard her spittle landed on my beautiful dupatta. Then he forced himself upon her and called to another who did the same. She was pure, poor, poor child. Too young to lose her womanhood. Now, I can never have another peaceful moment, because, always, her screams fill the silence. Grunting, groaning, and then the awful gurgling when they cut her throat. Zip! Like that.'

Ella's heart was crashing so hard against her rib cage, she was sure it would be heard.

'Zip!' Mrs Saleh repeated. 'When they rescued us—' her

voice had dropped to a whisper – 'I saw her body thrown to the side of the railway track, raped and cast aside.'

'Why does the good Lord sanction such atrocities?' Miss Hope asked, her usual chirpiness restrained. 'I wonder why he permits such things?'

'I don't wonder at all,' Mrs Saleh interrupted. 'Mr Saleh, God rest his soul, was also killed on that train, most horribly too. I believe the Lord wanted me to witness such acts to lead me to a calling, to give me a purpose in life, to serve others, so here I am, ever since Partition. If I don't believe that,' she added plaintively, 'what sense can it possibly make?'

What sense can it make? What sense can it make? Mrs Saleh's words kept repeating themselves in Ella's head. A snapshot of what she had seen in the maze exploded into her memory. Perhaps Aunty Marjorie had been losing her womanhood? Perhaps she was being dishonoured like the young girl on the train? Perhaps she had stabbed Uncle Ash to save herself? Or perhaps Mr Rockingham had killed him to save his wife? Or had Uncle Ash, like Mrs Saleh, played at being dead – but why?

Ella had no answers, but she knew that somewhere at the core of what she had witnessed was shame. That's why Shafi had fled. That's why the grown-ups had wanted her to accept that it was only a dream. Shame. Ella's eyes flew open. Would she become like Mrs Saleh? Had the Lord turned her into a witness because he had a calling for her?

'Are you awake, sweetie?' Miss Hope, her breath smelling of chewing gum and samosas, asked, bending over Ella's bed. 'You've had a nasty bump on the head, but that's what happens if you run in the bath house. Can I get you anything?'

Ella struggled to remember the appropriate phrase, used by those girls anxious to curry favour with Miss Patterson. She flushed slightly with embarrassment as she said, 'I want to invite the Lord into my life.'

The following evening, Ella returned to the dormitory. Watched by Zuhra, she retrieved her exercise book from its hiding place and, sitting cross-legged on her bed, for the first time since arriving at St Winifred's, she wrote at length, page after page. She described in meticulous detail what she had seen, Shafi's presence, and her failed attempts to tell the truth. She used no code, no initials. She was no longer fearful that an adult might take her away, as Tommy had warned; she had the Lord on her side. The entire episode had been for a purpose. The speed with which she was writing made most of the words illegible, so Zuhra gave up trying to read over her shoulder.

Miss Patterson had a man in her room. They sat at opposite ends of the small table she had placed by the window. The view they shared was of the hills, now snow free, and of acres of bluebells, and the girls in the playground below.

'Milk, Dr Mac?' Miss Patterson asked.

Her guest smiled acceptance. He raised his cup to his lips, then lowered it again, his hand shaking. Dr Mac had been teetotal all his life, he just looked like a drunk; a tremor to his hands, burst veins stencilling his cheeks, a body that was emaciated. He had been felled not by whisky but by almost every tropical disease known to man – amoebic dysentery, malaria, hepatitis – and a few yet to be detected. Like the figure splattered in a cartoon strip, he always bounced – or, more precisely, creaked – back to life.

Dr Mac was a travelling missionary, a charismatic preacher who, on top form, could persuade the most ardent Hindu, Muslim or Sikh to come to the Lord. He then left it to others to consolidate this fragile new-found faith, with mixed results once the convert's sense of uniqueness had passed. Dr Mac's skill did not come from a love of God. He had long ago grown bored with religion. And he loathed the intolerance it

YVONNE ROBERTS

bred. However, since he had no other skill, he went through
the motions, moving from one hill station to the next,
occasionally spending longer in Lahore or Pindi. It was an
easy life and it allowed him to indulge in his other interest
with a minimal amount of interference.

'Shortbread, Miss Patterson?' he asked. He always brought
a small gift from Lahore, where his female admirers looked
after him regally.

Denial came automatically to Miss Patterson, even
though, to her annoyance, she could imagine the sweet,
sugary, golden crumbs melting in her mouth as she spoke.
'Not for me, thank you, Dr Mac,' she answered brusquely.

The man didn't bother to coax her.

The doctor's origins were obscure. Miss Hope had once
tried to pin him down on his family tree. 'I'm like the grim
reaper,' he had replied flirtatiously. 'Like death, I have no past
and no future. All that matters is that I'm here with you now.'

Miss Hope had suddenly found herself extremely short of
breath and somewhat befuddled. 'Of course you have a
future, Dr Mac,' the young woman had insisted, sweating and
blushing. 'All the good works you do and all, isn't it? You'll
have a place in heaven, most certainly.'

'I wouldn't presume such a thing at all, Miss Hope,' he'd
sighed.

She recalled those words much later to an enthralled Mrs
Saleh. It was only then it dawned on Miss Hope that the
preacher had spoken not out of modesty but in truth.

Miss Patterson slammed the lid back on the shortbread, as
if capturing an evil genie. 'I've got a new recruit,' she began
abruptly. She shunned small talk, which she dismissed as 'the
shoehorn of seduction.' 'An English girl, one hundred percent English. Bright. Father a radio operator in the Foreign
Office. No indication that either parent is devout. She's
friendly with a girl called Zuhra, very troublesome, very
troublesome indeed. Muslim, of course.'

228

'How old?' Dr Mac asked casually. His fingers broke his shortbread into crumbs as fine as dust.

'Zuhra? Twelve or thirteen . . .' Miss Patterson replied.

'No,' he interrupted impatiently. 'The British girl.'

Miss Patterson picked up her binoculars and began to scan the playground below. 'Here she is,' she eventually said. 'Ella Jackson, aged nine. A strange girl in some ways. A bit lost . . .' She handed the binoculars to Dr Mac.

'Her mother hinted that she was inclined to be overimaginative, a little inclined to exaggerate, shall we say?' Miss Patterson added. 'Although, if anything, she's been rather withdrawn since she's been here. Naughty, because of the Muslim girl's influence, but withdrawn. Still, the good news is that, in these troubled and unpredictable times, she wants to come to our Lord.'

Dr Mac lowered the binoculars. 'I will endeavour to be her rock,' he murmured. Miss Patterson showed her approval by polishing her spectacles with great ferocity. It reminded Dr Mac how very, very gullible so many women could be.

Ella knew the Lord was on her side, not least because Caro and Milly had returned her confiscated magazine, signalling a truce had been called. The unstated terms were that, since she had kept her silence, the two seniors would leave her alone. Ella read God's support in other events too. She received a letter from her mother, promising to collect her for the first term break in ten days, and the nightmares which had fractured almost every night since she arrived at St Winifred's had begun to occur less frequently. Ella had even managed to finish embroidering her first daisy in needlework.

Best of all, Ella had Zuhra. She showed the British girl how to make plaits with extensions, taught her Pathan dances, and instructed her on the skill of using a chapati to eat curry with one hand. Ella was wanted; it had to be the Lord's work.

'Of course it isn't,' Zuhra said disparagingly. 'It's because your angel has been terribly lazy and now she's finally woken up. That's why it's making all these good things happen. Your Muslim angel,' she added mischievously. 'I can see it right there, on your shoulder. Where Miss Patterson thinks the devil sits.'

A day later, Miss Patterson informed Ella that it was time for her to meet Dr Mac. It was his habit to take small groups of potential converts – two or three at a time – into the hills for a picnic and to talk about the Lord. She would be among the chosen.

'Zuhra's seen the light too,' Ella replied eagerly, giving a generous interpretation to her friend's views on Christianity. 'She says she'd like to come too. Please, Miss Patterson, please . . .'

Zuhra stood with her eyes fixed on her own toes and said nothing. The teacher pursed her lips. Was this a miracle happening before her – or mischief in a different guise? 'Has someone told you about the cream cakes, Zuhra?' she asked sternly. 'Come on girl, it's the cream cakes, isn't it?'

'What cream cakes, Miss Patterson?' Zuhra asked, genuinely baffled.

The teacher decided to give Zuhra Iqbal the benefit of the doubt. The two girls were duly sent to the school hall to wait for Dr Mac. Ella heard the taps first. Tap, tap, tap, pause. Tap, tap. A lump came to her throat. It was as if she was receiving a signal from home. It sounded just like her father on his Morse key: dit da da da dit . . . tap, tap, tap . . . The taps grew louder. The door opened. A man in a cloak made a theatrical entrance, throwing out his arms. 'Suffer little children,' he roared enthusiastically. 'Come, my lambs, on the most exciting adventure of your lives. Join me, Dr Mac, in the wonderland that is God's love.'

Zuhra and Ella caught each other's eye and, nervously,

began to giggle. It was then Ella glanced down and saw that Dr Mac's left leg consisted of a wooden stump.

> 'Amazing grace, how sweet the sound
> That saved a wretch like me!'

Dr Mac sang at the top of his lungs.

> 'I once was lost, but now am found
> Was blind, but now I see . . .'

Dr Mac had his eyes closed and, while he bellowed out the hymn, he was tapping out the rhythm with his oak limb. Tap tap tap tap tap . . .

> ''Twas grace that taught my heart to fear
> And grace my fears relieved . . .'

Ella realised that Zuhra had joined in, her thin voice soaring above Dr Mac's.

> 'How precious did that grace appear
> The hour I first believed . . .'

Suddenly, to her surprise, Ella burst into tears and her sobs just would not stop. Dr Mac, the skilled deliverer, wrapped his arms around her and enfolded her in his cloak.

Chapter Twenty-Eight

'Oooh,' Zuhra said. The two girls and Dr Mac had taken a tonga a mile to the west of Chowdiagalli, then followed the riverbank up into the hills. Now, they were in a spectacularly beautiful clearing, ringed by pine trees. The roofs of St Winifred's were visible in a dip in the valley below. But it was not the view that had prompted Zuhra's pleasure. It was the cream cakes.

Dr Mac, unhampered by his wooden leg, had walked with a small bag strapped across his back. From it, he had drawn out a battered Bible, a bottle of lemonade, three mugs, and three cakes in a tin box. Layers of candy-pink and lime-green sponge cake cemented together with suspiciously white fluffy cream, the whole concoction decorated with hundreds and thousands.

'Eat,' Dr Mac smiled.

'Do you fear God, Dr Mac, sir?' Zuhra asked between mouthfuls, believing that she should do something to earn her treat. The three had been in each other's company for over an hour and, so far, the missionary had made no attempt to talk about hell and damnation. Alarmingly, he'd made no attempt to talk about anything much, just smiling to himself now and then.

'Do I fear God?' Dr Mac repeated the question as if he wasn't entirely sure of his response. He sighed and placed his hand on Ella's shoulder, and she hastily used the back of her

232

hand to wipe away her cream moustache. Dr Mac turned to Zuhra. 'No, child, I fear myself far more.'

'Truthfulness lends its own beauty,' Miss Patterson said. 'The leper who is horribly disfigured, if he speaks with an honest voice, never dealing in deception, will take on a radiance that holds its own attraction.'

The group of thirteen-year-olds – volunteers for this hour of Bible reading – looked unconvinced. Miss Patterson dismissed them and looked at her watch. Gone five. Dr Mac would return soon.

She walked out of the classroom, along the covered walkway, and stepped out on to the porch. Her head ached. She knew why. She must go to Peshawar in the coming break and have her spectacles replaced. She would stay at the convent and have a new summer-weight dress made.

One of the younger children came running over to her and curtsied. 'The deaconess says can she see you in her study after prep, please, Miss Patterson?' The little girl, her eyes round with fear, gabbled out the words and scuttled away.

This formal call had occurred twice before, each time before the holiday break. The head would chat aimlessly, then say how Miss Patterson was indispensable, and raise the issue of retirement. The veteran teacher, never flinching from the truth, would say that she would rather die first. In fact, that's precisely what she intended to do: die first. Until then, she would continue to protect her children and train them to resist Satan's ways.

Miss Patterson walked back into the reception area. On one wall was a roll-call of past staff. It told its own story. Initially, all the names had been British, then, gradually, in the late thirties, Anglo-Indian and Muslim names began to appear. Soon, she knew, the cry would be for an all-native staff. Such a mistake. Next, lessons would no longer be taught in the Queen's English. Trollope and Bunyan would be exiled from the curriculum, and values such as decency and honour and fair play would be treated as barely remembered eccentricities. Instead, indolence, laziness, fatalism and corruption would take over. It wasn't that she was biased towards the mother country, as silly little Miss Hope constantly complained, in her fake American accent. It was just that Miss Patterson knew British was best. It was as simple as that. It was to do with history and tradition and genes. If that made these Pakistani girls feel inferior, that's because they were. And no use pretending otherwise, no matter how much Miss Hope might prattle.

The old woman traced the stone-carved letters of the school motto at the bottom of the staff roll-call with her finger. '*In Veritate Virtus*': 'Virtue in truth.' She knew it wasn't just Miss Hope who objected to some of her views. A few parents had begun to complain too. Of course they found it painful; the truth always hurt. Virtue in truth? She had never had cause to doubt that yet.

Dr Mac's fingers gripped hard, digging into Ella's shoulders – so hard, that in an effort to free herself, she had moved from kneeling to sitting back on her ankles. Zuhra was alongside her, her mouth agape. It was all over in minutes, yet disbelief kept Ella locked in place.

After the cakes, the three had played hide and seek, then word games, then Dr Mac had suggested they pray together. At this point, Ella was convinced she would see a vision. Or at least, a voice might split the clouds asunder. God must have had a purpose for her, otherwise why had he placed her in the secret garden? Perhaps he would now be kind enough to make that purpose clear?

'Close your eyes, my children,' the man had whispered, his hand resting on her shoulder, quivering slightly. Ella decided it was as if he was drawing power from her. 'Close your eyes.' Ella immediately reopened one. Dr Mac was

234

dribbling. His left hand was under his cloak. His peg leg began to bang on the hard ground – TAP! TAP! TAP! Zuhra's eyes flew open. Dr Mac's body tensed and arched. He shuddered and groaned. His eyes still closed, he sank back on his heels and slumped. Was he dead? Zuhra made a noise that was a cross between a gasp and a chuckle. Ella turned and saw that her friend's face carried an expression she had never seen before. She wasn't laughing, she was afraid.

'God be with you.' His words drew Ella's attention back to the missionary. He was on his feet now, his back turned to them. He wiped his hand on a handkerchief and then blew his nose loudly. Throughout, he kept his gaze firmly on the ground. Ella slowly got off her knees, unsure how to behave. What had happened? Should she thank him? Or thank God? Or stay silent?

Tears were running down Zuhra's cheeks, but she was making no sound. Her reaction disorientated Ella even further. She had never ever seen her friend cry, not ever. Instead, the more oddly adults behaved, the more Zuhra's spirit glowed and her sense of fun thrived. Why was she reacting so differently now? Ella put her arms around her and tried to staunch her tears with the sleeve of her threadbare cardigan.

Dr Mac collected up the remains of the picnic. 'Now, now,' he said, smiling at the ground. 'No need for tears. You've been very good girls. Exemplary behaviour.

'Here.' He put his hand inside his cloak again. 'I'm going to give you a little present each – but don't tell Miss Patterson. In fact, you won't tell her anything at all about our skylarking, will you? You know how she hates me making a fuss of my girls.'

He drew out his hand. It held a fistful of glass bangles – green, blue, orange, purple, red – a bright, bright red. Ella remembered that Uncle Ash had given her a gift of bangles too. Zuhra grabbed the jewellery and put her hands together as if in prayer. As she did so, she very deliberately crushed the bracelets between the palms of her hands. Ella saw a thin trickle of blood between two of Zuhra's fingers. The girl backed away from the man.

Dr Mac ignored her behaviour and smiled at Ella. 'You and I must pray to the Lord again,' he said very softly. Then he turned and strode off, his leg and his stick knocking against stones. Tap-tap-tap-tap-tap . . .

Ella opened her hand and let her bangles fall one by one, before following the man of God back down the hill.

'We've got to tell someone what he did.' Zuhra was sitting cross-legged on her bed that evening, in the few minutes after prayers and before lights out. 'Stop writing for a minute,' she added crossly.

'I can't, it's important,' Ella replied.

'Stop,' Zuhra repeated.

Ella put down her pencil. 'You want to tell who about what?' she asked fiercely. 'For a start, they won't believe you, because they think you're bad. And second, they won't believe me, because, well, because . . .' She shrugged. 'Because they'll think I made it all up.

'Perhaps it was a God thing,' she added, more to give Zuhra comfort than out of conviction.

The other girl shook her head. 'He was doing something. I saw it. My cousin told me about it. She's married. He was doing what men do.'

'Saw what? What do men do?' Ella's heart beat faster.

'You know.' Zuhra appeared embarrassed. 'Well, I think I saw it,' she added quickly.

Ella was triumphant. 'See, as soon as you say, "I think", they'll say it's all in your mind. Then they'll ask all sorts of questions and you'll get muddled and then you won't know whether you saw it or didn't see it. And then they'll tell you you're wicked. And then you'll disappear.'

'Don't be so silly,' the Pakistani girl retorted, but her voice lacked confidence. 'I never want to meet him again. He's a horrible, horrible man. I wish Miss Patterson's bloody H-bomb would fall on him and burn him up.'

She buried her face in her pillow. Ella patted her friend's back awkwardly. She wasn't nearly as disturbed as Zuhra, partly because she was less clear about what had occurred, but also because she already placed the afternoon's event in that distant room, almost out of reach of memory, where she stowed all her most difficult times. Earlier, Ella had watched while Zuhra had scrubbed her hands and face almost raw, as if to rid herself of a stain impossible to move. Dr Mac hadn't even touched her, so why had she behaved so strangely?

Ella was the first to break the silence. 'Zuhra,' she said. 'Promise me, on your honour, on all your babies' heads when they're born, that you won't breathe a word to anyone about what happened? Your life may depend upon it,' she added gravely. 'Promise? Otherwise, it will all go really, really wrong. Honestly, it will.'

Zuhra sat up and turned to her friend. 'It's already gone wrong,' she said fiercely.

Ella looked uncertain. 'Well, if it has, don't say a word. It really is best. Trust me. Promise?' she insisted.

Before Zuhra could reply, Miss Hope called from the dormitory door. 'In your beds, sweeties. Hop in.' She switched off the lights. 'Nightie, night, girls.'

'Good night, Miss Hope,' twenty-eight voices parroted back.

Ella waited a few minutes until the sound of Miss Hope's flip-flops had receded down the corridor, then she whispered in the dark, 'Zuhra, you know when you said Dr Mac was doing what men do? Well, what exactly is it that they do?'

Dr Mac prepared to board the evening bus to Murree, a half hour's drive away. In a few months, he'd return for the confirmation of some of the older girls.

'Has Ella embraced the Lord?' Miss Patterson asked, as she came to say her farewells on the school porch.

'She's learning how to open her heart,' Dr Mac answered, as he hoisted his knapsack on his back, for the walk to the bus station.

'We'll see what we can do between now and your next visit,' Miss Patterson said. Her features rearranged themselves. Dr Mac observed there wasn't much to choose between a Patterson smile and a grimace. She was grimacing now. 'It's the older girl I don't trust much,' she commented.

Dr Mac was never at ease with Miss Patterson's assumption that he shared her jaundiced views of every other creed and colour. 'I don't know,' he answered amiably. 'In the end, we're all God's children, aren't we, Miss Patterson? To be used by him as he chooses?'

The following morning, after breakfast, Ella went to the area outside the kitchens where the young girls from the village worked. Some of the Muslim pupils treated the kitchen staff as beneath contempt. Ella had a different approach. Accustomed to the friendship she had with Surindabash, she had endeavoured to chat to some of the girls. One, Uzma, appeared friendlier than the rest. Now, Ella handed Uzma one of her film magazines – a sacrifice had to be made – a tin of Milo from her tuck box, three annas for a stamp, and the letter to be posted illicitly in Chowdiagalli.

This was the third time such a transaction had occurred. On each occasion, Uzma had bartered the price up. This time, Ella's letter was short, but the gist remained the same: rescue.

'Dear Mummy and Daddy,' she had written, 'I hope you are well. It is not cold any more. I am doing well in English and Arithmetic and Reading. Please, please, please, can you come and get me? I want to come home. I promise I'll be good. I miss you very, very much and the truth is, I am not at all happy. Actually, I am very miserable. This is urgent. Please do not tell a soul about this letter, especially not Miss Patterson, because complaining is forbidden. Lots and lots of love, Ella.'

Half an hour later, Uzma, walking back to her village, took the letter out of her pocket, crumpled it up, and threw it down a gully – a pale-blue speck on a river of sewage.

That night, Ella told herself it was just a matter of time. In two or three days, her mother and father would come, and then she would make sure that Zuhra was safe too. As each day went past and there was neither a letter nor any sign of her parents, Ella affected not to care.

On the fifth morning, a letter from Alice finally arrived. Ella rushed with Zuhra to the corner of the playground near the PE changing huts and the willow trees. Ella read quickly, and her face puckered in frustration. 'She doesn't believe me. She never believes me. I hate her, I hate her, I really do.'

Zuhra took the letter and read it carefully. 'It's not that she doesn't believe you,' she said quietly. 'It's because she doesn't know.'

Later that afternoon, Zuhra was called out of prep by Miss Hope. Mrs Chaudhary, the needlework teacher, had been patrolling the rows of desks, noisily chewing her way through a packet of sugared almonds, as if to remind the girls of one more privilege they were denied. Occasionally, she would stop and use the extra-long nail of her little finger to dig out fragments of nut embedded in her back teeth.

Zuhra did not come back into prep. Neither was she in supper.

After the meal, Ella ran from the dining room to the dormitory, not caring what rule she broke. As she ran, she made bargain after bargain. Please, God, let Zuhra be all right, then I'll never be rude to anyone ever again. Please,

please, God, let Zuhra be in class tomorrow and I promise to say an extra prayer in chapel every day. Please, God, I promise, I promise, I promise . . .

Zuhra's bed had been stripped bare, the mattress neatly rolled. She had had time to leave only her pencil-case under Ella's pillow, elaborately decorated by her on the outside. Inside, she had written, 'This is the property of Jayne Mansfield, Hollywood, USA. Keep Out.'

Miss Hope, at bed time, made no reference to Zuhra and nor did any of the other girls. She had been removed. What more was there to say? In the dark, Ella cried silently. She cried out of a sense of loss that, over the years, would dilute, but never go away. She cried because she believed she was to blame. First, Uncle Ash, now Zuhra, all gone. Who would be next? All gone, because of her. She had thought God was on her side, but, instead, he had punished her by taking Zuhra. The tears eased, replaced by defiance. Ella decided she didn't care about God or Miss Patterson or her stupid bomb or hell. She had no weapons with which to fight back, so she would retreat from their silly world altogether. If they didn't believe what she said, then what was the use of words?

In class, earlier that day, she and Zuhra had been chattering. Miss Patterson had punished only Zuhra, making her stand in the corner for the rest of the lesson, with her hands on her head. ' "He that hath knowledge spareth his words," ' Miss Patterson had instructed, as she often did. 'Proverbs seventeen, verse twenty-seven.'

Ella turned on her side, forcing herself to face the empty bed, and made a pledge. She, Ella Jackson, would strike herself dumb. 'He that hath knowledge spareth his words.' She would spare her words – no matter what anyone did, no matter how hard she was punished. See if she cared.

Chapter Twenty-Nine

Two days later, Miss Patterson happened to be in her room, making use of her binoculars, when she saw a woman, dressed in khaki slacks and shirt, walk down the drive from the gate. One of the girls in the playground spotted the stranger too and she was immediately engulfed by children, exuberantly shouting, 'Good morning, memsahib, good morning. Is your daughter coming to our school?' Mrs Saleh, on playground duty, tried to shepherd the girls back to their own territory, but they were too intrigued; strangers were rare at St Winifred's.

A few minutes later, Betty Brooking was ushered into Miss Patterson's small office, next to the head's study. The two women introduced themselves. Miss Patterson told herself smugly that Mrs Brooking was the woman she might have become, if she hadn't turned to the Lord first. Betty decided that any individual who wore fingerless net mittens and long sleeves in June had to be crazy.

'I told Ella's parents I'd be dropping by and they were delighted,' Betty said firmly.

'Yes, but did they give you written permission to take her out for tea?' Miss Patterson countered. 'I mean, you must appreciate we can't let our children leave with any Tom, Dick or Harry.'

The visitor raised an eyebrow. Miss Patterson observed

that the second button of her blouse was open, completely unnecessarily.

'Do I look like any Tom, Dick or Harry?' Betty asked dryly. Miss Patterson noticed that her lips were very red and matched her fingernails; a pampered woman, plainly accustomed to getting her own way. In Miss Patterson's world, all Americans were spoilt.

'Why don't you give Bill or Alice a ring?' Betty suggested, refusing to allow herself to become irritated.

'I could book a call, I suppose . . .' the teacher began hesitantly. 'But sometimes we can wait for several hours to be put through, you know.'

'Well, may I see Ella?' Betty requested. 'I've got a few things I'd—'

'We have a strict policy on term time gifts,' Miss Patterson interrupted.

The American woman sat back in her chair and folded her arms. 'Fine,' she answered crisply. 'Then I suggest you book a call to Peshawar and I'll wait for as long as it takes. Perhaps Ella might like to speak to her parents too, when they come on the line? Or is there a policy about that as well?' she asked, giving a forced smile.

Betty took out her cigarette case, lit up and exhaled. Through the dancing ribbon of smoke, she smiled and said, 'You don't mind, do you?'

'I'm afraid I very much do,' the teacher began, but she stopped. The American woman had leant forward and was exposing an indecent amount of breast – almost certainly on purpose.

Mabel Patterson fidgeted, unsure how to react.

Betty was speaking again. 'So, shall we book the call and see if Ella is available to chat to her mom and daddy?'

'She can't—' Miss Patterson stopped abruptly. Why did this woman make her feel so . . . jumpy? 'What I mean is, well, she can't, because she's lost her voice. Or, rather, she appears to have been struck dumb . . . temporarily, I'm sure . . .' her voice trailed away. It did sound rather absurd. But somehow, when everyone was closeted at St Winifred's, what was ridiculous to an outsider was regarded as perfectly normal practice within the confines of the school.

Betty stubbed out her barely smoked cigarette and gave the teacher a measured look. 'Struck dumb? What do you mean? How long is it since she said anything?'

'Not long,' Miss Patterson replied, then, anticipating the next question, she added, 'We didn't want to trouble her parents. In our experience, this kind of thing gets sorted out very quickly if we don't make too much of a fuss.'

'Too much of a fuss?' Betty made no attempt to hide her surprise. 'Forgive me, Miss Patterson, I've only had five children, but, in my limited experience, a child who chooses to act dumb and sticks with it for longer than five minutes is seriously disturbed about some damn thing. What exactly has been going on here?'

Mabel Patterson suddenly winked. Or, rather, a nervous tic gave her the appearance of winking. Americans were so rude, so loud, so absolutely disrespectful of one's status and seniority. It was this ridiculous obsession with all being equal. If the good Lord had wished us to be equal, he would have made us the same colour, speaking in one tongue.

Betty rose to her feet and, to Miss Patterson's alarm, she began to make for the door, the staff door, and entry to the interior of the school – not the visitors' door, and the exit to the outside world. 'If you refuse to bring Ella to me,' she said, 'then I guess I'll have to go find her for myself.'

Ella came into Miss Patterson's office unaware that she had a visitor. It took only seconds for Betty to make an assessment. The child's gymslip had a large hole where a darn had drifted apart, her knees were grubby and she looked even thinner than usual, but, otherwise, nothing drastic had changed.

243

'Ella, honey,' she said and swept the little girl into her arms.

Ella stiffened. She wanted to drown in the woman's lemon-perfumed hair, but wariness held her back. She said nothing. Betty sat the child next to her and held her hand. Fleetingly, Ella allowed herself to wonder what it would be like to have a mother like Betty.

'How have you been, Ella? We're all so looking forward to seeing you back home. Mommy and Daddy send lots of love. Daddy's real busy right now and Mommy's helping at the hospital. And Tommy's a lot better.'

Betty saw Ella's eyes flicker. She guessed she hadn't known about Tommy.

Ella decided to keep her gaze trained on her free hand, resting in her lap. Staying silent was easy amongst enemies, more difficult with those who brought comfort. But they were the most dangerous, the ones she could least trust. Besides, a pledge was a pledge.

Miss Patterson began to make clucking noises with her tongue. 'She's such a wilful child. We've punished, coaxed and cajoled her, but she insists on this silliness. I've warned her the way of transgressors is hard.'

Betty stroked Ella's cheek gently, and, without looking at Miss Patterson, she said flatly, ' "The way of transgressors is hard." Proverbs thirteen, verse fifteen. If I recall, Miss Patterson, that verse begins, "Good understanding giveth favour . . ." I have another thought from Proverbs which, as a teacher, I always tried to keep in mind. I'm sure you must be aware of it? "Acquire wisdom and with all that you acquire, acquire understanding . . ." Understanding, Miss Patterson, so important, don't you think, when handling children who are so impressionable?'

Betty turned on the older woman. Her anger was undisguised.

Who was the bigger sinner? she thought to herself. Was it herself, a drinker, an occasional fornicator, a person who now did too little for others? Or was it this waspish, sanctimonious bully of a woman, who prided herself in literally putting the fear of God into little girls? What test in life had this passionless, rigid spinster ever passed? What sin had she ever struggled to resist? If avoidance of life's pleasures was to be regarded as a virtue, the result would be the kind of world Miss Patterson inhabited, devoid of tolerance, forgiveness and understanding.

Betty had worked with teachers like Mabel Patterson. In the name of God, they took pride in exorcising a child's high spirits, her curiosity and confidence, and replacing them with only the deadening desire to please. That wasn't education, that was embalming. If she was going to break all her own rules and step into Ella's life, Betty told herself, what was the point of that, if it wasn't to make an improvement?

The woman gently lifted the girl's face towards her. 'Honey,' she smiled, 'I want you to pack your things. It's holiday time, anyway, in a week or so, so why don't you come back with me to Peshawar now, and maybe – who knows – we can find your voice on the way?'

Miss Patterson rose from her chair, her face taut with anger. She couldn't remember the last time the rules had been so thoroughly disregarded. 'I forbid you to leave until we have the approval of this child's parents.' Her voice was glacial. 'She is in my care until that duty is discharged. You wait until Mr and Mrs Jackson hear about this.'

'Well, Miss Patterson, if you recall, earlier in these proceedings, that's precisely what I was prepared to do – wait to hear from the Jacksons. But, hell, I don't think I'll bother after all. I'm staying at the Connaught Hotel. Ella and I will leave tomorrow. I'd appreciate it if you could arrange for her trunk to be sent over? And I hope, for your sake, Miss Patterson, that when Ella's voice does return she doesn't tell us something you might have cause to regret. It's been a pleasure meeting you.'

Betty Brooking and Ella Jackson walked up the drive, pausing briefly for the girl to wave goodbye to her classmates in the playground. Then, as Mabel Patterson watched, the child broke away from the woman and disappeared round the side of the school. She re-emerged minutes later, an exercise book, a green dupatta and a pencil-case held close to her chest. She and the American walked out of the gates without looking back.

Mabel Patterson went to the school secretary's office and obtained the Jacksons' telephone number. The operator made an immediate connection with Peshawar and she soon found herself speaking to Alice Jackson. She explained briefly what had happened, expressed her concern that rules had been broken, and decided against mentioning Ella's silence.

'I'm so sorry,' Alice apologised. 'I'll come immediately and try and sort this out. I'll telephone Mrs Brooking at her hotel. She's normally very reliable. Ella's all right, isn't she?' she asked anxiously.

'Now, you don't really think we'd let anything happen to her, do you, Mrs Jackson?' Miss Patterson said, as if she was talking to a naughty five-year-old.

The Connaught Hotel was the best hotel in Chowdiagalli. It was built on two floors in a triangular shape, around a central courtyard to offer views of the surrounding valleys and mountain ranges to all its guests. The rooms, even the most modest, led out on to spacious verandahs, partitioned by elaborately carved screens. Long before the end of the Raj, the Connaught had begun to slide into a shabbiness that added to its eccentricity. As a result, it attracted a certain type of more anarchic visitor. The rest kept away, preferring the Cecil Hotel in Murree, much to the satisfaction of the Connaught's staff, the youngest of whom had given thirty years' service. The dining room was filled with an eclectic taste in furniture, including two disused Victorian commodes. Bathrooms were more likely to house a stuffed tiger than an appropriate number of towels, while the library was home to a collection of pornographic drawings, a secret discovered by many a traveller seeking to learn more from the section labelled, 'Mughal Architecture.'

Betty Brooking had become a regular visitor over the months. She saw the Connaught as her retreat. She was warmly welcomed, not because she gave baksheesh generously, which she did, but because she delighted to hear the stories of days gone by. And each one of the hotel's geriatric but sprightly room boys was an historian in search of an audience.

Now, four of them stood to attention in a line, saluting, as Betty and Ella climbed the main stairs of the hotel. Betty returned their *asalam aleikums*. Once in her suite, a vast set of rooms which included a bedroom that Ella thought must be the size of a ballroom, a steady stream of servants – uninvited – busied themselves. One took Ella's sandals to be cleaned, another offered her iced water on a tray, a third produced a freshly peeled mango on a silver salver, while a fourth occupied himself on the verandah. Once he was done, beaming with pride, he beckoned the woman and child out.

Dizzy from the attention, Ella obeyed. A pretty English cream tea had been prepared. A snowy white cloth, a silver teapot, a tall glass of homemade lemonade, scones, cream, jam that looked more like raspberry sauce, wafer-thin cucumber sandwiches and, incongruously, a big bottle of tomato ketchup had been set out on an ornate table.

Betty put her hand on the girl's shoulder. 'The ketchup's for me,' she laughed. 'They think I have it with everything.'

The four bearers watched with great approval while the child ate and ate. Betty sat, sipping Scotch.

Ella's reaction to her rapid change in circumstance was cautious. For all she knew, she could be carted back to St Winifred's at any time, so she decided it was best if she didn't permit herself to overly enjoy what was on offer. Likewise, she tried not to consider the chances of an early return to Peshawar. That, too, would be too much like good luck. And Ella knew she'd done nothing to deserve that.

After tea, Betty asked only one question. 'Would you like a nap?' The nine-year-old shook her head. 'Well, let's go and have some fun,' the woman ordered lightly, linking her arm through her charge's and steering her through the door, followed by their entourage.

Chowdiagalli was at its best in the early evening. Each shop twinkled with fairy lights, visitors paraded in their finest clothes, and street entertainers provided impromptu shows – fire eaters, jugglers, conjurers. Betty and Ella strolled first up and then down and then up The Mall, like everyone else. In the small square in front of the church, a family of acrobatic dwarfs tumbled and flipped and occasionally collided. Nearby, a beggar with two withered legs clapped and cheered along with the crowd, as passers-by discreetly pressed small change on him. Betty took Ella into several shops, buying a couple of cotton dresses, some new sandals, a shalwar-qamiz and a dupatta, pyjamas, slippers and toiletries. Each time, Ella indicated her approval by a nod.

As the night drew in and the air grew crisper, Betty bought whisky, chocolate and a bundle of second-hand girls' comics. – School Friend, Girl, Girls' Crystal – the only ones on offer. Then, the two made their way back to the hotel, weighted down with packages. It was the first time that Ella could remember, when she had been the sole reason for an adult expedition. As the couple approached the hotel, she gave a little skip. Betty pretended not to notice.

In the suite, Ella was relieved to see that she hadn't been banished to the dark dungeon of the second bedroom. Instead, a small bed had been made up next to Betty's four-poster. The American sat propped up in bed reading while Ella settled down with chocolate and comics. Betty watched without comment as the child tucked her exercise book under her pillow. Later, Ella stole a glance at her. She really wished she could say thank you. But to her surprise, even though she wanted it to, the sound refused to come.

Breakfast was taken on the verandah, just after dawn. As they ate soft rolls and alarmingly yellow scrambled eggs, the colours of the day changed before their eyes – the dark blue of the distant mountains turned a pale lilac and the creamy mists of the valleys dissolved to reveal forests with tones of dark olive, khaki, apple and lime. Smoke from dozens of charcoal and pinewood fires spiralled up like silver corkscrews in the sky. Goats' bells clanged; copper pots clattered; the mullah called; babies wailed; old women shouted greetings; and a trio of small children danced on the tin roof of their shack, whistling and waving to attract Ella's attention. Much to their delight, she waved back.

Betty pointed to her right. 'See those mountains,' she said. 'That's Kashmir, beautiful Kashmir. That's where Ash is fighting the Indians. Your daddy says he should be home any day now. Won't that be great? Ash told me that you were his favourite nine-year-old.'

The glass of orange juice slipped from Ella's hand, smashing a plate and sending chips of china in all directions. 'Don't worry, honey,' Betty reassured her. 'Accidents happen.'

Later, she watched Ella as she played on the hotel's solitary swing. She noticed that the exercise book that the girl had carried with her constantly since leaving St Winifred's was gripped tightly in her hand, as if her life depended upon it. The child had begun to relax, but, since breakfast, caution had returned to her face. Betty figured what had triggered it was mention of Ash.

A man disappears without warning; a child grows

disturbed at the mention of his name. Betty understood now what had troubled her since the evening following the Queen's Birthday Party, when Ash had failed to meet her as arranged at the riding stables. She had thought that she'd been disappointed, her pride wounded. Now, she recognised it was not that, which had tormented her. It was a growing sense of trepidation.

'Ell-a, Ell-a.' Ella almost fell off the swing at the sound of the voice she knew so well. She looked up and there was her mother, standing in the hotel drive, her arms open wide. Ella ran straight into Alice's embrace. As she nestled into her mother's neck, relishing her familiar smells, loving the softness of her skin, the pleasure of the reunion was already overtaken by anxiety. She wanted to say, 'Promise you'll never leave me again. Promise, promise. Promise I won't have to go away to school ever again.' But she couldn't.

A little later, the two women and the child, a silent trio, walked through the hotel gardens. Alice held Ella's hand tightly. She ought to have visited her daughter more often, she told herself, she shouldn't have left Ella so long, she could have ignored Miss Patterson's advice to stay away. Why did looking after children always have to be so full of 'shoulds' and 'oughts'?

Alice glanced at Betty. She was embarrassed that the American woman had shown more involvement in Ella than Alice herself had managed. She was sure the child's throat would heal as soon as they were in the heat of Peshawar. It was probably just a mild infection. Of course, she would have sorted it out herself once Ella came home for the holidays, but Betty had to do it her way.

The American had offered several times to visit St Winifred's. She'd made the excuse that she was sightseeing in the area or going on a horse trek through the hills, so she could easily drop in. Each time, Alice had refused. But why?

If she had been too busy to make the trip herself, why hadn't she given Betty permission? Alice shook her head, as if to clear her thoughts. Of course, she knew why. Ella belonged to her. If anyone was going to visit the child, it had to be the mother.

She glanced down at her daughter. Her hair had grown, her gymslip was much too short; she smelt of wood smoke and her eyes were rimmed with pink. Alice experienced a pang: had Ella cried herself to sleep each night? Best not to think about it. What was done, was done. Besides, if she did ask Ella about homesickness now, it would only make it much worse when it was time for her to return.

'Dr Danvers will have you back to normal in no time,' Alice told the girl. 'A good dose of cough medicine and you'll be as right as rain.' Ella had expected her mother to be cross with her for all the trouble she'd caused. So, now, she was grateful for the warmth in her voice.

'Do you know if the school's taken her temperature, Betty?' Alice asked, anxious to demonstrate her concern.

The other woman stopped walking, so her companions followed suit. 'Honey,' she replied in her slow, lazy, drawl. 'I don't think with this problem a thermometer's going to be any help at all.'

Ella was asleep, clutching a new school satchel. She sat between her mother and Betty in the taxi hired to make the trip to Peshawar. The adults made aimless conversation, until Betty asked, 'Do you think something happened at the school?' She kept her voice low, so as not to disturb the child, and in neutral, so that her mother didn't become defensive.

'Oh, surely not,' Alice answered dismissively. 'Ella wrote home telling us how happy she was.'

Betty pressed on. 'Did you meet Ella's teacher?' she asked. 'She's a bit of a Bible-thumping dragon. Did you know she had photographs of the H-bomb pinned up all over one wall of her office? She told me that Ella had become very close to the Lord . . .'

'Of course I know,' Alice answered untruthfully. 'Miss Patterson's bite isn't nearly as bad as her bark, you know.'

'Miss Patterson and I had a conversation on the telephone yesterday afternoon,' Betty tried again. 'She mentioned that Ella's best friend, Zuhra, had been particularly naughty – and had recently been removed from the school over some incident or other. Do you think that's why Ella has become mute?'

'Nonsense,' Alice replied brusquely. 'If something had upset Ella, I'd be the first to know.'

Chapter Thirty

'Wires? What do you mean, man, wires?' Noel Hargreave-Smith had become increasingly irritable over the past few weeks. He was spending more and more time in his secret garden. So much so, that it was no longer 'secret', more a branch of his office. Now, he sat with Bill outside the hut. The latter was drinking an orange squash, Hargreave-Smith was gazing gloomily at a pre-lunch gin and tonic.

'Wires?' the Deputy High Commissioner repeated.

Bill attempted to explain that the small copper wires were for use in eye operations at the Quaker Hospital.

'And?' Hargreave-Smith prompted.

Bill tried again. 'If we could bring them in through the diplomatic bag. Just as a one-off. Enough to keep the hospital going for a year or so.' He cringed even as he begged the favour. 'It would make a huge difference. Some of the blind are just kids . . .'

The Deputy High Commissioner stared at his drink thoughtfully, 'You realise the bag is only for official purposes, don't you, old man? I mean, it's highly irregular to allow anything else . . . We could all be put in a most invidious position.' Bill began to feel optimistic

'I'm sorry,' Noel was saying, 'I'm going to have to say no on this. Where would we be if we each decided to break the rules whenever we chose? Look, I'll tell you what I'll do—'

he patted Bill on the back — 'I'll pretend we never had this conversation, no blot on the copy book, how's that?'

Bill sat flushed and utterly humiliated. Tell the bastard his reports home are shite, his wife's a bloody pea brain, his canter around the sodding countryside is a failed man's bloody folly. Tell him! Instead, Bill exchanged a few more pleasantries, made an excuse, and left.

Half an hour later, only Surindabash, serving his boss a solitary lunch, saw the sahib pour a very large whisky.

Just as Ella Jackson had discovered the existence of a different hierarchy at St Winifred's — saints and sinners, Anglican and Muslim, brown and white — so Marjorie Rockingham emerged from what her husband termed a malarial attack to a different social order prevailing in the compound of the Deputy High Commission.

In her absence, she had been usurped by Alice Jackson. So, when Alice was away in the hills and Marjorie heard a familiar cooee on her verandah, she was cheered. Sylvia stood twitching with excitement. In her left hand, she held a makeshift blindfold made from a scarf.

'I've thought of an idea. I've thought of something that we can do that's really, really useful. Isn't that most awfully exciting?'

Sylvia came towards her, waving the scarf. 'Just for a wheeze, let me put the blindfold on you and take you to my next little scheme. It's not far, I promise.'

Marjorie accepted her fate. Sylvia led her down the verandah steps, blindfolded her, spun her round, then propelled her towards what Marjorie guessed were the servants' quarters. 'Here we are!' Sylvia giggled, whipping off the scarf as she spoke. Marjorie blinked in the sunlight, then, to Sylvia's amazement, the woman began to shriek hysterically.

The sound of her screams roused Bill Jackson, who had

been sleeping off the effects of the whisky. He jumped out of bed naked, grabbed a bath towel, and ran in the direction of the sobs, wrapping the towel around him as he ran across the main compound lawn. He passed two chowkidars on the way. '*Jaldi, jaldi!*' he shouted. They looked at each other, bemused. They were paid to watch, not do. Piers Rockingham and Noel Hargreave-Smith, in the process of opening up the office after the afternoon siesta, began to half jog in Bill's wake.

Ahead, Bill could see Sylvia emerging from the door of the secret garden, her arm around a shaking and obviously distressed Marjorie. 'Someone's in there, I saw him, I did, I did,' Marjorie said tearfully as he drew closer, trying to explain her reaction. 'Did you see him, Sylvia?'

Bill picked up a brick and walked cautiously into the garden. On the few occasions he'd visited before, he'd paid no attention to the layout of the garden. Now, he was acutely aware – battered hedges, a small decrepit maze, clusters of bushes and then, suddenly, the clearing where he had sat earlier with Hargreave-Smith. A hut, two chairs, a table – nothing out of the ordinary.

'Are you all right, Bill?' Noel called from the door. 'Anything up?'

Then Bill heard Rockingham's voice. 'Best come out, old man, we'll send in the chowkidars. Don't want anyone getting hurt, do we?'

He was about to do as he was told when Piers shouted again. 'Come on, man. Come out.' His voice had an edge to it that Bill was certain had nothing to do with concern for his safety.

Instead of leaving, he turned one of the chairs to face the hut and sat in it, an incongruous figure in his bath towel and sandals. He heard the mutterings of the two chowkidars as they came nearer. Bushes ringed the clearing. A couple could be silently observed here, and never know they were being spied upon. What had Ella said? Ash and the Rockinghams had been together in the clearing? But why hadn't Shafi backed her story? Or had he lied and then fled from the compound out of fear?

As the two reluctant watchmen reached the clearing, Bill Jackson was on his hands and knees, trying to peer under the raised hut. He sat back on his heels, defeated. It was only in the cinema that vital clues dropped out of pockets. If Ash had spent time here on the night of the Queen's Birthday Party, he had left no mementos. Bill walked slowly towards the garden door, to be met by his two superiors.

'Not a soul in the place,' he reported to Piers.

A few minutes later, the car bearing Alice, Ella and Betty from Chowdiagalli turned into the drive of the British High Commission. At first, Alice thought Bill had organised a reception committee, since almost every resident of the compound was standing in a group on the lawn. Then, she took in Marjorie's distressed state and Bill's near-nakedness. Betty had put her arm around Ella, and felt the girl tense as she, too, caught sight of the odd gathering. A smile spread across Ella's face as she recognised her father. As soon as the car came to a halt, she was out of the door and in his arms, oblivious of the audience.

'How we've missed you. How have you been, my little peahen?' Bill smiled.

Alice gazed at the assembled company who appeared frozen, as if in a game of musical statues. 'What on earth's going on here?' she asked lightly.

Surindabash smiled broadly, revealing a new gold tooth. Ella admired it, then planted a kiss on his cheek, and ran to her bedroom. She saw with relief that nothing had changed. She immediately placed her exercise book under the sheet of newspaper lining the bottom of her wardrobe. Zuhra would have approved.

Later, as Surindabash hovered, Bill warned Ella not to go with the cook to the bazaars. 'Some people are a bit cross at the moment,' he explained. 'I've told Surindabash not to go himself, until all this dies down. I've told him to get the vegetable- and fruit-wallah to deliver to the house but—'

The cook interrupted, looking outraged. 'Vegetablewallah is dirty, rotten cheat. No damn good.'

Bill smiled. 'Just play in the compound, where we can see you,' he suggested gently to his daughter. 'Don't even go across to the park or play with the kids outside. It's not worth the risk, and it's only for a little while.'

That evening, Ella was sitting up in bed, *A History of Insects* open on her knees. She hadn't written anything since Zuhra's departure. Nor could she bring herself to write now. Earlier, Surindabash had been the first to tell her of Shafir's unexpected departure weeks before. 'Perhaps he'll come back,' the cook told the silent child philosophically. 'To say goodbye.' Ella heard a sound. Her father was watching her, standing in the doorway. He sat down on the bed and picked up the exercise book. She reached out and snatched it back, anxiety leaving her breathless. Her father made no comment. Instead, he took his fountain pen from his shirt pocket and gently opened the palm of her hand. In capital letters he wrote, 'DADDY LOVES YOU.' The scratching of the nib made Ella giggle. It was the first sound she had made for days.

'I told you she'd soon be back to normal,' Alice's voice broke in. She walked over to the bed and reached out to give her daughter a night time kiss. Ella curled her temporarily tattooed hand into a fist.

Three days later, Alice took her daughter to see Trixie Danvers at the hospital. She had admonished, threatened, punished and still Ella refused to speak. What's more, the child who previously was always a free spirit, wandering around the compound for hours, now refused to leave the bungalow, unless she was with her mother or father or Surindabash.

'I'm at my wits' end,' Alice told Dr Danvers. 'I don't know how she can do this to me.'

Ella blinked hard.

Trixie Danvers examined the girl, then questioned her gently. 'What happened at school, Ella?'

'She couldn't have been happier,' Alice replied.

Dr Danvers continued, 'Was there an incident? Did you see something unpleasant, perhaps? Or was there bullying?' She addressed her next question to Alice, but it was Ella she was watching. 'Have you talked to her friends?'

Alice shook her head.

Ella decided to see how far down she could push her left ankle sock with the toe of her right sandal. She concentrated hard.

The doctor reached out for Ella's hand. 'Have you been to visit Tommy yet?' she asked. 'I know he's longing to see you. Mummy's probably told you. He's a lot better than he was, but still very weak. Alice, perhaps you and Ella might like to pop in on him on the way out?'

Tommy was asleep in his hospital bed, his mouth slightly agape. Ella saw that his teeth were yellowing. She realised how much she needed him to wake up, to live, to hear everything she had to say, from beginning to end. She made a bargain with God. If he gave Tommy fresh life, she would overlook the business with Zuhra and try to serve him again. It would be difficult, of course, but she promised to really try.

Noel Hargreave-Smith hated cold consommé. It reminded him of strained ditchwater. Sylvia knew he disliked it, yet recently she had persisted in ordering it for several meals a week. It was time to make a stand. He placed his soup spoon by the side of the bowl and his hands in his lap. He opened his mouth to protest when his wife began to speak.

'I've got something to tell you,' she giggled excitedly. 'It's the most wonderful news for us both. Really, really exciting.'

Noel swallowed hard. He noticed for the first time that small whiteheads had appeared in a crop in the crease of Sylvia's chin.

'Are you ready?' his wife twittered.

He nodded his head numbly.

'Da-daaa!' Sylvia shouted with a flourish.

Daddy, did she say Daddy? Noel panicked. He shut his eyes, and opened them again to see that Sylvia had unfurled a rolled drawing.

'What do you think of that?' she challenged him triumphantly.

She was holding two drawings of his garden. One as it was now laid out; the second had been landscaped, presumably according to her own design.

'It's a Cobbett garden,' she trilled. 'You know, your Cobbett. Do you remember that book that Piers gave you for your birthday? The one you use to prop up furniture? Well, I borrowed it and had a look and the man had some quite good ideas really – roses, that sort of thing. I know you're not much interested but I thought we'd try and adapt a few and make you a lovely garden all to yourself. Isn't that exciting?'

Noel couldn't bring himself to speak.

'You'll have to stop her.' Piers Rockingham brought his fist down hard on the dining-room table, making the silver salt-cellar skitter almost its entire length. Marjorie showed no reaction. She supposed she must have ceased to care. She didn't care if he hit her or hated her; she didn't care if she lived or died. The strongest emotion she could rouse was contempt for the man she had once so treasured. At least catastrophe had brought clarity of vision. She saw herself and

Piers as a parasitical couple, only capable of flourishing when feeding off the misfortune of others. So, why hadn't she told the truth that afternoon when Sylvia had led her to the secret garden? Why hadn't she spoken out, then? She had recited the answers to herself over and over again. Because she was his wife and wives don't betray their husbands. Because what she owed him still outweighed all the rest. And because she was a coward.

Piers now had his face inches away from hers. 'Look at me, Marjorie,' he ordered, his voice soft. 'Persuade Sylvia not to touch the garden. Think of something else for the stupid woman to do. If she starts digging up and knocking down, Christ knows what she'll find. You do understand that, don't you, Marjorie?'

She nodded her head slowly. Marjorie had never doubted that her husband was clever enough to escape blame. What she couldn't fathom was how he also managed to evade the demons of guilt that plagued her every waking minute. Piers slept like a baby.

Rockingham resumed his meal. He was certain his wife would fail, so he was already beginning to formulate an alternative plan.

An hour after dawn the following morning, Bill Jackson arrived at the army riding stables. He had calculated accurately – Brigadier Sammy Sharrif was just preparing to mount. The Brigadier had a special responsibility for covert operations and figured often in Hargreave-Smith's despatches home, mostly for his alleged incompetence. Ash had been much less scathing about his superior officer. He had told Bill that, in his opinion, the Brigadier was informed, astute, cunning. He was a long-term survivor. In Pakistani politics, there was no greater compliment.

'Morning, Bill.' The Brigadier's British accent had been given further polish at Sandhurst.

'Got a minute, Brigadier? I'd be very grateful,' Bill asked. The last time they'd met, at the Queen's Birthday Party, they'd chatted about the pleasures of flying a Tiger Moth.

The Brigadier issued brief instructions and, within minutes, Bill found himself flanked by three young officers, tactfully riding out of earshot. 'Let me read your mind,' the Brigadier began, before Bill had a chance to speak. 'Then, if anyone should ask if you raised this particular question with me, we can both honestly deny that you brought up any such topic, if you get my drift?'

Bill nodded.

The army man looked ahead as he spoke. 'You are concerned about Colonel Khan. He is supposed to be on manoeuvres in Kashmir, but his wife hasn't heard from him, he missed your tennis game, he's made no attempt to contact you. You respect his right to private life – but you are naturally concerned, am I correct?'

'That's about it,' Bill agreed. He held back on the issue of what his daughter may or may not have witnessed.

'We have worries too,' the Brigadier continued. 'The Brotherhood have been making all sorts of allegations about the colonel. They've even claimed that he's a spy for our American friend, Mr Brooking.' The Brigadier flicked his whip. 'Such nonsense, of course.'

Bill thought the man sounded ambivalent. Christ, why was everything in this country so convoluted?

'Colonel Khan's activities have drawn the Brotherhood's attention to the army in a way that some of the colonel's less flamboyant military colleagues find . . .' he searched for an appropriate word, '. . . intrusive. Some of Khan's critics say that that is entirely his purpose. I myself believe that he is simply having a good time. Ash is nothing if not a bloody good hedonist.' The Brigadier gave a dry chuckle, then grew serious again.

'What we do not want is for Colonel Khan to have an

accident for one reason or another that might prove an embarrassment to the army. Particularly not so soon after the country has declared itself an Islamic Republic.' He gave a small shudder. 'Can you imagine the newspaper headlines in the *Frontier Post*? "Offices in disgrace . . ." In this country, as you well know, old boy, the army is more accustomed to pulling the strings than finding itself the subject of ridicule from a bunch of Islamic clerics. Next thing, by God, they'll be demanding a purge of the whole damn military.'

'So where is Ash?' Bill asked bluntly.

The Brigadier turned in his saddle to observe the Englishman's reaction. 'We don't know,' he answered flatly. 'But there have been other occasions when he has removed himself from the scene without explanation.'

'So he's not in Kashmir?'

The Brigadier smiled wearily. 'He might be but certainly not on army business. We have a record of his movements until the day of the Queen's Birthday Party. Then, nothing.'

Bill's stomach lurched. 'Did Ash know he was being watched?' he asked.

The army man gave a short laugh. 'But of course, old boy. You don't go around helping yourself to other men's wives and expect to go unobserved, do you? The officer responsible for organising Khan's surveillance claims that the reports for the day he went missing have been mislaid – not by him, of course. More like Khan provided him with a monetary reward for a temporary lapse in concentration. Perhaps Ash has cleverly arranged to slip away for a few days in the hills with a lovely lady?'

Bill struggled to make sense of the information the Brigadier was providing. 'Are you saying he's has chosen to disappear? You don't think . . .' Bill couldn't quite bring himself to say the words.

'Do I think he's been hurt? Eliminated by the Brotherhood, perhaps? Or taught a lesson by a cuckolded husband?' The

Brigadier gave an enigmatic smile. 'Ash's wife has suggested to me that he's at this very moment repenting at his leisure in Chitral or Sindh. She believes he will return, eventually, a chastened boy.'

'And you? What do you think?' Bill urged.

The Brigadier sighed. 'I think it's possible. Or perhaps, my friends, the fundamentalists, have chosen to listen to the mullahs. Every day they have been telling the young and eager that Islam's time has come; Gamel Abdul Nasser is the new leader. They tell the crowds they are Muslims first, Pakistanis second. Ash is, at times, more Raj than the Raj. His taste for white women is seen by some as an affront. Someone may have decided to give him a good hiding and he will appear when his wounds have healed. Perhaps.' The Brigadier pulled up his horse. 'Your friend is a clever man, Mr Jackson. An enigmatic man. I believe he is not nearly so easily read as my Muslim brothers believe.'

'What should I do?' Bill asked. He was aware of a growing sense of shame. He should have taken Ella at her word. Perhaps she had seen Ash's death. But if so, where was the body? And how could the Rockinghams – especially Marjorie – sustain such a picture of innocence?

'What should I do?' he asked again.

The Brigadier waved his hand regally. 'Do nothing,' he instructed. 'Something messy has occurred. It's a damn nuisance because it will give us all a terrible headache. But until we know precisely what the size and nature of the mess might be, my advice is to do nothing. For now, this is a little local difficulty. Do you understand me, Mr Jackson?'

Bill nodded his head – but he didn't understand at all. Why had the Brigadier taken him so fully into his confidence? Was he warning him off Ash's trail? – or goading him into action?

After Ella's return from St Winifred's, Betty had suggested that she give her a regular swimming lesson at the Peshawar

Tennis Club. Alice had been relieved to have the child off her hands for a couple of hours. Betty picked Ella up each morning at 7.30 am, before the fiercest heat of the day. Now, after his conversation with the Brigadier, Bill decided to make a quick detour to the club, to catch Betty before returning to the compound for the morning shift.

When he reached the pool, she was standing on the diving board, showing Ella how to prepare for a dive. Her hair was tied back and she wore a simple black swimming costume which showed a slim, almost muscular, figure. Bill knew exactly why he found Betty so attractive. She was sensual because she appeared unafraid. *Unafraid.* Why were so many of the other women he knew so timid? Living in fear of their own emotions and desires, afraid of each other, afraid of what others thought, afraid of being in the wrong? Betty gave the impression that being in the wrong was the one place she relished. Just like Ash.

Bill continued to watch, unobserved, while Ella, sitting on the side of the pool, threw back her head and laughed noisily as Betty pretended to topple into the water. His daughter could laugh, why could she not talk? Might Betty infuse Ella with something he lacked completely – a bloody-minded belief in herself? Bill put his head in his hands; there lay the catch. For Ella to believe in herself, she first had to know that she was believed by others. And she hadn't been – not at all.

Still, he reminded himself, if Ash had been harmed that night, there had been two witnesses, not one. Ella, for now, was mute – but Shafi the gardener had a voice.

He stood up and called a greeting to his daughter and the American woman. He knew now what had to be done. Shafi must be found – and the best person to winkle him out no matter where he was hiding in the North West Frontier Province was Peshawar's premier expert in the business of the gutter, Mr CJ Brooking.

Chapter Thirty-One

Two days later, on 4 July, CJ gave an American Independence Day supper party at the Peshawar Tennis Club. A number of the older staff, reared in reverence of the British Empire, went about their business, sullen and grumbling, hauling up the Stars and Stripes. The younger servants, who couldn't care less about the Raj, also began to protest when they discovered that the American sahib was insisting that they give up their uniforms for cowboy outfits, check shirts, jeans, stetsons and holsters especially shipped in from the States.

The potential for a mutiny became more apparent as the preparations proceeded. CJ, playing tennis with Bill Jackson, chose not to intervene, since Norman Vincent Peale had instructed in *The Power of Positive Thinking*, 'Never participate in a worry conversation.' At six-thirty, the staff were requested to change. Twenty minutes later, Abdullah, the head bearer, stepped out of his sweltering mock-suede chaps and sat down, arms akimbo, refusing to continue to lay any more tables.

CJ was called in from the courts. In the garden, where he had expected a stupendous barbecue – complete with a chuck wagon as a prop – he found a dozen sedentary sweating Pakistani cowboys and, as spectators, a gaggle of excited local children, who always found ways of illegally entering the club. Even Belle Masters had come out of her salon to watch the fun.

Bill, still on the court, could hear CJ's bellows. 'It's only a goddam costume, for Chrissakes. Look, I'll pay all you sons of bitches double, just get the fuckin' clothes on and get back to work.'

Money and insults had worked reasonably well on both the sewage plant and the runway, now almost back on schedule. A young bearer stood up, took off his fringed cowboy bolero complete with sheriff's star and threw them forcefully at the officer.

'Hey, you, pal, just wait a minute . . .' CJ began. Two more 'cowboys' stood up and moved towards him. 'What? What?' he challenged. 'You looking for trouble? You feeling tough?'

A servant's hand reached out for a knife from the long line of trestle tables. Belle Masters gave a shriek. Abdullah spoke sharply in Urdu and attempted to turn one of the bearers away from CJ's path. Four were now advancing on him. The American calculated rapidly; this was the shower hour. The club would be deserted while members prepared for the evening. What had got into these sons of bitches?

Suddenly, as if from nowhere, Bill was standing at his shoulder. '*Koi bat nai* . . . No worries . . . Give me the outfits . . .' As the men began to peel off their ridiculous clothing, Bill kept smiling his thanks, acting as the collector of wardrobe. '*Shukria . . . shukria . . .*'

Abdullah, now deeply embarrassed, avoided CJ, and nego tiated with Bill.

Ten minutes later, the rebels had melted away, preparations had been resumed and CJ was standing at the bar with a beer, rewriting contemporary history.

'Shit, man, I had them within an inch of doing what they were told,' he insisted. 'Now they get their way, plus double pay, and I lose my cowboys – that's one helluva deal you struck. If that's me winning, I hope to Christ I'm on the opposite side next time you strike a deal, buster.'

Bill let the comment pass, ordered a tonic water and dreamt about a Johnnie Walker with ice.

CJ paused, then asked reflectively, 'What the hell do you think that was really about?'

'Men not wanting to look like fools, maybe?' Bill suggested dryly.

'It was more'n that,' CJ insisted. 'They really didn't like me telling them what to do.' Bill raised an eyebrow. CJ conceded. 'OK, they never like it. But they don't usually get aggressive . . . It was almost as if they were looking for trouble. We've had a couple of incidents recently. Maybe it's the weather – or maybe it's all building up to something. Your chowkidars in the compound got guns?' he suddenly asked. Bill shook his head. CJ slapped his hand on the counter. 'Well, make damn sure they do.'

Thirty-six hours later, the American sent his driver round to the British High Commission with a note. It told Bill that Shafi Akhtar had been traced. He was working as a gardener under a different name, for wealthy Pakistanis near Mardan, a town twenty-five miles north-east of Peshawar. The address was enclosed.

After the showdown at the tennis club corral, Bill had had no problem at all in persuading CJ to use his network to seek out Shafi. One favour deserved another. The American didn't even ask for an explanation. What surprised Bill was that it had taken him so long. If Shafi had merely been running from local debtors, as Surindabash had reported, why hide himself quite so thoroughly?

Since returning home, Ella had found herself spending more and more time sitting on the steps of the Jacksons' dining-room verandah, facing the secret garden, just waiting. One day, she was sure, Uncle Ash would come striding out through the door, and across the lawn, laughing and calling for her, his Cinderella. Ella often dreamt a similar scene at night. But then, as Ash approached, he would turn and the back of his shirt would change colour from white to crimson. Ella would rush to stop the bleeding with the pale green dupatta he had given her; the colours dancing and clashing inside her head – white, crimson, green, red; white, crimson, green, red. And she would see herself lying in her bed, under a sheet sodden with blood. But the next morning when she awoke, it would be as white as white again.

For several days, each time Marjorie looked out of her bedroom window, the child would be there, sitting on the steps opposite, missing nothing. Once, she had become hysterical and told Piers that she was sure the little girl knew something. She could read it in her eyes. Piers had told her to pull herself together and not be so silly. Soon, he would have the whole matter sorted.

'What's happening about Sylvia and the garden?' he'd asked. 'Tell her it's sacred bloody ground or something. I just need a few more days.'

But twenty-four hours later, a battered digger appeared in the compound drive, operated by a man who was so skeletal and scaled in filth he might recently have been exhumed. Noel Hargreave-Smith, dressed, since this was Saturday, in a casual safari suit, came out on to his verandah, followed by his wife. Apart from this trio, and a couple of chowkidars, the compound was deserted.

'He's just going to make a bit of a start, Noel darling. I did tell you. You'll love it when it's done. I promise. It will be the pride and joy of the compound. A horticultural treat . . .' she ended lamely.

Noel raised his finger and pointed at the owner of the digger. 'You,' he roared. '*Imshe, imshe* . . . Off . . . out . . . out. Out now . . .'

The man ignored him, jumped down from his machine and came scurrying over to the memsahib, his hand extended, demanding payment. Sylvia swayed and promptly fainted, landing with a thud on the verandah floor. The driver paused. If the memsahib was dead, he should leave immediately to avoid blame. If she still drew breath, he must remain to receive payment.

Suddenly, a fistful of rupees were thrust into his hand. Hargreave-Smith glared as the man scuttled back to his machine, revving it loudly before noisily exiting. Noel was aware that Alice had run over from her bungalow and was helping his wife to her feet. Rockingham, too, was halfway up the steps.

'Sylvia . . .' Noel politely extended his arm to his prostrate wife. His voice was now devoid of emotion. 'Please don't go near the garden again. I don't want it touched. Do you understand? I like it as it is. Please leave it alone . . .'

He was about to add, 'Please leave me alone,' but that would have been too discourteous. He had entered into a contract with this woman, and he must fulfil it as best he could.

For a minute, it looked as if she might stamp her foot. Instead, Sylvia smiled weakly at her husband. 'Of course, darling,' she said.

He turned to Rockingham. 'Could you make sure the lock on the garden door is changed and only I have a key, please, Piers,' he ordered.

'Right away, Noel,' Rockingham said. He had to restrain himself from skipping back down the steps.

Marjorie, watching from her bedroom as the digger retreated down the drive, sat down and cried – not from relief, but from disappointment. She had so wanted it to be over.

Bill Jackson intended to visit Shafi Akhtar immediately but as the heat fried its way through the beginning of July, work kept him in the office for longer than usual. Ella remained without speech, unable now to converse even if she'd wanted to. She visited Tommy often in hospital, accompanying her mother when she did her voluntary work. Ella would sit by the boy's bed and occasionally write in her exercise book, or just watch. Tommy too was without words, lying sedated. In his company, in their mutual silence, Ella believed there was safety. Or at least, a haven from the unpredictability of the grown-up world. 'Speak the truth,' they said. But what they meant was, 'Speak the truth – sometimes.' The problem was knowing when that 'sometimes' was. She decided that only the very clever could get it right, and they had to be cleverer even than Zuhra. So, it was probably impossible.

Dr Danvers had suggested to the Jacksons that they take Ella to a specialist in Karachi. Alice preferred to wait, certain that the trouble would clear up on its own. She had suggested to Bill that Ella might be attention-seeking. 'Well, give her some attention then,' had been his curt response.

On one of her visits to the hospital, Alice had been surprised to bump into Mabel Patterson, on holiday from St Winifred's, and attending the eye clinic.

'Nothing serious, I hope?' Alice had asked, immediately polishing up her vowels; teachers, like diplomats, she regarded as a cut above her.

'A spot of bother with a cataract,' Miss Patterson had replied. 'Nothing the good Lord can't remedy. Has Ella found her voice yet?' Alice had shaken her head. 'She will,' the older woman had asserted grimly. 'When she is ready.'

Alice did not mention Miss Patterson's presence in Peshawar to her daughter. Instead, when she was kissing her good-night that evening, she said, 'This can't go on for ever, you know, Ella. Think what it's doing to Mummy.'

On 11 July, Noel Hargreave-Smith ordered the bearer to open a bottle of champagne before dinner. As her glass was filled, Sylvia watched her husband quizzically. Since the altercation around the Queen's Birthday Party and her

thwarted attempt to redesign the secret garden, their relationship had resumed its surface rhythm of cool courtesy
while Sylvia secretly battled on with her private goals. She
fantasised that one day her husband might be raising a glass to
his unborn son. But on this occasion, it wasn't birth the
Deputy High Commissioner had chosen to toast, it was
death.

Ceremoniously, he stood up and saluted with his glass. 'To
the Lords,' he intoned solemnly.

'To the Lords?' Sylvia squeaked – the champagne made
her burp.

Hargreave-Smith frowned. Then, in a patronising tone, he
began to speak slowly as if to make himself clear to a
simpleton. 'The House of Lords, darling.'

Sylvia attempted to look as if the truth had dawned. But of
course it hadn't, not remotely. Her husband tried again. 'The
House of Lords . . . in Westminster . . . it voted yesterday
against the abolition of capital punishment. Damn fine show.
Trust the hereditary peers to get it right.

'To the Lords!' he repeated again.

Sylvia looked at this stranger who was her husband and
thought she was about to burst into tears.

Ella and Betty had returned from swimming. While Betty's
driver waited in the compound, they walked across the road
to the park for a mango ice-cream. As they were making their
way back, a tonga began to gallop towards them at high
speed. Betty and Ella ran to remove themselves from its path,
reaching the open iron gates of the compound just in time.
They turned to see where the tonga was heading. Suddenly, a
body was thrown out at their feet. The face was bloodied and
beaten to a pulp. Under the man's arm was a large green
cabbage.

Ella opened her mouth and shouted at the top of her
lungs, 'Surindabash, no, no, no . . .'

The cook, on his daily trek to the vegetable bazaar, had been badly beaten. His greatest regret, however, was not the missing teeth or his cracked ribs, but his beloved bicycle. Immediately after he was ejected from the tonga, the bike, buckled and missing its wheels was also deposited at the gate of the compound. 'Bloody bastards,' Surindabash attempted to say.

Alice took him to hospital to be stitched and bandaged. Hargreave-Smith lent his Humber so that Bill, whose pleasure at the return of his daughter's voice had been overtaken by anxiety about Surindabash, could persuade the cook's family to move into the compound's servants' quarters until he was healed.

'Why did they hurt Surindabash?' Ella asked, on the journey to the outskirts of Peshawar.

'Because of us,' her father answered shortly.

Bill turned to chat to the driver. Casually, he asked him how long it would take to make the trip to Mardan.

'You want to see Buddhist ruins?' the driver asked.

Bill shook his head. 'Do you remember Shafi, the gardener?' he explained. 'I'm hoping to pay him a visit.' Even as he said the words, he regretted them, aware that he had yet to explain the gardener's departure to his daughter.

Ella looked out of the window and pretended she hadn't heard.

Chapter Thirty-Two

The next morning, the Hargreave-Smiths were eating breakfast on their verandah; Marjorie was lying on her bed with a migraine; her husband was opening up the office; David Carnow was an hour's drive away en route to Lahore; Alice was in Surindabash's kitchen, attempting to master the hitherto unused electric stove, to make scrambled eggs. Ella was in the servants' quarters playing with Surindabash's young children. According to Dr Danvers, it was the shock of seeing the cook so badly injured that had restored Ella's voice. 'Trauma correcting trauma,' the doctor had explained. Alice had sniffed disbelievingly.

At 8.00 am as usual, the chowkidars opened up the compound's battered iron gates. A dhobiwallah wheeled in his bike, followed by a witless beggar and a couple of stray dogs. Dogs and beggar were evicted amiably. A gardener watered the flower beds lackadaisically. The sun baked the soil dry almost as soon as it was dampened.

Bill abandoned the idea of breakfast. He went out on to the verandah with a cup of coffee in his hand. Something was different about this morning. He walked to the verandah steps, the leather of his sandals squeaking as he did so. Then he realised what was strange – it was the early morning sounds of the city, the racket made by the traffic. He could hear both, but much subdued. A jeep pulled up outside the Deputy High Commissioner's office. Bill recognised the army

officer who climbed out as Colonel Abdul. Ash had introduced Bill to the Colonel, an austere, reserved man, several
months earlier. He appeared uncomfortable now, as if
performing an unpleasant duty. Noel had emerged from his
office and was extending his hand in greeting. The two
disappeared into the building. Bill took a seat, put his feet
up on the verandah railing – and waited.

Fifteen minutes later, the Colonel emerged again. He
walked into the centre of the drive, a junior officer ran
towards him and within minutes a dozen soldiers had fanned
out across the compound.

Alice came out of the kitchen, attracted by the commo-
tion. She took one look at the military and began to run to
the servants' quarters, calling for Ella. The girl came out into
the drive with Surindabash's baby son on her hip. As she did
so, two or three of the servants, a few belongings tied in
bundles on their heads, slipped out of the gate.

'What's happened?' Ella asked. 'Are we being arrested?'
She gave the baby to his older sister and took her mother's
hand.

Alice looked at the walls which separated the compound
from the outside world. Suddenly, they didn't look nearly
high enough. She noticed for the first time that much of the
glass which topped the walls had been removed.

Bill came up behind her and gave her shoulder a reassuring
squeeze. 'We'll be fine,' he said, as if reading her mind.

'Are we being arrested?' Ella asked again, excitedly.

'No,' her father answered. 'We're being protected.'

An hour later, the chowkidars on the gate had been
replaced by nervous-looking armed soldiers. Several jeeps
were parked in the drive. Scaffolding had been erected on
three sides of the compound walls, to allow soldiers vantage
points looking down on to the streets. A private residence
backed on to the fourth side, and that too was patrolled.
Sylvia endeavoured to discover who or what might be the

enemy, but the response from one officer was hardly illuminating. 'Students,' he answered vaguely. She busied herself by setting up a soft drinks depot on her verandah and kept plying anyone in a uniform with Peak Freans assorted biscuits and lemon barley water.

Then, for hours, nothing happened. Vigilance was soon replaced by heat-induced sleepiness. Sylvia had collected parasols from the compound staff and the soldiers were handsomely looked after – at least in terms of shade. The perimeters began to resemble Blackpool beach.

As the tension seeped away, Ella slipped out of the bungalow. One soldier showed her his gun. A second, probably aged only sixteen or seventeen, said his name was Zattoor, and asked her to converse with him in English. 'I am a very brave soldier,' were his first careful words. After that, his vocabulary ran out.

The wives in the compound checked their stocks and found themselves with sufficient tinned food to last for weeks, should events lead to a siege. 'But why do we need half the army here, if it's only a handful of students?' Sylvia plaintively asked anyone who would listen. 'I mean, students are generally nice people, aren't they?'

By late morning, the women had resumed more familiar routines. Marjorie returned to her migraine. Alice prepared a chicken casserole and Sylvia, in The Residence, wrote letters home to old school friends, describing the marvellous time she was having.

In the office, the men listened to the news on the BBC World Service. It announced that the World Bank had followed Britain and the United States in refusing Egypt funds for the Aswan Dam. Hargreave-Smith switched off the wireless and addressed Rockingham.

'Piers, you and Albie draw up a list of nationals in the city and we'll ask the army chaps to pick them up and bring them here – if they're willing. Awkward so and sos, some of them.

Thank God, a lot of them are away in the hills.'

In the evening, a mobile kitchen was set up on the lawn to feed the soldiers. Ella sat on the verandah steps and watched, unobserved. At the foot of the walls, just visible through the undergrowth, lights flickered on and off as the soldiers bedded down for the night. A young male voice began to sing a popular Urdu song.

Later, when Ella went to say good night to her mother, she found Alice dancing alone in the sitting room to her favourite singer, Dean Martin, holding a gin and tonic. 'Memories are made of this . . .' he crooned as she swirled. Ella watched, wishing her mother didn't look so sad.

'Will they come in the night for us?' Ella asked, more out of curiosity than fear.

'Of course not.' Alice attempted a smile. 'We're as safe as houses.'

By the following afternoon, the army numbers were halved. The crisis was officially over – informants suggested a false alarm. Betty called to say that she was at the Air Force Club, where some of the Americans had been taken for security reasons. They were not yet being permitted to go home.

'The Yanks are always so namby-pamby. They panic at the slightest thing,' Alice remarked scathingly to her husband. 'They should've lived through the Blitz. Then they'd know what it is to be frightened.'

Bill returned the bottle of whisky he'd been holding to the drinks trolley. He liked the smoothness of the glass, the smell of the alcohol.

'What do you think?' Alice prodded.

Bill picked up a two-month-old copy of the *Illustrated London News*. If he could tell his wife about just a fraction of the material which passed through his fingers at work, it would instantly prick the sanguine bubble in which she attempted to float through life.

'I think the Americans know more than we do,' he answered quietly.

Mabel Patterson took off her new glasses and replaced them with her old ones. It always took her time to adjust to spectacles. Her room in the convent was whitewashed and simple: a bed, a chair, a rug, a crucifix, a ceiling fan, a curtained area containing a rope and several hangers for her clothes, a bedside table with candles in case of a power failure. The room had French windows which led straight out on to a dusty, arid area of ground, around which the six guest rooms were positioned. To the left was the school, ahead of her was the church and behind her were the living quarters of the four nuns – three Irish, one Pakistani. Except that now only the Pakistani nun remained, since the others were at a conference in Lahore. They were always at some conference or other. In Mabel Patterson's opinion, the way to the Lord wasn't through jawing.

A knock at her door drew her attention. A young servant girl opened it, curtsied and asked if the memsahib would come to the sitting room, she had a guest. Surprised, Mabel Patterson followed her. A young army officer was looking at a four-foot statue of Mary with some interest. He explained his mission and suggested that Miss Patterson might wish to accompany him to the British Deputy High Commission, where he could guarantee her safety.

Mabel Patterson peered at him as if he must be quite, quite mad. 'Young man, do I look as if I'm in need of rescuing?' she asked indignantly. 'Nothing will happen to me until the good Lord decides – and, when he does decide, no army in the land will be able to prevent the inevitable. I'll stay put, thank you very much. Tell your superiors you couldn't find me. Tell them, I've returned to the hills. That way,' she added more gently, 'nobody needs to make a fuss.'

When the conversation was reported to Noel in full, he sighed. He had had one like Mabel Patterson in every single post – aspirational martyrs. They caused the most frightful logistical problems.

Chapter Thirty-Three

O n 26 July 1956, the quartet of soldiers on the gate of the British Deputy High Commission came off duty to be replaced by a fresh shift. In the park opposite, a man with a dancing monkey on a lead attempted to attract an audience to watch the animal's performance by monotonously banging on a drum. In Alexandria, on the fourth anniversary of the overthrow of King Farouk, the Egyptian president, Colonel Nasser, began his address to the nation also with a drum roll. He spoke, via the wireless, for two hours and forty minutes. In Peshawar, Bill Jackson took all of it in Morse.

President Nasser announced that he had nationalised the Anglo-French controlled Suez Canal Company. If the imperialists objected, 'They could choke on their fury'. The revenue would go towards building the dam at Aswan on the Nile which would double Egypt's cultivable land and provide invaluable hydro-electric power. 'We shall industrialise Egypt and compete with the West,' the President roared. 'We are marching from strength to strength.'

Some of his speech was a lesson in economics. He explained how the Aswan Dam would cost thirteen hundred million dollars to build. The USA had promised fifty-six million, Great Britain fourteen million and the World Bank two hundred million, so long as nine hundred million came from Egypt. He expressed his anger that the promise of Western funding had been broken. He had had no choice but to nationalise the Suez Canal Company, nearly half of whose shares were in the hands of the British Government. Compensation would be given. President Nasser went on to tell the Egyptians that he had personally negotiated with Eugene Black, President of the World Bank.

'I started to look at Mr Black, who was sitting in a chair, and I saw him in my imagination as Ferdinand de Lesseps,' he reported. De Lesseps was the French-born creator of the Suez Canal. Nasser mentioned the man's name fourteen times during his speech.

The Egyptian leader announced that Major Mahmoud Younis, a fellow army officer, would become chairman of the newly created Suez Canal Authority – and responsible for its continued efficiency.

What President Nasser's listeners did not know was that the repeated mention of de Lesseps' name was a coded message to Major Younis to move into action. He ordered the immediate cordoning off of the Suez Canal company's offices in Cairo and Ismalia.

An MI6 spy, code-named Lucky Break, had worked for months within Nasser's inner circle. The information he gleaned had been relayed to British Embassies, High Commissions and Deputy High Commissions in the relevant areas around the world. According to Lucky Break, among Nasser's aims were the destruction of Israel, the removal of the West's influence from the Arab world, and the creation of a Pan-Arab union based on the precepts of Islam. But no mention had been made of the Suez Canal.

The Egyptian cabinet had been informed of the canal's nationalisation only an hour before the Egyptian people. So, Lucky Break experienced what must be one of the more unhappy lessons in espionage. He was among the last to know. Even as President Nasser was broadcasting, a British tanker entering Port Said was ordered to turn around and make the six thousand mile journey around the Cape of Africa.

Noel, listening later to fragmented reports on the radio, offered his views. The Egyptians would be unable to make nationalisation work. They lacked the technical and managerial skills and, in any case, they were an altogether inferior bunch. If Nasser was the recalcitrant child of an under-par empire, then all the more reason to teach him — and others — a lesson they'd never forget. 'Who knows what might happen if we let the Nassers of this world become too big for their boots?' Hargreave-Smith asked, in the same pedestrian style that he adopted in his reports. 'This whole fiasco will be over in days, make no mistake — but not before Nasser's learnt a bit of humility,' he added, with, Bill thought, an excessive amount of smugness.

On his way back to the bungalow after work that evening, Bill noticed the thud of the drum in the park opposite had begun again. He walked to the open gates and a little way down the road, hidden by the shadows. The monkey man's audience had grown from a handful to three or four dozen. Something was odd about the scene. It took Bill several minutes to realise what it was. Then he got it: the monkey man's crowd was entirely made up of young men. Every woman and child in the park had disappeared.

Casually, Bill turned and sprinted back into the compound. As he ran, he shouted orders to the soldiers on guard to shut the gates and call up reinforcements immediately. 'Say the *burra* sahib has ordered it. *Jaldi! Jaldi!* Fucking hurry!' He ran to the bungalow, calling for Alice. He told her to find Ella and stay inside, closing all the doors and windows. Next, he bolted up the stairs of The Residence, opened the door and literally slid along the polished floor of the hall. Noel was sitting at the end of the dining-room table and gazing forlornly out of the window. Bill rushed into the room. The Deputy High Commissioner was not alone as he had first thought. Instead, his wife was at the opposite end of the table, chattering away more or less to herself.

'Excuse me, Noel,' Bill interrupted. 'I think we're in for trouble. Real trouble. They're gathering in the park. They've probably heard about Suez on the wireless. I've told the soldiers to radio for reinforcements. Albie's told me that Mabel Patterson is at the convent and so far has refused to come here – and then there's the Larkhalls. Blossom will be an easy target, because of Albie. Everyone in Peshawar knows they live on the Jamrud Road.'

As Bill was speaking, Hargreave-Smith had risen and begun to move out on to the verandah. Now, he stopped, his face expressionless.

'We'll make arrangements for Miss Patterson, but I'm afraid the Larkhalls will have to do the best they can to look after themselves.'

'What do you mean, "look after themselves"?' Bill knew he was shouting. 'They've got a sick boy for Christ's sake and a grandmother who's bloody a hundred and one. If an anti-British crowd gets hold of them, they are very definitely bloody butchered. We owe them more than that. Albie's worked here for years. His family's got a right to expect more than a bloody self-preservation order. Come on, man.'

Bill expected Noel to shout back, fight his corner, justify his decision – lives were at stake, for Christ's sake, and his judgement had been challenged. Instead, the man merely looked pained and embarrassed, as if he was dealing with a particularly uncouth guest at a weekend house party. Bill wanted to shake him until his teeth splintered.

Noel sighed heavily. 'Rules are there for a reason, Jackson –' the use of Bill's surname was deliberate – 'we especially need them during these more difficult periods . . . If we let Mrs Larkhall and her entourage in, every Anglo-Indian in Peshawar will try and follow in her footsteps. We'll be besieged. You know that. Now, see if Albie can contact his wife on the telephone, there's a good chap. Perhaps the hospital might offer a place to hole up for a bit?'

Bill, shaking with rage, put his hand on Hargreave-Smith's arm and spun him round with more force than he intended. 'Blossom doesn't own a telephone, Noel. They can't afford a telephone, not on Albie's wages or hers. Have you any idea how they live? They can't even afford a decent bloody wheelchair that works. I'm going to get the Larkhalls and bring them here and I hope to God, for your sake, that it's not too late.'

'I absolutely forbid it,' Noel barked, his anger finally roused. 'Do you hear me?'

But Bill was already running back across the lawn. As he did so, he saw out of the corner of his eye that the soldiers had briefly opened the gate, allowing entry to an open-topped Pakistani air force jeep. In it was a driver, and Betty Brooking, dressed as if ready for a picnic: dark glasses, sundress. Across in the park, the beat of the drum was now accompanied by a voice using a megaphone and cheers and shouts from the crowds.

'Hi, Bill,' Betty called out.

Bill needed transport to bring the Larkhalls back. The keys to the official cars were kept in Rockingham's locked desk-drawer and were issued by him only after a driver or member of staff filled in a form, the top copy to be filed, the carbon copy to be retained by the user of the British Deputy High Commission's vehicle at all times while driving.

'What are you doing here?' he asked abruptly.

Betty smiled. 'Welcome to you too,' she answered. 'I've come to pick up Ella. They've got a cartoon show at the Air Force Club. I asked if I could bring her, and they were delighted.'

'Any trouble on the way?'

She shook her head. 'Why should there be? I thought we'd had our scare.'

'Nasser's nationalised the Canal,' Bill said curtly. 'Can I use your jeep?'

Something about his tone persuaded Betty not to waste time. In Urdu she told the driver to wait on the Jacksons' verandah. Then, she moved into the driving seat.

Bill objected. 'Out,' he said curtly.

'In,' she answered flatly.

'I'm going for the Larkhalls,' he said.

'So,' she replied, beginning to pull the hood up overhead and wind up the windows, to make it more difficult for those outside to see the skin colour of the jeep's occupants. 'You'll need more than one pair of hands and I speak better Urdu than you do. And, if we get stuck, I'm also a helluva lot prettier than you – and I've got a sweeter tongue. Get in the saddle, sonny Jim. Or shall we sit here and argue until the riots are underway?'

As she began to manoeuvre the jeep, Alice emerged from the bungalow. 'What's happening, Bill? Why are the gates closed?' she asked agitatedly. 'Where are you going?'

Bill contemplated lying, since he knew Alice would object. He decided that the truth would be a lot quicker. 'I think we're in for a spot of trouble. I'm off to bring the Larkhalls in. Noel's not happy about it, so Betty's lending me a hand. Noel says we can't look after the Anglos—'

'Bastard,' Alice interrupted.

Bill was surprised. He'd expected his wife to tell him not to be an idiot, not to mark his card, to do as the boss said.

'What a bastard,' she said again.

'It's not him,' Bill answered. 'It's the rules. And, without the rules, Noel is like a jellyfish caught at high tide. Give my love to Ella,' he added.

A minute later, the jeep was out of the gate and heading down The Mall. After the last frenetic five minutes, the tranquillity of the street made Bill feel that his earlier reaction had been slightly absurd. The jeep hurtled down almost deserted roads.

Fifteen minutes later, Betty and Bill were in the Larkhalls' drive. Blossom, Thomasina and Tommy, improved and recently released from hospital, had been chatting on charpois on the verandah. Bertha was away in Rawalpindi. Bill explained the problem briefly, omitting the Deputy High Commissioner's reluctance to give them shelter.

'What shall we bring?' Blossom asked calmly.

Betty replied first. 'As much medical stuff as you've got. And whisky,' she added dryly. 'For medicinal purposes.'

Tommy insisted that the family's two lovebirds and Kedgeree, their adopted mangy yellowish stray dog should accompany them.

'What about the servants?' Blossom asked.

Betty and Bill exchanged glances. The jeep was full.

'Tell them to disappear for a while, Blossom. They'll be OK,' Bill advised, hoping he was right.

Tommy, Blossom, Thomasina and the pets were wedged into the back. Bill squeezed a bag of supplies under his legs in the front.

'Hold tight,' Betty ordered, pressing her foot down hard on the accelerator. As the jeep spun back on to the road, gunfire was heard coming from the university area, further to the west of the city. No one in the jeep spoke.

Then Thomasina raised her wavering voice and began to sing, 'Father, hear the prayer we offer/Not for ease that prayer shall be/But for strength that we may ever/Live our lives courageously . . .'

By the fourth verse, Tommy, Bill, Blossom and Betty had joined in, singing at the top of their lungs, driving down the middle of deserted streets. 'Be our strength in hours of weakness/In our wanderings be our guide/Through endeavour, failure, danger/Father be—'

'Shit!' Bill interrupted.

The jeep had reached the junction of Khyber Road and Hospital Road. Apart from a few bullock carts and a handful of bicyclists, traffic was still sparse. It was then that he remembered Mabel Patterson. The convent was across the railway line, off Dabgari Gate Road, close to the Old City. The Old City and the university were the twin homes of mayhem – be it religious, political or personal. Why drive into trouble? Bill calculated the odds. If he was right in his prediction, once they reached the compound, it would be extremely difficult to leave again. The army would be reluctant to provide an armed guard, since the old woman had already declined one invitation to seek protection. On the other hand, if they drove to the convent now, all five of them plus Mabel Patterson might be put at risk. For what? To hear the tough old trout say no thank you?

'Take a left,' Bill instructed.

Betty did as she was told.

'Mabel Patterson,' he explained.

Betty grimaced and asked wryly, 'Dear God, do we have to?' Then, she concentrated on driving.

Miss Patterson was writing letters in the communal sitting room used by the nuns. The room was on the far side of the convent, so she didn't hear the jeep pull up, nor Betty and Bill calling her name as they ran through the darkened, empty classrooms and corridors. She had made herself a cup of tea, since the servants had disappeared. Another week and then it would be time to return to St Winifred's. To her great excitement, on the previous day, she had received a letter from the Right Reverend Thomas Buckingham, Bishop of Lahore, her employer.

At first, as she read it, she believed illogically that her new spectacles were somehow affecting the words. So, she replaced them with her old pair. But the Bishop's instructions remained unaltered. The Board had decided that, after twenty-four years of excellent service, it was time she moved on to fresh pastures. 'Fresh pastures' indeed. The letter told her that a young woman would be arriving from Karachi to take up Miss Patterson's post at St Winifred's at the beginning of the August term and the Board therefore requested her presence in Lahore, to discuss an alternative placement. Perhaps she might like to consider taking up a teaching post in a church school in the UK, where her qualities would surely be warmly welcomed?

Miss Patterson had given herself time for reflection. Now, she was scribbling a furious response. She knew exactly what the Bishop hadn't got the courage to say. The Board was trying to purge all the British staff from its schools and employ locals, in order to ingratiate itself with the government, as well as boost the number of pupils, now on the decline. She believed in being frank. She would inform the Bishop, newly appointed, that that kind of purge would lead to a complete collapse in educational standards, not to mention the destruction of the school's moral fibre. Of course, the Bishop had never seen what Miss Hope looked like, dressed up to go into Chowdiagalli on her evening off. Nylons and painted toenails! He couldn't hear the trashy American music she listened to every night. Loud and *lewdly* rhythmic. What kind of an example was that to set?

Miss Patterson resumed her letter-writing. She was crisp and to the point. She would return to St Winifred's, she would continue to teach, she would ignore the Bishop's wishes on the straightforward basis that she knew her school better than he did. St Winifred's needed her, now more than ever. 'I should advise you that on matters of educational policy,' she added, 'I have rarely been proved wrong.'

An exercise in certainty always reinvigorated Mabel Patterson; an absolute tonic. It was then she heard someone calling her name. She opened the door of the sitting room. 'I'm here,' she shouted back. 'Who wants me?'

Betty and Bill ran in the direction of the teacher's voice. When the teacher set eyes on the American woman, her formal smile of welcome turned cool.

'Miss Patterson –' Bill Jackson held out his hand – 'how

do you do. I'm Ella's father. This is extremely urgent,' he added. As he spoke, he attempted to steer the older woman by the elbow, back the way he had just come. 'We need to leave now. You must come with us to the compound. It's not safe here, if . . .'

Mabel Patterson stamped her foot several times. 'No, no, no,' she repeated tetchily. 'Why should I run for cover like some wretched animal? As I told the young man, I've never had to be rescued in my life, and I don't intend to start now. I know these people,' she added. 'I used to teach here. They won't touch me. They won't touch the place at all. Far too much respect—'

'Bullshit,' Betty snapped. 'The world's moved on since you were here, Miss Patterson. We're talking about kids barely out of diapers on the streets now, not their parents. It'll be the young ones who come looking for you. The ones who want to walk a different path from their fathers. And slicing you up would be the perfect proof that they're big enough to do it. A gift from Allah, you might say.'

Mabel Patterson resolutely shook her head.

'Fine,' Betty said angrily. 'Let's go, Bill. Miss Patterson is adult enough to make her own mind up. Although I wish we hadn't risked our necks to find that out.' She looked the woman squarely in the eye. 'Is it sacrificial lamb time, Miss Patterson? Is that it? How does it go, "Precious in the sight of the Lord is the death of his saints . . ."? Personally, I'd rather continue as a living sinner than end up a dead saint.'

Miss Patterson gave a small, prim smile. 'I don't doubt it,' she said.

Betty bowed in an ironic acknowledgement, then she began to walk across the quadrangle. Bill reluctantly followed. The American looked back once. Mabel Patterson was standing to attention like an old soldier, her bony shoulders hunched up near her ears, her skin withered by lovelessness. As they turned a corner, Bill pulled Betty to a stop.

288

'We can't leave her, they'll tear her apart,' he insisted.

Betty raised one eyebrow and replied laconically. 'OK, I'll hit her over the head, you stuff her in the sack, and then we can tie her to the jeep's roof . . . Look,' she added in a softer tone, 'she's a believer but I don't think it's a taste for martyrdom that we're dealing with here. It's pride. The old billy goat doesn't know how to give in. If we force her to come with us, if we take her pride away, what has she got left? It's the only defence she has in a world that's changing so fast she doesn't know where she belongs.'

Bill shrugged. 'Personally, I'd rather stay alive and forfeit a bit of dignity any day . . .'

Betty reached out and very gently stroked his cheek with the back of her fingers. The gesture, so intimate, so unexpected, so unlike Alice's exercises in affection, made him shiver involuntarily.

Betty gave a small smile. 'No you wouldn't,' she said firmly.

A few minutes later, the jeep driven by Betty, recrossed the railway line and turned back into The Mall. It slowed down briefly as a bus, repatched and plated like a metal armadillo, lumbered across their path, leaving clouds of filthy black smoke. Something landed on the roof of the jeep with a thud.

'What is it? Can you see?' Betty asked, as she rammed her foot down hard on the accelerator.

Bill looked up. A stain was beginning to spread across the canvas. He stuck his head out of the window. A teenager was on the roof of the now stationary bus, jumping up and down jubilantly, his shirt billowing out like a giant white kite.

'By the smell, I think it's a petrol bomb of some sort,' he shouted, trying to manoeuvre himself out of the side of the moving jeep.

'Wait,' she ordered. She swerved the vehicle violently from one side of The Mall to the other, in an effort to dislodge the unwanted luggage. Inside, passengers and dog and lovebirds collided and crashed. A sound like a balloon bursting was heard and, suddenly, flames were licking the roof. In the rear-view mirror, Betty could see a crowd emerge from behind the bus, carrying placards and waving sticks.

'Keep driving,' Bill yelled.

Kedgeree the dog, sitting on Blossom's knee, began to howl mournfully as he smelt the smoke. Tommy was coughing, Thomasina's quavering voice began to sing. 'Abide with me . . .'

Furiously, Bill turned the two screws above the windscreen, which secured the roof. Betty took a left into the side road that led to the British High Commission. Some of the crowd running down The Mall behind them splintered off, running across the park to cut the jeep off.

'Duck,' Bill shouted to the passengers in the back, as, standing in the jeep like a chariot driver, he pushed the roof back with all his might. Thomasina was on her knees on the back seat, her cotton blanket at the ready. As the canvas folded back, concertina-like, she threw a thick cotton cover over it, killing most of the flames. Wordlessly, she sat back down.

'Not bad, ma'am,' Betty shouted into the wind. 'Not bad at all.'

On the right of the jeep, in the park, the numbers had grown to well over a hundred, armed with staves, knives and rifles. For the first time, Bill's stomach took a trip to the basement. If numbers increased further, they'd need more than half-a-dozen members of the military to save their skins inside the compound.

Betty's shirt was sticking to her skin with perspiration. As she wiped sweat from her eyes, she said out of the corner of her mouth, 'That's the trouble with the seventh cavalry — they're always saving someone else when you want them most. Shit!' she added. A stone hit one of the jeep's windows and bounced off. She put her hand on the horn and kept it there, in an effort to alert the soldiers on guard behind the closed doors of the compound. Three or four figures rushed out of the crowd and grabbed hold of a street vendor's cart full of soft drinks, pushing it in the jeep's path. A deep ditch ran on either side of the road to help with drainage during the rainy season. Blossom covered Tommy's eyes with her hand and shut her own tightly. The dog whined. Betty spun the wheel, the jeep appeared to head straight for the ditch, then she turned it back. The jeep's front left-hand wing clipped the cart, sending the flagons of lurid-coloured liquid splashing across the road, creating an instant rainbow. Bill stuck his head out of his window, banging the side of the jeep with his hand, and bellowed at the compound gate, 'Open the fucking door. It's me, the wireless operator sahib. *Jaldi, jaldi.*'

It was a moment frozen in time. The jeep slowed to a stop. The crowd in the park, which had begun to advance, halted. The occupants of the vehicle sat, paralysed. The gates remained shut. Then, a voice gave a blood-curdling battle cry and the crowd, as one, began to run. A soldier opened the gate a crack and peered round sleepily. The jeep lurched forward, ramming the doors open and sending the soldier flying. Bill, Betty and Blossom jumped out and ran together to close the gates behind them. A soldier manning one of the artificial turrets created from scaffolding on the army's earlier visit fired several shots. The crowd surged on. The battle had begun.

Chapter Thirty-Four

Adrenaline drained, Bill and Betty leant their backs against the compound gate, while a shower of stones thudded into it on the other side. Once his heart had stopped pounding, Bill realised that the American woman was so close, the heat of her body was warming his.

Then Ella was flinging her arms around his neck, kissing his face. 'Daddy, Daddy, Tommy's going to stay the night. Mummy says he can,' she babbled, oblivious of the circumstances.

He looked up to see Albie Larkhall carrying his son and the lovebirds into the bungalow, followed by Kedgeree and Grandma. Noel Hargreave-Smith was standing on the steps of The Residence, his face impassive.

Later, Ella sat cross-legged at the end of her bed. Tommy lay asleep, exhausted. She had told him all that had occurred at St Winifred's, including Dr Mac's peculiar form of worship and Zuhra's removal. She also said that her father had begun to ask her questions about the night of the Queen's Birthday Party, but she had decided that she would say nothing.

Tommy had told her this was the best move. 'If your Ash is alive, he'll turn up,' he'd told her authoritatively.

At the time, Ella thought this surprisingly wise. Now, she thought it a rather silly comment. Of course Uncle Ash would turn up if he was alive. The problem was what should she do, if he was dead?

An hour later, more rifle fire could be heard across the city. Bill, back in his office, was working flat-out; much of it to do not with the present emergency but the protocol around the imminent visit of minor British royalty and his preferred brand of hot chocolate and whisky.

During a couple of minutes of respite, Bill smiled bleakly at the irony of his situation. For all his efforts to keep his views to himself, to desist from comments on religion, republicanism, sovereignty, socialism and sub-standard public school boys, he was still out on his ear. And for what? For playing at John Wayne.

His disregard of Noel's instructions, he was certain, had saved the Larkhalls' skin – and because of that he had no regrets – but it would also result in his dismissal. He'd end up working in a factory, just like the other blokes after all: clock in clock out; Friday night in the pub; two weeks' holiday in Rhyl; fags; beer; the *News of the World*; monotony; atrophy then death.

Bill got up and walked out of his office into the main reception area, Albie Larkhall's domain. Betty was sitting on his deserted desk, smoking a cigarette. 'How's the hero?' she mildly mocked. Bill suddenly felt bold.

'Come into my office,' he said. It sounded more like a command than a request. Betty stood up, stubbed out her cigarette in the glass ash tray depicting the Houses of Parliament, and followed him through a heavy iron door. This was normally closed and secured on a combination lock with the code known only to Bill and his immediate superiors. Should the situation outside escalate, he would be obliged to incarcerate himself behind it and continue communicating on the Morse key until fire or a bomb or tear gas seeping through the cracks drove him out. Then, later, he would no doubt watch as somebody else collected the medals.

'Do you need help?' he asked, sitting down and putting his feet up on the desk. His mouth was dry. Betty smiled. Much to his annoyance, he flushed. She lit another cigarette.

'I was trying to get a message through to CJ,' she said. 'He'll be protecting the sewage plant but when he stops to think, he'll try to get hold of me at the Air Force Club.'

'He'll be worried,' Bill commented.

Betty shook her head. 'Uh-uh. No, he won't. He'll be annoyed,' she corrected him without rancour. 'He'll be annoyed that I'm not where I said I'd be. You know CJ, he's a man with a mission. He's a believer, like Mabel Patterson. They're big on ideas, but individual people and their needs? Hell, we're just the slipped stitch in their otherwise perfect sweater.'

Betty exhaled slowly, and narrowed her eyes to the screen of smoke. She was an arm's length away. Bill took his legs off the desk, leant forward, raised his hand a fraction – and put it down again.

She was speaking again, 'Do you know something, Bill? I used to be a believer like them once – a crusader for marriage, motherhood and the American way of life. I was right and everybody who disagreed with me was wrong.

'Then one of my kids died, a couple of other events occurred and I gradually realised that the trouble with belief is that it lives on self-delusion. So, these days, I believe in nothing. I have no faith. I have no self-delusions, no delusions at all. I don't imagine, like CJ, I'm the vanquisher of the Red Peril; that the only freedom worth having is the one I'm fighting for . . . I don't cherish notions, like Miss Patterson, that I am God's channel on earth . . .'

'And the bad side of being without belief?' Bill probed.

'You tell me,' she countered.

He protested. 'I have got a belief. I believe in my child, in making a better future for her. I have to believe that it won't be the same for her, as it was for me, otherwise what the hell is the point of it all?'

Betty shrugged. 'Aah yes, the things we do to our children

in the name of love. We pummel and pound them, until finally, when they buckle and give up their fighting spirit, we say, "Look, what a good kid you are . . ." And we are so pleased with ourselves that we have forever locked them in the prison of our prejudices.'

Bill rubbed his hand through his hair. 'Christ, you're a bigger cynic than I am, Betty, and that's saying something.'

She pointed at him with the cigarette held between her two fingers and affected astonishment. 'Gee, you're right,' she answered sardonically. 'That's what happens when you have no faith – you get scared and lonely and grouchy. But most of all, you have to learn how to live without the hope that you can make a difference. I miss that. I really miss that.'

She blinked hard, and for a second, Bill feared she was going to cry. Instead, she stood up and threw her still smouldering cigarette into his waste paper bin. Then, she waggled the fingers on one hand in a goodbye wave.

'If you can send a message to CJ, I'd appreciate it. Your wife has kindly offered me a bed for the duration, so I'll see you later, honey.'

Bill watched her hungrily as she walked away.

Shortly after, Colonel Khalil returned at the head of a small convoy of jeeps. The crowd gathered again and, at first, watched silently as the first three vehicles turned into the compound. Then, as if to a hidden signal, the crowd swarmed around the tail end of the convoy, rocking the jeeps in an attempt to turn them over. Oblivious of who might be under the wheels, the jeeps pressed forward. Several guns were fired, voices screamed. Makeshift ladders appeared out of the crowd and were propped up against the compound wall. Young men, matchetes in hands, began to climb. Inside the compound, the soldiers scrambled to resume their positions on the scaffolding.

One shocked young soldier almost fell out of the last jeep. His cheek had been neatly divided in two. It lay open like a couple of chicken breast fillets. Ella ran out of her bedroom and into the sitting room. Alice and Blossom immediately went to the wounded man's aid, carrying him into the Jacksons' bungalow. Surindabash, still stitched and bandaged, came hobbling out of the servants' quarters, his family in tow. He directed the children to sit under the kitchen table, then rolled up his sleeves. 'I am a Pathan,' he announced amidst the confusion, to nobody in particular. 'You saved my life. Now, it is my duty, my honour, to save yours.'

'Wonderful,' Alice said dryly, struggling under the weight of the soldier. 'You can start by boiling water. Lots of it.'

Marjorie and Sylvia came running over to the bungalow, directed by Colonel Khalil's sergeant. Now, they hovered, as Blossom and Alice laid the soldier on the settee. Ella watched from the door.

Marjorie had begun to weep. 'Oh, God, we're all going to be killed. Oh, God, I knew something like this would happen. We're all going to die horribly. They'll cut us to ribbons. They'll rape us. They'll . . .'

Blossom shook Marjorie hard. She, in turn, rounded on the woman. 'How dare you touch me, you filthy little chee-chee. How dare you presume to lay a finger on me. Look at you, you're so brown and drab, you're positively disgusting.'

For a moment, Ella thought that her mother was also going to attack Blossom. So she reached for the Anglo-Indian's hand. But, instead, Alice, her eyes ablaze, addressed Marjorie in a way the little girl had never seen before.

'Don't you dare speak to my friend like that in my house, or in any house,' Alice demanded angrily. 'Blossom is worth ten of you any day. For God's sake, Marjorie, stop snivelling and whining and bitching. For once go and do something useful. Help Surindabash in the kitchen. Or, if you can't stomach him, find a corner somewhere and stay there and keep quiet. Do you understand?'

Marjorie opened her mouth — and shut it again.

The shouts and slogans and rifle shots began to gather a frightening momentum on the other side of the wall. Alice knelt down and took Ella in her arms. She kissed her on the forehead. 'Listen to me, sweetheart,' she said, smiling. 'Mummy was in London in the war. Do you remember how I told you lots and lots of bombs fell?' Ella nodded obediently. 'And there were fires and houses falling down?' she continued. 'Well, do you remember I told you I was right in the middle of it and not a single thing happened to me? Not a single hair on my head was harmed?

'Look at me, Ella, and listen carefully,' Alice spoke softly. 'Your Mummy is a very, very lucky person. And, because you're mine, you are going to be lucky too. No matter how noisy and upsetting it sounds out there, we — all of us, you, me, Daddy, Blossom, Tommy, Sylvia — we are all going to be as right as rain. Do you understand?'

Ella nodded her head again. Her mother smelt wonderfully of the talcum powder in her bathroom. In truth, Ella wasn't feeling at all frightened by events outside the compound walls. She'd seen it all at the cinema. What did cause her concern was the Rockinghams. Would her mother's luck also protect her from them?

Alice stood up, went over to Bill's tape recorder, selected a tape and wound the spool into position. Then, she pressed 'Play', and turned up the volume high. Sarah Vaughan almost drowned out the cacophony in the street.

> 'Ooh, make yourself comfortable
> Ooh, make yourself comfortable,'

Alice sang along.

'Ooh, make yourself comfortable, baby,
I've got some records here to put us in the mood,
The phone is off the hook, so no one can intrude . . .'

Sylvia began to giggle nervously. 'Oh, I say, how very funny . . .' she gurgled. Blossom took the risk and reaching out, patted the young woman's arm. She was rewarded with a shaky smile.

'Right,' Alice instructed, 'to work, ladies.'

She and the two other women, hindered by Surindabash, rapidly moved most of the furniture out of the sitting room, set up camp beds for the wounded and cleared a book shelf to house medical supplies. As they worked, Ella found herself drawn to the dining room. She peeked through the half-open door. On the table Surindabash had placed glasses, ice, soft drinks and a plate of sweaty tinned cheese, cut into squares and stuck on toothpicks with pineapple chunks, as if he was expecting a cocktail party rather than a riot. Marjorie sat alone at the table, staring ahead. Ella decided she didn't look much like the person in the garden that night. Perhaps, after all, it had been a dream? Then Marjorie, lost in her own thoughts, turned to Ella's hiding place and, unseeing, stared at the child. And the girl knew the woman was afraid.

'We're going into the garden for a breather, Ella,' Blossom called from the sitting room. The voice made Marjorie start. Obediently, she rose from the table as if she had been summonsed too. Ella turned and fled.

She found her mother with Sylvia, Blossom and Betty, standing on the lawn in semi darkness. The military bustle of the compound was shut out by the garden's bamboo fences but not the continuing chants of the rioters and the crack of rifles. Ella looked up. It was as if the black sky had acquired a hem of brightest orange.

'They're burning buildings in the cantonment,' Betty explained, following the child's gaze.

'Not to worry,' Sylvia interrupted. Alice noticed the younger woman's hands were shaking. Betty lit a cigarette and handed it to Sylvia. 'No, I can't, thanks awfully,' she said, shaking her head. Then she gave a wan smile. 'At least, we're all in this together, what? Aliens under one sky and all that.'

Blossom and Alice exchanged glances.

Betty blew out smoke from her cigarette. Then, softly, she began to quote. 'English men and women in India are . . . members of one great family, aliens under one sky.'

Ella assumed the words were meant to make them all feel better, but she couldn't find much that was reassuring in being called an alien.

Sylvia beamed at Betty with pleasure. 'You've read Maud Diver too?' she squealed. 'How marvellous. She wrote that over forty years ago, but it's absolutely true, isn't it? We are members of one great family. And we really are aliens here.' Sylvia suddenly remembered Blossom's presence. She blushed. 'Oh, I say, I hope you realise that I include you in the family too, of course I do. I mean, you're virtually the same as us. British and all that. Almost. Isn't she, everyone?'

Sylvia's discomfort was curtailed by Albie and Bill appearing, to check on their safety. As they did so, a blood-chilling roar went up from the park and there was an enormous bang at the gate. Instinctively, the women moved closer together. Ella gripped her mother's hand tightly as they all made their way to the drive of the compound.

Colonel Khalil emerged from the chowkidars' room, which he had commandeered as his headquarters. 'Petrol bombs,' he explained. 'More rioters are on their way. Students from the university. They're younger, so they'll be more foolhardy. I've sent for extra help.' He shrugged, as if to say it was a matter of Fate whether more troops would be delivered.

'Oh, I have great confidence in you, Colonel.' Sylvia beamed her approval. 'You're not actually shooting them, though, are you?' she added, as if the thought had only just occurred to her. 'That would be awfully unpleasant.'

The Colonel's face was expressionless. 'We would prefer not to shoot. On the other hand, should any of the rioters breach our security—'

He was interrupted by two soldiers half dragging a third across the adjacent lawn. Bill and Albie went to help. Ella was transfixed. The man's chest was changing colour from khaki to a brilliant crimson. She was distracted by a whooshing noise and the sound of dull clunks coming from the men stationed on the walls. Suddenly, a cannister appeared high in the sky, clattering down into the compound. It spun round on contact with the drive, hissing with what the girl thought was steam.

'Tear gas – they're throwing it back,' Bill shouted. 'Ella, put your skirt over your nose and mouth. Get back inside, quick, quick . . .'

Sylvia also ran, but tripped on the verandah step. A second and third cannister came over. Ella stopped to help the woman, now splayed flat like a discarded rag doll. A thick fog descended. Ella could barely see for the tears that were pouring down her cheeks, and could hardly breathe for a choking cough.

'My baby,' Sylvia was sobbing. 'Don't hurt my baby.'

Ella stood there, flabbergasted. What baby?

The crowd, swollen to three or four hundred, was terrifying in its vocal power, but utterly chaotic and without tactics when it came to trying to breach the defences of the compound. Sporadic assaults were maintained for the next three hours. Hargreave-Smith and Colonel Khalil had discussed what must be done should the rioters decide to split into four groups and attack each of the compound's walls. They would succeed within minutes. The staff, families, servants and soldiers would all retreat to The Residence and hope that the repeated request for reinforcements would be heeded in time.

The rioters, however, remained disorganised, apparently satisfied with home goals: casualties inflicted on the soldiers, mostly cuts, bullet nicks and injuries sustained due to flying stones and missiles. A tinder-dry bush in the compound ignited, as if a miracle from God, as an amateur petrol-bomb went astray. And, periodically, the soldiers would fire tear gas into the crowd, only to have it returned. By evening, a grey pall hung over the compound. The Jacksons' sitting room had become a fully functioning first-aid room. Alice was in command, Blossom acted as her chief medical officer, Betty bandaged and Surindabash kept up a continual supply of food. Ella acted as messenger boy.

'Take this to Daddy, in his office,' Alice instructed her daughter, giving her two cold bottles of beer in a basket and a plate of chicken sandwiches. Surindabash hadn't been able to resist piping mayonnaise, dyed rose pink, around the plate's rim. Alice smiled as the child's fingers became covered in the goo. 'Never mind,' she said, as she kissed her cheek. 'You've been such a brave girl today. I'm really proud of you.'

'In true life?' Ella asked.

'In true life,' her mother answered.

Ella made for her father's office, dancing on air.

Shortly after nine, Bill, who had been on duty permanently since arriving back in the compound in the afternoon, left his office to stretch his legs. Colonel Khalil was making his way across the lawn. He was holding a handkerchief to his forehead.

'Are you hurt, Colonel?'

The officer stopped. 'It's a small cut, a stone,' he replied. 'When this is over, I'll get a couple of stitches.'

'Why not let Blossom have a go now? It looks nasty,' Bill suggested.

He shook his head. 'If I stay in the bungalow even for half an hour, it would be bad for morale.' He gave a wry smile. 'We're soldiers. We have our duty. But a few of my men believe it's also their duty to help their brothers on the other side of the wall.'

Bill gave a small shudder. 'So what's stopping them from opening the gates and letting them in?' he asked.

Colonel Khalil patted his heart with his right hand. 'Me,' he answered dryly.

Bill found himself warming to the man although he had none of Ash's charm. 'It doesn't look as if extra help is coming,' he commented.

'Are you surprised?'

Bill shook his head. 'Not really. I don't suppose that, politically, it would look very good to have half your army wiping out a handful of rioters for a pack of Brits.'

'At the same time—' Colonel Khalil raised his finger – 'we don't want to see any dead foreigners either. So we hope this squall will eventually blow itself out.'

'Do you hate us?' Bill asked bluntly.

'I judge as I find,' Colonel Khalil replied, then paused. 'And, if I'm honest, I don't find a great deal that appeals. Britain is where? Kenya, Malaya, Cyprus . . . it will have to learn what it means to be a very small country.' As if the compound was his domain, the officer indicated with his hand for Bill to take a seat in one of the Deputy High Commissioner's garden chairs. The two men sat alone on the floodlit lawn.

'You have a few minutes?' the military man asked politely. Bill nodded. 'Do you know what this is really all about?' the Colonel asked. 'It's not just anti-British sentiment, or pro-Islamic enthusiasm. It's more than that. It's about what we call *ghairat* – self-respect. And Nasser has had a lot to do with it. It's he who has given the Egyptians something to be proud of at last, a reason to believe they are not second-best

302

to the Americans or the British. That they have a right to forge their own destiny. And, in response, what do your estimable Sir Anthony Eden and his civil servants desire? President Nasser's assassination, no less. Such civilised behaviour from the oldest democracy in the world, don't you think?'

The Colonel gave a small, tired smile before continuing. 'Pakistan is a new country — we crave someone to give us that sense of self-respect too,' he said. 'That *ghairat*. I hear everyone in the UK is predicting that President Nasser will be incapable of keeping the Canal in operation. I have been listening to the World Service, of course. I'm told that the Egyptians will fail, not just because they lack the professional expertise, but, by inference, because they are brown and therefore inferior. That is not very pleasant, is it, Mr Jackson? That's why those people are out there tonight. That's why they are so angry. They have had too many years of that — and they resent it.'

To his surprise, Bill found himself defending what he had so often criticised himself. 'Have we done nothing right?' he asked mildly. 'I mean, some of the drains we installed still work well,' he added, sounding more flippant than he intended.

The Colonel nodded. 'I think you understand what I'm saying, Mr Jackson. Many people in your country, just like some people in mine, are keen to see a new order. If we allow ourselves to feel gratitude, that change will never come.'

By late evening, the park had taken on a carnival atmosphere. Vendors offered food; men had set up impromptu camps; the smells of cooking wafted over the walls; music blared out from speakers, alternating with long altercations in Urdu. Still, each time the compound gates were opened even a fraction, it triggered a shower of stones and bottles.

Alice had provided bedding for Surindabash and his family,

and they were now asleep on the dining-room verandah, since the servants' quarters, close to the walls, had been hit continually. The Rockinghams' sons had been expected for the summer holidays in four days. Piers had been due to travel to Karachi, a two-day journey by train, to pick them up from the airport. Arrangements were now made to postpone their arrival. Marjorie showed no emotion at the news.

'Sometimes, I wonder if she's actually got any interest in those boys,' Alice commented, as she and Blossom and Betty Brooking watched the Rockinghams disappear into their house opposite. 'She never says much about them.'

'And how do you feel about having a kid?' Betty asked casually.

'What a silly question,' Alice answered.

At midnight, Noel asked Piers to make a tour of the compound, to check on the extent of the damage. In the course of his inspection, he stopped to chat to one of the drivers. The man asked if the sahib had heard the news? Shafi the gardener had been found outside Mardan.

Piers had anticipated such an event. He later let himself into the secret garden and retrieved a small bundle from the heart of the most overgrown section of the maze. As he did so, a stray dog howled in the night. He stopped dead, the bundle under his arm. He waited until his loss of nerve had passed, then he walked into the clearing. Close to the hut he heard something crack under his foot. He looked down, and saw that he had broken the leg of a miniature horse.

Piers' mouth went dry. This, he had not expected. Why would a child's toy be in the garden?

At dawn, the mullahs' call to prayer, relayed on loudspeakers in the park, acted as the compound's wake-up call. Five injured soldiers had slept in the Jacksons' sitting room. An officer arrived to check on their progress. Ella was sitting quietly in one of the chairs on the dining-room verandah when the officer and her mother began to make small talk.

'By the way,' Alice eventually said. 'Any news of Colonel Khan?'

'Oh, he'll be back very, very soon,' the officer replied, nodding his head vigorously, as if to reinforce his message.

As the officer said goodbye, Alice caught her daughter's eye – and reddened.

Chapter Thirty-Five

During the course of the morning, the rioters of the previous day rapidly began to melt away from the park, the novelty of violence eroded by the more mundane requirement of earning a living. In forty-eight hours or so, those who had contemplated murder would be content to resume normal relations with their intended victims – such had been the ebb and flow of sectarian conflict in this area for generations.

Surindabash peeked out of the gate and swore that he had spotted his attackers. Now, he grew bolder. He shook his fist and shouted at the dwindling numbers opposite, 'Bloody bastards!' Then with a satisfied smile, he returned to the bungalow and resumed cooking breakfast: a hero at last, if only in his own eyes.

Before the army departed, Rockingham suggested that they comb the entire compound. 'Top to bottom, offices and servants' quarters included. Better safe than sorry.' His argument was that infiltrators might have slipped over the less well-guarded walls during the night – or, perhaps weaponry might have been hidden by collaborators among the staff, for use at a later point?

Hargreave-Smith thought his number two's reasoning rather far-fetched. On the other hand, he didn't want to be on record as withholding permission, should further trouble ensue.

The Deputy High Commissioner also had to consider how he should best deal with Jackson. Reports were coming in that the British consulate, the university, the offices of several aid projects, and a number of private homes had come under attack. George and Trixie Danvers at the Quaker Hospital had been unharmed – as they always were. No word had been heard of Miss Patterson. So, Noel was inclined to delay his judgement until her safety, or otherwise, was established. The man had to be disciplined – the question was, how severely.

At 11.05 pm, Colonel Khalil requested a meeting with the Deputy High Commissioner. Accompanied by two NCOs, Khalil placed a small, bloodied bundle on Hargreave-Smith's desk. Without speaking, he untied the knot and spread the bundle out. It was a man's vest, containing a wallet. Noel opened the wallet gingerly. It was empty except for half-a-dozen business cards.

'We found this behind a cupboard in the servants' quarters,' the Colonel reported. 'The third room on the right as you enter the quadrangle. It appears unoccupied. We must handle this situation extremely carefully,' he continued. 'It could have ramifications which would be embarrassing both to you and to us at a very delicate time. Do I have your agreement?'

Noel nodded as he handed back the wallet. 'This is the last thing I need,' he said. 'What an almighty bloody nuisance.'

CJ Brooking had had a very good disturbance. The sewage plant and runway had been left untouched. Not least, because, applying himself assiduously to a bout of positive thinking, he had come up with the idea of placing signs in Urdu and Pashtu all around the perimeter. The signs read, 'Beware! Land-Mines. God be with you!' He had also recruited a gang of thugs from the bazaar who would have intimidated the most bloodthirsty crowd, never mind the snivelling cowards that had briefly presented themselves at the gates. Now, he was looking for his wife.

CJ had assumed she would be at the Air Force Club, along with a number of other Americans. Someone had reported she had been seen driving to the convent. He liked his life tidy, a missing wife irritated him hugely. 'Fuckin' woman,' he shouted again and again, hitting the jeep's steering wheel with the flat of his hand in anger.

Of course, if CJ had had more self-awareness, he would have understood that it wasn't irritability he was experiencing, but acute anxiety at the thought of a loss he wouldn't have a clue how to bear.

The convent gates were open when he arrived. Inside, slogans had been daubed on a couple of the walls, and some of the classrooms had been vandalised. The chapel had fared even less well. The pews had been hacked, the altar overturned, the statue of the Virgin Mary decapitated. CJ was about to leave when he heard whimpering coming from the vestry.

He picked up a lump of wood and moved quickly. Pulling back a curtain, he saw a small black-and-white mongrel, tied to a bench. One of its haunches had been cut open. A woman in a burquah was attempting to bandage it with torn-up strips of curtain material and the dog was protesting hugely. 'Come, come, Patch,' she was saying in English. 'You're making a fuss about nothing.'

Mabel Patterson duly explained how the crowd had come to the convent on the previous evening. Before they arrived, she had decided the Lord's protection also required a little inventiveness on her part too. So, she had borrowed a burquah from one of the servants' rooms and had crossed the road from the convent, to watch the proceedings from the doctor's surgery opposite. Now, standing in the courtyard, she indicated with her head. Through the open gate, CJ could see a sign which read, 'Dr A Siddiqui (Hons) Homeo Pathic Expert. Liver A Speciality.'

'He was most understanding. Far more so than your wife, I might add. Why are you Americans always in so much of a hurry?'

In the end, CJ succeeded where others had failed, by the simple device of appealing to Mabel Patterson's sense of duty. He told her that the British Deputy High Commissioner would require an immediate first-hand account of the events in the convent, in order to make an official report to London. Only she could provide it. It would be utterly irresponsible for her to remain in the convent a moment longer.

Shortly afterwards, the American entered the gates of the British High Commission wearing a broad grin. Next to him was a woman dressed in a black burquah, holding a wounded mongrel on her lap.

'Where the hell have you been?' CJ greeted his wife, as Betty emerged from the bungalow.

Miss Patterson pulled back her burquah, her face triumphant. 'Ah, Mrs Brooking,' she said.

'So, you've agreed to be rescued after all, Miss Patterson,' Betty remarked.

The older woman stepped out of the jeep majestically. 'Agreed to be rescued? Certainly not,' she snapped. 'I've come to testify.'

Later that afternoon, Ella sat at the table on the lawn between Miss Patterson and her mother. The bungalow had been restored to its normal order. The guests, apart from Mabel Patterson, had returned to their homes. She had spent some time with Noel, who was so relieved to see her unharmed, he had offered the loan of his driver and a car to expedite her return to Chowdiagalli on the following morning. Sylvia, officially pregnant, much to her husband's despair, had been insistent that the teacher should spend her last night in Peshawar with them at The Residence.

'I retire very early,' Miss Patterson had said, by way of acceptance.

Now, she was taking tea with the Jacksons. She had expressed approval that Ella's voice had returned. The two adults were questioning the child about her time at St Winifred's. It was, Ella thought, a very peculiar experience.

'You were happy there, weren't you?' Alice addressed her daughter.

Ella opened her mouth.

'Settled in right from the word go,' Miss Patterson answered on her behalf.

'And made lots of friends too?' Alice enquired.

Ella opened her mouth.

Miss Patterson spoke for her again. 'Lots – but not all quite as suitable as one might have wished. Isn't that right, Ella? Still, let bygones be bygones.'

'I didn't like Dr Mac,' the girl suddenly blurted out. She knew from the heat of her cheeks that her face had coloured crimson. 'He was horrible to me and Zuhra. He made her cry. He made her disappear.'

Very studiedly, Miss Patterson placed her cup and saucer on the table. 'Ah yes, Dr Mac,' she said. 'I've been meaning to tell you about Dr Mac, Mrs Jackson. Perhaps Ella might like to do some reading in her room?'

As she spoke, Mabel Patterson was simultaneously sema-phoring furiously with her eyebrows. Ella knew that when adults did this, it meant either secrets or trouble. Perhaps, in this case, it meant both.

Ella, in her pyjamas, sat on her bed, her parents on either side of her.

'Did this horrible man, Dr Mac, touch you?' her mother was asking, her voice wavering.

310

'Yes,' she answered, assuming she wouldn't be believed.

To her surprise, her father hugged her and said, 'Poor kid.'

'Where?' The word came out of her mother like a high-pitched screech.

Ella looked blank for a second. 'On the shoulder,' she replied.

'Nowhere else?' her father pressed.

She shook her head.

'Nowhere . . . private?' her mother asked.

Ella shook her head again. 'He didn't touch Zuhra at all, but she said she saw something. And they took her away.'

To her alarm, her mother was now sobbing on her shoulder. 'You know you can tell Mummy anything, don't you?' Alice said through her tears. 'Mummy's always here for you.'

'Dr Mac didn't touch me,' Ella answered, seduced into openness by her mother's words. 'But Shafi did. He touched the top of my leg . . . and things . . . He was only being friendly,' she added quickly as she watched the expression on her mother's face change from distress to alarm.

'He didn't mean anything, honestly.'

Shafi Akhtar was arrested at dawn four days later, in his room at his place of work. He was beaten severely during the course of his arrest and again in the cells in Peshawar. He was accused of the murder of Colonel Ashraf Khan Afridi sometime in late April. He was also charged with robbery. One of the drivers swore that he had seen Shafi with the dead man's wallet in the servants' quadrangle. He denied everything, even though, as a result of the beatings, he was now coughing up blood. The police told him they had discovered a knife at his place of work, which they believed to be the murder weapon.

Shafi knew then that he was going to die. He was hung upside down, tied by the ankles, and the soles of his feet were whipped with a bamboo cane until they were so lacerated, he passed out. This was a favourite way of eliciting 'the truth' from suspects. He duly confessed all.

According to a report in the *Frontier Post* on the following day, Shafi Akhtar, a former senior gardener at the British High Commission, 'confessed with many tears of repentance to the stabbing of the much esteemed Colonel Ashraf Khan Afridi, a soldier of great standing and hero of many battles'.

The criminal said that he had 'pounced' on Colonel Khan as he was leaving the Queen's Birthday Party. He had pulled him into the bushes, stabbed him, and removed his body later. The motive was robbery, since Shafi Akhtar had serious gambling debts, 'against all the laws of Islam'. The *Frontier Post* also described Shafi as a heroin addict, on the basis of no facts at all.

'The guilty man will come to trial shortly and will be hanged for his wicked deed according to the esteemed judge's directions thereafter,' the *Frontier Post* report concluded.

Each day, except Friday, one of the compound's drivers would be sent out to buy several copies of the newspaper. It was then distributed to staff and a copy was placed in the reception area of the offices. News of Shafi Akhtar's arrest was therefore received simultaneously in several households. Piers Rockingham read it, and savoured his relief. Marjorie never bothered with newspapers.

Sylvia was bearing up well, even if she said so herself. She felt jolly sick quite a lot of the time, and Noel was being terribly grumpy, but he hadn't told her she couldn't have the baby. So Belle had been absolutely right. Touch wood. Or, rather, touch the broken pieces of the taweez which Sylvia kept in her drawer, alongside the photograph of Starburst.

Now, she was in a state of great excitement. 'A murder! In our compound! Oh gosh! And that nice Shafi. Well, actually, I always did think he was a bit creepy, didn't you, darling?' she addressed her silent husband, who was staring disconsolately at her stomach. 'Poor Colonel Khan. What an awful way to go. Where exactly in the compound does it say he was stabbed? Do you think there'll be blood? Gosh, it's just like Agatha Christie.'

Noel woke as if from a dream. 'Have you seen my miniature horse?' he asked. 'It's gone missing. Everything's going missing. You really need to get a better grip on this place, Sylvia. Nothing used to go missing before . . . Sorry, darling, sorry,' he added quickly, as he saw his wife's eyes begin to fill with tears. 'Too many loose ends . . .'

In the Jackson bungalow, it was Surindabash who broke the news to Ella, as her parents read it for themselves over breakfast. She had been sitting at the kitchen table, digging out the damp salt from the salt cellar before refilling it. She had just told Surindabash that she would not be returning to St Winifred's. Dr Mac had done something bad to a student teacher who had complained. 'She's almost grown up, so it counts more,' she explained. In turn, the cook recounted what he had heard in the bazaar about Shafi. To his surprise, Ella, jumped up, knocking the tub of salt flying.

She rushed into the dining room to confront her parents. They looked up, startled, from their scrambled eggs.

'Is it true about Shafi?' she asked. 'Is he going to die?'

Alice buttered her roll. 'Quite right too. He should be boiled alive for what he did to you.'

Ella ran to her bedroom, retrieved her exercise book from its hiding place in the wardrobe, and locked herself in the bathroom. She sat on the stone floor, back against the bath. It was cool on her skin. She began to flick through her book, stopping now and then to read how Shafi had bought her bangles; how he had shown her the hiding place of the key to

313

the secret garden; how he had rescued her from something horrible that night in the maze. Shafi hadn't hurt her or frightened her. She should do something to help him now. That's what you did for a friend. But how could she – if nothing she said was believed?

The two women sat opposite each other. Betty had been compelled to visit Ash's widow as soon as she'd heard about the gardener's arrest. She'd told herself it was to convey her condolences, but she knew that it was also because she wanted to be with someone who knew Ash as he'd been behind the veneer, behind the gloss of charm and 'clubbability', a word he'd used so often.

'He didn't do it,' Faryal Khan Afridi said. 'The gardener didn't do it. You know that, don't you?'

'What do you mean?' Betty asked, surprised.

'I mean that Ashraf wasn't killed by the gardener. Ask yourself why he would choose Ash. If he wanted money, why not steal from one of the houses in the compound, take jewellery, cameras? Why rely on the contents of a wallet?'

Betty shrugged. 'It was a crime of opportunity. Ash happened to be in the wrong place at the wrong time . . . I guess . . .'

'Ashraf had been seeing a woman in the compound. He had been seeing her for a couple of weeks,' Faryal Khan interrupted.

'Who? Not Sylvia, God forbid. And it couldn't have been Alice Jackson, could it?' Betty said. 'She's a beautiful woman, but Ash was fond of Bill. Very fond. He told me so.'

Faryal gave a brief smile. 'Ash was a spoilt child. If he wanted something, he had to have it. But in things that mattered, his loyalty would have been absolute. He would lay down his life for a friend . . .'

'So what do you think happened?' Betty asked.

314

Ash's widow folded her hands in her lap. 'I don't know, but Shafi Akhtar might. Go and see him. What has he got to lose? He's going to die anyway. And, unless he speaks out now, the truth will die with him. I want to bury my husband,' she added with dignity. 'I need to find Ashraf's body and bring it home.'

'But why ask me?'

'It would be seen as inappropriate for me to visit my husband's killer,' Dr Khan replied. 'As a Western woman, your wishes will carry more weight – and you can tell the authorities you want to visit the condemned man because—'

'Because I'm an interfering do-gooder. Something patronising like that?' Betty interrupted, and the other woman gave her a fleeting smile.

Betty fell silent again. It was ironic. Ash had often accused her of standing on the sidelines, refusing to become involved. Well, now, he had reached out from the dead and pulled her right into the very centre. If she did as his wife asked, she knew the outcome. Little would be achieved, a lot of her time would be taken up, there would be some hurt and disappointment – and a great deal of annoyance on the part of others, who would accuse her of meddling.

The woman opposite broke into her thoughts. 'Will you help?'

'Nobody will thank you – or me – for uncovering a scandal,' Betty replied, annoyed that she had been presented with an unwanted dilemma.

'I want my husband's killer caught and his body recovered,' Dr Khan replied tersely.

'So what's in it for me?' Betty asked crudely.

The woman held her gaze. 'That, surely, is your private concern,' she answered. 'Something between you and Ash.'

Betty rose from her chair. 'OK. I'll do it. For one terrible moment, I thought you were going to start talking to me about guilt and conscience.'

'You're not that easily manipulated, Mrs Brooking,' Dr Khan answered, extending her hand in farewell.

Betty took it as a compliment.

CJ grumbled and cursed and then did as his wife asked. He expedited her request with the appropriate authorities. Or, to put it another way, he paid a hefty bribe to ensure that, the following morning, Betty sat in a spartan room in the Dabgari Jail. The room contained only a table and two chairs. She placed a packet of Camel cigarettes, a bottle of lemonade and five Hershey bars on the table. Inside the chocolate wrappers, she had carefully inserted fifty rupees, easily several months' salary for Shafi Akhtar.

As she sat, she recalled the conversation she'd had with Ash in the grounds of Deane's Hotel. Now, it was as if he'd had a premonition of his own death. *The truth lies . . . in seeking out what you have not been told . . . in unearthing the witnesses who would otherwise have no voice . . .*

Betty caught her breath when the gardener hobbled into the room, his legs tied together with old rope. Several teeth were missing, his left cheek was swollen, one eye was closed, dirty, bloodstained rags were wrapped around his feet. He averted his eyes.

'Thank you for seeing me,' she said. It sounded ineffectual, but she wasn't sure where to begin. Besides, the smell of fatalism hung about the man so strongly, it almost prompted her to give up and go home immediately.

'Did you stab the soldier sahib?' she asked gently. The man looked at his hands. Betty pushed the cigarettes and soft drink in his direction. He ignored her offering. 'Do you know who killed Colonel Khan?' she pressed again. 'If you know, and you tell me, I'll do all I can to help you and then you will be freed.' This time Shafi Akhtar gave her a look of profound pity.

Betty persisted, asking question after question, in the hope that one might trigger a response. But it was as if the truth had literally been beaten out of him. Frustrated, she said it was time for her to go, but she would return in a few days in case he might have remembered something. 'Do you have family?' she asked. The man shook his head. It was his first direct response. Spontaneously, she added, 'Your roses in the compound look lovely.'

The man gave a smile, the plum-coloured skin of his bruised cheek and eye crinkling. Betty winced in sympathy. The gardener opened his mouth and it appeared to fill with blood. Betty thought he was haemorrhaging. Then, he cleared his throat and spat betel juice on the grey cement floor. She was still looking at the dark stain when he said, 'Ask Missy Ella.'

Chapter Thirty-Six

Zuhra had endeavoured to teach Ella some of the basic history and beliefs of Islam – a subversive activity in St Winifred's. She had told her how there were no images of Allah, because he was everywhere. The Koran said, 'Wherever you turn, there is the face of all.' She had said there were ninety-nine names for Allah in the Holy Book, including, All-Seeing, *al-Basir* and The Expander, *al-Basit*.

Zuhra had explained how Mohammed was twenty-five when he met his wife to be, and she was forty and very clever. Mohammed had received God's message relayed through the angel, Gabriel. She had told Ella that a good Muslim prays five times a day; gives alms; fasts regularly; makes a pilgrimage to Mecca; and is prepared to give their life for God in a holy way, a *jihad*. She had also informed Ella about the Shi'ites.

Ella had recounted all this to Surindabash. He had sucked air in through his teeth noisily. He was a Sunni. Ella failed to grasp the complexities of the reasons for the split between the Sunnis and the Shi'ites, but she knew it came to a head during Muharram, the first month in the Islamic calendar year. Zuhra had said that Shi'ites honoured the memory of Imam Hussain in a very different way from the Sunnis. He was descended from Ali ibn Abi Talib, the first Imam, married to Fatima, the blessed daughter of the Prophet. Hussain had been martyred at Karbala in Iraq, defending the values of

Islam hundreds of years ago. His death was commemorated on the tenth day of Muharram, known as Ashura. Days of mourning followed, then Shi'ite men took to the streets in a public display of their grief. 'If you saw it, Ella,' Zuhra had said, 'you'd be really, really scared.'

The day Betty visited Shafi Akhtar was the day before the Shi'ite procession through the streets of the Old City. Betty's tutor, Mr Ali Shah Shaukat, had invited her to watch it from the balcony of his house. She, in turn, had extended the invitation to the Jacksons and the Rockinghams.

'Although why Betty would want to spend time with the Rockinghams is anybody's guess,' Alice had remarked to Bill. 'She always gives the impression she has nothing but contempt for them both.'

'You know there's a lot of blood in the procession, don't you?' Ella asked Betty solicitously, as they sat on the bench outside the secret garden.

The woman blew out smoke from her cigarette. 'Have you ever seen a lot of blood, Ella?' she asked casually.

The child kicked the side of the bench with her sandal. If she could knock it five times without killing one of the army of ants which always swarmed around its legs, Betty would forget that she had asked the question.

'Have you, honey?'

Ella squashed a solitary ant, and changed her self-imposed rules. If she could kick the bench three times . . .

Betty stubbed out her cigarette. 'I went to see Shafi today, in prison. He said you knew what had happened here that night. He said you might tell me. He's your friend, isn't he, Ella? You'd want to help him, wouldn't you?'

'Nobody will believe me. Nobody listened before.' The words were out of her mouth before she could stop herself.

'I will believe you,' Betty said and she took the girl's face

319

between the palms of her hands. 'You must have seen something horrible. You must have been really frightened. Tell me what happened. If you tell me, we could try and help Shafi. We might be able to save his life. That's important, isn't it?'

The struggle to decide on the best course of action was visible on the child's face. Betty knew, if Ella trusted her enough, she might recount what she'd seen. What puzzled Betty was why she saw the truth as such a terrible risk.

Ella jumped up. 'Let's go back,' she demanded flatly. And she ran across the lawn before the American could stop her.

At 5.00 pm, Bill took his daughter over to Tommy Larkhall's house for an hour, while he had a chat with the clerk. Albie was convinced that Bill had sacrificed his job for his family's sake. His gratitude made Bill so uncomfortable that he had avoided him for a few days. Now, Albie had relaxed back into his old ways. What Bill had no intention of telling him was that he was absolutely right. Noel had informed him that he would be recommending his dismissal from the Diplomatic Wireless Service. He would lose his right to a pension. It would take six weeks to send out a replacement.

'You're a fine chap in many ways, Bill,' Noel had added uncomfortably. 'But dependability is at the core of your job. And once one rule is broken, where will it end? I'm sorry.'

Now, while Bill and Albie chatted, Ella discussed with Tommy what she should do about Shafi's arrest.

The experience of his most recent collapse and medical treatment had left Tommy with even less reason to trust adults than before. His advice was unequivocal. 'You're only a girl. Whatever you say won't make a difference anyway,' he pointed out flatly, absolving her of responsibility.

Ella thought she'd feel better. But she didn't.

The exterior of the house was finely decorated in rose-coloured carved wood and wrought iron. Marjorie tried not

to look at the cracks in the plaster which were the width of
her fist, or the manner in which the entire construction
appeared to lean to one side. She and Piers and the Jacksons
had waited since 10.00 am in the street outside because the
American woman was late. Marjorie's head throbbed from
too many Tom Collinses on the previous evening. It always
throbbed these days. So, she'd had a brandy this morning, or
maybe two, to ease the pain.

Belatedly, Betty arrived and knocked on the door. It
opened and the group walked into the most delightful
courtyard – cool, dark. Marjorie could hear water tinkling;
large green palms created filigree shadows on the mosaic
floor. Two women, veils held across their faces, watched and
giggled. A baby, dressed only in a cotton vest, crawled on
hands and knees, pursuing a mangy cat with half a tail.

'Mrs Brooking, how good to see you,' said a thin, elegant
man with white hair. 'And all your friends. *Asalam aleikum.*'

Kawa, green tea, and *mit'hai*, brightly coloured cubes of
lentil flour cooked in syrup, were served in a room dominated by two large sofas, still covered in their protective
wrapping.

Marjorie said little and drank and ate even less.

Mr Shaukat murmured a few words to a servant girl and
she returned with three or four dupattas to cover their heads
as a sign of respect. 'Choose one, please,' the host directed his
female guests.

Bill took one and wrapped it around his head. Everyone
laughed.

The balcony was hardly spacious. It permitted room for
six chairs and a small table. The visitors shared the site with
several twittering budgerigars in cages tied to the balcony
railings. In the distance, as they waited, the group could hear
drums and bells and chants, which rose and fell with increasing volume. The chant, at first, was indistinguishable. As a
mass of men, naked to the chest, came into view, the words

became plain. 'Ya Allah! Ya Hussain! Ya Allah! Ya Hussain!'

The vomit rose in Marjorie's throat and she fought it back. She closed her eyes, then looked again. Immediately below her she could see ramshackle lines of young men. Every man held in each hand what looked like a flail, made of several chains, each chain bearing a small blade. Rhythmically, over and over again, they lashed their own backs, first with one flail, then the other. If one man wilted or fell, another would take his place, mortifying himself even more fervently than his predecessor.

All Marjorie could take in was how blood came in so many tones and shades: crimson on the men's white trousers, almost black where the blood had coagulated around older wounds, rust-coloured on the potholed asphalt, and streaked maroon on the men's chests. The smell of blood, the sight of blood, the slippery, sticky sensation of blood was every-where. Even on her hands. Furiously, Marjorie began to wipe her palms down the side of her dress, over and over again. She stood up and, pulling the dupatta from her head, she began to stuff it wildly into her mouth, her body shaking. Betty reached out to pull the scarf away, and Marjorie's screamed words were drowned out by the bellows of the crowd below. 'Ya Allah! Ya Hussain! Ya Allah!'

Only Alice was close enough to hear what the woman had said. Instinctively, she looked at her husband and put a finger to her lips.

'Sunstroke,' Piers explained, as he escorted his wife down-stairs. They waited in a corner of the courtyard until the procession had passed. Mr Shaukat insisted on keeping the couple company while they waited, much to Piers' barely concealed annoyance.

Upstairs, on the balcony, Betty confronted the Jacksons. 'What did she say?' she asked.

Alice frowned at her husband.

Bill ignored her. 'The others were making such a racket, I

couldn't hear a thing,' he replied.

'Alice?' Betty tried again.

'She was mumbling. I'm not sure she said anything. Just mumbling . . .'

Betty exploded. 'Oh, for Chrissakes, Alice! Shafi's about to die, Marjorie's clearly unstable, and Ash is missing. What the hell does all that add up to?'

Alice tightened her lips.

Anger swept over Betty. It had been a long time since she'd allowed herself to experience emotion at full strength. Now, she had no choice. 'Shall I tell you something about yourself, Alice?' she snapped. 'One day, very soon, you're going to have to step out of your fantasy world and deal with life as it really exists. You're going to have to see in yourself what is of true value. Gain some self-respect. And you're going to have to stop directing Ella's every thought and word.

'You've got the girl so confused, she can't fathom the rules you live by. And do you know why? Because your rules are phoney. They're not rules, they're ballasts against the fear that you're only second-best. Hell, look at the standard of what's touted around you as a superior class of human being. You're better than the lot of them twice over, honey – so why can't you see that? For Ella's sake if not your own?'

'Have you quite finished?' Alice asked icily.

'No,' Betty replied. 'All three of us will carry the blame if Shafi dies and Ella bears the guilt of his death. She has to be encouraged to talk. Why not let her tell us what she knows?'

'Let? Let? Let?' Alice's voice rose a decibel each time she repeated the word. 'What do you mean let? I wouldn't dream of standing between her and the truth. You're talking bullshit. Frankly,' she added with relish, 'it's what you Yanks do best. Don't think I haven't realised that you've been trying to charm Ella away from me, from the minute you first saw her. Well, it hasn't worked, not one bit.'

Alice turned to her husband determinedly, as if she saw

him too as a prize to be wrenched from her grasp. 'Bill, are you coming?'

Dutifully, he got up to follow his wife. As he passed Betty, he bent to whisper in her ear.

'You persuade Ella to talk,' Bill urged. Betty took a step back. He reached out his hand. 'Please,' he said.

Chapter Thirty-Seven

'Snap!' Tommy murmured weakly, his hand flopped down on the pile of cards. Ella slammed her hand on top and recoiled at the sensation. His flesh was clammy and cold, like freshly-made sticky paste. Surreptitiously, she examined him again, as if she expected the boy to turn into flour and water.

'Can I ask you something, Tommy?' she asked. She was sitting on the edge of his charpoi on the Larkhalls' verandah. Today, she avoided looking at him because his lips were chapped and sore. Ella wondered if Tommy might be dying now before her very eyes. Her mouth set in anger. She wouldn't let him go. She absolutely wouldn't. She wanted him to stay as her friend for ever. It was all God's fault, he'd created this horrible world.

Tommy collected up his cards. 'You shouldn't play this game,' he remarked snootily. 'You're like all girls, you can't concentrate properly.'

'Yes, I can.'

'No, you can't . . . And if you upset me, they'll have to call the doctor in and then you'll be in even more trouble,' Tommy added, milking his frailty again.

'I'm not in trouble,' Ella protested.

'Oh yes, you are,' the boy insisted. 'I heard your mother tell my mother that your dad's been given the sack and I bet it's because of all the things you've been saying.'

Tommy drew some satisfaction from Ella's reaction. He

wasn't naturally malicious but he was bored with being bedridden, as he had been now for several weeks, and his grandmother always said boredom bred wickedness.

'That's not true,' Ella yelled, jumping to her feet. 'I haven't said a word to anyone about anything – not for ages. I hate you, Tommy Larkhall. My dad hasn't had the sack. That's a lie – and I wish you were dead.'

Half an hour later, Blossom negotiated a truce.

Tombola Night at the Peshawar Tennis Club proceeded as usual three days after the riots, signalling a return to normality. Mr Jeremiah Durrani, proprietor of an electrical goods emporium, called the numbers as he did every Thursday. The players dutifully chorused the catch phrases: 'All the nines, ninety-nine . . . Legs eleven, number eleven . . .' Alice played four cards, while Bill took Ella for a swim.

At the nearly deserted pool, the fairy lights that ringed the area played on the surface of the water like multi-coloured fireflies. Only the occasional swimmer broke the pattern. Bill and Ella swam steadily side by side and without speaking, both finding the darkness and the rhythmic lapping of the water soothing. Bill glanced at his daughter bobbing up and down at his side like a baby tugboat, determined not to fall behind – and suddenly, he heard himself laughing out loud with the simple pleasure of it all. Ella was his little girl, and he loved her. He opened his mouth to tell her so but, instead, he shouted, 'Race you to the shallow end!' And then, he let her win.

Betty was waiting at the steps, as she had prearranged with Bill. He affected surprise so he could tell Alice, if she asked, that the meeting had been accidental. Why antagonise her further? Betty suggested that she wait with Ella while he went for drinks. The two duly sat and chatted, dangling their feet in the water. After several minutes of discussion about Tommy and swimming and Surindabash's bruises, Betty asked, 'Have you ever seen a film called "White Christmas"?'

Ella looked at her. 'Does it have Doris Day in it?'

Betty shook her head and laughed. 'No, it stars Bing Crosby and a couple of others – and a lot of snow. They're showing it at the open air cinema next week. Would you like to come? I don't know why they're putting it on in the middle of summer, maybe they're trying to cool us all down after all the riots . . .'

Ella giggled – and replied excitedly, 'I'll have to ask Mummy.'

Betty readjusted the girl's towel around her shoulders. Then, she added, 'You remember I told you I visited Shafi in prison? I just wondered if you might remember better now what happened. He did say you would tell me . . .'

The girl said nothing but drew her feet out of the water and hid them under her towel. She stared straight ahead. Betty waited.

Ella took her time and chose her words carefully. 'Shafi told Daddy that he hadn't seen anything because he wasn't there. So, how could he know that I'd been there?'

The woman gave a wry smile. 'True, very true,' she commented. 'I guess that means one of you is lying, doesn't it, honey?'

Ella pondered her options before speaking again. 'It was me. I was lying. I made things up. I didn't see anything. I couldn't because I was in bed – having bad dreams,' she added, crossing her fingers.

'You know Shafi says he killed Uncle Ash?' Betty pressed gently.

Ella nodded her head and began plucking at her towel distractedly. The woman continued, 'Ella, sweetheart, I know this is difficult, but he really needs somebody to speak up for him. He needs somebody to say that they were with him, that he isn't a person who hurts people.'

'And what if the other person isn't believed either? Then they're both in trouble, aren't they?' the girl responded guardedly.

'Sometimes, you can't avoid trouble, not if you think it's important to do what's right. Deep down, you know what's right, don't you, Ella?' Betty urged gently. 'Somebody out there hurt Uncle Ash. Why should he get away with it? That's not fair, is it?'

The child responded with a flash of anger. 'But Mummy says there's a lot of things in life that aren't fair. We just have to learn to put up with them. Tommy dying isn't fair, is it?'

'No it's not,' Betty countered evenly. 'But you do understand what I'm asking of you, don't you, Ella?'

The girl turned to her and the woman could see confusion and conflict written on her face. Of course she couldn't understand the contradictory, hypocritical, upside-down world of the adult.

'I think so,' she replied.

'Treat it as a game,' Betty instructed Sylvia firmly. Perpetual nausea in the early weeks of pregnancy had given the wife of the Deputy High Commissioner an uneven yellowish tinge, as if she'd sat in a bath of tea for hours. 'Treat it like the closing pages of a detective novel. You and I are going to solve the mystery of who killed Colonel Ashraf Khan.'

Sylvia's eyes gleamed. She clapped her hands. 'What fun!' she answered, then her face clouded with disappointment. 'But I thought they already had a culprit?'

Betty folded her arms. 'Well, here's where we prove them wrong. Okay, babe?'

Sylvia gave a little skip of pleasure. 'Okay,' she replied, hunching her shoulders excitedly.

A little later, she sent the bearer scurrying around the compound with delicately perfumed handwritten notes. They were invitations from her husband to drinks before lunch, for a surprise celebration. Sylvia forgot to inform Noel of this event, so he arrived at The Residence to find his sitting room overflowing.

Sylvia barely acknowledged her husband's presence as she addressed the assembled company. 'Allow me to thank you all for coming,' she beamed. 'I'm going to place you in the capable hands of Mrs Brooking.'

Betty asked everyone to take a seat. She said she intended to be brief and to outline the circumstances in which Colonel Ashraf Khan Afridi had died. Nobody moved, nobody said a word. Then Piers Rockingham yawned and sat back in his chair, stretching his legs. Ella slipped her hand into her father's and he gave it a little squeeze.

The American woman spoke clearly and without faltering. She hoped this conveyed the false impression that her words were based on facts, not hypothesis.

'Colonel Khan enjoyed women. He was having an affair with Marjorie Rockingham,' she began.

'No!' Sylvia exclaimed delightedly.

Betty continued, 'He had been having an affair for a relatively short time. They met often at the riding stables. On the night of the Queen's Birthday Party they went into the maze together. Perhaps they believed that it was the safest place. Perhaps it added to the excitement. Apart from Mr Hargreave-Smith no one else ever ventured into the place. Or so they thought.

'I don't know why or when, but Piers Rockingham followed them into the secret garden.'

Betty glanced at Rockingham, who continued to affect boredom. 'Piers or Marjorie stabbed Ash Khan and Piers later disposed of the body.'

Rockingham was shaking his head.

Alice broke in, 'That's ridiculous, absolutely ridiculous.'

Betty ignored her. She continued, 'He thought they were

329

alone when the killing occurred, but he was being observed by the gardener and Ella.'

Piers smiled.

Alice interrupted again. 'That man Shafi is a disgusting little pervert. He should have both hands chopped off before he's hanged.'

Bill stepped in front of his wife and, kneeling, turned his daughter to face him. 'Ella, what have you got to say?' he asked softly.

Hargreave-Smith stood up, raising his hands like a conductor on his podium. 'Please, please, this is most unconventional. Extremely difficult indeed . . .' Then, he realised he had the attention of no one in the room. They were all watching the wretched Jackson child.

'Ella?' Bill pressed

The child looked at her father, then at Betty and finally at her mother, before speaking in a small voice. 'I did see Aunty Marjorie and Mr Rockingham and Uncle Ash,' she began.

Sylvia sucked in her breath noisily.

'I did see them but not in the secret garden. They were talking at the party.'

Hargreave-Smith heaved an audible sigh of relief. 'Thank God for that,' he said. 'Let's accept the child's word.'

Alice extended her arms as if to embrace Ella, but her daughter darted past her and down the steps of The Residence, and was gone.

'Happy now?' Alice demanded angrily, turning on the American woman.

The following morning, Betty returned to the compound. She had come from the prison to tell Bill that a judge sitting in camera had decided that Shafi Akhtar should be executed at dawn.

'Shit,' he excaimed. 'What in the hell are we going to tell Ella? No one can get within ten yards of her,' he explained. 'She locked herself in the bathroom yesterday and hasn't come out since. Surindabash has left her food, but she won't talk to me or her mother. Perhaps she might listen to you?'

A little later Betty, with a highly disapproving Alice by her side, spent almost an hour attempting to elicit a response from Ella through the bathroom door. Then, some instinct made Betty put her hand on the handle. It turned easily. The bathroom was empty.

Ella had seen the scene often enough in films. She climbed out of the tonga, paid the driver one rupee, walked into the police station near the fort in the Old City, and very politely made her request. 'I'd like to see the Chief of Police, please. I want to make a confession – about a murder.'

She was taken without fuss to his office. It was a large room and clearly belonged to an important man since four ceiling fans whirred at full pelt and there were three telephones on the biggest desk that she had ever seen. The room also held a rattan sofa, several odd chairs and an ornate, heavily carved coffee table.

A policeman directed Ella to a seat and went out again. She sat alone in the room and waited. She had placed her exercise book in her satchel, which she now eased off her shoulder. She patted it, as if for reassurance. She had swung her legs backwards and forwards twenty-three times before someone came back into the room.

'May I help you, young lady?' asked a voice. Ella, occupied with watching her feet, looked up to see the tallest, thinnest man with the biggest moustache in the world walking towards her. She suddenly felt very, very small.

'Lemonade?' the man asked kindly.

During her bathroom vigil the night before, Ella concluded that, as everything that had happened since the night of the birthday party was linked to her, she must be to blame. She also decided that no matter how terrible she might be, she would not turn her back on a friend, more precisely three friends – Uncle Ash, Shafi and Zuhra. Honesty was all she had to offer.

'So, young lady,' the police chief asked, taking a chair next to her. 'How can I help?' As Ella began her story, she was encouraged by the fact that he didn't interrupt her once. But perhaps that was always the way if someone had a confession to make.

'My name is Ella Jackson,' she began. Then added, 'Don't you need to write this down?'

The man shook his head and smiled. 'If you don't mind, I'll listen first,' he answered. 'Please continue when you are ready.'

Ella lifted her chin a fraction and pushed her plaits back determinedly over each shoulder. She didn't want him to know how very, very frightened she was.

She began again. 'I live in the compound in the British cantonment. My daddy, William, is the wireless operator. We live with other people too and there's a very big garden. In one corner of the garden, there's another smaller one which has a big wall and it's all locked up. Do you understand?' she asked anxiously. The man nodded, watching her intently.

'I often go around the big garden on my own. It's quite safe,' she added, in case he might worry. 'That night, there was a big party. It was so lovely . . . lots of lights and dancing and Uncle Ash gave me a green dupatta. I've got it in my satchel, if you'd like to see it?'

The man indicated with his hands that this was not necessary, so she continued.

'Uncle Ash used to tell me that I was his Cinderella and he always made me laugh.' She paused. 'And then there's Aunty Marjorie. She lives with us. Well, opposite us. Mummy says she's very nervy and a bit of a snob. She always looks as if she's been crying but she's quite pretty although not as pretty as Betty, who is just gorgeous, like a film star. Prettier even than Doris Day.'

If the man was phased by this rush of names, he didn't show it. A servant knocked and entered bearing a tray with a bottle of lemonade and a small glass. He placed it in front of Ella. She sipped her drink, beginning to feel ever so slightly important.

'Shafi, the man you've got in prison, is my friend.' She gave the shadow of a smile. 'He is . . . he used to be our gardener. Not our gardener exactly, the compound's gardener. He showed me how to grow things, and he gave me little presents. I don't care what Mummy says, he was nice, he really was,' Ella burst out, surprised at how angry she sounded. She expected the man to tell her she was being rude, children should be seen and not heard, but still he said nothing.

'Shafi promised to show me the secret garden but it was ages before he actually did it,' she went on. 'I suppose he didn't want to break the rules. But it was my fault, I made him break the rules and show me. Mr Hargreave-Smith, the Deputy High Commissioner, my dad's boss, sits in the secret garden, in the middle of the maze a lot. I mean, he has a chair and books and things and . . . toys.' She slid the word in casually, to gauge the man's response. He simply nodded gravely, as if this was not uncommon among middle-aged men.

'Anyway, that night, the party was over. Everyone was in bed and I couldn't sleep. I often wake up at night. I'm supposed to stay in bed . . .' her voice trailed off. The man shrugged. Ella took this to mean that he regarded this as a mild misdemeanour. She liked him more and more.

'I went to the secret garden. It wasn't locked but there was a big pile of stones at the door. I . . . I . . . I . . .' To her horror, Ella realised that, quite without warning, her eyes had filled with tears – and they were now spilling down her cheeks. She took in a shuddering breath and wiped her nose on the back of her hand. The man took a large white handkerchief out of his pocket and gave it to her. Ella thought it smelt too clean to use but he flapped his hand to indicate that she must.

She wiped her eyes and looked again at the man and somehow, she knew, she was being believed. He could see she was telling the truth. She gave a small sigh of relief and for the first time, allowed herself to relax back into the chair. She began to speak again.

'I wanted to get my exercise book. It was hidden in the garden. It was just an adventure really. That's why I was tip-toeing. Not to spy on anyone, just as part of the adventure, make-believe, if you know what I mean? I crept close to the hut and that's when I heard all these funny noises. Then, when I was behind one of the hedges, I saw . . . I saw,' Ella swallowed hard. 'I saw Colonel Khan sort of squashing a lady. At first, I thought it was Mummy because they are really quite good friends. Then I realised that the lady was making crying noises so I thought he must be hurting her and I hid my eyes. Then there was a horrible sound and when I looked again, I saw that the lady was Aunty Marjorie. She had her back to me so that's how I knew. And Mr Rockingham, her husband, was there too and Uncle Ash was lying face down and it was horrible, all red and bloody. I remember now,' she added, as the details came pouring back.

'They had a blanket on the ground, a light blue blanket. It must have been quite hot and itchy. But it was turning bright red. I was going to run out and offer to get help but Shafi stopped me. Suddenly, he was there – and he told me to stay quiet and say nothing. And he was right, he was right.' Ella was on her feet, her fists clenched.

'I tried to tell Mummy and Daddy. I tried to explain but nobody would hear what I had to say, not even Dad. He said he'd looked and there was nothing there. He said Uncle Ash was away. He said that Shafi had said he'd seen nothing. He said he wanted to believe me but how could he? So they sent me away. They did. They really did. And now Shafi is in prison because of me.'

The man leaned forward and very softly asked, 'So who did hurt Colonel Khan, young lady? Aunty Marjorie or Mr Rockingham?'

Immediately after the lunch-time gathering at The Residence, Marjorie had begun to drink. She duly collapsed later that evening and had to be carried to bed by Piers and the bearer. The following morning, sick and wan, she appeared at breakfast just as Bill Jackson came running up the steps of the verandah two at a time. She watched with a sense of satisfaction as he grabbed hold of her husband, who was sitting at the dining-room table drinking coffee, and shook him by the collar of his shirt, ripping the cotton.

'If you've touched a fucking hair of Ella's head,' Bill spat into his superior's face, 'you will breathe your bloody last in my hands, that I promise. What the hell have you done with her? She's the only bloody witness to what you and your half-cracked wife did, and by God, she's going to tell her story. And be believed. Do you hear me?'

Piers coolly removed the hands of the wireless operator from around his throat. Over and over again on the previous evening, he had reminded himself that there was no evidence; only the word of a child and a Pakistani gardenwallah. 'My dear chap, I haven't seen Ella since yesterday. And I think we've all heard enough of the story she has to tell, don't you?'

Bill turned to Marjorie. 'What the hell's going on?' he pleaded. 'Did you know Ella's disappeared?' He saw the woman's eyes register shock. He persisted. 'Were you having an affair with Ash? If you had any feelings for him at all, why in God's name don't you say something? Or has he bullied you into silence?' Bill indicated with his head towards Piers.

Marjorie moved as if sedated. She sat down at the table slowly. 'I didn't,' she answered woodenly. 'Have any feelings for him, I mean.' Bill saw that a muscle had begun to jump in Piers' cheek. 'I went to bed early. Ask Belle. I left her chatting to Piers. I think she told you where I was, didn't she, Piers?' Marjorie added, a challenge suddenly in her voice.

Piers smiled emolliently at Bill. 'You won't get much sense out of her this morning, old man. She's feeling a little frail, aren't you, darling?'

Bill walked to Marjorie's end of the table and bent down, their faces inches apart. He whispered so softly that Piers had trouble hearing what he said. 'Do you know why Ash liked to fuck white women, Marjorie?' Bill asked evenly. She held his gaze.

'Because he wanted to have a go at their husbands. He was like the kid in the playground who always wants the other boys' toys. He didn't give a damn about you. Told me so himself. He—'

Piers' voice interrupted. 'I think that's quite enough, don't you? Marjorie's told you, she barely knew the man, never mind liked him. Go home, there's a good chap. Go home and wait for Ella to turn up. She always does. The sooner we can get this mess sorted and everything back to normal the better.'

Only after the Rockinghams heard Bill's footsteps on the gravel, did Piers speak to his wife, contempt coating every word. 'If you keep your mouth shut, we will stay unblemished. Nothing connects us – do you understand? Nothing. You owe it to me, after all I've done for you, to keep your nerve. A couple of months from now, it will all be forgotten. Christ, people die all the time in this bloody place.'

He watched as his wife's face appeared to dissolve before his eyes, like melting candlewax.

She gave a small whimper. 'I didn't mean to hurt him. I

only had the knife because I was frightened coming into the garden alone. You shouldn't have pushed him . . .' She paused as if composing herself and then asked flatly, 'Do you have any idea at all why I had an affair, Piers? Do you know why I finally allowed myself to be seduced after all these years – and by a man with a dark brown skin, a wog as you so eloquently phrased it?'

She didn't wait for her husband to reply. Instead, she continued almost dreamily. 'Ashraf made me laugh – but it wasn't that. He made me feel whole and I don't mean the sex – it wasn't that either. He treated me with respect – but that's not why . . .'

Piers banged his fist down on the table. 'So what the fuck was it then?' he shouted. Until this point, he had refused to discuss the detail of his wife's philandering. Now, he felt like giving her the hiding of her life.

Marjorie read the danger signs but she had no wish to retreat. 'I'll tell you why I slept with Ash, Piers. It's because I'm a coward. I've come to hate almost everything about my life. But most of all I detest my own weakness. I haven't the courage to make any change so I walked into a situation which I knew, one way or the other, would make change happen. Bill's probably right. Ash may well have used me, but I used him too. Isn't that the point of infidelity, Piers?'

Marjorie got up from the table, and, wrapping her arms around herself, began to sway and turn, as if in a slow, sensual dance. In a baby voice, while her husband watched, transfixed, she crooned,

> 'I'm aware that my heart is a sad affair
> There's much disillusion there—
> But I can dream, can't I?
> Although we are oceans apart
> I can't make you open your heart
> But I can dream, can't I?

Can't I pretend that I'm locked in the
    bend of your embrace
For dreams are just like wine
And I'm drunk with mine . . .
I can dream, can't I . . .'

An hour later, the police chief had completed the last of
several telephone calls. One, in particular, proved crucial. He
had contacted Trixie Danvers at the Quaker Hospital and she
had confirmed a small but vital piece of Ella's tale.

'So, can Shafi go free now?' the child had immediately
asked. The police chief avoided answering. Instead, he
busied himself issuing instructions for the Jacksons, the
Rockinghams and Noel Hargreave-Smith to be brought to
the station.

The Jacksons were the first to arrive. 'Where on earth
have you been? Don't you know we've been worried sick?'
Alice chastised, simultaneously holding her daughter close.

Almost immediately, Piers Rockingham and the Deputy
High Commissioner were ushered into the room. The police
chief thanked them all for their attendance and asked them to
sit. He pulled up a chair close to him for Ella and patted her
shoulder as if to give her courage. She tried not to look at her
mother. Slowly and carefully, he repeated what Ella had told
him, before asking the Jacksons and Ella to wait in one office
while Piers Rockingham waited in another, so that he could
have a private word with the Deputy High Commissioner.

Fifteen minutes later, the group reconvened. This time,
Noel addressed them.

'The information I elicited convinces me that the following facts are true,' he said crisply. 'Shafi Akhtar did not kill
Colonel Khan. The Chief of Police and I have agreed that Mr
and Mrs Rockingham will catch the first train to Karachi en
route to the UK – under escort.

'We will make reparations to Colonel Khan's widow,' he

added. 'Nothing else will emerge about the facts of this case for the good of public order.'

Rockingham was on his feet. 'You've got no proof at all. I refuse to accept this. She's a manipulative little bitch.'

'Sit down, Mr Rockingham,' Hargreave-Smith ordered abruptly.

Piers took no notice. 'She's produced a pack of lies.'

'I haven't, I haven't, not this time,' Ella burst out indignantly. 'I told them about Aunty Marjorie's back. I . . .'

Piers moved across the room towards the child but, just as swiftly, the police chief stepped in his path. 'Please, Mr Rockingham,' he requested urbanely. 'Do be seated.'

'Her back?' Alice repeated, mystified.

The police chief turned to Ella. 'May I?' he asked. The girl nodded permission. He duly went on to explain that on that night in the garden, Ella had seen the left side of Marjorie Rockingham's unclothed back. She had described it as looking like a dent in a car's wing.

The policeman continued, 'I've now checked with Dr Danvers at the Quaker Hospital, who has treated the lady in the past. She confirmed for me that Mrs Rockingham sustained a serious bomb injury during the war. It resulted in extensive scarring and required a large number of stitches. At one point, it was assumed she would be unable to have children. Am I right, sir?' He addressed himself to Piers.

Rockingham sneered. 'So what? The girl could have seen her any time. Swimming, sunbathing . . .'

Bill sprang to his daughter's defence. 'But Marjorie never goes swimming, does she, Piers old man? She hates the water.' As he spoke, Ella began to cry.

'I'm sorry, Mummy,' she kept saying over and over again. 'I'm sorry. Don't send me away, will you? Promise you won't send me away?'

Alice and tried as best she could to give her daughter comfort.

★ ★ ★

On their way back to the compound, the Jacksons, loaned the Deputy High Commissioner's car, made a detour to Betty's house, on Ella's insistence. She was the first out, flinging her arms around the startled woman. 'You've got to help, Betty. I told them the truth. They've got to let Shafi out now. You will help him, won't you?'

Betty swung the child round triumphantly. 'You're a star, Ella Jackson!' she shouted triumphantly and kissed the top of the child's head. Then she realised that Alice was watching her with an expression almost akin to envy.

'What made you change your mind and speak?' Betty asked the girl later.

Ella looked exhausted. 'I knew Mummy would be cross if I did, but when I was in the bathroom on my own last night, I remembered that I'd told Uncle Ash that if anything happened to him, I'd try and pick up the pieces – and all the grown-ups laughed. Well, they were wrong to think that that was a joke, weren't they, Betty?

'I have tried to pick up the pieces, haven't I?'

That evening, a typed memo was placed on Bill's desk. It informed him that, in the light of Piers Rockingham's unexpected departure, and other unforeseen events, it would not now be appropriate for his tour of duty to be terminated prematurely. His dismissal was therefore withdrawn. It was signed by Noel Hargreave-Smith.

Bill crumpled the paper into a ball. The news brought him relief, but no joy.

Shortly after, a letter arrived at the compound addressed to Miss Ella Jackson. It was from Zuhra Iqbal. She wrote at length and exuberantly with exclamation marks scattered across every page, like an epidemic of stick insects.

'I am very well!!!! I do want you to come and stay and my

340

mother is saying that is OK!!!! Please write as soon as possible!!!!'

Zuhra explained that she was alive and well and had engineered her own escape from St Winifred's by telling her parents of how the missionary man 'had done things'. Her parents had acted immediately – but the school had refused to take steps until a student teacher who had been molested as a child made an official complaint.

'You must come and stay with me and write soon!!!' the Pakistani girl had concluded, and signed herself, 'Your very best friend, Zuhra, a.k.a. Miss J. Mansfield.'

A day later, at dawn on the first of August, 1956, Shafi Akhtar was hanged. Betty broke the news to Ella in her bedroom later that same morning. She told the girl that she had pleaded and bargained and even pressed CJ to exert some influence, but she had failed to win the gardener a reprieve.

What she chose not to explain was that at a time when religious and nationalist emotions were so easily stoked, the British Government, the Americans and senior military figures in the country had decided that it would be unwise to put a white man on trial for the murder of an adulterous Pakistani army officer. Nevertheless, a culprit was required. Shafi Akhtar was considered inconsequential enough to meet requirements.

Instead of recounting all this, Betty described to Ella how she had told the gardener of the child's efforts to save him. How the girl had gone to the police alone and found the courage to speak out.

'Shafi told me to send you his thanks. And to tell you that you have always been his very good friend.'

Ella stared at Betty aghast. 'Shafi dead? He can't be. You promised,' she raged. 'You promised that if I said something he'd be free, he'd be all right. And now you've broken that promise. You're no different from the other grown-ups, you're all the same.' The girl beat her fists against the woman's chest.

'I tried, Ella, at least I tried,' she pleaded. 'One day, when you're older, you'll know why that matters. Trust me.'

Ella pulled away, her face streaked with tears. 'Trust you?' she sobbed. 'Trust you? Why should I trust you?'

Betty took the weeping child by the hand and, sitting down with her on the bed, put her arms around her and rocked her gently to and fro.

'This is the real world, Ella, bad things do happen,' she said gently. 'People often say what they don't mean, make promises they can't keep, cause too much pain. But I want you to understand that quite a lot of the time, they are trying their best. Part of growing up means learning to accept that, sometimes, that's all they can do. That's all we can do. Do you know?' she added. 'You and Ash taught me that lesson all over again. It is better to try, even if you fail, than to do nothing at all and live without hope . . .' Betty's voice trailed away.

She expected the child to give vent to still more disappointment and grief. Instead, Ella's sobs gradually became calmer. She wiped her eyes and her nose with the hem of her sundress. Her face was streaked and blotchy and Betty mourned for the new wariness that was in the little girl's eyes.

Ella slowly reached out and patted Betty's shoulder. 'I think I understand. It's all right,' she said gravely. 'You did what you could.'

She got up, walked over to her wardrobe and pulled out a beautiful pale green, heavily sequined dupatta. 'Here,' Ella said. 'This is special – you have it.'

Betty watched as she retrieved an exercise book and took a pair of scissors from the drawer. Then, the girl left the room without saying another word.

Ella eventually found herself sitting on the bench outside the secret garden. She made a space for Shafi. Next, she nicked her thumb with the scissors, and let the blood flow. Silently, she made a vow. She would never become a grown-up. Ever.

Opening '*A History of Insects*', Ella picked up her pen and, taking great care, she wrote on its final page only two words: 'The End'.

RONAN BENNETT

The Catastrophist

Shortlisted for the 1998 Whitbread Novel Award.

Gillespie, an Irishman, goes to the Congo in pursuit of his beautiful Italian lover Inès. Unlike her, Gillespie has no interest in the story of the deepening independence crisis, nor in the charismatic leader, Patrice Lumumba. He has other business: this is his last chance for love.

'Bennett's writing is as lush and sensual as ripe mangos ... The tone, which is perfectly pitched, and the exotic setting collude to evoke an era of colonial decadence' *Financial Times*

'Glowing with psychological insight ... I have not read such a good thriller in years ... The prose is as sharp as a whip, though subtle and poetic' Ian Thomson, *Evening Standard*

'A great achievement, an impressive testament to the appeal of strong narrative and sympathetic characterisation' *Sunday Telegraph*

'A memorable book, with a ring of deeply felt authenticity' Hugo Hamilton, *Sunday Tribune*

0 7472 6033 8

review

JENNIFER JOHNSTON

Two Moons

In a house overlooking Dublin Bay, Mimi and her daughter Grace are disturbed by the unexpected arrival of Grace's daughter Polly and her striking new boyfriend. The events of the next few days will move both of them to reassess the shape of their lives. For while Grace's visitors lead her to consider an uncertain future, Mimi, who receives a messenger of a very different kind, must begin to set herself to rights with the betrayals and disappointments of the past.

'Superbly executed . . . both enchanted and enchanting' *Daily Telegraph*

'A marvellously affirmative and exhilarating novel which satisfies like a gorgeous piece of music. More please' Clare Boylan, *Image Magazine*

'Mesmerising . . . a richly atmospheric coupling of fairy-tale conceit and raw emotional urgency' *Daily Express*

0 7472 5932 1

review

If you enjoyed this book here is a selection of other bestselling titles from Review

MY FIRST SONY	Benny Barbash	£6.99 ☐
THE CATASTROPHIST	Ronan Bennett	£6.99 ☐
WRACK	James Bradley	£6.99 ☐
IT COULD HAPPEN TO YOU	Isla Dewar	£6.99 ☐
ITCHYCOOBLUE	Des Dillon	£6.99 ☐
MAN OR MANGO	Lucy Ellmann	£6.99 ☐
THE JOURNAL OF MRS PEPYS	Sara George	£6.99 ☐
THE MANY LIVES & SECRET SORROWS OF JOSÉPHINE B.	Sandra Gulland	£6.99 ☐
TWO MOONS	Jennifer Johnston	£6.99 ☐
NOISE	Jonathan Myerson	£6.99 ☐
UNDERTOW	Emlyn Rees	£6.99 ☐
THE SILVER RIVER	Ben Richards	£6.99 ☐
BREAKUP	Catherine Texier	£6.99 ☐

Headline books are available at your local bookshop or newsagent. Alternatively, books can be ordered direct from the publisher. Just tick the titles you want and fill in the form below. Prices and availability subject to change without notice.

Buy four books from the selection above and get free postage and packaging and delivery within 48 hours. Just send a cheque or postal order made payable to Bookpoint Ltd to the value of the total cover price of the four books. Alternatively, if you wish to buy fewer than four books the following postage and packaging applies:

UK and BFPO £4.30 for one book; £6.30 for two books; £8.30 for three books.

Overseas and Eire: £4.80 for one book; £7.10 for 2 or 3 books (surface mail).

Please enclose a cheque or postal order made payable to *Bookpoint Limited*, and send to: Headline Publishing Ltd, 39 Milton Park, Abingdon, OXON OX14 4TD, UK.
Email Address: orders@bookpoint.co.uk

If you would prefer to pay by credit card, our call team would be delighted to take your order by telephone. Our direct line is 01235 400 414 (lines open 9.00 am–6.00 pm Monday to Saturday 24 hour message answering service). Alternatively you can send a fax on 01235 400 454.

Name ....

Address ....

....

....

If you would prefer to pay by credit card, please complete:
Please debit my Visa/Access/Diner's Card/American Express (delete as applicable) card number:

Signature .... Expiry Date..............